"ANNABELLE! OVER HERE!"

"Annabelle, how does it feel to have to come bail your mom out of jail in the middle of the night?"

"Annabelle, do you think this is because her career has totally tanked since she left the show, or was she always a lush?"

Okay, that was just wrong. As much as I tried to follow my *Thou shalt not look paps in the eye* mantra, I turned to see which one had asked that last question. Just in time to see Ben pull up all five feet eleven of himself as if he was going to take a swing at the guy.

Despite the fact that he drove a fancy car and lived in a million-dollar, famous-architect-designed house, Ben was a hippie at heart. He was Buddhist Lite and not into violence, but when people said mean things about Mom, something kicked in and he got all macho. "Just ignore them," I murmured, pushing our way through the crowd. He settled down, and we walked through the doors of the police station.

Each flash of the paps' cameras was a reminder that the truth about my mother—the one that I had tried so hard to hide—was about to become public.

Books by
ROBIN PALMER

Cindy Ella
Geek Charming
Little Miss Red
Wicked Jealous

For younger readers:

Yours Truly, Lucy B. Parker 1: Girl vs. Superstar
Yours Truly, Lucy B. Parker 2: Sealed with a Kiss
Yours Truly, Lucy B. Parker 3: Vote for Me!
Yours Truly, Lucy B. Parker 4: Take My Advice!
Yours Truly, Lucy B. Parker 5: For Better or For Worse

THE CORNER OF BITTER AND SWEET

ROBIN PALMER

speak
An Imprint of Penguin Group (USA) Inc.

SPEAK
Published by the Penguin Group
Penguin Group (USA) Inc.
375 Hudson Street
New York, New York 10014, U.S.A.

USA / Canada / UK / Ireland / Australia / New Zealand / India / South Africa / China
Penguin Books Ltd, Registered Offices: 80 Strand, London WC2R 0RL, England

For more information about the Penguin Group visit www.penguin.com

First published in the United States of America by Speak,
an imprint of Penguin Group (USA) Inc., 2013

CIP DATA IS AVAILABLE

Speak ISBN 978-0-14-241250-3

Printed in the United States of America

1 3 5 7 9 10 8 6 4 2

The publisher does not have any control over and does not assume any responsibility for author or
third-party websites or their content.

ALWAYS LEARNING   PEARSON

For Nicole Dintaman

ACKNOWLEDGMENTS

Immense gratitude, as always, to my editor Jennifer Bonnell, who never fails to get my characters . . . and me. Huge thanks to Eileen Kreit and Kristin Gilson at Penguin and Tina Wexler and Kate Lee at ICM for their ongoing support. Special thanks to Arianne Lewin, who initially helped me flesh out this idea. And, finally, to all those who have shared their experience, strength, and hope with me through the years.

For more information about Alateen, please visit http://www.al-anon.alateen.org.

PROLOGUE

"Santa Monica Police Department" is not a popular check-in destination on FourSquare at L'École—the private school in Brentwood, California, full of Hollywood royalty, where I'm a junior.

Especially at 4:15 a.m., which is where I found myself on Mother's Day morning, staring at a ripped vinyl chair and wondering whether it was okay to swipe at it to remove any of the germs that had accumulated from the various butts that had been there before me, or whether that would make my assorted neighbors in various stages of consciousness peg me as some fancy white girl as they waited for their mothers or whoever they knew who was behind bars there.

"Stay here," ordered Ben when he deposited me in front of the bank of chairs. My mother's entertainment attorney, Ben was the closest thing to a dad I had. Mostly because I never knew my biological father. My mother had

1

gotten pregnant with me during a two-week stand when she was twenty-six; then she'd used the money the guy gave her for an abortion to buy a pair of Prada wedges at the Barneys Warehouse sale. Ben wrinkled his nose at the stench of stale cigarette smoke and burned coffee. "But try not to breathe too much."

Not a problem, I thought as he walked away. Not because I was worried about getting lung cancer from secondhand smoke and dying young because my life was so awesome. It was because over the last year, ever since *People* cover girl Janie Jackson, aka four-time Emmy Award-winner for Best Actress in a Comedy Series, aka my mother, had walked away from the hit sitcom that had made her so famous that women at Supercuts all around the country asked for "the Janie," breathing was becoming harder and harder to do.

Splitting the difference, I sat down with just the end of my butt on the chair and tried to avoid the stare of the African American woman down the row wearing a faded Beyoncé shirt and stretched-out jeggings.

Finally, I flashed her a smile. "Hi." *Thou shalt be nice to everyone or risk being called a bitch by gossip bloggers and tabloids* was one of the Ten Commandments when you were a Daughter Of Someone Famous.

The woman raised an eyebrow before crossing her arms and glaring at the floor.

Things to keep in mind when waiting to bail out your

mother from jail. Number one: small talk in police precincts is not necessary.

A few chairs down from her, a Hispanic guy in his twenties who was pretty hot snored away. I took out my iPhone and clicked on the Notes icon so I could continue my list of other things to keep in mind if I ever found myself in this situation again.

I was a big list girl. They made me feel safe. At first, I just made them in my head as I was lying in bed before going to sleep. I started about a year after the series began, when I noticed Mom was drinking more than usual. The lists were pretty random back then: things I had eaten that day; what I had watched on television; what I would name a kid if I ever had one. But recently, in the last few months, it felt important to start writing the lists down. There was something about seeing the words on paper or a screen that made me feel a little safer; a little more grounded; a little more tethered to the earth, like I wasn't going to blow away. First in a few Clairefontaine graph notebooks I had gotten at Monoprix (the French equivalent of Target, my favorite store) during the Let's-celebrate-the-fact-that-for-the-first-time-in-seven-years-I-don't-have-to-go-to-work-on-Monday! Paris trip that Mom had booked after she left the show. When I had filled those up—all written with a Pilot Super Fine SW-R Razor Point II Marker Pen (they looked better and more official when written with a Super Fine versus a regular Razor Point II)—I started using my iPhone for the lists. (Not only were the Super Fines difficult to find, but they were also expensive.) I preferred the notebooks to the iPhone—something about the shiny covers made the lists a little less pathetic and a little more elegant—but it was easier to pass as normal with the smartphone. As if, instead of listing the people to call in case my mother fell into an alcohol- and prescription-drug-induced coma, I was jotting down must-have spring accessories or something.

Trying not to cringe at the string of drool that had begun to dribble out of the sleeping guy's mouth (from "hot" to "not" in seconds flat), I clicked on one of the lists I had made a few days earlier during gym class, after using the excuse of period cramps to get out of volleyball for the third week in a row.

THINGS THAT MAKE ME FEEL SAFE
- ★ Lists
- ★ Most chain stores, i.e., Targets, Walmarts, 99 Cent Stores. Basically any store where, if I wanted, I could buy a Diet Coke with Lime, a pair of pajamas, and a lawn mower. (Maybe I couldn't get a lawn mower at the 99 Cent Store, but I could get a baby Jesus action figure.)
- ★ The rubbery plastic smell of the inside of a Barbie's head. I have one stashed in a box

in the back of my closet—the entire Barbie, not just the head, so that I don't come across as some sort of Barbie serial killer. When I'm feeling nervous, I just pop the head off, take a whiff, and then pop it back on.

★ The smell of Play-Doh. Which, when I'm feeling really nervous, I have been known to huff from the can.

★ My camera. When it comes to talking about how I feel about something, I often find myself rendered mute, and photos help me to express things I can't put into words.

★ Ben.

So basically, a perfect day for me would be a trip to Target with Ben and my camera, where I would buy a Barbie and some Play-Doh.

Sitting in the lobby of the Santa Monica Police Department in the middle of the night? Not on the list.

Luckily, I had one of those mini Play-Doh cans in my purse. I got up and headed for the ladies' room, which, from the smell of it, hadn't been cleaned since about 2002. With one hand on the door to hold it closed (the lock was broken, and although as far as I knew huffing model clay wasn't a crime, I didn't want to take any chances), I took three quick sniffs, holding the smell in my lungs for a bit the way I had seen kids do when they smoked pot. I waited for the relief to kick in—the feeling that everything was okay, and I was just overreacting—but it didn't come. All that happened was that my foot slipped on some mysterious substance next to the toilet and made me drop the lid of the Play-Doh can in the toilet.

Once back in my chair, balancing on my left butt cheek, I closed my eyes to try to bring up the vision of myself walking into Target. I tried to conjure up the soft *whoosh* of the automatic doors, but I couldn't—maybe because of the stream of angry Spanish that was coming from over near the vending machine along with the sound of someone pounding on it. So I switched gears and instead tried to go back in time a few hours and hear the soft trickle of the fountain that lived outside my bedroom window and often served as a sort of aural sleeping pill on the nights I was really worried instead of just kind of worried about my mother. The really expensive antique fountain from China that Mom's decorator had insisted she buy because it was good feng shui and would protect us from bad things.

The one that, given the fact my mother had been booked for drunk driving as she sped the wrong way down the Pacific Coast Highway, was obviously defective.

CHAPTER ONE

There was nothing about the forty-eight hours leading up to my balancing on a germy ripped vinyl chair that made me think that life as I knew it was about to be over.

That Friday had been a typical one.

TYPICAL FRIDAY IN MY LIFE PRE–ARMAGEDDON
- ★ Wake up.
- ★ Make sure Mom is still alive and hasn't choked on her own vomit or accidentally overdosed on Ambien or Klonopin, two of the many prescription-drug bottles she keeps on her nightstand.
- ★ Throw on silky Indian-y shirt that I sneak from her closet while she's passed out because it's Friday, which means I don't have to wear the itchy navy-blue L'École school uniform that makes me look like a flight attendant.

★ Text Mom to get out of bed as I listen to my best friend Maya go off on our other best friends Olivia and Sarah during the drive to school in her powder-blue BMW convertible. She was pretty sure they were total homophobes, as evidenced by the fact that ever since Maya announced she was a lesbian, the two of them wouldn't get undressed in front of her in gym class.

★ Call Mom during lunch to see if she is out of bed or if this is one of her depressed days.

★ Realize from her groggy voice that it's one of her depressed days.

★ Make her promise to be out of bed and showered and dressed by the time I get home and to please call her psychiatrist to see if he can up her meds to deal with the depression.

★ Hold the phone away from my ear as she yells at me that she's *not* depressed—she's just tired—and there's a difference. (Mom gets very upset when anyone brings up the D-word. You would've thought they were accusing her of drinking too much. Which, you know, she does.)

★ Rinse and repeat.

Ever since Mom had left the show in order to be a big movie star, only to not have that happen because she ended up doing romantic comedies so stupid that even Jennifer Aniston and Katherine Heigl turned them down, she had gotten more and more "tired." Tired to the point that sometimes her hair went unwashed for so long it left grease marks on the couch pillows. Tired to the point that I would hear her crying into her pillow through her closed bedroom door. Tired to the point that I had stopped making a hash mark on the Ketel One vodka bottle in the freezer to compare it to the one I had made the night before with a Sharpie because she was going through them so fast. (Semi-useless bit of trivia: because of the condensation from the freezer, Sharpies are the only thing that work.)

That Friday, I held my breath when I walked into the house after school, not knowing what I'd find. But when I heard the TV on in the den, I relaxed a little. She was out of bed—that was progress.

"Bug? Is that you?" Mom called out. Bug was Mom's nickname for me because of the way I apparently flailed my arms and legs in my crib when I was a baby.

I flinched. It probably wouldn't have been noticeable to most people, but I could hear a slight slur in her voice. Dogs and their extra-sensitive hearing had nothing on me and my ability to tell from just one word when someone was wasted.

"Uh-huh," I said.

"Come say hi," she said.

I cringed. Mom was sprawled on the white slipcovered

couch in a black silk nightgown and a ratty pink chenille robe, a toe sporting chipped red polish peeking through the L.L. Bean slippers she had had since I was little. As if that wasn't bad enough—and it was—she was eating gherkin pickles straight from the jar. The sight was not exactly in line with the elegant-yet-inviting-beach-house-chic decor that *Architectural Digest* had written about in the cover article about our house a few years earlier.

When I got to my room, I was going straight to my closet for the Play-Doh. The blue kind because for some reason it gave off the strongest, most calming odor.

With a pickle between her fingers like a cigarette, my mother opened her arms. "Come give me a hug," she demanded.

I sighed. And the Barbie's head. Definitely needed some of that. Trying to say no would get me nowhere. Even when she was drunk—*especially* when she was drunk—Mom had a way of getting what she wanted.

I walked over and leaned down so I could be swallowed up by her, sucking in my breath and holding it so I didn't have to smell the alcohol or BO. I looked at the ninety-two-inch plasma TV. "Are those . . . *kittens*?"

Mom nodded as she pushed me away and began to crunch on a pickle. "Uh-huh. It's this show called *Too Cute*," she said with her mouth full as she fished another pickle out of the jar. "Kittens are so . . . *life-affirming*. I wonder if there've been studies that show that they raise your serotonin level." She turned to me. "What do you think, Bug?

Do you think we should get a kitten?" Her eyes got all misty. "You know, when you were a baby, before I started calling you Bug, I used to call you 'puppy.'"

That didn't even make sense. But when Mom was drinking, lots of things didn't. I wasn't sure there was enough Play-Doh in the world to fix this.

"You promised you were going to be dressed when I got home," I said.

"I *am* dressed. This nightgown,. Bug? It's La Perla." She sniffed. "Forgive me for wanting to relax a little after spending eight years working my ass off." She hiccuped. "Excuse me."

I shook my head. "And you wonder why I never want to have people over anymore," I muttered under my breath as I stomped back to my room. Back when Mom was on the show, my house was ground zero for hanging out, but over the last few months I found myself constantly coming up with excuses as to why I couldn't have friends over: *The painters are there. The kitchen is being retiled. It's raining. It's sunny. It's Tuesday.*

"I'm your mother, Annabelle," she called after me. "I will not let you speak to me like that!"

She was in luck. I wasn't interested in speaking to her, period.

I was in the middle of a new list titled Ways to Support Myself If I Ever Emancipate Myself and Move Out (I knew you needed a master's degree to be a psychologist and I hadn't graduated high school yet, but I put it down as an option anyway) when there was half a knock on my door before it opened. A closed door meant nothing to Mom. Even if you were in the bathroom on the toilet.

"I know you're mad at me, but I needed to share something with you." She sniffled. It was a good thing she hadn't gone to the trouble of putting makeup on today, because if she had, it would have been all cried off.

"I never said I was mad at you," I corrected. I mean, I *was*, but I hadn't come out and said it. Mostly because I didn't want her to be able to use it as ammo to pour herself another drink.

"Carrie called." Carrie was Mom's agent. "Katherine Heigl changed her mind and decided she wants to do that movie I was going to get the offer for."

Ouch. Losing a role to Katherine Heigl was ten times worse than losing it to Jennifer Aniston. Especially when it was a very unfunny, dumb comedy about an uptight businesswoman who's downsized and forced to take a job at a day-care center where she falls in love with a wacky Jim Carrey–like music teacher. "I'm sorry, Mom."

She nodded, her eyes all teary. "Me, too." She reached into the pocket of her robe and took out a crumpled tissue. "Well, I'll let you get back to whatever you're doing."

I turned over my iPhone to hide the list. I felt guilty just thinking about leaving her. As if she'd ever let me get away with it. Mom was so clingy that one of her old assistants had once bought her an embroidered pillow that said *If you ever leave me, I'm going with you.* "Are you sure you're going to be okay?" I asked.

She tried to smile. "Of course I am. I'm always okay."

I got off the bed and walked over and gave her a hug. In the last year I had grown three inches, so now, at five feet six, I was two inches taller than she was. For some reason, looking down on her rather than up made me anxious, as if I had just jumped out of an airplane and couldn't open the parachute. "Things are going to turn around."

She nodded into my chest.

"They are."

"You promise?" she asked my left boob.

"Yes, I promise."

"When?"

I sighed. "I don't know, Mom. Maybe you should call Gemini and ask her." Gemini was the psychic to whom Mom had been going for eight years, ever since Gemini told her she was going to get a role in a series with a number in the title that was going to make her super-famous. (The sitcom—a total *Friends* rip-off—was called *Plus Zero.*)

"You think?"

"Actually, no—don't call her." Now that she was a Psychic to the Stars rather than a recovering crackhead working at the Psychic Eye Bookshop, she charged three hundred bucks an hour. "Just trust me."

"Okay."

As I started to let go, she clutched harder. "Bug?"

"What?"

"Do you love me?"

I stopped myself from sighing. "Of course I do."

"How much?"

Really? We had to do this now? "All the way up to God," I replied impatiently.

"That's it?"

"Past God, past God," I sighed. That was our thing, something I had come up with when I was seven that she had held me to ever since. The thing that we had said to each other back when she used to tuck me in and, when I got older, when she'd call me from the set to say good night. The thing she'd force me to say when we were in a fight and she was feeling needy. You have never known embarrassment until you're standing in line at the ArcLight movie theater hissing into your phone, "Fine. I'll say it. I love you all the way up to God, past God, past God. Now will you please stop calling me?"

She smiled and kissed me on the forehead. "That's how much I love you, too. Thanks for cheering me up," she said as she shuffled off.

After she was gone, I reached over to my nightstand and picked up a photo in a silver frame. It was a picture of the two of us on our back patio, on a sunny August afternoon six years ago, the first time she was nominated

14

for Best Actress in a Comedy Series for her sitcom *Plus Zero*. I was six at the time and she was thirty-two, even though all the magazine articles said she was twenty-eight. With her sky-blue one-shouldered vintage Halston gown, and her honey-colored hair cascading down her back in perfect ringlets, she looks like a Greek goddess. This was the version of my mother that I wanted back — the one who was bursting with life. The one surrounded by light.

The one who showered.

I, on the other hand, look like a Hostess Sno Ball. I'm squeezed into a strapless pink taffeta dress that — although, thankfully, you can't see it in the photo — gave me back fat; my brunette curls are stubbornly pinned back into a French twist, which had already fallen out by the time we got out of the limo, resulting in bobby pins dripping from my hair and into my food throughout the evening.

In the photo, Mom stands behind me, her pale white hands with their perfectly polished red nails planted firmly on my olive-colored arms. We're both smiling — hers made up of straight white teeth; mine a mouth full of metal braces.

To anyone looking at the photo, it looks perfect. The big house. The sparkling pool. The fancy clothes. The cloudless sky. But because this is Hollywood — where the main export is make-believe — the picture doesn't tell the whole story.

The morning of the Emmys — after a few slaps on the face and the espresso I managed to get down her

15

throat—we were in business. I'd already stumbled out of bed somewhere around 3:00 a.m. to check that she was still breathing (holding mirrors up to a passed-out person's mouth is useful only in the daytime; middle-of-the-night checks require leaning down and putting your ear right up to her mouth). By the time Ozzie and Alix—her hair and makeup team—arrived to get her ready, Mom was about 80 percent sober. And by the time the camera crew from *InStyle* arrived to document the whole thing for the "Countdown to the Emmys" article, you would've had no idea that things were anything less than perfect at Casa del Jackson.

Just like no one can see how, in that photo, Mom's not just touching my arms. She's clutching them. So hard that there would be red marks on my skin when she let go, because that's how it always was.

But instead of reaching up and removing them, or wriggling away, I had reached up and grabbed on to one of her hands.

And was holding on just as tight.

———————————————————————

After a few hours, I went back into her room and found her lying in bed on her side, staring at the wall. It was a good thing my dream in life wasn't to be a cheerleader because obviously I sucked at it.

"Are you hungry?" I asked.

She rolled over onto her other side. This was how we communicated a lot of the time lately. I asked questions, and she rolled over and ignored me.

"Well, I'm going to make us dinner," I said as I turned around and went to the kitchen.

At our house "making dinner" meant nuking Lean Cuisines. I had grown up on them. When Mom became rich, you would've thought we would have stopped, but I think they put some sort of drug in them that made you addicted, because they were still the thing we grabbed for on the nights when Esme, our housekeeper, hadn't cooked for us. "It's ready!" I called out as I brought a Fettuccine Alfredo and a Ginger Chicken to the dining room table.

She padded out. I was happy to see that she had brushed her hair, at least one side of it. Happy until I saw her detour to the kitchen so she could fix herself a vodka and tonic. When I was little, I had loved the sound of the ice cubes jangling in the glass. Now I thought of them as screaming. Glass in hand, she plopped herself down at the dining room table, sinking heavily into the chair as if she had just finished a triathlon.

I forced myself to look at her. "You want the fettuccine or the chicken?" I asked as I balanced them on my palms.

She pointed to the fettuccine. ("All this cheese and pasta for only nine points! Where else are you going to find that, Bug, huh?" she was always marveling.)

I had wanted the fettuccine. "I don't think I'm going

to go to that party tomorrow night," I said, putting the dinner in front of her. I walked around to sit down. The ten-foot table, made of wood from a 250-year-old barn from somewhere in Vermont, totally dwarfed us. As did most of the stuff in the Spanish-style hacienda that, thanks to the Hot Property section of the *Los Angeles Times*, everyone knew had cost $2.75 million. The house was beautiful, but sometimes I still missed the two-bedroom West Hollywood apartment we had lived in until the middle of the first season of the show. It was small, and we had had to space our showers out because the hot water always gave out, and the smell of stuffed cabbage that had wafted up from Mrs. Spivakowsky's apartment downstairs always made me want to vomit, but it had been home. Even after seven years in this house, a lot of the time I still felt like Alice after she drank from the bottled marked DRINK ME.

Mom looked up, the unbrushed side of her hair sticking to her face. Normally sunkissed and blonde, angry dark roots were now sprouting from the top. "But you've been looking forward to it all week," she said.

That was true. I had been. I didn't know the kid throwing it—some girl from hippy-dippy Crossroads School named Zazu—but my friend Olivia had promised there were going to be lots of hot guys there. "Get a boyfriend" had been on my How to Avoid My Mother list the other night, and a party with cute boys would be a good place to

18

start on that. Even though I sucked when it came to flirting with boys and therefore hadn't had a boyfriend before.

I shrugged. "It's okay. There'll be another one." In my mind's eye I saw my shrink Dr. Warner's eyebrow go up as she gave me a look that was not exactly disapproving, because shrinks were supposed to remain neutral, but was definitely disapproving-ish. According to her, missing out on social events just so I could sit at home to watch Mom drink and be depressed wasn't helping the situation. In fact, what I was doing was called "enabling," which, from what I had gathered, was a fancy word for "co-signing people's bullshit." The thing was, when I did leave Mom while she was depressed, I just ended up spending my whole night calling to check how bad she was slurring, which wasn't exactly social.

She picked at her pasta. "Really? You'd do that?" she asked. I could tell she was trying not to sound too excited. But it still came through.

"I just said I would, Mom," I snapped. Immediately, I felt bad. I hadn't inherited her acting ability. I mean, I had been the one who had offered.

She hauled herself up from the table, walked over, and pulled me up into a huge hug, despite the fact that I was midbite with a forkful of chicken and rice in my hand. "Oh, Bug, what would I do without you?" she asked into my neck as I watched a clump of rice disappear into her hair. Because it was already so dirty, I didn't bother to get it out.

Instead, I shifted so that my breathing was only halfway constricted. It was if I could literally feel the need rolling off her in waves and settling on my body. Like I had been slimed or something.

I moved my face so that her breath, metallic from the pills she took (Ambien for sleeping, Zoloft for depression, Klonopin for anxiety), wasn't filling my nostrils. I hated that smell. Almost as much as I hated the smell of vodka, even though she swore that vodka didn't smell. "Well, lucky for us, you won't have to find that out," I sighed.

She let go of me and clapped her hands. "I know— we'll do Movie and A Manicure!" she said, all excited. "Just like the old days." Back before *Plus Zero* (read: when we were poor) we'd spend Saturday nights giving each other manicures in her bed while watching cheesy 1980s comedies like *Mannequin*. (I didn't know which was more painful—the way Mom always pushed too hard with the cuticle stick or Kim Cattrall's performance.)

"Okay. Sure. Sounds great," I said. Recently, Mom had been on this whole "old days" kick. Maybe because the here and now kind of sucked.

"You're *sure* you're okay staying home with me?" she asked. "Because I don't want you to do it just because you feel like you *have* to and then resent me for it. Because that's at least two more therapy sessions right there. If you do it, I want it to be because you *want* to."

"Mom, it's fine," I said firmly.

The fog that had been hovering around her face for the last week lifted, replaced by the bubbliness that had made her such a big TV star, causing one blogger to once write "Janie Jackson—the most carbonated star on network television!"

"This is going to be so fun." She pushed her Lean Cuisine away and stood up. "I'm going to go check the nail polish supply to make sure it hasn't thickened."

————————————————

The next morning Mom decided that instead of just Movie and A Manicure, we would spend the entire day together.

"And do what?" I asked as I watched carefully to make sure she didn't pour anything but milk into her coffee.

"Go to Be Here Now?"

Be Here Now was a big New Age/self-help bookstore in Venice that Mom loved. The problem was that when she got the books home, she usually passed out before she got more than a few pages in, so they didn't really help.

"You know the incense in there always makes me sneeze," I replied.

"Okay, okay. How about...ooh...I know! We'll *bake*."

"Bake."

"Yeah. We'll make cookies! Those ones you made with the pretzels and the butterscotch chips. The—whatsit-called—recycling cookies."

"You mean the Momofuku Milk Bar Compost Cookies?" I corrected.

"Yes. Those."

Those *were* pretty awesome. I had seen the recipe on the Pinterest board of some girl named Jen who lived in New Jersey. Basically you took anything you wanted — pretzels, potato chips, Reese's — and put it all in there. They were like a legal version of crack cocaine.

"Baking's a good mother/daughter thing to do, don't you think?"

I shrugged. I would have preferred hanging out in my room making a list of the ways I'd rather spend my Saturday other than hanging out with my depressed mother, but if baking was going to help kick Mom out of her funk, I was up for it.

She stood up. "We'll go to Whole Foods and get the stuff. Give me two minutes to get dressed."

A half hour later, I was still waiting for her. I plopped down on the couch and picked up a copy of *People* with the actor Billy Barrett's smile beaming out at me. "He's *Rad and Righteous*, But Will the King of Hollywood Ever Find True Love?" the headline read. You couldn't say that Billy Barrett was the flavor of the month. He was more the flavor of the last two years.

According to the article, Billy was a "combination of the Ryans (Reynolds and Gosling) and the Brads (Pitt and Cooper)." He did both comedy and action, and his new movie *Rad and Righteous* (an action comedy) had been number one at the box office for the last three weeks in a row. He wasn't my type—for the most part I liked guys who were a bit nerdier in both looks and personality—but I could see the appeal. Every girl I knew thought he was super-hot. Including Maya ("Just because I'm into girls doesn't mean I can't appreciate the gorgeousness that is Billy Barrett."). If you took a poll at my school and asked which Hollywood actor most girls would like to lose their virginity to, he'd win by a landslide

"Mom, we're going to the supermarket—not a premiere!" I yelled.

"Yes, but it's Whole Foods, Bug," she yelled back. "You never know who you're going to run into there."

———————————————————

She was right. You never knew.

Half an hour later, right there in the produce aisle, we saw Billy Barrett himself, staring at a pair of big boobs on a very thin, very flirty brunette who was helping him pick out artichokes.

"Eww. Gross," I said out loud. Mom was busy being fawned over by an old couple who were telling her how no one in their retirement community missed a rerun of *Plus Zero*.

Suddenly, Mom stopped talking. "Is that . . . oh, my God . . . it is. It's Billy Barrett." She fluffed her hair. "I have to go say hello."

I held her back. "Mom, you don't even know him!"

"I know. But we're both actors." The only thing worse than one celebrity in a non-movie/TV-set public place was two of them. It was like there was this weird law-of-physics thing that kicked in: whenever two famous people were in the same room, they had to say hello to each other. She grabbed my hand. "Come with me."

Before I could stop her, she had dragged me over with her. "Excuse me, Billy?" Mom said as the brunette stuck out her boobs a little more and did a hair flip. While her flip wasn't as smooth as Mom's, it was pretty good.

Please let him recognize her, I thought as he turned around. Billy Barrett didn't look like the type of guy who watched a mainstream 9:00 p.m. sitcom. He looked like the type of guy who was just getting up from an early-evening nap after a wild night of partying and preparing to go do it all again.

As he focused on her, a big smile appeared on his face. It wasn't just his mouth that smiled—it was his eyes as well. In fact, if it was possible for a person's nose and chin to smile, they were, too. He was cute. Like I-don't-know-if-I'd-give-it-up-for-him-but-I'd-definitely-start-thinking-about-what-kind-of-birth-control-I'd-use-in-addition-to-condoms-if-I-did kind of cute.

"*Wow*. I can't believe I'm standing in front of *Janie Jackson*," he marveled. "That's just . . . *wow*." He turned to the brunette. "Isn't it?" The action-hero deep voice that he used in interviews and on red carpets wasn't there.

He sounded . . . normal. Like some sort of Midwestern-churchgoing-star-quarterback guy. Which made sense, because according to the article I'd read, that's exactly who he was.

The brunette looked less impressed than Billy. "I guess," she said as she stuck her chest out even farther.

Mom did her patented smile-as-she-ran-a-hand-through-her-hair move. (It was such a trademark of hers that it was actually cited in one of those *How to Get a Guy and Keep Him* books as a flirting technique.) "You're so sweet to say that," she laughed.

I was confused. What, exactly, had he said?

"You know, I used to watch your show all the time my senior year." Billy winked. "When I was supposed to be studying."

Ouch. He may have been hot, but obviously he had not downloaded any sort of *How to Talk to Older Women Without Making Them Feel Old* e-book.

Mom's smile flickered. "Well, thank you," she said. "I appreciate that. I think."

"Although now that I'm standing in front of you, it's obvious that you were like, *twelve*, when you shot that," he laughed.

His save made Mom turn the smile back up to full wattage.

"But seriously. You're, like, an *idol* of mine," he said. "Your comic timing in that show was *genius*."

I cringed. Putting emphasis on words like that—that was definitely a kind of flirting, wasn't it?

"You know, I did a guest role on *Two and a Half Men*," he said, "so I know how tough sitcoms can be."

That was, like, the nicest compliment Mom had gotten in the last few months, other than when the homeless guy we passed on Ocean Avenue a few nights earlier had told her she had killer knockers. "You're so sweet to say that," she said again.

The way his eyes kept drifting down toward those knockers, I wasn't sure *sweet* was the word for Billy Barrett at that moment. According to the blogs, he was a bit of a commitmentphobe. He had an on-again, off-again thing with a screenwriter named Skye, who was known as much for her habit of dressing like a 1940s movie star as she was for her ironic indie comedies. Skye did not have a last name. Well, she did—Bernstein—but after being nominated for her second Academy Award, she decided to chuck it, and Hollywood decided to let her. She broke up with Billy every other week because of the photos that popped up with him *thisclose* to other girls, and then overshared about the whole thing on her blog and Twitter.

"And the fact that you just walked away from a hit series to pursue your art?" he asked Mom. Huh. Billy Barrett was a reader—at least of feature articles in *People* and *US Weekly*. "Talk about inspiring."

Pursuing her art. It hadn't exactly panned out that way,

seeing as how barely any offers for roles in any films had come in, let alone for ones in arty, indie films.

"Do you realize the guts it takes to do something like that?" He shook his head. "Wow. *Wow.*"

Okay, we were definitely in flirting territory. Why couldn't we have run into him in Target instead of Whole Foods? At least if we were in Target, I could have excused myself and gone and bought some Play-Doh and ducked into the bathroom for a quick huff.

He grabbed her arm. "Do you know who Joseph Campbell is?" he asked, as if the fate of the universe hung on her answer to the question.

Mom gasped. "Omigod—I *love* Joseph Campbell!"

There was a book by this Campbell guy in Mom's bathroom, which was where she did a lot of her self-help reading.

"Oh, me, too," Billy said. "The makeup woman on my last movie gave me one of his books to read before I went to Costa Rica last year—we weren't involved or anything, just friends," he added quickly and a little guiltily. "I have to say, the dude just nailed it, you know? Totally blew me away."

"*Meee, tooo,*" Mom agreed, clutching at his arm. "Absolutely genius."

"Right?" Billy said. "Now that I have this production deal at Universal, I've been thinking about developing a biopic about him. You know, for me to star in?"

"I *love* that idea!" Mom exclaimed. "I've never seen a picture of him, but I bet you'd be perfect!"

"Who is he?" I asked. I was somewhat intrigued because of the way they were gushing, but also a little annoyed. Mom clearly forgot there were other people around. Like, say, people who were a tad uncomfortable watching their mothers flirt with guys who were in college when watching her TV show.

Billy turned to me. "He was the one who came up with that awesome phrase 'Follow your bliss,'" he explained. He turned back to Mom and smiled. "And that's exactly what you did."

She sure did . . . she followed it right out of a career.

She sighed. "You know, I can't tell you how nice it is to feel so . . . *understood*."

This needed to stop. For many reasons. And I needed to get home to my Play-Doh and my Barbie head, and make a list. I pulled at her arm. "Mom, we need to go."

Billy looked surprised. "This is your *daughter*?"

"It is. This is Annabelle," she said proudly, with some lash battage. Whenever she introduced me, it was as if she were introducing the baby Jesus. "I had her when I was quite young," she made sure to add.

Billy turned to me and smiled. "Well, I definitely see the resemblance."

Actually, there wasn't much of one. Mom was blonde and blue-eyed and English- and Swedish-looking, while I, with my dark curls and brown eyes, resembled my father's

Italian side. But because I just wanted to get out of there, I smiled back before pulling on Mom's arm again. "Mom. Seriously. We need to go. You know, to make the cookies."

"Okay, okay." She turned to Billy. "Well, it was so nice to meet you."

Please don't ask her for her number, I thought to myself.

"Yeah. You, too," he said. He patted around his jeans and took out his wallet and pulled out a receipt. "Let me give you my number—"

Really? This was even worse. Anyone who knew how to Google knew that the passive-aggressive move of a guy giving you his number instead of asking for yours was the kiss of death. At some point down the line, usually right after you had totally fallen for him, he'd freak and do the pullback thing that at first you'd try to convince yourself would pass in a few days but would ultimately prove to be the beginning of a big blow-off. Which, if you were my mother, would then cause you to drink even more heavily and go that much longer without washing your hair.

"Do either of you guys have a pen?" he asked us.

Oh, he was good. From the outline of his smartphone in his jeans, it was evident he could've just texted or e-mailed her the info, but some reptilian guy wisdom made it so he knew the importance of ensuring that he avoided having her contact information in his possession.

"Nope. Sorry," I said at the exact same time Mom said, "But I bet Annabelle does. She's very organized." Without even asking, she took my bag and started rummaging in it.

"Here you go," she said, flashing him another full-wattage smile as she started to hand him one of my Pilots.

"No—wait!" I said, snatching it away from him. I pulled out a regular old blue ballpoint one instead. "Use this one. That one doesn't work." I was not letting him touch the good pen. He'd ruin it, and I'd have to find a whole other brand for my lists.

As he scribbled down his number and e-mail, I read the receipt upside down. Six hundred bucks at Soho House, which was a members-only club in Hollywood that constantly showed up on the gossip blogs. I had been there a few times for some Sweet Sixteen parties, and every time I had felt like some Midwestern *Price Is Right* contestant compared to the model-like waitresses with their Keratined hair. Radiohead's "Creep" blared from Billy's butt. He stopped writing and flashed an apologetic smile. "Sorry. If I don't take this, it'll just be more trouble later." As he fished his iPhone out of his pocket, I saw Skye's picture and name flash across it.

"Hey," he said as he answered. "I'm at Whole Foods. Let me call you back in a few, okay?"

I couldn't make out the words that rushed out of the phone, but I could hear the annoyance in them.

"Yes, I'm in Whole Foods," he replied, just as annoyed. "Would you like me to take a picture of the sign and text it to you?"

He closed his eyes and pressed on the spot in between

his eyebrows as he listened to her response. "Okay, I can't deal with this right now," he said. "I'm hanging up." She said something else. "Actually, that's not passive-aggressive at all, Skye. That's pretty straight ahead." He clicked off and shoved the phone back in his jeans before morphing back into the smiling, laid-back dude he had been pre–phone call. He continued writing down his information. When he was done, he held the receipt out to Mom. "So, yeah, we should, I don't know, get together and talk more about Joseph Campbell."

"Oh, I'd *love* that," Mom said, snatching it from him.

He turned to me. "Nice to meet you, Annabelle."

"You, too," I said. I wondered how I could make it so that the receipt accidentally ended up ripped up and in the garbage.

He flashed another smile. "You've got a great mom here," he said, looking straight at her rather than at me.

"Yup. I do," I said, pulling some more while Mom just stayed put, grinning.

"Well, I should let you guys go," Billy said, making no attempt to do so. "Creep" started back up from his pocket, and his smiled faded.

"Probably a good idea," I agreed. "Seeing that, you know, we have lots of stuff to do." I dragged Mom behind me.

"What were you doing?" I demanded when we got to the aisle with all that baking stuff.

"What are you talking about?" she replied, peeking

around the corner to get another look at him as he paced around the bananas while on the phone.

"You were totally flirting with him!"

"Oh, please."

I looked at her. "Mom, he's like almost half your age."

"Annabelle, you're such an exaggerator," she said. "He is not. He's, like, ten years younger than me."

I whipped out my iPhone and Wiki'd him. "Twenty-six. Actually, he's *sixteen* years younger than you," I corrected.

She cringed. "He is? Oy." She fluffed her hair. "Anyway, it doesn't matter. It's not like it makes a difference. We're just two actors who admire each other's craft and took the opportunity to tell each other that and might get together to talk philosophy."

"You're not actually going to *call* him, are you? Mom, he's on the phone with his *girlfriend* right now."

"Well, he sounded annoyed by her, and from what I read in *People*, they're very on-off," she sniffed.

"If you have a ringtone and picture for someone when they call, that's pretty much 'on,'" I replied. Mom had been single for a whole three months, which was like three years for normal people. Her last guy was James, this yoga teacher who had a reputation for giving his students lots of adjustments that included his hands on their butts. But as desperate as she could be for male attention, she *never* got involved with people who were involved with other people.

As she reached up and began to rub the area in between her eyebrows, just like Billy, I couldn't help but laugh. Usually she didn't start morphing into the guys she went out with until after she had slept with them. "Annabelle, he's an attractive man. This is Hollywood. You can't swing a cat without hitting one. I didn't say I was going to call him." She started grabbing stuff off the shelves. "Now let's bake those cookies."

I tried to grab the receipt/phone number out of her hand, but she slipped it into her bag before I could snatch it.

CHAPTER TWO

A HISTORICAL LOOK BACK AT WHAT HAS PASSED FOR A TYPICAL SATURDAY NIGHT DURING THE COURSE OF MY TIME ON THE PLANET

Ages 0–9 . . . Handing Mom tissues while she cries about how she doesn't have the energy to go to yet one more audition, then giving her one of the five pep talks I rotated through about why she shouldn't give up on the acting thing and how it was only a matter of time before she got her big break so we could stop eating Lean Cuisines and go out to the movies instead of watching things on Netflix.

Ages 9–15 . . . Monitoring how much Ketel One vodka Mom poured into her glass of club soda as she got ready for an A-plus-list party held at a Malibu Colony beach house/famous-architect-

34

designed modern thing in the Hollywood Hills/
Spanish hacienda north of Montana in Brentwood
given by a smarmy agent/producer/network
executive, then giving her a pep talk about how,
yes, she did deserve all the fame and acclaim she
was getting and, no, people didn't think she was
a fraud. And, yes, I had the credit card number
to give the guy at Nobu when I ordered sushi for
my friends and me, and of course I would thank
them for making an exception and delivering it
to me all the way in Santa Monica because I'm
Janie Jackson's daughter.

Age 15–up until two months ago . . . Pouring
out some of the straight Ketel One Mom was
drinking and replacing it with water as she got
ready for a C-plus-list party held at a smaller/
not as nice/nonfamous-architect-designed house/
condo/restaurant held by a just-as-smarmy agent/
producer/network executive, then giving her a
pep talk about how, yes, she was right to follow
her gut and walk away from the number-one-
rated sitcom on the air so she could fulfill herself
creatively with dramatic roles in feature films even
though those roles were not being offered to her.
And, yes, I would not overtip the Domino's guy
because I understand that while we're totally okay

35

as long as those residual checks keep coming, we're no longer made of money now that Mom doesn't have a steady job.

Present day . . . Fighting with Mom about her drinking/pills/the fact that, actually, she's not tired—she's depressed. Door slamming (sometimes her, usually me). Apology from her about how sorry she is for being so moody—it's just a really rough time, but that's no excuse because she's the mother and should know better, and don't worry, all that's going to change because she's going to get it together this time. She swears. Really. Me accepting apology because it's either that or watch her stare at me like a puppy that's been kicked until I do. Going out with my friends to parties but spending more time checking up on her than trying to talk to guys.

But instead of going to parties, I seemed to be spending more and more time Googling "what to do when a parent's drinking gets worse," or working on my photography. Photography is my thing, and I'd found it only recently. Ben and I always hung out on Sunday afternoons—we started doing it about four years ago, first to let Mom catch up on her rest after having spent the week on set and, once she left the show, to sleep off her hangovers. About a year ago Ben took me to a Diane Arbus exhibit at the Getty Museum one Sunday. Photography hadn't been something I had paid much attention to before, but there was something about the shots—they were from her "Freaks" series—that floored me with how powerful they could be.

Before then I had never realized how a photograph—even a simple one—could tell a story that was just as descriptive as a four-hundred-page book. It was as if the lighting and composition and angles all worked together and told you a secret. Something you couldn't put into words. Maybe didn't feel safe putting into words. But it was there.

I became obsessed with the Nikon Ben bought me for my fifteenth birthday. Sure, things like Instagram and Hipstamatic were fun, but I preferred old school. The heft of a camera in my hand. Black-and-whites that weren't Photoshopped to look prettier or heightened with filters. Which, if I ever admitted that out loud, would probably result in my being run out of L.A.

Dr. Warner thinks that the reason I love photography so much is because it's something my mom has never had an interest in, so it's a way for me to define myself as separate from her. Maybe. Or maybe it's because photography is about expressing things without words. Mom's not good at being quiet, and I am. I don't know.

But I do know that I never feel more like myself than when I'm out and about shooting. When I'm taking pictures, it's as if the pane of glass that I always feel is between the world and me disappears for a while. Which, seeing that I'm behind a camera, doesn't make sense, but it's true. When I'm shooting, it's like I'm part of the world rather than separate from it.

Post–cookie making (as usual, Mom's ADHD made it so that she got bored and wandered off before we had even finished assembling the ingredients, leaving me to make the cookies myself), I was in my room posting a photo I had taken of a homeless woman pushing a shopping cart past a tricked-out Escalade in Venice onto my Tumblr when Mom came barging in, holding two of the many vintage 1970s Diane von Furstenberg wrap dresses that she owned.

"This one?" she asked, holding up a brown and pink print. "Or this one?" She gestured with a purple one with red squiggles.

I picked up my Nikon and fired off a shot of her.

"Annabelle, we talked about this—no pictures of me without makeup," she warned.

"But you look good. You look like yourself." I may have been the only person who preferred her without makeup than with.

"Put the camera down, please."

I did. "I missed the part on the Movie and A Manicure Evite about dressing up," I said, rubbing at a smudge on my white duvet in an attempt to get it out but only making it worse. Like the rest of the house, my room was all Shabby Chic whites and creams. It wasn't my style, but the decorator had said that it was dangerous to screw with the chi, or energy, of the house.

"Oh, honey, we're going to have to do that another

time," she said, walking over to my full-length mirror and holding both dresses up. "I just got a call from Carrie that these reality-show producers from Germany are in town. They want to take me to dinner to talk about doing a show about me, and this is the only night they're free." She turned to me. "So which one? The brown or the purple? Keep in mind that one of the guys is single."

There was so much about this that was wrong I wasn't sure what to be more upset about. Was it: (a) Mom didn't sound even the least bit sorry that not only was she blowing me off after I had canceled my plans for her but she was just telling me in passing; (b) her career was so in the toilet that she was considering doing a reality show; or (c) she was dressing to impress a German guy whom she had never even met? I decided to go with (d) all of the above.

"Really, Mom?" I demanded.

She turned away from the mirror. "So you don't like either of them." She began to walk out of the room. "Not a problem. I'll bring some more choices—"

"I'm not talking about the dresses!" I cried. "I'm talking about the fact that I canceled my plans to stay home to cheer you up and then you go ahead and totally bail without—"

She stood up straight. "I do not need 'cheering up,'" she said defensively. "Because people who need cheering up are people who are depressed, and *I am not depressed*."

"Yeah? Then who was that crying in your room until three o'clock in the morning every night this week?" I demanded.

She stood up even straighter and smoothed her imagi-
nary skirt, like some maid in one of those boring English
movies that always won a bunch of Academy Awards. ("Just
once I'd like to be offered one of those," Mom was always
saying. "I can look plain. I mean, I don't *prefer* it, but it's not
like I wouldn't do it for my art.") "Okay, Annabelle, that's
enough," she said, all serious. "We'll have this conversation
later, once you've calmed down." She began to walk out but
then turned. "And don't worry about helping me pick out
something to wear—I'll figure it out myself."

If she had delivered that line in a TV show or movie, it
would've gotten a laugh. But the thing was, she was serious.

We spent the rest of the afternoon fighting. Or rather,
I spent the rest of the afternoon huffing Play-Doh and trying to ignore her while she manufactured all these bogus
questions to try to get me to start talking to her because
she was too stubborn to apologize. At six, she *click-clacked*
into the living room as I was going through one of my
favorite photography blogs. It belonged to some guy in
Iceland where he posted photos of really depressing stark
settings that he then planted this mechanical smiling dog
in. "Well, I'm off," she said.

Not ready to forgive her yet, I ignored her.

"Do I look okay?"

I sighed and looked up. I was never good at the silent
treatment. Giving or getting it. In her peach-colored DVF
and vintage Frye boots, you couldn't tell that she had spent

the last three days in bed watching bad TV while drinking vodka and eating peanut butter-filled pretzels. "You look fine," I said grudgingly.

"Fine or good?"

"Good," I replied.

She smiled. "Thanks, Bug."

"But . . ."

"But what?"

"Are you wearing Spanx?" I asked.

"*No*," she said, offended.

"Oh." I went back to Tumblr.

"Do I need them?"

I shrugged. "No."

Out of the corner of my eye I could see her glare at me before she stomped off.

Not nice, true. But I couldn't help it. It was bad enough how selfish Mom could be sometimes, but to be so clueless about how selfish she was being and expect me to just forgive her like that—that was the part that drove me nuts.

A minute later she returned. "Better?"

I looked over and nodded.

She applied some of the Fiercely Fresh lipstick that had been named especially for her (a deep red called Jeweled Janie) to her already perfect lips before coming over and sitting down next to me. She smelled good. Agent Provocateur perfume. Warm and spicy and jasmine-y. Mom-ish.

"Annabelle, I'm sorry," she said softly, pulling me

toward her. "I realize that was selfish of me to do that. I wasn't thinking."

So she wasn't that clueless. I tried not to, but I leaned into the smell and closed my eyes. That smell was Mom at her best. When she was happy and together and made me feel like she had everything under control. The way you should feel when you're with a mom. At least I guessed so. I wasn't sure because it didn't happen that often.

"It's okay," I sighed into her head.

She let go of me. "You're sure I look okay?"

"Yes," I said. Actually, some of her eyeliner had smeared, but I was still mad so I wasn't going to point that out.

She flashed her trademark Janie Jackson smile. "Great. I'm off then. The restaurant's all the way in Malibu, so don't wait up for me. I'll see you in the morning."

"Two-drink limit!" I called after her.

"Annabelle, don't worry about me, okay?" she said in her best I'm-the-parent voice. "I'm the adult here. Not you."

In what universe?

The lack of typos in her replies to my texts throughout the night was a good sign. Her spelling, which wasn't great to begin with, got worse the more she drank. Around midnight, when she wrote that I would be happy to know that she had had only one glass of wine and was now drinking Pellegrino, I decided it was okay to go to sleep.

A few hours later I felt a hand on my shoulder.

"Annabelle," a man's voice said.

I smiled. Even three-quarters asleep, I'd know that voice anywhere.

"Annabelle, you have to wake up," Ben said.

I kept my eyes closed. Maybe Mom had had one of those movie moments where she had realized she was in love with him and she had gone to his house to tell him, and now they were waking me up because we were going to fly to Hawaii and they'd get married on the beach, like in some cheesy TV movie.

"Annabelle, you have to get up and get dressed, okay? We have to go get your mother out of jail."

Hearing "get your mother out of jail" will wake you right up. I shot up in bed. "What are you talking about?"

"DUI," he said as he rummaged through my pile of clothes to be put away on the antique bench at the foot of the bed, those that I never actually got around to putting away. He grabbed a pair of jeans and a T-shirt and tossed them over to me.

DUI stood for Driving Under the Influence. As in alcohol. So much for that two-drink maximum. Or the water that she swore she had switched to.

"She was driving on the wrong side of the PCH."

At that I slid back down under the covers. This was not happening. The PCH was the Pacific Coast Highway, which ran along the ocean and was sometimes hard to

43

drive on during the day. I screwed my eyes shut again and tried to go back to the Mom/Ben/me/Hawaii scenario while I waited for a "Just kidding!" from Ben. None came. I peeked out from under the covers. "Please tell me there were no paps around?" It was as much a prayer as a question. Paps were short for paparazzi, which was short for scum of the earth.

"There were," he sighed. "Annabelle, you need to get up. We need to go get her."

I pulled the covers over my head.

After a few sniffs from a can of blue Play-Doh that I then shoved into my purse, I threw on my clothes and pulled a brush through my hair. (It wasn't that I was vain, but things were bad enough without pictures of me looking as if I had just stuck my finger in an electrical socket making their way across the Internet.) During the drive over, I made a mental list of my favorite places in the world (the top of Fryman Canyon, the Marais in Paris, Palm Springs on a summer night). Ben, being Ben, tried to make me feel better by asking how my week had been; how I had done on my trig test; what new music I had heard on KCRW that he should be listening to so the assistants in his office wouldn't think he was totally uncool. Leave it to him to try to act as if we were on our way to get ice cream rather than to bail my mother out of jail.

Ben came into our life when I was eight. Mom met him because he was the entertainment attorney for the guy who lived in the apartment next door, this screenwriter named Scout Rosenstein ("It says Scott on my birth certificate, but that's just so . . . *common*, you know?" he liked to tell me when he babysat me while Mom was out on auditions). Back then she didn't have an agent or manager, so when she finally booked a voice-over gig for a deli-meat commercial, she needed someone to make the deal for her. Ben—who was not just a big-time attorney with big-time actor, writer, and director clients but also a vegetarian— wasn't in the business of doing rinky-dink deals like that, but Scout convinced him to do it as a favor.

As Ben likes to tell it, he took Mom on as a client not because of her, but because of me. From the minute we met, in his office—Scout, who was away in Thailand rewriting a big action movie because the star decided on the first day of shooting that he couldn't find his character's motivation, couldn't babysit me—we had this instant connection.

As for him and Mom, not so much. In that first meeting, she launched into this whole thing about how she had just taken a workshop about abundance and manifestation. And the fact that she had drawn him into her life like this to jump-start her career was proof that the crystals she had bought with the money that should have gone toward the electric bill had obviously worked. I had grown up with this particular brand of insanity, so I was used to it. Ben is *not* a New Age-y kind of guy, so he just thought she was bat-shit crazy. And then, when he politely tried to tell her that while he was sure that her psychic was right when she had

45

said that one day Mom would win an Academy Award, and while he was happy to do this *one deal* for her *as a favor to Scout*, he really wasn't taking on new clients, she completely ignored him and went right on talking.

My mother may have been crazy, but she was also charming, and you kind of couldn't help getting swept up in her excitement. Which Ben did. Maybe it was because unlike all the unformed guys in Mom's life—the pot-dealer-who-really-wanted-to-direct, the waiter-who-really-wanted-to-write, the personal-trainer-who-really-wanted-to-be-a-stunt-double-for-Johnny-Depp—Ben was solid. He didn't just have a job, he had a career. And a house, which meant he didn't have to crash at our place like the pot dealer did. And a car that was clean and didn't smell like cigarette smoke or break down on Sunset Boulevard, like the waiter's did. And instead of borrowing money from Mom like the personal trainer did (not that she had any to lend at the time, but she did anyway), Ben lent us some but never in a creepy way that made it seem as if he was doing it just so she'd go out with him.

In fact, unlike most straight guys, he never hit on her. At the beginning, it was because he had just broken up with this screenwriter he had lived with for three years and "needed to grow my balls back after she had busted them into a million pieces." (Overheard one night as the two of them hung out in the living room when I was supposed to be asleep. Instead, I was standing at my door with one ear to a glass listening to their conversation.) Then, after a while, when he had become family—to the point where Mom let him see her without her makeup on—the idea of them together seemed kind of creepy. Ben was the one who checked my math homework and listened to me practice my oral reports on such boring subjects as how the Grand Canyon came to be. (Mom said that as much as she loved me, listening to all those facts and figures gave her anxiety and was going to force her to take a Xanax.)

And Ben was the one I called the first time Mom passed out so hard I couldn't wake her up and I was terrified she was dead.

Nothing happened between them. Perhaps because, with an undergraduate degree in Russian literature from Princeton and a law degree from Yale, he was really smart and therefore knew that his shelf life in Mom's orbit would be longer if he used his brain when dealing with her instead of his penis. Until one night when I was thirteen. I had slept over at Maya's that night, but the next night when Mom, Ben, and I went to King Fu for our weekly Sunday night Chinese dinner, the whole thing was Awkward-with-a-capital-A. So awkward that, right after the waiter put down our egg rolls and moo shu pork, I turned to them and asked, "Okay, what's going on?" Mom, with her oversharing problem, blurted out the whole story. About how, the night before, after the season's wrap party, Ben had been trying to make her feel better about her latest breakup, from this German director named Thaddeus ("I do not make movies—I make *films!*" he was always correcting me). And how one thing had led to another and before she knew it, they were kissing and then . . . At that point I put my hands over my ears so I wouldn't have to listen—that's how grossed out I was. Luckily, Ben reined her in, and she skipped to what she called the long and the short of it.

"The long and the short of it, Annabelle," she had announced as Ben stared at his eggroll as if it held all the secrets of the universe while I stared at my sneakers as if they were in there instead, "is that, after a very long and honest conversation, Ben and I have decided that what happened between us last night, while it was beautiful and loving"—that was really how my mother talked sometimes, like a Hallmark card—"is better off . . . fading into a memory instead of blossoming into a full-blown flower." (A really cheesy Hallmark card.)

At that I had cringed. Not so much because I was still thinking about the fact that she and Ben had done it but because I was realizing how corny she could sound when she came up with her own dialogue. I hoped for her sake that she wasn't going to be one of those actresses who decided what she really wanted to do was write.

She turned to Ben and smiled. "Right, Ben?"

He paused before smiling back. "Right," he replied. He didn't look at me. But he didn't need to. Because in the moment between the pause and his "Right," I saw it all in his eyes. How much he loved her and how hurt he was by the fact that she didn't love him back that way.

Something changed after that night at King Fu. To anyone else, it probably wouldn't have looked any different, but to someone whose report cards over the years were covered with comments like *Annabelle is very perceptive of other people's feelings—perhaps to a fault, as she tends to take them on sometimes*, I picked up on it right away. Ben was still part of our lives—at my violin recitals, with the video camera because Mom was hopeless with anything that had more than one button; at birthday dinners; holidays; awards shows. When it was just the two of us—like during our Sunday outings—he was still the same Ben, giving me his full attention. But whenever Mom was around, I could see how at some point it was like a part of him got up and left the room. Maybe because it made it hurt a little less. After a while, it just became this unspoken thing that we lived with—the idea that Ben loved Mom, but Mom didn't love Ben "like that," and as long as no one (i.e., me) brought it up, we could keep pretending it wasn't there.

We got to the Santa Monica Police Department to find a swarm of paps waiting outside. You could always tell them from regular people: they were the ones chain-smoking and knocking back Red Bulls with pissed-off expressions on their faces as if they still hadn't gotten over the fact that they had been chosen last for volleyball in gym class in fifth grade, and that's why they had devoted their lives to making other people's lives hell. When they got a look at Ben's shiny BMW 750, they came to attention like soldiers. Well, if soldiers were doughy and in serious need of some sun and vegetables.

"Annabelle," he said, putting his hand on my arm as I started to open the door.

I turned. "Yeah?" My voice sounded garbled and far away, as if it were coming via an underwater speaker in a very deep pool.

"It's going to be okay. I promise."

Although Ben was pretty much the only person I knew who consistently made good on his promises, it was hard to believe him on this one. "Sure," I replied rather unsurely.

Something about the way he squeezed my arm made my eyes fill with tears, which I quickly put a stop to by biting the inside of my lip. I knew if I let myself start crying, there was a chance I might not stop. As I opened the car door I was gunned down by the *click-click-click* of their cameras. Growing up with a famous mom meant that I had perfected my blank stare when it came to this stuff years ago. It was just the right amount of I'm-just-going-to-ignore-you without being too bitchy and verging into you-guys-are-the-scum-of-the-earth territory. (Which they were. One time one tried to get into the examining room when Mom was having her gynecological checkup.)

"Annabelle! Over here!"

"Annabelle, how does it feel to have to come bail your mom out of jail in the middle of the night?"

"Annabelle, do you think this is because her career has totally tanked since she left the show, or was she always a lush?"

Okay, that was just wrong. As much as I tried to follow my *Thou shalt not look paps in the eye* mantra, I turned to see which one had asked that last question. Just in time to see Ben pull up all five feet eleven of himself as if he was going to take a swing at the guy.

Despite the fact that he drove a fancy car and lived in a million-dollar, famous-architect-designed house, Ben was a hippie at heart. He was Buddhist Lite and not into violence, but when people said mean things about Mom, something kicked in and he got all macho. "Just ignore them," I murmured, pushing our way through the crowd. He settled down, and we walked through the doors of the police station.

Each flash of the paps' cameras was a reminder that the truth about my mother—the one that I had tried so hard to hide—was about to become public.

———————————————————————————

I was about to go back to the bathroom for another round of Play-Doh huffing a while later when a thirtyish woman with blonde cornrows wearing a leopard-print halter top smiled at me. She would have been pretty if it weren't for the pockmarks on her face. And if she got her chipped tooth fixed. And if she lost the black liquid eyeliner. But she did have a nice nose.

"Cute top," she said.

"Thanks," I replied. "I, uh, like yours, too." It wasn't really my style, but it felt like the right thing to say during a chat in the waiting room of a police station while talking to a woman who may or may not have been a hooker.

She smiled big, showing a few more chipped teeth. "Yeah? I got it at Marshalls. In Chatsworth. I only got it, like, a few weeks ago, so there might be some left."

Chatsworth was deep in the San Fernando Valley. It was also the capital of the porn industry, a fact I had heard on the news the other night. "Great. I'll try and swing by there and pick one up," I replied, probably a little too enthusiastically.

She leaned in closer to me. As she did, I saw that she had a tattoo of a pentagram on the back of her right shoulder. Maybe she wasn't a hooker but a witch. "Personally, I like T.J. Maxx a lot better, but what are you gonna do, right? I mean, every single Marshalls—they all have this . . . *smell*."

"I know what you mean," I agreed. Actually, I didn't, but I was hoping that if I agreed with her she'd go back to her *People* so I could start surfing the top gossip sites to see what they were saying about Mom's arrest. After she didn't say anything for what seemed like a safe amount of time, I went back to my iPhone.

"Like a hospital, right?"

I looked up again. "Huh?"

"All the Marshalls. They smell like hospitals," she replied. "Or old age homes. But not T.J. Maxx. They smell like . . . one of those scented candles."

I couldn't believe I was having a conversation about the smell of different discount-clothing stores at five o'clock in the morning while the guy I wished was my father bailed my mother out of jail. Although that would definitely win me some sort of Most Original Facebook Status Update award.

As she put her *People* into her purse and settled back in her chair, I knew I was in trouble. "So who you here to get?" she asked. "Boyfriend?"

As I shook my head, the sleeping guy let out another snore and some more drool.

"That's who I'm here to get," she said. "Actually, he's my fiancé. We haven't gotten around to getting the ring yet, but we're going to. They're just so expensive, right?"

I nodded. As much as I was dying to know why the fiancé had been arrested, I didn't dare ask, afraid it would be a very long answer.

She pointed at Ben at the window, who, after signing a bunch of forms, was now on the phone. "That your dad?"

I shook my head.

"Oh. So *he's* your boyfriend."

Okay, I was definitely not in Kansas anymore. Ben was

twenty years older than I was. In L.A. you saw that a lot but not with, like, *teenagers*. "Uh, no. I'm here for my—"

Before I could finish, the door opened, and Mom came *click-clacking* out. Her steps were a little more wobbly than usual, but she still walked better in heels drunk than most people did sober. Her hair was a bit mussed up, her blue eyes were a little bloodshot, and her eyeliner was smeared, but other than that she looked fine.

"Omigod—that lady looks just like that actress!" my new friend gasped. "The one who used to be really famous! From that TV show...the *Friends* rip-off...what's it called?"

"*Plus Zero*," the African American woman offered.

The cornrowed T.J. Maxx fan nodded. "Right. Right."

When Mom saw me, she slowed, and her flawless posture—the posture she had perfected by doing the old-school-walking-with-a-book-on-her-head—disappeared. Her shoulders slumped, her face bloomed with sadness and regret and guilt and all the other stuff that I some-times saw on it when she hadn't closed her bedroom door entirely at night and I peeked through the crack. Or when she was standing at the sliding glass door that led to the backyard, staring out at the pool as she smoked a cigarette and blew the smoke outside, because in her mind, if she did that, she wasn't really smoking.

It sounded warped, but it actually made me happy to see my mother like that. Not because I wanted her to be miserable, but because it was honest and true and not an act. The times I loved Mom best were when she wasn't overly happy or overly beautiful. I loved her when she was human, because it made me feel as if it was okay for me to be human, too.

But then, in a split second, she put her (former) super-star face back on, threw her shoulders back, and continued *click-clacking* toward me. When she reached me she pulled me into a hug.

"Omigod, it *is* her!" I heard the woman gasp.

"Yup. You're right. I recognize the walk," the now-awake Hispanic hottie agreed.

"Oh, Bug. I guess I kind of screwed up, huh?" she said into my ear.

Kind of? "I don't know, Mom. You think?" I said, unable to keep the anger out of my voice.

I felt her stiffen. "You don't have to be so *hostile*," she said, hurt.

Before I could reply, I heard the familiar click of an iPhone camera.

With the money she could get selling that to one of the tabloids, my new friend would be able to buy every-thing in T.J. Maxx.

As the two of us let go of each other, Mom ran a hand through her hair. "You don't have a mirror by any chance, do you?" she asked me.

"Are you serious?"

"I'm a huge fan," the cornrowed woman gushed to Mom.

Mom smiled big. "Oh, that's so sweet! Thank you so much!"

"Do you think I could get a picture with you?" she asked. "'Cause no one's gonna believe me when I tell them I met you."

"I don't see why not," Mom said.

Ben and I looked at each other. Maybe on a normal day the fact that Mom was posing for pictures with fans in the middle of a police station at 5:00 a.m. after having been arrested would have seemed completely insane, but because this wasn't a normal day, it just seemed par for the course.

The woman handed the phone to Ben. "Would you mind?"

As Mom posed, I plopped down on the chair and did a Google search of her name to see what came up.

I cringed when I saw the first result. "Oh, no."

Ben looked over. "What is it?"

"Simon," I sighed. Simon was Simon Sweet, a blogger whose real name was Edwin Machado. Despite the fact that he was only twenty-eight, Simon had almost as much filler in his cheeks as Mom did. Who would've thought that not answering some dorky fan's e-mail with his request for an autograph all those years ago would have resulted in his remade self gleefully dragging Mom through the mud of cyberspace after her life imploded? Apparently, Simon was not great at letting things go because whenever he could write something snarky about Mom or print unflattering photos, he did.

Mom took her arm away from the woman's shoulder and reached for my iPhone. "Give me that." She held the screen up close to her face. "*What* . . . ? She squinted. "I can't see this without my glasses," she said as she handed it back to me. "Can you read it to me, Bug?"

I looked at it and cringed. "How about if I read it to you in the car?"

"No, I want to hear it now."

"Mom, I don't think this is—"

"Annabelle. Read it."

I sighed. "Okay. 'SIMON SEZZ.... What former sitcom queen who hasn't been able to get arrested finally *did* . . . driving the wrong way on the PCH at two a.m.? According to the police report, Ms. Washed Up and Has Been drank a little too much vino. . . . like, say, three times the legal limit. And from the mug shots that are about to be released, it appears that someone's been skimping on the highlights.'"

Mom was so mad some lines popped up on her forehead, which, given the amount of Botox that had built up over the years, was close to a miracle. "First of all? It was not two a.m.— it was three. And I was drinking vodka, not wine. And I was only two-point-nine-eight times over the legal limit."

"I don't know what that Simon person is smoking, talking trash about your hair," the cornrowed woman said. "'Cause I think it looks great."

"Thank you," Mom said.

She had been trying to get it done for about a month, but ever since Miki, her hairdresser, had gotten his own show on Bravo, he was now more famous than she was and had trouble fitting her in even though she had been his first celebrity client.

Ben walked over to the door and peered outside. "Janie, we need to go. There's a ton of paps out there."

She turned to the woman. "You wouldn't happen to have a mirror, would you?"

I grabbed Mom's arm. "Mom, come on."

"Okay, okay." She looked me over and pulled out a lipstick from her bag. "Bug, you look pale. Just put a bit of this on, will you?"

"You're insane," I said, shaking my head as I pulled her toward the entrance.

"You ready?" Ben asked me before he opened the door.

"Do we have a choice?"

"Nope."

"Then, sure. Why not?" I replied.

CHAPTER THREE

I spent my sixteenth birthday in rehab.

Well, visiting Mom in rehab. She hadn't wanted to go ("Rehab is for people who have a *serious* drinking or drug problem," she kept saying. "Not someone like me who has a drink once in a while to unwind.") Ben, her agent Carrie, and her publicist Jared thought it was a good idea. ("Don't take this the wrong way," Jared said during the Team Janie meeting at our house the morning after the arrest, "but I'm thinking we might be able to get you a book deal for a memoir out of this. Or at least a column in Oprah's magazine.")

So two days, countless snarky blog posts underneath Mom's mug shot, and a very unflattering photo of me taken by the T.J. Maxx lady making the rounds on the Internet later, Ben arranged for Esme, our housekeeper, to stay with me during Mom's time away, and he drove her down to Oasis, a "full-care facility for the recovery of mind, body, and spirit" (read: fancy way to say rehab). He took her when I was at school. More specifically, while I sat in class trying to focus on the trig quiz in front of me. Fully aware that no one else in class was focusing because they were sneaking looks at me to see if I'd end up losing it like Lara Newberry (the Daughter Of a stand-up-comedian-turned-movie-star) had the day after *her* mother had been shipped off there. ("All I can tell you is when you go for Family Weekend," she told me in the bathroom, "make sure you go hungry, because the food in the dining hall there is awesome. Totally organic. And because alcoholics crave sugar when they're detoxing, the dessert and snack selection is super-great.")

I may have looked as if I was keeping it together on the outside, but inside was a different story. That following Wednesday, before joining my friends in the cafeteria, I stopped in the bathroom. Luckily, I was close to the nice one—the one that they had just redone over spring break so that it no longer smelled all vomit-y. (Private school for girls = beaucoup de bulimia.) Once in, I went to the handicapped stall and managed to plop down on the toilet and grab on to the metal rail before my heart started to pound so hard it felt as if it was going to come through my throat.

"It's not a heart attack," Madame Jennings, the school nurse, had said two days earlier, on Monday afternoon when I got Mademoiselle Burton to let me out of history class to go see her.

"How do you know?" I asked doubtfully. Ever since a school nurse had told me my foot was fine the day I fell off the balance beam in third grade and then it had turned out to be broken, I tended to question their expertise.

"Because it's a panic attack."

I shook my head. "No, it's not. I don't get panic attacks."

She shrugged. "Well, now you do," she said curtly, as she opened up a carton of tongue dispensers and put them in a jar. "Welcome to the club."

I wondered if being a school nurse was like being a gym teacher. Kind of a those-who-can't-get-a-job-in-a-real-hospital-because-they're-missing-a-sensitivity-chip-end-up-in-a-school-arranging-wooden-Popsicle-stick-looking-thingies situation.

"You really think it's a panic attack?" I asked as I put my hand on my chest. It was as if behind my back my heart had gone to 7-Eleven and chugged a six-pack of Red Bulls.

"Yes," she grunted, not even looking up.

She was worse than a lunch lady. I guessed the fact that she sounded so bored should have made me feel less anxious, because obviously in her mind I wasn't going to die, but it was actually making me feel more so. "So what am I supposed to do about it?"

"Breathing helps."

"But that's part of the problem. I can't breathe."

She shrugged. "I don't know what to tell you. I suggest having your mother make an appointment with your primary-care physician."

I would have, had my mother not been busy doing something called "equine therapy," where you got in touch with your inner child while brushing a horse. Something I learned in an e-mail she sent from the BlackBerry that belonged to one of the chefs who was a big *Plus Zero* fan and had lent it to her even though it was technically against the rules for the rehabbers to have contact with the outside world.

Even though a Google search later showed that I had six of the eight most common symptoms of panic attacks, I continued to insist that wasn't what was going on with me. Mostly because there had to be at least one person in the family who was keeping it together. Esme, who was like a second mother to me, wasn't handling things very well. Ever since Mom had left, she spent most of her time crying and praying for Mom's soul while I patted her on the shoulder and handed her tissues.

Even the Play-Doh wasn't helping. The only time I seemed to be completely free of the anxiety was when I was standing in a very hot shower, which had left me with perpetually pruned fingers.

Sitting in the girls bathroom, I took a lot of deep breaths and was finally able to calm myself down enough to sit through lunch. I joined my friends at the table with a very L.A.-approved brown rice, veggies, and tofu bowl. "Hey," I said. "What's up?"

Olivia reached out and put a Cotton Candy–polished hand on my shoulder as I sat next to her. "How are you doing?" she asked quietly, as if she worked at a funeral home.

"Yeah. How are you doing?" Sarah echoed. Sarah was big on echoing whatever Olivia said. The thing was, she lacked Olivia's smoothness, so when she said it, it was a little too loud, to the point where a group of Sylvia Plath–loving depressives at the next table glanced over, excited to see who else was having a hard time.

I shrugged. "Turns out a parent in rehab does not get you excused from trig pop quizzes."

"Mrs. Tashlick's such a bi-atch, I bet she would've made you take it even if it had been an attempted OD situation," Maya said, shoveling fries into her mouth.

As warped as that was, I had to laugh. A lot of people found the fact that Maya was missing a filter between her brain and mouth a little off-putting, but that was one of the things I loved most about her. Along with the fact that she had recently chopped off her long blonde hair into a short bob and died it jet black, "just because."

Olivia flinched as Maya shoved three fries at once into her mouth. Up until last summer Olivia had considered fries a major food group herself, and had had the butt to prove it. Four weeks at fat camp and one eating disorder later, she existed on steamed veggies with a dollop of sriracha sauce for almost every meal, and the butt was a thing of the past. As was her previously frizzy brown hair—now it was blonde and keratin straight.

"Has Billy Barrett tweeted about it?" she asked.

The vein on the side of my forehead that had been pulsing on and off ever since picking Mom up at the police station started up again with a vengeance. "Why would he do that?" I had made the mistake of telling them about meeting him in Whole Foods, and now they wouldn't drop it.

She shrugged as she dipped a piece of broccoli in the sriracha and began to nibble at it. "Because they're now friends because of Whole Foods."

"Yeah. The Whole Foods thing," Sarah agreed as a glop of her tuna fish sandwich ended up on her shirt on its way to her mouth. With her frizzy red hair and freckles, she looked like the L.A. version of Pippi Longstocking. "Celebrities always tweet about other celebrities when they die and stuff like that. Not that, you know, your mom is *dead*," she began to backpedal. "What I mean is that they tweet when some crazy drama that's all over TMZ happens."

"Nice, Sarah," Maya hissed as she grabbed one of her sweet-potato chips.

"What?" Sarah hissed back, moving her chips closer to her.

"Way to take her mind off it."

"No, he hasn't tweeted about it," I replied. "Because they're not friends. They talked for two seconds."

"And he gave her his number and e-mail," Olivia added.

"And he gave her his number and e-mail," I agreed. "Which she won't be using because in light of everything that's going on, hooking up with some actor—who, by the way, has a girlfriend—is the last thing on her mind." At least I prayed it was. Not to mention I had managed to snag the receipt from her bag after we had gotten home from the market that day and tuck it away in my sock drawer.

As I managed to change the subject to the guy from Harvard-Westlake whom Olivia had met at the Crossroads party over the weekend, I flashed on a photo that I kept on one of my nightstands of the four of us. It had been taken two years ago, at the Oscar party Mom threw every year at the house. Her parties were almost as famous as the post-Oscar *Vanity Fair* party. In the photo, we're all crowded together, me in the middle, holding us all together, which was essentially how it had been since the four of us became friends back in seventh grade. When there were fights, I was the one who played Oprah and got everyone to make up. I was the one who decided what we'd do for our birthdays. I was the one who made a yearly scrapbook and gave them out to everyone on the last day of school.

Because it was just Mom and me—no siblings or even cousins—these guys weren't just my friends. They were my sisters.

Having a famous mom definitely raises your stock in terms of popularity, and sure, I had been invited to hang out with the super-popular girls—shopping, sleepovers . . . you name it. One spring break, Yancy Shapiro had even invited me to go to Hawaii with her and her family. But I just wasn't popular-girl material. I wanted to hang out with Maya and Olivia and Sarah. Like me, they were a little off. Maya had the whole IDI (inappropriate disclosure of information) thing going on. Olivia liked to eat her feelings, after dipping them in hot sauce. And Sarah was a hypochondriac who had a symptom-navigator app so she could try to diagnose all the diseases she was sure she had. While we weren't *un*popular, no one would be mistaking us as characters on *Girls* anytime soon.

"So are you still up for Arcade Fire next weekend?" Olivia asked. Because her father was the head of the television department at one of the big talent agencies, he was always able to get us tickets to concerts. Or, rather, his assistant did.

"It's, uh, Family Weekend at the . . . thing," I replied. I still couldn't bring myself to say *rehab*. In fact, the night before, as I lay in bed unable to sleep, I had made a list of synonyms for it—such as *wellness center, health spa, place people go after they fuck up royally*.

"Can Jade have her ticket then?" Maya asked. "She loves them."

Olivia and Sarah exchanged a quick look. Jade was Maya's new girlfriend. With their matching black bobs, they sometimes looked like twins, which was a little weird.

"Actually," Olivia said, "so does Parker. I think we should ask her." Parker was Parker Wren, sister of an actress who, in addition to supposedly going out with Ryan Gosling a few times, had just snagged a role in Wes Anderson's new film, a combination that gave Parker official Sister Of status. Olivia put her hand on my arm again. "We'll miss you."

"Yeah. Totally," Sarah agreed. "Some other time."

"Yeah. Of course. Another time," I said. Although it made me feel like the world's worst daughter, I hated my mother at that moment.

The only place where my mother had good timing was in front of the camera. Other than that, it sucked (see: getting knocked up by almost total stranger), so it made sense that the two weeks following her arrest were super-slow on the gossip front. Not one celebrity (a) announced he or she was gay; (b) got caught cheating via cellphone pictures; or (c) got into a public brawl with the ex of a current boyfriend or girlfriend. Which meant that for the first time since she announced she was leaving *Plus Zero*, Mom—and, by default, I—were in the news again.

There were pictures of me on the blogs walking into school with captions like "Devastated by Her Mother's Breakdown, a Distraught Annabelle Jackson Attempts to Trudge Through the Day!!!" (Actually, on that particular day, I was not distraught. I was exhausted because I had stayed up until two o'clock in the morning watching

The Way We Were and crying, not just because it always made me cry but because it was Mom's and my favorite movie to watch together.) And me outside Whole Foods chugging down a smoothie with the caption "It May Look Healthy, But What's Really in That Smoothie? Is Annabelle Jackson Going Down the Same Road of Destruction as Her Mother???"

That one bugged me, mostly because it was never going to happen. Maybe it was because Mom was a poster child for how annoying drunk people could be, or because vomiting wasn't on my list of fun ways to spend my time, but the one and only time I had gotten wasted had been enough for me. Every time I came close to throwing up, I found myself overcome with the fear that I wouldn't be able to get to the toilet in time, which would then render me immobile, and so I ended up hurling wherever I happened to be. Which, in that case, happened to be on a very expensive sofa at this girl Sparrow's house. I already felt out of control enough. I didn't need alcohol to feel even more out of control and then have a headache to boot.

Although as I pulled into my driveway on my bike post–Whole Foods smoothie pap attack, I kind of wished I could just walk into the house and pull out the bottle of whiskey I knew was stashed in the head of the giant Ganesha statue on the patio and drink until I passed out. (Although Ganesha was the Indian god who was the remover of obstacles, obviously, he—like the fountain—wasn't operating on all cylinders.) To be able to shut off my head for a few hours. Or at least turn the volume down on the running commentary about how Mom's arrest was just the beginning, things were going to get worse, and somehow (even though I wasn't quite sure how) this was all my fault. Like if I had been a better daughter, watched her more, and told Ben how bad things really had gotten with the drinking and pills, then I could have stopped it. If a drink (or five) would've done that, then I totally would've poured myself one. But I knew that the half hour (or five minutes) of peace I would've gotten would've then been followed by even worse fear and worry and regret. Plus, because I would be drunk, it would take that much longer to get back to a state of mind where I could then do something about it. Or at least *think* I could do something about it.

Esme was at her book club, and even though the sun was just starting to go down, she had put every light in the house on because she thought it made it a happier place. But when I walked in, there was nothing happy about it. If anything, the space and quiet I found myself standing in the middle of brought all the anxiety that I had been pushing down since Mom left bursting to the surface.

If I had been Olivia—or at least the old Olivia—I would've gone to the kitchen and started stuffing my face with any carb that wasn't nailed down. Instead, I went straight to my bedroom. Out of habit I locked my door, even though I was the only one there. I went to my closet and took out the pillowcase on the left-hand corner of the floor. As I brought it to my bed and turned it over, four cans of Play-Doh, two Barbies, a Skipper, and a Ken (maybe it was the lack of hair, but none of the Ken heads gave off that rubbery smell that I loved so much) came tumbling out. Followed by some assorted random Colorforms, their smell long gone, that I couldn't bring myself to throw out because they reminded me of the West Hollywood apartment and a time when Mom was happy and hopeful and had a glass of wine only on very special occasions.

Picking up the red can, I popped the top off and brought it to my nose, closing my eyes as I inhaled deeply. I counted to five as I held it in my lungs, waiting for the familiar feeling of safety to wash over me, like when I wrapped myself in the blanket that Esme had crocheted for me, but nothing happened. It didn't happen when I tried the yellow can, or even the blue one. Or with any of the Barbie heads. Instead, my heart beat faster as yet another anxiety attack kicked in.

Nothing was working.

Feeling even more anxious and uncomfortable than before, I went over to my desk and took my Nikon out of its case and walked into Mom's bedroom. Back when we still lived in West Hollywood, she'd go through decorating magazines and tear out photos of bedrooms she loved, talking about how one day her bedroom would be in a magazine. And it had been. A bunch of times.

Even though she'd been in rehab for a week her smell was still there — the musky smell of her Agent Provocateur perfume mixed with the tart citrus and sweet gardenia of the different body lotions that were scattered around the room. ("Let me tell you something, Annabelle," she liked to say. "Sure, dental hygiene is important, but soft supple skin? Just as important, if not more so. I mean, if need be, you can *buy* new teeth, you know?") I half expected her to come strolling out of her walk-in closet, wearing only her underwear. Even though it drove me nuts when she did that. ("Sweetie, the human body is a beautiful work of art," she'd always say when I tried to convince her to put clothes on. "Especially before things start sagging.") I would have done anything for her to do that right then.

I walked into her bathroom. All sorts of makeup tubes and bottles and compacts littered the countertops, untouched since she had left. She had enough to open up her own makeup counter. Or at least work at one. Which, once she got out of rehab, might be the only job she'd be able to get.

I aimed the camera. *Snap.* I loved the sound of the shutter opening and closing. There was something so purposeful about it. Something that said, I'm not sure why, but this image — this moment — it matters. It's something I want you to know about me and my life and what I think and what I feel and what I can't really tell you in words. Because if I try, it'll just end up sounding stupid and make me feel weird, like my insides are hanging out because I took the risk to let you in, so I'm going to do it in pictures, but then I don't want to discuss it after. Because if I do, we'll somehow start talking about my mother because somehow the conversation *always* ends up getting around to her; and it's too painful, and right now I'm too angry and too sad and too scared. So if I just don't talk about it, maybe I can keep pretending that it's not really happening, or that it's not really so bad, or that if I wish hard enough, the whole thing will just go away and we can go back to things being normal, whatever that means.

I opened the medicine cabinet. A row of amber-colored prescription bottles stood at attention like soldiers. Unlike the rest of the room, these were in perfect order, their labels facing out. Xanax. Ativan. Klonopin. Ambien. Prozac.

Snap.

Even before I had Googled each one to see what they were for, and the various side effects, and the things you were supposed to avoid when taking them (like, say, alcohol), I had known what they did. What they did was take my mother away from me. The way they made her eyes all glassy and her speech slow was bad enough. But when she took them, it was like I could see part of her—the part that was fun, and funny, and loved life, and had this amazing energy that swept you up whether you wanted it to or not, and got you out of bad moods, and made you laugh when maybe fifteen minutes before you wanted to cry—it was as if I could literally see it waft up and out of her, like smoke trailing out of a chimney. And what was left was just a beautiful five-foot-four, Pilates-ized, yoga-ized shell.

I opened the door to her closet and walked over to her Diane von Furstenberg dresses, wedging myself between them and breathing in her smell. Out of the corner of my eye I saw an old Payless shoebox, up on top of the shelf, its sides dented. I couldn't believe after all this time she still had it. I carefully took it down and went over to her bed, crawling under the covers and putting two pillows behind me, like we did when we watched TV together. To anyone else looking inside the box, it would've just looked like a random bunch of junk. Different-colored crystals and stones, fortunes from fortune cookies, inspirational quotes scribbled on paper about having faith and never giving up, one of those little clip-on koala bears missing its right eye, an empty bottle of a Young Living Essential Oil called Into the Future.

For good or for bad, this junk was what my mother was about—magic and wishes and hope. And—after years of struggling and going without so I could have and choosing to look at our life as an adventure instead of what it had been for so many years, which was chaotic and a little scary—it had paid off. Big time. Mom had gotten what she wanted—she had become famous, and the world knew who she was, and they loved her like her family never had. While Mom suffered from verbal diarrhea most of the time, her childhood was one subject she stayed quiet about. She had grown up in a small town near Pittsburgh that, from the few photos she had in an album she kept stashed on the other side of the closet, looked run-down and depressing. Her father was a mechanic, and her mother had been a secretary for an accountant. It would have been one thing if there had been a lot of love to make up for the fact that there wasn't any money, but from the stony look on Mom's face whenever I brought them up, there hadn't been.

At the bottom of the box was a piece of yellowed notebook paper.

> I, Annabelle Meryl Jackson, hearby proclame that I have the best mother in the entire world and that I love her more than anything—all the way up to God, past God, past God—and always will.
>
> (Even though she won't let me get that cute beegle we saw in the window of Pet Luv because she says that pet stores are evil because they get their dogs from puppy mills.)
>
> Signed,
> Annabelle Meryl Jackson,
> Age 7, Los Angeles, CA 90046

I smiled as I remembered the look on her face when I gave it to her. That was what started the "all the way up to

God, past God, past God" thing. I smoothed the paper and leaned it up against the box on the bed and reached for the framed picture on her nightstand—the same one from the Emmys that I had in my bedroom—and put it next to the box. Then I grabbed my camera.

Snap.

It was a good thing I just got the viewfinder wet with my tears and not the lens.

That Saturday, before we drove down to Laguna for Family Weekend, Ben insisted that we go to John O'Groats—a little restaurant on Pico Boulevard that, over the years, had become what we both considered our place. Unlike so much of L.A., it was down to earth, with oatmeal that was just the right consistency and even better biscuits. I so associated it with Ben that once, when Mom was dating this architect named Theo (he was Swedish, with blond hair and pale skin, and he never smiled) and she suggested the three of us go there for breakfast one Saturday, I lied and said that it was closed for remodeling.

Ben also insisted on singing the entire "Happy Birthday" song off-key when Sioban, our favorite waitress with a thick Irish brogue that took me years to understand, brought over a biscuit with a candle in the middle of it. Although I acted embarrassed, the truth was, the reason I kept my face turned down with my hands covering my eyes wasn't because Ben was such a bad singer (though he was) but because I was afraid that if I looked at him, the tears that I could feel lodged in my throat—the ones that had signed a lease at the police station and were so settled there they were almost done decorating—would decide to go on a field trip and come out through my eyes.

"Happy Sweet Sixteen," he said once I had blown out the candle. Like so many birthdays before, my wish was that my mother would finally get her shit together and marry Ben. "How's it feel to be the bravest, most beautiful sixteen-year-old on the planet?"

Ben was always going on about how pretty I was. And even though I always told him he was nuts, every time he said it, my heart was forced to expand to make room for the extra love that I felt for him because of it. Maybe it was because he knew that it kind of sucked being the semi-pretty Daughter Of one of *People*'s Most Beautiful People, but if he complimented Mom on how she looked, he always complimented me just as much, if not a little bit more. I didn't actually believe him, but I sure was grateful.

I shrugged. "I wouldn't know."

"I love you so much, Annabelle. You know that, right?" I nodded. I did. It was one of the few things in life I was sure of. "I love you, too."

He smiled and reached into his pocket and pulled out an envelope. "Here's the third part of your gift." The first part had been a new portrait lens that I had been stalking at Samy's Camera on Fairfax, and the second part was a book of Francesca Woodman's photographs. She had been this amazing artist who took these dreamy black-and-white self-portraits before jumping off a building when she was twenty-two. ("What a fascinating story," Mom had said when I told her about it. "Maybe I should develop a movie about her. With the right lighting I could probably pull it off, don't you think?")

The smile on my face flickered as I opened the envelope. It was an application for the CalArts photography program summer fellowship for high school students. I had mentioned it in passing to him about a month earlier, and because he was Ben, he remembered. I would have loved to go. "That was really sweet of you to remember, but with everything going on . . ." I shook my head. "I can't."

His own smile faded as well. "Look, obviously this is not a great time. For any of us. But I'm not going to let you put your life on hold because of her, Annabelle. You've done that enough."

"I have not," I said defensively.

His left eyebrow raised the tiniest bit, the way it did when Mom tried to tell him she had only had two drinks and was therefore fine to drive.

"Even if I did apply, I wouldn't get it," I went on.

"How are you going to know that if you don't apply?"

I hated how logical he could be. It had to be the attorney in him.

He reached for my hand. "Annabelle, give yourself this opportunity. You're an amazing photographer. Let the world see that. You need to stop hiding."

"I am not hiding." He may have not been my father, but sometimes I sure got mad at him like he was.

"Will you at least think about it?"

"Fine," I lied.

"This is it?" I asked later as we drove up a rolling green hill toward Oasis. In front of us stood a ginormous mansion complete with a gazebo surrounded by blooming flowers, and behind it the sparkling Pacific Ocean. I took out my camera and snapped away.

"Uh-huh," he replied. "It's like something out of *The Great Gatsby*," he said as he nodded to a smiling gardener, whom I half expected to break into song.

I wasn't sure what I had been expecting a rehab to look like. Glassy-eyed people zoning out in front of a TV tuned to bowling? Some sort of waterboarding setup? Oasis, however, was more like one of those resorts you saw in *Condé Nast Traveler* magazine—the ones that cost more a night than most people made in a week, where your every need other than someone wiping your butt was taken care of for you before you even realized it was a need. (The first Christmas Mom was on the show, we went to one of those places, in Mexico, and I was so uncomfortable with people coming up behind me and saying "Is there anything I can get you?" that I ended up spending the last two days in the hotel room watching television.)

"They're all so *happy*," I whispered to Ben as we stood in the lobby watching well-dressed people lounging on the overstuffed sofas, laughing. They turned to us and smiled. "Shouldn't there be, I don't know, . . . crying or something?" I murmured as I smiled back.

"Maybe that only happens at the cheaper rehabs," Ben whispered back.

"Bug!"

I looked up to see Mom sailing down the stairs. Wearing jeans and a light blue T-shirt, her hair hanging loosely around her makeup-free face, she really did look thirty-seven, like it said on her bio on IMDb, instead of forty-two, her actual age. Although she'd probably yell at me, I quickly reached for my camera and started snapping away. She looked too beautiful and too much herself not to.

In our last therapy session, Dr. Warner told me that when this moment came—seeing Mom for the first time—it was totally okay if I didn't want to let her hug me. I didn't even have to talk to her if I didn't want to. According to Dr. Warner, anger was a perfectly acceptable response to the situation and it was important to let that out rather than let it get stuck inside me and come out in all sorts of weird ways, like screaming at customer-service people in India with very American names.

"Mom!" I yelped as I ran up to her and threw myself at her, almost tackling her to the ground. Sure, I was pissed. But that could wait. As she hugged me and I breathed in her scent, I realized that for the first time in I didn't know how long it was free of that gross metallic twinge that the pills gave her.

She clutched at me so hard I could barely breathe. "Oh, Bug, I'm so sorry."

"It's okay," I said, scrunching my eyes tight to try to hold back the tears.

"No, it's not okay," she said tearfully. She pulled me to her closer. "I know I'm supposed to wait until we have our official session with Rain—she's the counselor who's going to be running group today . . . oh, honey, you're not going to *believe* her story. . . . Her mother was a crackhead, and then when she was sixteen she started . . . actually, you know what? It's her story to tell, not mine, so forget I said that," she rambled. "Anyway, what I wanted to say is that I know I owe you a giant amends for everything I put you through, and I don't expect you to forgive me right away—really, I don't—but I just hope that—" As a very tall African American man with long dreadlocks walked by, Mom waved. "Tony! Tony! This is Annabelle, my daughter!"

I wasn't sure what was worse—a hungover mom who moved at the pace of a snail or a sober mom who had so much energy it was as if she had drunk a pot of coffee in one gulp.

Tony came over. "Nice to meet you, Annabelle. I've heard a lot about you."

At that, Mom pulled me into another giant hug. "Do you see how much I love you, Bug? I talk about you all the time."

"She does," Tony agreed. "Like . . . all the time."

"There's Alexis!" Mom said as a skinny scowling girl around my age, her platinum-blonde hair streaked with magenta and wearing a nose ring, walked down the stairs. "I really want you to meet her. She's just lovely. Or will be when she finally lets me give her some makeup tips. Wonderful personality."

Alexis looked like she wanted to hurt someone.

"She could really use a friend," Mom went on. "Which is why I told her that once we get out of here, she should come out to the house for a weekend!" She pointed to an older woman wearing a silk caftan puffing away on a cigarette outside as she paced around a tree. "I also invited Marianne to come up for a few days . . . I know she looks fabulous—that's Halston, by the way—but the truth is her drinking and drugging have basically left her *destitute*," she went on. "Although I told her that there's absolutely no smoking in the house. Bug, I know I've only been here for two weeks, but I swear to you, I am *done* polluting my body—Ben! Oh, honey, it's so great to see you!" she cried as he walked up. She smothered him in a hug as well. "I know I fought you on it at first, but, honestly, I think coming to rehab is going to prove to be the single most important decision I've ever made in my life. Well, after having Annabelle, obviously." She turned to Tony. "You know, I was *thisclose* to having an abortion. But the night before I was supposed to go to Planned Parenthood, *Terms of Endearment* came on—did you see that? Shirley MacLaine is just *magnificent* in it—and—"

I cringed. Maybe rehab helped you stop drinking, but apparently it didn't help with oversharing. As I looked at Ben, I saw that he looked as freaked out about the new and improved Mom as I felt. Luckily, before she could embarrass me or herself even more, a very tan, very short man who looked vaguely familiar blew a whistle. "Hello, family. May I have your attention, please?"

Mom leaned over to us. "Look! It's Dr. Arnie!"

That's why I recognized him—Dr. Arnie was the founder of Oasis. Between being the addiction specialist for a news show called *This Morning* and a reality show called *Intervening . . . with Love*, he was on TV more than Mom nowadays.

"Before we start the weekend's festivities, I just want us all to take a minute"—the minute thing was Dr. Arnie's trademark—"to turn to the person on your left, and then your right, and to look them in the eyes—when I say this, I mean *deep* in the eyes, not the barely-scratching-the-surface way that we tend to go through life, making us feel alone and isolated and feeling like a drink is our only solution to that isolation—"

"Oh, I love when we do this," Mom sighed.

"—and because you're all probably standing next to your loved ones, what I'd like to do so that you can really go to your edge and get something out of this exercise is for everyone to move around and get in a circle"—Dr. Arnie was very big on circles—"and make sure that you don't know the person on either side of you."

All of us family members glanced around uncomfortably.

"Come on, family. Let's get moving," Dr. Arnie said.

At that, all the happy shiny rehabbers began to scurry while the rest of us looked longingly at the door, as if we wished we could make a break for it.

"Let's start *connecting*!" Dr. Arnie urged.

I had come here to connect with my mother. Not total strangers like the little old lady on my left who, later on, I would come to find had once robbed a bank to support her prescription drug habit.

"Now turn to the person on your left and look him or her deep in the eyes . . . that's it . . . deeper."

I tried. I really did. But when I'm uncomfortable or nervous, I laugh. A lot. Like a very-inappropriate-amount a lot. Which I started doing with the old lady who was boring into me with her eyes behind her smudged glasses.

Mom looked over from where she was gazing into the

eyes of an accountant-looking guy who looked so nervous to be standing so close to one of *People*'s Most Beautiful People that I could see the sweat beading on his forehead. "Annabelle," she hissed.

Instead of quieting down, I began to laugh more.

"Annabelle. Stop it," she ordered, louder.

I couldn't help it. The whole thing was just so bizarre.

"It's okay, Janie," Dr. Arnie assured her. "This is just Annabelle's way of self-protection over her uneasiness about being vulnerable. It's completely understandable. By the end of the weekend, she'll be in a very different place. You'll see."

Yeah, like back home in my room making a list of the reasons I wished I had someone else's life.

CHAPTER FOUR

SUMMARY OF FAMILY/FRIENDS WEEKEND AT OASIS

★ # of times Dr. Arnie said the phrase "Hello, family" = 52

★ # of times Mom hugged me = 47

★ # of times I was forced to wriggle out because she was suffocating me = 45 (the other two I forced myself to stay in it because I couldn't stand one more you-killed-my-puppy look when I pushed her away)

★ # of times I sneaked off to the bathroom to huff Play-Doh = 7

★ # of times I sent Maya a text that said something along the lines of "There are no words to describe the amount of touchy-feeliness going on here" = 21

★ # of times she texted me, saying, "I know you want to be a photographer but I really

hope you're taking notes bc this is so part of
a memoir. = 5
★ # of photos I took for what I had started to
think might make an interesting photo series
= 26

As corny as the whole thing was (see Saturday night talent
show put on by patients, which included spoken-word
performances and interpretive dance about addiction), it
was obvious that the place worked. Because the patients
and their families got to work out their stuff in front of
the entire group ("Family, alcoholism, and addiction are all
about secrets, which is why rule number two at Oasis—after
no drinking or drugs—is no secrets," Dr. Arnie said), it was
like having a front-row seat at a reality-show taping.

"Okay, Janie and Annabelle, you're up," he announced
on Sunday afternoon.

As Mom took out her lipstick and put on a fresh coat, I
tried to look at the bright side: at least her depression had
lifted to the point where she was back to being vain. She
turned to me and held it out. "You want some?"

I shook my head. "I'm good."

"Honey, I know this isn't really the time," she said, "but
once I'm home I'd really like to talk about your passive-
aggressive attempt to process your rage toward my addiction by avoiding makeup at all costs."

"Huh?"

"I've been talking a lot about this with Elan"—she stopped to turn and wave at her assigned counselor, whom she had daily therapy sessions with, an Israeli guy who, with his tight pink T-shirt, looked like Adam Lambert— "and we think that your avoidance of makeup is an act of hostility. Against me. Because it's such a part of my life."

I looked around to see that everyone was watching us.

"Not that it's not understandable," Mom went on. "You know, the hostility."

"Very good, Janie." Dr. Arnie nodded. "Especially the part when you get outside of yourself to acknowledge how Annabelle might be feeling. I know how hard you've been working on that."

How about how hard I was working not to yell at Mom for totally embarrassing me in front of all these people?

She may have given up drinking and pills, but as we sat facing each other in the inner circle with a carved Native American talking stick that Dr. Arnie had gotten from some medicine man during a trip to New Mexico, it became clear that she sure hadn't given up her other bad habit: taking every conversation and turning it around so it was about her.

"Annabelle, it would be very healing for me . . . I mean, for us"—at her correction, Dr. Arnie nodded approvingly— "if you could tell me the different ways in which I hurt you back when I was under the influence of alcohol and pills."

"You want me to do that right now?" I asked doubt-fully. "In front of all these strangers?"

"We're not strangers," Dr. Arnie boomed. "We're *family*."

I slid down in my chair. "Please, can we do this some other time," I mumbled.

"No, we can't," Mom said firmly. "According to Dr. Arnie, this is a very important part of my recovery."

I looked over at Ben, who gave me one of his please-just-do-what-she-wants-in-order-to-keep-the-peace looks. Usually accompanied by an even-though-you're-younger-sometimes-you-just-need-to-be-the-bigger-person speech. Which, according to my calculations, would mean that when it came to Mom, I was as big as the continent of Africa.

I cleared my throat. "Okay. Well, then I guess—"

Mom shoved the stick to me. "Honey, you need to use the talking stick. It makes the whole thing more sacred."

At that moment I wished I kept a blog. Because you couldn't make this stuff up. I took it from her. "I guess ..."

Mom leaned forward. "What, sweetheart? What is it you guess?" she asked anxiously.

"Janie, remember the exercise we did in group last week about respecting people's boundaries and personal space and not smothering them by finishing their sentences?" Dr. Arnie asked.

"Yes. Right," Mom replied. She grabbed the talking stick from me. "I'm sorry for interrupting you, Annabelle.

That wasn't very respectful of me. Please go on," she said as she offered me the stick again.

I took a deep breath. The faster I got to it, the sooner I could go lock myself in the bathroom with my Play-Doh. "When you were drinking . . . I don't know . . . sometimes I'd get . . . really scared," I said softly, feeling as though I was going to throw up. Talking about my feelings was not at the top of my "Favorite Things to Do" list.

For once, Mom stayed quiet. In fact, it was so quiet, I could hear Larry, this guy who had wrecked his lungs because of all the crystal meth he had smoked, wheezing in the corner.

"Excellent, Annabelle," Dr. Arnie said. "Can you tell your mom why you got scared?"

I pinched the top of my thigh so I wouldn't cry. "Because sometimes . . . when I'd go into your room to check on you, you were barely breathing," I said quietly. "And I'd have to go into your bathroom and get a mirror and hold it up to your mouth to make sure I could see your breath."

I heard Ben draw in his breath. As close as we were, I had never told him that. I had never told anyone that. It made me feel ashamed, as if it was my fault. Like if I were better or different or didn't fight with Mom so often, she wouldn't drink so much.

I watched as Mom's shoulders fell. All of the Janie Jackson of her was gone. She was just . . . a person. And as warped as it sounded, I really wished I could have taken a picture of her at that moment. "I'm sorry," she whispered.

"Do you know how many times I thought you were dead?" I snapped. The anger was definitely starting to come.

Her eyes filled with tears. "Bug, I am so, so sorry—" To her credit, she didn't try to take the talking stick from me.

"And do you know how many times I've heard that?" I yelled as my own eyes started to leak.

"I know," she said. "Annabelle, I'm sorry. You know, everyone thinks an amend is an apology, but that's not what it means," she said quietly. "I looked it up on diction-ary.com." She glanced at Dr. Arnie. "What I meant was that I had someone else look it up because Internet access isn't allowed here. Anyway, it means 'to change.' And that's what I'm going to do. I'm going to do my best, one day at a time, to try to be the best mother I can possibly be." She reached for my hand. "That's all I can promise you, Annabelle. I can't even promise I'll be successful at it. But I can promise I'll try."

How many promises had she made to me over the years? And how many times had she dropped the ball on them? I wanted so badly to believe it was going to be dif-ferent this time, but I didn't have the energy. I was too tired. Tired of being angry. Tired of being scared. Tired of not trusting her. Tired of being let down when I did trust her. I was so tired that when Mom went to hug me, I didn't try to get out of the line of fire like I usually did.

But I didn't hug back.

I just couldn't.

Later that afternoon, as Mom and Ben had tea and gluten-free scones, I grabbed my camera out of the car and took a walk. While I made sure not to take any shots where people's faces could be seen because of the whole anonymity of it all, over the weekend I managed to get some good stuff. The liver-spotted hands of a seventy-five-year-old man named Herb, his fingers gnarled by arthritis, clutching the bronze medallion he had been given for the thirty days he had been clean and sober. ("Obviously I'm thrilled for Herb—he's a lovely man, not to mention a huge fan of the show," Mom had whispered as everyone clapped for him, "but to get sober when you're that old? The pain of having to feel your feelings will kill you that much faster.") A copy of what was known as "the Big Book"—written by the people who had started Alcoholics Anonymous—open to a page that had certain passages underlined, with handwritten notes in the margins. Mom and Ben sitting on a glider on the front porch, her head against his shoulder, the two of them staring into space as they swung back and forth.

I was just about to take a shot of a cigarette butt next to a giant stone that had the word *Breathe* etched into it (talk about an oxymoron) when I heard Mom's familiar *click-clacking* behind me. (She may have let go of alcohol and pills, but heels were another story.)

"Do you want to take some shots of me?" she asked.

"No thanks," I said, snapping away.

"Oh. Okay," she said, disappointed. My mother still didn't quite understand why I liked taking photos that didn't have faces or people in them. Specifically, people who were not her.

"Ben said he got you a new lens for your birthday."

I stood up and turned and aimed the camera at her. "Yup."

"Honey, don't," she said, putting her hand up to shield her face.

"You just asked if I wanted to take a picture of you."

"Yes, but I meant, you know, *later*. When I have some makeup on."

I clicked away. "Why? You look good now."

"I do? Really?"

I nodded and clicked some more.

She put her hand down and relaxed a bit. As she did, Janie Jackson started to come alive again. A big smile. Her trademark head tilt.

I put the camera down.

"What's the matter? You just said I looked good!"

"You do. It's just...I don't feel like shooting anymore." I didn't want to take photos of things everyone took. I wanted the truth. And that Janie Jackson—the one with the high-wattage smile—she was never really real to begin with.

She walked over and sat on a bench and began to pull at a sunflower. "When I get out of here, I'm going to get you your present."

"You don't have to."

"Of course I have to. It's your Sweet Sixteen!"

I aimed the camera again, focusing on the quarter chin she had going because of the angle of her head. She'd kill me for that later, but she looked good.

"Okay, but it better not be makeup or anything like that."

"Please. I know better than that," she sighed. She stroked the sunflower. "Did I ever tell you what I got from my parents for my sixteenth birthday?"

I shook my head.

"A coupon for a free introductory class at Très Jolie Beauty School," she said.

They had never supported her dream to become an actress. They had wanted her to become a beautician.

"Did you go check it out?" I asked.

"Nope. Saved my money from the ice cream place I worked at in a paper bag that I kept in my sock drawer and then used it to buy a one-way bus ticket to L.A. right after graduation."

I smiled. My mother may have been a lot of things— crazy, annoying, melodramatic, maddening—but she was also brave. We had gone to visit my grandparents once, when I was four, but Mom had had a huge fight with my grandmother and we had left early. I didn't remember much about the trip other than Mom taking me to that ice cream place and me crying as I dropped my mint chocolate chip cone on the sidewalk, but I do remember how neither of my grandparents seemed to see my mother. Even though she wasn't famous yet, everyone who came into contact with my mother was pretty dazzled with her—me, most of all. But the two of them—I remember that they just looked through her, as if she wasn't even there.

It all felt very Shrink 101, but as I watched her on the bench, I thought about how maybe that was what this— the wanting to. be famous, the drinking—was all about. About not having been seen by the people who are supposed to see you. Most of the time I wished my mother gave me less attention, but maybe she did it because she hadn't gotten any.

As if she could read my mind, my mother held out her hand, and I went over and let her pull me down next to her.

"I know you don't believe me, but I really am sorry."

"I know you are."

"I am, Bug. I really am," she said as she twirled one of my curls around her finger.

"And I just said I know you are."

"I love you, Bug."

"I love you, too," I sighed.

I felt her relax. "Thank you."

We sat there quietly for a few moments. I closed my eyes so I could better hear the sound of the ocean in the distance.

"How much?" she asked.

I sighed. "All the way up to God, past God, past God."

She squeezed me to her. "That's how much I love you, too. Things are going to be different, Annabelle," she said. "They're going to be okay."

I heard a wave crash. "Okay." Suddenly, I felt sleepy. Like now that the storm was over and I didn't have to worry about the roof being ripped off, I could finally rest.

I heard footsteps and opened my eyes to see Ben striding over, his usually tan face looking pale. "We have a problem," he said gravely.

I sat up straight. So much for resting.

Mom shook her head. "Problems aren't really problems. They're just opportunities for growth." She turned to me. "Isn't that catchy? I heard that at an AA meeting the other night."

"Well, then, what I'm about to tell you is a very, very big opportunity for growth," Ben said.

"How big?" I asked nervously.

"On a scale of one to ten?"

I nodded.

"Ninety-five."

"When did you become such a drama king?" Mom laughed. "This is so not like you. Unless you're about to tell me that you just found out you have some incurable

95

disease, whatever you're about to tell us cannot possibly be that bad."

"Barney's dead," he said.

Barney was Barney Merloff, Mom's business manager—the one who had taken care of all her money since *Plus Zero* started and invested it in stocks and paid all the bills and drove over in his red Cadillac every Friday afternoon with checks for Mom to sign and homemade rugelach that his wife, Arlene, had baked for me. I loved Barney. He was like the sweet, balding, coins-jingling-in-his-pockets, how'd-that-quarter-get-in-your-ear-magic-trick grandfather I never had.

At that, Mom burst into tears. "No! *No no no no no no!*" she wailed.

"That's not the bad part," Ben said.

"What do you mean, that's not the bad part?!" Mom demanded. "Don't you know that Barney was like a *father* to me? What happened? Was it a heart attack?" She shook her head. "I've been telling him for years that all that pastrami was going to catch up with him. I even gave him a gift certificate for ten sessions with my trainer for his last birthday!"

"He . . . killed himself."

Talk about a bad part.

"What?!" cried Mom. "How could I not have seen that he was in such emotional pain?! I guess I was just so stuck in my own misery . . . oh, God . . . how long was this going on?"

"The emotional pain? Probably from the time that the police showed up and arrested him for embezzling close to a hundred million dollars from his various clients and wiping them out completely," Ben said.

"*Whoa*," I said.

"Oh, my God . . . those poor, poor people!" Mom cried.

Oh, no. "Uh, you're not going to now tell us that we're *part* of that poor, poor people group, are you?" I asked.

Mom turned to me. "Annabelle. Stop with the catastrophic thinking, please," she ordered. "It's really not good energetically."

Ben sighed. "Unfortunately, Janie, it's not catastrophic thinking."

"Yes, it is," she said. "She always goes to that place. I mean, I understand why, I really do, but—"

"It's the truth," he said.

We just stared at him. Waiting for him to say "Just kidding!" even though Ben was not a "Just kidding!" kind of guy. Mom stood up and began to walk around in circles, dazed.

"Mom, watch where you're going!" I called after her as she began to stumble into some roses. I turned to Ben. "Okay, maybe he took *some* of our money, but we're not part of that wiped-out-entirely group, right?" I asked nervously.

His look alone told me that, actually, yes, we were.

So much for the things-being-okay part.

CHAPTER FIVE

Although it hadn't hit the blogs yet, when I got back to school that Monday after Family Weekend, I could tell from the whispers and stares that the news had gotten out. And seeing that the only people I had told were Olivia, Sarah, and Maya, it had to have come from one of them. Maya had been in full obsession mode with Jade for the last month, during which, if she wasn't talking to Jade on the phone, or texting her, she was talking about her, so I knew she wasn't responsible. Not to mention she was out sick that day.

When I had FaceTimed with Olivia and Sarah the night before and told them, they seemed genuinely concerned. ("You're not going to have to move to one of those shelters, are you?" Sarah had asked, all freaked out.) But by third period the next day, when they weren't at our regular meeting place in the quad before the morning bell, or in the bathroom where we checked in during passing time, I started to think something was up. The fact that they quickly stopped talking when I got to our table at lunch didn't help my paranoia, even though they made sure to keep the conversation light as we ate and focused on this new raspberry/yogurt/spinach/egg white diet (Olivia's contribution) and the symptoms of Lyme disease (Sarah's). And when I ran into them at Om My Gawd, our favorite coffee place, after they had told me they couldn't come over after school because they both had their SAT tutors, I knew.

"Annabelle," Olivia said nervously. "We ... um ..."

"Both your tutoring sessions happened to get canceled?" I suggested.

They looked at each other, relieved. "Uh-huh," Sarah said.

They may have been my best friends, but good liars they were not.

"And we were thinking of texting you to see if you wanted to come," Olivia said, "but we thought, you know ..."

"That I wouldn't want to be out in public because my life has been blown to bits?"

"Well, *yeah*," Sarah agreed.

I watched as Olivia cringed. Sarah's lack of tact was something we were used to and just accepted. But every time Sarah had a foot-in-mouth disease flare-up, it always had to do with someone on the outside—not one of us. And that cringe or eye roll would be done together.

If Dr. Warner had been there, she would have told me that

instead of letting my fear of confrontation get the best of me and just ignoring the fact that my best friends had lied to me, I needed to call them on it right then and there. Not lie in bed that night and go through all the different things I should have said at the time but didn't because I was a wuss.

I decided to try it. Right after I fortified myself with some Play-Doh. Once I was safely barricaded in the bathroom (between calls to check on my mother, panic attacks, and hiding from paps I could have written an insider's guide to restrooms across the greater Los Angeles area, and despite the thrift store decor of the coffeehouse, the bathroom was surprisingly clean), I whipped out the full-size can of blue Play-Doh.

I sniffed in and stared at myself in the mirror, willing myself not to pick at the two large zits that had decided to take up residence on my chin. "You can do this," I gasped before emptying my lungs. "These are your best friends. If you can't be honest with them, who *can* you be honest with?"

And then the door opened.

"Ah!" I yelped.

"Whoops. Sorry about that," a girl said.

The bathroom may have been clean, but the lock was tricky. And it wasn't just any girl—it was Parker Wren, the Sister Of from my school.

She moved forward so she could get a better look. "Annabelle?"

I tried to hide the can behind my back, but my hand

was shaking so much, I dropped it and watched helplessly as it began to slowly roll toward her.

She leaned down and picked it up. "What are you doing with Play-Doh?" she asked, confused.

I was usually good at coming up with a believable lie on the spot. But at that moment, I was at a loss. I just stood there, my mouth opening and shutting like a guppy. "I, uh . . . I just found it in here," I finally mumbled. "And I was . . . checking to see if it was really Play-Doh, or, you know . . . something else."

She took a sniff, wrinkling her nose as if it were dog shit. "Ugh. Yeah, it's Play-Doh." She tossed it into the trash as if it were contaminated and turned to leave. "I'll see you out there."

"Yeah," I mumbled. After she left, I walked over to the door and locked it again. Then, with my butt against it for further reinforcement, I stretched as far as I could to reach the garbage to fish out the can, knocking it over in the process so that the top came off, the clanging echoing off the concrete walls.

"*You,*" I said to myself in the mirror as I sniffed in a moment later, "are beyond pathetic."

When I got back to the table, the three of them quickly stopped talking.

"Hey," I said as I looked around for a chair. Parker was lounging in the one I had been sitting in, so laid back that she was almost reclining.

"Oh, *hey*," Olivia said, as if it had been five years since we had seen each other rather than five minutes.

"That totally sucks about losing all your money," Parker said, slurping her iced latte.

"Yeah, it pretty much does," I agreed.

"And that you can't go to Cabo now," she said. For the last three years, the four of us had gone to Olivia's parents' vacation house there right after school let out. Obviously, after the Barney news I had been sure I couldn't go, but as we were driving home from Oasis, Ben made a point of telling me that there was no way I was canceling, and that it would be another birthday gift from him.

"I didn't say I couldn't go."

"Although I guess your loss is my gain," Parker said, slurping some more.

"What are you talking about?" I asked, confused.

At that, Olivia fiddled with a lock of her brunette hair while Sarah moved her jaw from side to side—habits that came out when they knew they were busted.

"Parker, we—" Olivia started to say.

Parker shrugged. "The fact that I'm going in your place."

"—hadn't exactly decided that was the deal," Olivia finished. She turned to me. "It was just something we were thinking about. If, you know, it turned out—"

"—you couldn't afford it," Sarah finished, so loudly that the table of fedora-wearing hipsters turned to see who the poor loser was.

"I thought you said she *definitely* wasn't going," Parker said.

I waited for them to tell her that of course they hadn't said that; that she had misheard them; that I was their best friend and this was a tradition; and that, actually, because she was acting like such a bitch, it was probably best if *she* didn't go. Instead, they just looked away.

Which was the only answer I needed before I ran out of the coffee place to Mom's surprise Sweet Sixteen present to me—a Prius. Which was probably going to be repossessed. Having just gotten my license, I wasn't a great driver to begin with, but trying to navigate pre-rush-hour traffic (which, because it was L.A., was just as bad as rush-hour traffic) with tears streaming down my face got me more angry honks than usual. As I drove, I flashed on a documentary on the Discovery Channel that I had once seen about how, in the wild, when an animal is sick and weak, sometimes the other animals, instead of protecting it, will just go in for the kill because they know that it can no longer be of use to them and pull its weight in keeping the whole ecology of the animal kingdom going. That didn't just happen in the wilds of Africa. It happens on the Westside of Los Angeles, in all-girls private schools, too.

Once home, I got into bed and wouldn't come out— even though Esme, in an attempt to deal with *her* feelings about the life-blown-up thing and the fact that she was losing her job of nine years, had been on a manic cooking binge and had made her famous homemade empanadas. I had never been a big crier—I guess after the first few times I cried over Mom and nothing changed, I decided it was a waste of time—but that night I couldn't stop. First, I tried to stave it off with some lists, but as I felt the feelings rise up, I finally just curled up and let it go. I cried until snot ran out of my nose; I cried until my gasps for air sounded more donkeylike than human; I cried until I was emptied out of all the anger and fear and sadness that could fit in my body.

I cried through the texts from Maya saying she had heard what happened and those guys were assholes and we didn't need them anyway and she totally wanted to talk to me but was with Jade at some spoken-word thing in Venice and would call me later. And the ones from Ben asking how I was doing and—staying with the theme that if we continue to pretend everything is just business as usual, maybe it will be—telling me that there was a documentary on HBO about the photographer Annie Leibovitz that I might like. And the e-mail from Mom—typed on an Android belonging to Sam, the Reiki energy healer at Oasis who really wanted to direct—telling me how excited she was to come home tomorrow night and to keep an eye out for some curtains she had ordered online from Anthropologie and that before I started freaking out because our financial situation was a little "up in the air at this moment," they were on sale—"VERY ON SALE!!" she wrote in caps—so it would be just fine.

And then I cried some more.

=====================

In the movies, after someone falls apart like that, they wake up the next morning feeling better. As if a tsunami ripped through and although there's all this destruction that's been left behind, there's also a feeling of peace and calm and the motivation to start over again and build something better. Not in my case. In my case I woke up pissed off that I was still alive and promptly pulled the covers over my head and stayed in bed. It turned out that, like Mom, I was really good at staring at the wall for hours on end. Maybe it was hereditary.

I didn't even want to make lists, which, had I had the energy, would have been centered around things like Possible New Friends Now That I Only Had One and That One Was Totally Obsessed with Her Girlfriend. (I was thinking of zeroing in on foreign-exchange students from Middle Eastern countries who didn't know who Mom was because they didn't get *Plus Zero* there. Finally, around 4 o'clock, I dragged myself out of bed and into the shower, where, as I scrubbed away any physical evidence of my depression (lying in bed for almost twenty-four hours resulted in very oily skin), I also practiced various upbeat renditions of "Hey, Mom! Welcome home! Why are my eyes all swollen? Allergies, I think." The last thing I wanted was for her to come home from rehab, get all stressed out about the fact that I was all stressed out, and end up drinking again.

Not that I needed to worry about that. She was too busy going through the Google Alerts about her that had accumulated while she had been gone the last twenty-eight days and reading me the comments that people had posted on the photos of her leaving rehab that had surfaced on some of the gossip sites that afternoon to notice. ("Listen to this one, Bug!" she yelled out from the bathtub. "'Janie Jackson looks about ten years younger now that she's sober. I'd totally do her.' Isn't that so nice?")

There's no guidebook that tells you how to act after your mom comes home from rehab. I wanted so badly to trust her; to believe that things were going to be different; but certain habits were hard to break. Like how, after we had spent some time going over some listings of condos to check out that weekend, I got ready for bed and walked over to her bedroom to say good night, carefully avoiding the creaky parts of the hardwood floors so that she wouldn't have a chance to stop doing whatever it was that she wasn't supposed to be doing.

I got there to find her door almost closed, but open just enough for me to be able to spy on her. What I saw totally freaked me out: my mother was reading quietly while drinking from a mug.

She looked up. "It's okay, Bug, you can come in," she said, all calm.

I pushed the door open. "How'd you know I was there?"

She smiled. "You're a loud breather."

"I was just checking . . . to see if you needed anything," I said. *To see if you were drunk. Or zonked out on pills.*

"Nope, just reading," she said, holding up a book called *Perfectly Imperfect*. Apparently, rehab hadn't cured her addiction to self-help books.

I walked over and sat on the edge of her bed, reaching for the mug. "Can I have a sip?" So maybe I was still working on raising my trust level a little.

"You hate tea," she said.

That was true. "Not *all* tea," I said. "So can I?" If she said no, I was picking up the phone right away and calling Ben—

"Of course you can."

I took a sip and tried not to gag. Why was tea so disgusting? After I swallowed, I relaxed. No alcohol. Unless there was a certain kind of alcohol that didn't actually *taste* like alcohol, which you—

"Annabelle. There's no alcohol in there. It's tea. Just plain old Peach DeTox tea, okay?" Mom said, a little pissy.

"I didn't think there *was*," I said, just as pissy. So maybe we had a lot further to go with the trust stuff than either of us would have liked. "Anyway, I just wanted to say good night."

She smiled. "Good night, Bug." She leaned over and hugged me. "I'm so glad to be home."

"And I'm glad you're home," I said.

For as long as we had one.

I don't know if Mom believed me the next morning when I told her that I still wasn't feeling well and should therefore respect my fellow students by staying home so as to not inflict them with germs, but she didn't fight me on it.

Although I wished she had after everything hit the fan later that morning.

"That's two weeks away!" she cried after she read the certified letter she had just received—the one addressed to Janet Eleanor Jackson, her real name. ("Janie just sounded so much cuter," she had explained to me when I first discovered the discrepancy. "Plus I didn't want anyone confusing me with Michael Jackson's sister," as if the difference in skin color wasn't a big enough giveaway.) According to Mr. Dinshaw Patel from Wells Fargo, we needed to be packed and moved out of our house by the end of the month. Apparently this was not the first time that Mr. Patel had attempted to contact Mom to let her know there was a problem, but Barney had intercepted the letters.

Picking up a pen from the table and holding it to her mouth as if she were smoking it, Mom paced around the living room as the silver statue of Lakshmi, the Indian goddess of abundance, seemed to mock her. (Yet another very expensive yet obviously defective good-luck charm.) "Okay,

okay. What am I supposed to do?" she asked herself. "I'm supposed to breathe, and I'm supposed to . . . call my sponsor!" In Twelve Step programs, a sponsor was a person who had been in the program longer than you, whom you called for advice. According to Mom, it was like a shrink mixed with a priest or a rabbi. "But I don't have a sponsor yet! Because I'm supposed to be going to meetings so I can find one." She turned to me. "I think I should go to a meeting."

"Go," I replied. It seemed like a much better solution than.popping a pill.

CHAPTER SIX

CHANGES MY MOTHER, AS MY MOTHER, DECIDED
WOULD BE OCCURRING NOW THAT SHE WAS MY
MOTHER AGAIN (OR MAYBE WAS MY MOTHER FOR
THE FIRST TIME)

★ Meals would be eaten together. Without the aid
of magazines, books, TV, or iPhones. (That one
went away after day two, when we resumed
eating dinner the way we always did: on the couch
making fun of the hosts on *Access Hollywood*
and *Entertainment Tonight*).

★ Every day would include twenty minutes of
non-meal-related together time, when we
did things like "communicate, listen to, and
appreciate" each other. (Thank you, Dr. Walter
Bienstock, author of the bestseller *We're
Family, But I Realize I Barely Know You*, one of
the many books she downloaded.)

★ Homework would be looked over to make sure it was completed before bed. (This one went away after day two, due to Mom's ADHD and lack of math ability.)

★ Her Facebook friend request must be accepted so that she could monitor my online activity and make sure I was not interacting with people (i.e., men) who were age-inappropriate. (Not happening. I knew she'd just spam my wall with comments written in caps with exclamation points and inspirational videos about spirituality.)

"What would you like me to cook for dinner?" she asked a few nights later as we drove home from the two-bedroom condo on Darlington Avenue in Brentwood that I had found on Craigslist and that we had just signed a lease on. Mom thought that the fact that we'd be the only non-Iranians in the building other than the woman across the hall from us and her three cats would be great. ("What a wonderful way for us to expand our cultural horizons!" she exclaimed as Persian music wafted through the open windows as we stood in front of the smoked-glass mirrors in the living room. "And we don't have to spend money on plane tickets!")

"You mean, what do I want you to defrost?" I asked as

I took the wheel while she reapplied her lipstick.

Satisfied that her lips were kissable—even though one of the things they said at rehab was that you shouldn't get into a relationship for the first year of your sobriety or make any other big life changes—she took the wheel back. "No, I mean cook."

"Pushing buttons on a microwave and opening takeout containers is not cooking."

"I'll have you know that during my meditation this morning I ended up *visualizing* myself cooking," she said. "So I downloaded a bunch of cookbooks onto my ereader and—"

"Mom, you can't be buying books right now!" I cried. "You need to be *selling* them!" I had started listing her stuff on eBay. I had gotten pretty good at writing up catchy postings about once-in-a-lifetime opportunities to own clothing, shoes, and accessories belonging to an A-list Hollywood celebrity. (The word *former* really should have come before A-list, but I needed to move the stuff fast.)

"Annabelle, stop worrying about our finances," she said firmly. "You're not the mother, okay? I am."

I snorted. "Since when?" Whoops. I hadn't meant to say that. And from the hurt look on her face, it had come out pretty harsh. "I'm sorry. I didn't mean—"

She nodded. "No. It's fine. I understand where you're coming from," she said softly, making me feel worse than

I already did. She reached for my hand. "Annabelle, I want you to know I completely validate this hostility you've been feeling toward me since I've been back. I really do."

"I don't have any hostility," I said.

She was the one who now snorted.

"I *don't*," I repeated.

"Honey, you're allowed to have feelings around all of this," Mom said. "In fact, you *need* to have them."

"I don't have any feelings," I snapped.

"Yes, you do. You're having feelings. End of story," she snapped back.

I sighed. Mom not passing out every night was a positive change. But the fact that suddenly she was pulling rank and going so overboard trying to be the responsible mother was annoying.

Soon our conversations were limited to which box to pack what in. But even if I didn't want to talk to her, I couldn't stop myself from keeping tabs on her like I had before Oasis. As much as I wanted to believe that when she said she was going to an AA meeting, that's where she was, or that the pill I had just seen her swallow was, in fact, a multivitamin, it was hard. Especially after we moved to the new apartment.

One of the most difficult things about Family Weekend at Oasis had been hearing just how much of a sneak Mom had been. The way she had poured vodka in the fresh-squeezed juices that Esme spent a half hour making her when she went on her health kicks. The way she'd play all her doctors against one another in order to get more pills. According to Dr. Warner, having everything out on the table was ultimately a good thing because now Mom and I could start with a new foundation, but it didn't feel like that. It felt like hell. If you couldn't trust your mother, who *could* you trust?

Maybe snooping around in her bathroom drawers in our new apartment to see if she was hiding anything wasn't a cool thing to do on my part. And not calling to find out her ETA after her AA meeting, before I went to snoop through her bedroom—that was a stupid move. But I *did* snoop, and I *did* get busted, which resulted in her freaking out, which resulted in *my* freaking out, which resulted in her calling Ben to come over to "handle" me because she couldn't. Which resulted in my asking her if she really thought it was fair that she was always asking Ben to do the kinds of things that you'd ask a boyfriend or husband to do—like, say, get a person into rehab or handle their kid—but she wouldn't actually *let* Ben be her boyfriend or husband even though it was clear to everyone that nothing would make him happier. Which resulted in her telling me to mind my own business because I was not mature enough to understand how complicated these things were. Which resulted in my going into my room and slamming the door before firing off a text to Maya that said, *God, I freaking hate her sometimes!!!!*

The good news about Ben getting involved was that even though he was not-so-secretly-if-you-could-read-him-like-I-could in love with Mom, he also knew that, although she was sober, she was still nuts. I knew that when he got there, he'd totally agree that she was going way overboard with all this I'm-the-mother-end-of-story stuff. And that while maybe rummaging through her private stuff when she wasn't home wasn't very nice, it made sense.

I was in my new bedroom working on a list when Mom and Ben came in.

PLUSES TO HAVING A VERY LIMITED SOCIAL LIFE

★ Don't have to worry about buying birthday gifts for friends, which means all that money can go toward new camera gear.

★ Don't have to worry about clothes that you lend to friends getting stained/ruined.

★ Time that would have been spent texting with friends/shopping/getting mani-pedis can instead be spent making lists about the pluses of not having a social life.

★ Lunches can be spent alone under a tree pondering the meaning of the universe rather than talking about boys, movies, or gossip.

"Annabelle, there's something . . . ow!" he said as he smacked one leg on a table that had been in the living room of our house. Like the rest of the apartment, my bedroom was stuffed to the gills, to the point that if the producers of the TV show *Hoarders* saw our place, they would've booked Mom in a minute, and probably for a double episode. We had downsized from five thousand square feet to a thousand, but instead of selling most of our furniture, Mom had insisted on keeping as much as she could. ("We're going to need it when things turn around and we move again," she kept saying.) But instead of putting it in storage like a normal person, she moved as much as she could into the apartment. I had a king-size bed in a room that was meant to fit a queen (snugly, at that) and bruises all over my shins from bumping into things whenever I tried to make my way out the door.

He turned to Mom. "Janie, you've got to get rid of some of this stuff."

"And give in to small-minded thinking that is all about lack instead of abundance? No, thank you," she replied as she maneuvered her way around the slipcovered love seat that had been in our cabana near the pool.

He sighed. "Fine." He looked at me. "Annabelle, your mother and I have been talking and—"

"You're going to Alateen," Mom finished.

He gave her a look.

"What's *that*?" I demanded.

"Remember when we were at Oasis and we went to that Al-Anon meeting?" Ben asked.

I nodded. Al-Anon was the Twelve Step program for family members and friends of alcoholics, whether they were still drinking or sober. They had meetings, just like AA, where speakers shared their stories about what it had been like living with the person who was drinking, and what happened that ultimately made them start coming to meetings and how their life was different now. Then, after they were done, other people got a chance to share for a few minutes. Because it was a Twelve Step program—which, according to Dr. Arnie, was not a religious program but a spiritual one—there was a lot of talk about a Higher Power, which seemed to be another word for God. I wasn't sold on the whole God thing (see: the Holocaust, innocent people starving in Africa, the success of the Kardashians), but I do know that when Ben and I had been in that meeting I did feel like something had my back.

"Well, Alateen is a group for younger members of Al-Anon," Ben explained. "Kids your age."

What was going on here? This was the part of the movie where he was supposed to agree with *me* that Mom was overreacting. Telling me I had to go hang out with a bunch of strangers and share my innermost secrets and let them pat me on the shoulder or, even worse, *hug me* was not part of the script. Unless it was a horror movie. I shook my head. "No way. I already go to therapy."

"This is different than therapy," Ben said. "It's a support group. With kids going through the same thing you are. You know, I've gone to some Al-Anon meetings in the last few weeks and—"

117

Had everyone gone nuts? "You guys can spend all the time you want going to meetings," I said as I stood up, "but that's not how I'm spending *my* time."

Unless I was bribed.

"So I probably shouldn't mention that the reason I'm here is because I was promised a Holga camera in return for giving up an hour of my life to listen to complete strangers share their innermost secrets," I said to Ben as we sat in his car outside a church on Wilshire Boulevard that Saturday morning.

"Yeah, I'm thinking leave that part out. Might not go over well with the crowd," Ben said as he ruffled my hair before pulling my door open. "I'll be back at one to pick you up."

Luckily, there was a decent coffee place that was about three blocks away, which meant that if I started walking back at quarter of, I'd have plenty of time to get inside and then walk out with the group at one.

"And just so you know, I'll be waiting out here around twenty of," he said with a wink. "In case, you know, you were planning on just ditching the meeting altogether."

Or not. I sighed. It was both amazing and annoying to be known so well.

The meeting was held in a mildewy-smelling basement with a furnace banging away somewhere down the hall.

I walked in to find a fat kid with reddish-brown hair

and freckles who looked to be a few years younger than me wearing a vintage Donkey Kong T-shirt with his hand in the Munchkins box that was sitting in the middle of the scuffed table.

He looked up, startled. "I'm only taking one," he said defensively.

I glanced at his hand, nails bitten to the quick, clutching at what looked to be at least three, probably four, greasy-looking dough balls, before sliding into the folding metal chair closest to the door.

He pushed the box toward me. "You want one?" he asked with his mouth full.

"No thanks," I said as I began to rummage in my bag. When I had turned twelve and started carrying a purse, I had discovered the usefulness of rummaging as a way to avoid having to talk to people when I was nervous.

"You're new, huh?" the boy asked.

I looked up in time to see him go to grab another Munchkin. A mission that he reluctantly aborted when he saw he was busted. "I didn't get a chance to have breakfast this morning," he said, just as defensively.

I shrugged. "I don't care how many Munchkins you eat."

Which then made him grab two. "Am I right? You're new? 'Cause I've never seen you here, and I've been here every Saturday for the last eight months." I wasn't sure why he sounded proud of that fact, but he did.

"Well, yeah. Kind of," I replied. "I mean, I'm *new* in

that I've never been here before, but it's not like I'll be coming back. . . ."

"How do you know if you'll come back if you haven't even sat through a meeting before?"

I shrugged. "I just know."

"But how? Don't take this the wrong way or anything, but that's really judgmental of you."

When someone told you you were being judgmental, how *were* you supposed to take it?

"So who's your qualifier?"

"My what?"

"Your *qual-i-fier*," he said, as if dragging the syllables out was somehow going to explain it. "Jeez, you *are* new. The person in your family who drinks."

I shook my head. "I never said anyone in my family *drank*."

He snorted. "Denial's not just a river in Egypt, you know."

Who *was* this kid? "Okay. Fine. My mother . . . she used to drink . . . but she doesn't anymore. She just got out of rehab," I said proudly.

"I remember when my dad got out of rehab the first time. That was"—he counted on his fingers—"five times ago."

If everyone was like him, I definitely wasn't coming back. Before I could go to the bathroom for a Play-Doh break, some more kids started to file into the room. Most of them seemed to be around my age, a few younger, a few older. And—in the case of this one girl—a lot younger, like elevenish. In addition to the Munchkins lover and me, there were a few other white kids, some African Americans, a few Hispanic kids, and one Asian girl who took the seat on one side of me. Who—from the kimchi she was eating that smelled insanely delicious and was making my stomach rumble—was most likely Korean. It reminded me of my elementary school back in West Hollywood back before Mom got famous and put me in the L'École, where suddenly everyone around me was white and rich.

In addition to the kids, there was what I was later told was an Alateen meeting sponsor, someone older who was in Al-Anon who sat back and made sure that things ran properly. In this case, the sponsor was this girl Amanda, a woman in her late twenties with auburn hair, kohl-rimmed eyes, and a tattoo across her left wrist that said GRACE. She didn't say much, and a few times I saw her checking her phone even though one of the announcements at the beginning was "Out of courtesy for the other members, please do not text during the meeting." But I also saw her nod a bunch of times with a grateful smile on her face as people were talking, as if she totally identified and understood what they were saying and feeling, which made me jealous. It had been a long time since I had felt that way.

"Are there any newcomers who would like to introduce themselves at this time?" asked Laticia, who was running the meeting. The reason I knew her name was because when she began she said "I'm Laticia" and the group—well, everyone in the group but me—responded, "Hi, Laticia" in unison in this singsongy way.

I slunk down in my seat and started examining my cuticles, but even with my head down I could feel everyone staring at me.

"Introduce yourself," whispered the Munchkin kid, who had somehow ended up sitting on the other side of me.

I gave him a look before I mumbled, "I'm, uh, Annabelle."

"What'd she say her name was?" a Hispanic boy wearing a TUPAC 4EVA T-shirt across the table loudly asked the girl next to him, who was busy texting. "Angela?"

"She said Annette," the girl replied.

"Annabelle," I said louder.

"Hi, Annabelle," they sang. I tried not to flinch. Even if I got something out of this thing, I didn't think I could ever come back if only because I could not deal with the "Hi" thing. It just felt so . . . cult-y.

Luckily, no one began grilling me after that. (Annabelle what? Who's your qualifier? Why are you picking at your fingers?) Instead, Laticia went back to reading a bunch of handouts that I didn't listen to because I was too busy thinking. Where exactly did things go so wrong that I'm spending a beautiful Saturday afternoon not with my friends, or a boyfriend, but in a smelly church basement at some self-help group meeting? A few words stuck out—*understanding, hope, acceptance*. Like, say, the way I *hoped* that Mom and Ben would be *understanding* when I told them they needed to *accept* I wasn't coming back here.

"Okay," Laticia said when she was finally done reading through the *Twilight*-size notebook of announcements. "Well, Eddie was supposed to speak, but he texted me last night that his dad was getting out of jail today and he was going with his mom to pick him up, so—"

Okay, I'm sorry. But *jail*? Then I remembered: it was only a few weeks ago that my mother had been in jail as well. So much for thinking I was all that different than these guys.

She turned to Munchkin Guy. "Walter—would you do it?"

"Sure," he said, wiping his mouth with the back of his hand. As he stood up and walked to the head of the table, I saw that he had a bit of plumber's butt going on. Once he settled himself in his seat, he cracked his knuckles. "Hi, I'm Walter—"

"Hi, Walter," boomed the group.

I was just about to get up, slip out, and go hide in the bathroom when something clicked and the Charlie-Brown's-teacher *wompwompwomp* noise coming out of Walter's mouth morphed into regular English, and what I heard shocked me. Even though there was a lot that was different about us—he was a fourteen-year-old boy and mentioned Call of Duty, like, three times—I completely related to much of what he was saying. The way that he couldn't stop himself from snooping in his dad's briefcase and throwing out pills when he found them. The way that he hated to have friends over because he never knew if his dad was going to embarrass him by being drunk. The pressure to remember what lies he had told to other people in order to cover up the truth about what was going on inside their house.

When he talked about that stuff, I knew exactly how he felt. And because I knew how he felt, I felt understood—like Amanda did, when she nodded—and not so alone. And because I felt understood and not so alone, I felt. . . . *better.*

When Walter was done, and we went around the room and people started to share, I related to them, too. I even found myself nodding a few times. That being said, I had gone this long without help from anyone but Dr. Warner in dealing with Mom—I didn't need to bring my problems to complete strangers. Finally, after the Korean girl shared about feeling if she could just try harder to be perfect, then maybe her mother would stop drinking (hi, been there, done that), it was my turn.

I cleared my throat. "Well, uh, this is really—"

"Who are you?" Walter demanded.

"Huh?"

"Your *name.*"

"I already said it," I replied, feeling my cheeks getting red. "It's Annabelle."

"Yeah, but you have to say it each time you speak," said the Hispanic boy.

I sighed. "Fine. I'm Annabelle, and—"

"Hi, Annabelle," the room sang back.

I flinched. "Hi. And, uh, I think this is a really great thing you guys have here. So thanks for letting me sit in and listen today. . . ." I trailed off. They all looked at me, as if waiting for me to go on. "And . . . that's it."

Luckily, it was 12:59. When Amanda said it was time to close the meeting, I shot out of my seat.

"Where are you going?" asked Walter.

"She just said it's over."

"No, it's not. We still have to close."

As everyone got in a circle and grabbed hands, I half wondered if we were going to start skipping around and singing "Ring Around the Rosie."

"Annabelle, would you like to take us out with the Serenity Prayer?" Amanda asked.

"What?" I asked, confused.

"She doesn't know what that is. She's new, remember?" Walter reminded her.

"I know what it is," I insisted. Mom had put a copy of it up on the fridge.

He shrugged. "Fine. Go for it."

Everyone looked at me, waiting for me to start. "Ah . . ."

"God . . ." —Walter began, before everyone joined in — "grant me the serenity . . . to accept the things I cannot change . . . the courage to change the things I can . . . and the wisdom to know the difference."

Other than the God part, it wasn't very religious, which was a relief.

At the end of the prayer, while still holding hands, everyone moved them up and down.

"Keep coming back," they said in unison.

Even though I may have related to what they were saying . . . *that* was not going to happen.

Awards shows are the L.A. version of religious holidays. The Golden Globes are Rosh Hashanah; the Grammys are Easter; and the Academy Awards are Christmas, Yom Kippur, and Kwanza all rolled into one. Each one is an opportunity for a party, including the MTV Movie Awards, which Mom decided would be a great opportunity to make into a house—or to be more accurate, apartment—warming party.

It was a good thing we had been poor before Mom became famous because it meant that we knew how to clean. And because our apartment was about one-sixteenth the size of the Santa Monica house, we had it party-ready pretty quickly. One of the worst things about going broke was having to let Esme go. She ended up taking a full-time job in Malibu working for a director and his wife because her mom was coming from Guatemala for good and she needed a steady gig, but she promised that she'd be back. ("Wait until I get on *The Price Is Right* and win," she said. "After that, I'll come back and take care of you for nothing.") Her last day with us was so sad that I ended up eating the entire *dulce de leche* cake she had made me as a good-bye present while Mom was at back-to-back AA meetings.

"That Wendell boy seems very nice," Mom yelled from her bedroom as she tried on half her closet looking for just the right outfit for the party, even though there would be only six of us. "I'm glad you invited him to the party."

"It's Walter," I called out while I set out the food. Nothing fancy—just guacamole, hummus, chips, spinach dip. A little different from the time Mom had convinced the chef from Nobu to cater our Oscar party. "And I didn't invite him—you did."

The day before, while Mom was over in the bath-and-body-cream aisle of Whole Foods, even though I told her that buying fifteen-dollar vanilla body cream was not how people without money shopped, and I was in the middle of checking the ripeness of some avocados and wondering whether we could get away with not having guacamole and serving just salsa, seeing how much the avocados cost, I felt a jab in the back.

"Is that you?"

I turned around to see Walter—the Munchkin-eating kid from the Alateen meeting—chomping away on one of the jumbo chocolate chip cookies from the bakery shelf.

"Yup. I thought it was," he said with his mouth full. "Annabelle, right? I'm Walter. In case you forgot."

"Hi, Walter," I said in the singsongy way the kids had used in the meeting. I was trying to be funny, but from the look on his face I had missed. Like by a mile. I glanced over to see that Mom was now demonstrating her signature pratfall from the show to a small group of shoppers. "Mom," I called out. As she glanced over at me I shook my head in an attempt to get her to stop.

"That's your mom?" Walter asked, surprised.

I nodded.

"The woman who got busted going the wrong way down the PCH?"

Apparently, even fourteen-year old gamers read the gossip blogs. "Yup."

"That was *epic*. My dad only hits mailboxes. But he's gotten pretty good at it." He held out his cookie. "Want some?"

"Thanks," I said as I broke off a piece. Maybe he wasn't *that* bad.

"I said a *piece*—not *half* of it."

Then again.

Mom made her way over. "Did you see that older couple? They're from Des Moines, and it turns out they have

128

every single episode of *Plus Zero* on their DVR. It's like they're . . . what do you call that . . . superfans!" She flashed her signature Janie Jackson smile at Walter. "Hello, I'm Janie Jackson."

"I'm Walter."

"So do you two know each other from school?" Mom asked.

"Mom, I go to an all-girls school, remember?"

"Oh, right." She laughed. "Early sobriety space-out, I guess."

I shook my head. So much for anonymity.

"I know Annabelle from . . . *around*," Walter said. He made it sound like we were part of the CIA, rather than two people who ended up in a smelly basement because our parents drank too much.

She turned to me. "Did you invite Walter to the party?"

"Um—"

"What party?" he asked suspiciously.

"We're having a little soiree for the MTV Movie Awards tomorrow night," Mom replied. "A combination awards/ housewarming thing. We recently had to move because—"

"Mom, Walter probably already has plans—"

"No, I don't," he said. "That sounds like fun."

"You don't have to come," I said quietly as Mom turned away to pose for a picture with the couple from Des Moines.

"Why would I have said I wanted to if I didn't mean it?" he asked. "If I had done that, that would've been

people-pleasing, and that's one of the things that attend-
ing meetings helps us to stop doing."

I sighed. "Fine. Give me your number. I'll text you the
address."

When I had recently given the praying thing a try, like
those kids had been talking about at the meeting, and had
asked if maybe God could bring me some friends now that
mine were gone, this wasn't what I had in mind.

"Bug, come quick!" Mom yelled. "Look who's on!"

Camera in hand, I walked to the door of her filled-
to-the-gills-with-slipcovered-furniture bedroom, where a
shirtless Billy Barrett was running away from a burning
building in an ad for *Rad and Righteous*.

"Isn't that *weird*?" she asked. At least she was wearing
a towel instead of walking around naked, like usual.

"What?" I asked as I snapped away at her nightstand,
which was littered with self-help books and little Twelve-
Step meditation books.

"That at the exact second I turned on the TV, there he
is!" She turned to me. "What do you think it means?"

I aimed the camera at the heap of dresses on her bed. If
she had sold them—which she refused to do ("Annabelle, this
is your *legacy*," she kept saying, even though they were all size
twos, and I was a six)—I bet we could have paid our rent for
a year. I shrugged. "I think it means his movie's number one at
the box office, and they want to keep it that way."

"No, I mean the *deeper* meaning," she said. "You know what they say . . . 'Coincidence is God's—'"

"'Way of remaining anonymous,'" I finished. "I know. You've mentioned that." That was the latest slogan Mom had picked up at meetings. I just prayed there wasn't a bumper sticker for it. Her car was already covered with ones that said things like ONE DAY AT A TIME, EASY DOES IT, and LIVE AND LET LIVE. ("Are you sure you don't want me to get you one for your car at the Twelve n' Twelve?" she had asked the other day. "Not only is it such a great reminder for you, but you're actually being of service to other people when they're driving behind you!")

"I've actually been thinking of calling him," she said. "Except I can't find that piece of paper with his number on it. . . ."

Because it was still in my sock drawer.

"So I was thinking of e-mailing Carrie's assistant to see if she could find out who his publicist is and—"

"Please don't," I pleaded.

She glanced up from the pile of dresses. "Don't what?"

"Don't—" The look on her face made me stop. Like she was this innocent kid, and I was about to tell her that Santa Claus was just something made up by Walmart and Target to justify people getting pepper-sprayed on Black Friday. "Nothing."

She shook her head. "Nope. Can't get away with that, Bug. That's not clear and open communication." She pushed the dresses aside so she could stretch out on the bed and put out her hand, motioning for me to join her.

Thank you, Oasis, for that. "It's just . . . he's sixteen years younger than you!" I said as I walked over and lay next to her.

She cringed. "Do you really need to keep bringing that up?" She shrugged. "So there's a bit of an age difference. It worked for Demi and Ashton."

"No, it didn't! They broke up!" I reached for the camera and aimed it at her. I loved the little lines that were starting to come in on her face now that she couldn't afford Botox as often.

"Well, it worked *until* they broke up." She put her hand up. "Not so close, Bug."

Instead of pulling back, I actually zoomed in closer. "Yeah, and then she had a total meltdown and became anorexic and started doing Whip-Its and got carted off to rehab."

"Hey, there's nothing wrong with rehab," she said. "It's the beginning of healing."

I put the camera down and curled up beside her. "I thought the AA people told you you can't get into a relationship for a year."

"It's not that you *can't*," she replied as she tickled my arm, "it's just something that's *suggested*."

I closed my eyes. For years I had been the one to tickle her arm. It felt good to be on the other end of it. "How come?"

She shrugged. "I don't know. Probably because if it doesn't work out you'll want to drink or something."

My eyes snapped open. "Well, there you go. That's a good enough reason right there," I said. I hated how much I still worried that at any moment things could go back to how they had been. "Don't you think you have enough going on at the moment without getting involved with some ginormous star who's closer in age to me than you?"

"What are you talking about? I have nothing going on," she replied. "That's the problem."

"That's not true," I said. "You just got a voice-over."

She sighed. "For *dog food*, Bug. *Dog. Food.*"

I was glad we weren't facing each other so she couldn't see me cringe. That sounded a lot worse when said out loud. "Well, it'll pay the rent for next month at least."

"Nope. Half the rent."

If Ben weren't helping us out, we would have been even more screwed. Because he didn't want to make Mom feel worse than she already did, he tried to do it in ways that weren't so humiliating. Like how he said the reason he was paying my tuition was because he wanted an excuse to go to the East Coast and visit me when I went to college. And how he took over the car payments because he cared about our safety and didn't want us to have to deal with some used car that might have bad brakes.

Mom got up from the bed. "I don't want to talk about this anymore. It's too depressing."

She was right. It was.

"Getting back to Billy —"

Okay, that was as depressing as the fact that we were broke.

"It's just . . . I really felt a connection with him," she said. "Like at a very, very deep level."

"Um, did you *see* SimonSez's Not-So-Blind item on his blog this morning?" I asked.

"No. Willow suggested I try and detox off the gossip stuff for thirty days." Willow was Mom's sponsor. She was only twenty-five but had been sober for five years. An ex-heroin addict, she now worked at Neiman Marcus in the Chanel department. "What'd it say?"

I picked up her iPhone and surfed for it. "It says . . . *What Hollywood hottie, recently crowned Hollywood's most eligible bachelor, is also a major commitmentphobe as evidenced by the canoodling with cuties that was going on last night at Soho House?*"

She shrugged. "It doesn't say it's him."

I looked at her.

"At any rate, I'm telling you, Bug. The way I feel is very strong. It might even be a past-life thing."

I sighed. "Mom, people are going to be here in, like, an hour, and you haven't even put your makeup on yet." I picked up a purple-and-tan-striped wrap dress. "Here — how about this?"

She took it from me. "Bug, I'm serious. Why are you so against my getting in touch with Billy?"

I might have answered her if I had known the answer, but I didn't. It was partly the age difference. Partly that I worried that if they hooked up and then he dumped her, on top of everything that had gone down this past month, she'd start drinking again. Partly the fact that I knew the bloggers would have a field day with their snarky comments. But it was more than that. I just wasn't sure what the more was.

"You know what? You should just do what you want," I said.

"Annabelle, you don't have to get *hostile*."

"I'm not *hostile*," I said. Only a little hostile-ly.

"I didn't get sober to sit here and watch my life pass me by."

I stood up. "Oh, I'm sorry. I thought part of why you got sober was to make sure you didn't *die*. Or kill someone," I retorted. "I didn't realize it was so that you could get a new boyfriend."

"Now you're being ridiculous." She let her towel drop, as if being butt naked in front of another person was the most natural thing in the world, and pulled on a pink-and-gray Halston dress that crossed so low in front you could almost see her belly button. "Well?" Mom asked as she turned from side to side in front of her three-way mirror.

"Are you trying to get Ben back?"

"Of course not."

I shrugged. "Then I'd lose the cleavage." I wouldn't

have dared bring it up, for fear of its sending her over the edge, but I had noticed that over the last few months Mom's perky boobs—for which she was just as famous as her haircut—had started to droop a bit. Not that you could blame them. There wasn't much to be perky about lately.

Pulling the dress off, she began to rummage around on the bed for another outfit. I cringed.

"What about this one?" she asked, wriggling into a turquoise silk shift.

"You look like you should be salsa dancing at a club in Miami."

"Oh, you're no fun." She pouted. "This is a *celebration*."

I had to laugh. My mother may have been annoying, but her ability to interpret the glass as being half full when it was almost bone dry was pretty impressive. Seeing a flash of red on the bed, I fished it out. "Here, wear this." It was a cleavage-lite Diane von Furstenberg.

She wrinkled her nose. "But it's so . . . bland."

"Mom, we're not *going* to the awards—we're just watching them on TV."

"Okay, okay," she sighed, walking over and scooping me up in her arms, hugging hard. "Do you love me?"

"Of course I do," I said into her hair.

"How much?"

"All the way up to God."

She hugged harder. "And?"

"Past God, past God," I replied as I pulled back a bit.

And I did. Really. Which is what made the whole thing so frustrating.

———————————————

One good thing about not being able to afford to throw a big party for an awards show was that you could actually see and hear everything. Including the *Rad and Righteous* commercial. The one they played, like, three times within ten minutes.

"Again?" Ben asked as we all sat in the living room on assorted, oversize, mismatched furniture. In the few minutes everyone had been there, Carrie had banged her hip on an end table and tripped on a Persian rug; Ben had knocked over a lamp; and Walter had spilled some Coke on a white slipcovered chair.

I glanced toward the kitchen, relieved to see that Mom still held Walter hostage and was talking his ear off about this horrible romantic comedy she had done after she left the show—in which she played Katherine Heigl's older sister, and the entire cast and crew got food poisoning on the first day—while he popped shrimp after shrimp in his mouth. (I had tried to veto the shrimp because it was expensive, but Mom overruled me.)

"Again," said Alice, Ben's date. When he had called the night before to ask if it was okay if he brought Alice to the party—this D-girl he had been out with a few times—

I felt a twinge in my stomach. It was one thing to take someone to dinner, or to foreign movies with subtitles at the Nuart, but bringing someone to an awards party meant something. Even if it wasn't the Oscars and was being held in what looked like the set of *Hoarders*, with the smell of *khoresht-e fesenjan*—lamb stew—coming in through the windows. Secretly, I had hoped that Ben bringing a date would freak Mom out and finally make her realize that he wasn't going to sit around forever waiting for her—but all she had said was, "Absolutely! The more the merrier! And would you be a total love and pick up some coconut cupcakes at Joan's on Third?"

I was all set to not like Alice. D-girls—"development girls," aka women who spent their days tracking scripts that might go on to sell for a million of dollars—had a reputation for being super-annoying. Like grown-up sorority girls. But Alice was different. Maybe it was because she had a fab English accent. Or the fact that she was wearing a long tweed skirt with Doc Martens boots and a black lace shirt with cap sleeves, through which I could see a yin and yang tattoo on the back of her right shoulder. Or how, as she handed me the box of cupcakes, she said, "You're lucky I didn't inhale all of these during the drive over, because while I've been able to swear off ciggies, I will never be able to turn down a cupcake."

Or maybe because when the commercial for Billy's movie played, she paused in her conversation with Carrie, glanced at the screen, rolled her eyes, and said, "You can't swing a cat in this town without seeing that bloke's abs on a TV screen or billboard." Then patted Ben's abs and said, "Good thing I'm not into that kind of stuff."

"Whose abs?" Mom called from the kitchen.

Because Mom spent so much time worrying about *her* abs (we had owned every infomercial-advertised ab buster/shaper/zapper on the market before we sold them at our garage—or, as Mom insisted on calling it, "estate"—sale the weekend before we moved), it made sense that Mom would perk up at the word.

"Billy Barrett's," Ben yelled back. The pre-show resumed, and there were Billy and Skye walking the red carpet. If the MTV Movie Awards were prom, Billy and Skye would definitely be crowned king and queen. With her jet-black bob, ruby-red lips, kohl-lined eyes, and six-inch stilettos, she'd probably also win Most Likely to Have Slept with the Entire Football *and* Debate Team.

Mom *click-clacked* into the room just as there was a close-up of Billy giving one of the interviewers a bro hug. "See, Annabelle? I told you."

"Told her what?" Ben asked.

"Nothing," I said.

I watched as Alice took his hand. He didn't let go. In fact, I could see him squeeze hers, which made me both happy and sad in the same moment. Ben deserved to be happy. I just wished he could have been happy with us.

Carrie looked up from her BlackBerry and brushed her Brazilian blown-out brown hair back from her eyes. When she signed Mom ten years ago—still an assistant, without an office—her hair had been super-curly, and she had worn these shapeless dresses she got at Loehmann's. Now, at only thirty-three, she was the head of the motion-picture talent department at one of the biggest agencies in town and had a standing appointment every Monday at the hottest hair salon in Beverly Hills. Although she was looking at us, her fingers continued typing away. "I just read the script for his next movie this morning," she said. "It's amazing."

"That *Hope Is the Thing with Feathers* thing?" Alice asked. "You're right. Unless he royally screws up, he might get an Oscar nomination out of it."

"What's it about?" Mom asked.

"It's about this townie in a small town in upstate New York—think Matt Damon in *Good Will Hunting*," Carrie replied. "He ends up falling in love with a female professor in her early forties who specializes in Emily Dickinson—think sexy librarian type—who's fifteen years older than him and a recovering alcoholic. Kind of a reverse *My Fair Lady*, in that she's the one who educates him." With a quick glance at her BlackBerry, her fingers began to fly again. "Except then she's diagnosed with cancer. But before she dies, he smuggles her out of the hospital and takes her to Emily Dickinson's house, where they sit outside and he swears his undying love to her before she dies in his arms. Think *Terms of Endearment*, but with sex instead of the mother/daughter relationship."

"*Terms of Endearment?!*" Mom turned to me. "Bug, did you hear that?"

She turned to the group. "Annabelle wasn't exactly . . . planned," she explained. "And I had scheduled a procedure at Planned Parenthood, but the night before I was supposed to go *Terms of Endearment* was on cable, and I took that as a sign that I was supposed to cancel the appointment. I didn't realize it, but even back then I had a connection with a power greater than myself."

Alice glanced at Ben, who gave her a what-can-I-tell-you shrug. "Well. *That* was a good thing," she said brightly.

"Your mom's awesome," Walter whispered to me as he grabbed a handful of the chocolate-covered espresso beans Carrie had brought, which were probably a regift.

"Yeah. In a completely inappropriate way," I whispered back.

"Who's playing the woman?" Mom asked.

"They haven't cast her yet," Carrie replied. "Sandy was supposed to do it, but she dropped out." The bigger the star, the less need there is to mention a last name. Which is why in Hollywood, everyone knew "Sandy" was Sandra Bullock.

Maybe there *was* something to this coincidence stuff. I wasn't into fate—I left that stuff to Mom—but between the Billy thing, and the fact that the lead character was the same age as Mom and a recovering alcoholic, the whole thing just kind of smacked of it.

I felt goose bumps pop up on my arms. "This could be the one," I blurted out.

Carrie turned to me. "The one what?"

"The one that'll get Mom back in the game."

Agents don't like it when you fill a client's head with visions of fame and fortune. Especially when you do it in front of them, which means they have to do damage control in the moment.

"I know it *sounds* great," said Carrie, "but Janie, I'm not sure it's for you."

"What are you talking about?! It couldn't be *more* for me!" Mom countered.

"She's not wrong," agreed Ben. Which was surprising. Ever since things fell apart, Ben had been dropping hints that maybe Mom might want to look into another line of work. Like maybe get her certification to be a yoga teacher. ("You do it all the time anyway," he'd said, "so why not get paid for it?")

"I could definitely see you in the role," Alice added. "I'd probably be thrown in D-girl jail for this, but I see you even more than Sandy."

I smiled. Yeah, kind of hard to hate her.

"I agree," Walter said. "It's hard for girls to do action movies, but she was great in *Speed*. But then she had to start doing stupid romantic comedies. Sandra Bullock should do more action."

While totally off point, Walter seemed to be in the supportive zip code, which I appreciated.

Mom turned to Carrie. "I don't understand why you're so against this."

"It's not that I'm against it"—Carrie said, not looking Mom in the eye—"'it's just that they're very close to making an offer to someone."

"Who?"

"I think I heard it was . . . Carey Mulligan."

"Carey Mulligan is, like, *twenty-five*," I said.

"She's younger, but she plays older," Carrie said. "Plus, you know, she's *Carey*. And she's English. That English thing alone makes her able to do anything."

"Well, I bet if I could just meet on it—" Mom said.

"Janie," Carrie interrupted, "here's the thing. . . ." At that moment Carrie didn't look like one of *Hollywood Reporter*'s 50 Most Powerful Women, as she had been named a few weeks earlier. She looked like someone who felt awful about the fact that what she was about to say was going to hurt someone who had remained her loyal client for many years, even when bigger, more established agents had tried to steal her away. Or—worse yet—she looked like someone who knew she was about to hurt a friend. "There's no way it's going to happen," she said quietly.

As I watched Mom's face begin to fall, I felt my heart crack.

"Janie, believe me, no one knows more than me how perfect this would be for you," Carrie pleaded. "In fact, I put in a call to the casting director twenty minutes into reading the script, to try and get you in to read, but she was very clear about it: they want a name."

"But she is a name," I said. "Everyone knows who she is." Maybe nowadays they knew it because the tabloids printed really unflattering photos of her all sweaty after yoga, with captions like "Has Janie Jackson Gone off the Wagon Because of the Stress of Losing All Her Money???!!!" But still—in Hollywood, publicity was publicity.

Mom stood up and smoothed her dress. "Annabelle, it's okay. I get it."

"Janie, I'm so sorry," Carrie said.

"Don't worry about it," Mom said, squeezing Carrie's hand. "I appreciate your trying."

None of us looked at one another as we listened to Mom make her way toward her room, this time with a sad-sack-sounding shuffle rather than her optimistic *click-clacking*. Instead, we all stared at the floor.

But in my mind I was totally giving God the finger.

CHAPTER SEVEN

I didn't completely believe that my giving God the finger had anything to do with Mom falling into a ginormous depression about the fact that, from here on out, our groceries would be bought with money made from dog-food and feminine-product voice-overs. ("Listen, I may not be able to get her in to read for the Billy Barrett movie, but I do have some really good news," Carrie said after Mom left the room. "I think I may have gotten her a gig as the new voice of Tampax!") But it probably didn't help.

"Hey, God?" I whispered as I took out my key to open the door that Tuesday after school. The day had started out bad (woke up to a photo on one of the gossip blogs of me walking out of Om My Gawd with what looks like three chins and the caption "Janie Jackson's Daughter Turns to Food to Deal with the Stress of Her Mother Going Bankrupt!!!"). And it got worse when I happened to find out while hiding out in the bathroom during a panic attack that, other than Kristin Farelli, who spent most of her time alone writing poetry about the moon and menstrual blood, I was the only one in my class not invited to Sharona Kline's Sweet Sixteen. Which hurt even worse, seeing that back when we were thirteen and no one liked Sharona because she smelled like a combination of mothballs and Lysol, I made sure to invite her to all my parties. (I had to take two huffs of Play-Doh after that.) "I have a proposition for you," I went on. "If I open this door and Mom's out of bed and showered and dressed in something other than those flannel cat pajamas, I will go back to another one of those Alateen meetings."

The night before, as I lay in bed listening to the muffled sound of her crying, I had come to the conclusion that, if I were just a better person—a person who tried to be good and didn't think mean thoughts about other people, like, say, the way that, as I watched Olivia chewing on the one piece of Twizzlers that she allowed herself once a week, I kind of hoped she'd choke on it—things might go back to normal.

"Mom?" I called out.

Nothing. Not even the sound of women screeching in Spanish coming from the TV from one of Mom's tele-novelas. As I walked toward her room, my stomach did cartwheels. Was it drama queen-esque of me to worry that one of these times I might find my mother checked out permanently in the bathtub à la Whitney Houston? Not only had Mom not been to one AA meeting since the party, but she had stopped answering her phone, which, post-rehab, was constantly ringing with calls from Willow and a host of permanently chipper sober people.

Through the crack of her door, I saw her lying in bed, staring at the wall. Greasy brown roots sprouted from her head.

"Hi! I'm home!" I said as bubbly as possible as I flung open the door. It came out sounding pretty flat, though.

Her reaction was to pull the blankets up over her head to block out the light that was coming in.

"So, did you have a good day?" I asked hopefully.

Nothing.

I sniffed. "Well, I can smell that a shower wasn't part of it." I fished her arm out from under the covers and cringed at her chipped red nails as I tried to yank her up. *Thou shalt never walk around with chipped nail polish* was Commandment Number 8 in Mom's world. "Look, Mom, I'm sorry you're a little bummed out here, but bathing is not optional."

It was like trying to pull a five-foot-four log. "Mom. Please," I pleaded. All the fizz was gone from my voice. I sounded like an opened can of Diet Coke that had been left out in the sun all day. "Please get up."

"I think there's some Lean Cuisines in the freezer," she said through the blanket. Her voice sounded tinny, as if coming through a radio station with bad reception. "Or just order in. But no pizza. You need to stay away from dairy, Annabelle. It's really doing a number on your skin."

147

I sighed. It was probably a good sign that, while she didn't care about how she looked, she was still concerned about how I looked.

"Mom. Come on."

She yanked the covers up higher.

"Mom."

She flipped back over and peeled the covers down so that her face was showing. The dark circles under her eyes made her look about ten years older. "Annabelle, *please.* Just leave me alone."

"I just—" I was going to say something nice. Something along the lines of "I just hate seeing you so sad. And I miss you. And I want my mother back." But before I could get any of that out of my mouth, I saw it.

A bottle of Ketel One vodka rolled off the bed and toward my feet.

Mom shot up like someone had lit her butt on fire. "It's not open!" she said, all panicked when I bent to pick it up. "See? The seal isn't broken!"

For months I had imagined how I'd feel if I discovered Mom drinking again—maybe because if I went over it in my head enough times, it wouldn't hurt as much when it happened. Sometimes I was pissed. Sometimes I was scared. Sometimes I was sad. But no matter how many times you play something out in your head, the way you think it *will* feel, versus how it *does* feel, never seems to match up. Because at the moment, I just felt numb.

I held it out toward her. "Just go ahead and drink it," I said quietly. "Doesn't matter to me."

"Annabelle, I wasn't going to open it. I was just—"

"You were just what?" I demanded. "Using it as a hot-water bottle for cramps?" I asked, my voice rising.

"No, I had it . . . It's here because . . ."

I shook my head. "You know what? I don't care why you have it." Now I wasn't angry at *her*—I was angry at myself. For being stupid enough to have trusted her again. To have been dumb enough to have believed that things had actually changed. To have thought that my mother had finally grown up and gotten it together and decided to act like a parent, the kind who took care of her daughter and made her feel that no matter what was going on, no matter how sucky things were, things would work out.

As I put the bottle on her night table, I knocked over the photo of us that had been taken at the Emmys.

She leaned over to pick it up. "Bug, please—"

"Like I said, it doesn't matter." And then I got my legs to move.

Back in my room, I picked up my phone and dialed Maya. "Hi. Can you talk?" I said, sniffling when she picked up. Olivia and Sarah had given up with even pretending to be friendly to me anymore, but at least I still had Maya. When she wasn't with Jade.

"Hey," she said over the din of what sounded like a restaurant. "I'm with Jade at Chin Chin. Can I call you later?"

"Don't worry about it," I said.

"Is everything okay?"

"It's fine."

"You don't sound fine."

"I am. I have to go," I said before clicking off. I scrolled down my contacts list. There were a lot of entries, but they were more the kind of people whom you called when you were feeling okay, or at least okay enough to know that you could get away with the lie that you were okay. I couldn't call Ben because he and Alice were going to Mexico for a long weekend. From the number of times he'd cleared his throat, I could tell how hard it was for him to tell me, but I was happy for him. In fact, I was so happy for him I was tempted to see if they'd adopt me if they got married.

"I can't believe this is what it's come to," I said out loud as I came to an entry toward the end. I clicked on the name and reached for a can of Play-Doh.

"Hello?" a voice said.

I didn't say anything. Mostly because I literally couldn't, because my lungs were full of the smell of kiddie clay.

"Hello?" it demanded.

What was I doing? I was just going to hang up.

"I know it's you, Annabelle."

I cringed. Of course he did. He had me in his phone, too. "Hey, Walter," I said as I exhaled.

"What are you doing?" he asked suspiciously.

"Nothing."

"Well, you sound weird. Why are you calling?"

Someone was missing a small-talk chip. "I don't know. No real reason," I lied. "Just to say hi."

"Oh."

We sat on the phone in silence, save for the sound of faint wheezing coming from his end. "So, uh, how are you?" I finally asked.

"Fine."

I waited for him to ask me how I was, but he didn't. Those meetings may have taught kids how to deal with someone's drinking, but apparently they didn't throw out social skills tips.

We went back to being quiet in what was possibly the most awkward conversation ever. "What about you?" he finally asked.

"What about me what?" I asked warily.

"Are you fine?"

I was all set to say, *Yeah, sure, things are great.* Wasn't that what most people wanted to hear anyway? I mean, most people, when they asked how you were, barely even listened to the answer because everyone just said "Great." What would people do if you told the truth and said, *Actually, things suck—life as you knew it has fallen apart and sometimes when you go to sleep you hope you won't wake up in the morning?* Not like you wanted to kill yourself or anything like that, but just that you wanted out of your life and into someone else's.

151

What was I doing? I didn't know this kid. He was a fourteen-year-old *gamer.* Sure, when he talked at the Alateen meeting, I had related to a lot of the stuff he'd talked about, but what was going on with my mom now—that was different. It was *private.* No one other than Ben knew about Mom's depressions. I hadn't even told Maya how bad she actually got. I couldn't tell this semi–complete stranger.

"No. I'm not fine," I finally said. I bit the inside of my lip so that I wouldn't start to cry, but that plan failed as well.

"Is your mom drinking again?" he asked quietly.

I sniffled. *"No,"* I scoffed, as if that was the dumbest thing in the world.

"Then what is it?"

In that moment, I felt as if I was at one of those forks in the road that had all those signs to different cities all around the world. Except, instead of cities, these signs said things like LIES I'VE TOLD SO MANY TIMES THEY NOW SOUND BELIEVABLE, WISHFUL THINKING, JUST FIGURE IT OUT YOURSELF, and IT'S NOBODY'S BUSINESS. But there was one more sign—it was near the bottom, and the paint was chipped and faded, but I could still make it out. What it said was, JUST TELL THE TRUTH ALREADY.

Maybe it was living in L.A.—the capital of make-believe, where people got paid to make up stories and pretend to be other people. Maybe it was growing up with my mother. Or maybe it was because I had been down those other roads so many times and it had gotten me nowhere.

I took a deep breath and, without meaning to, told Walter the whole story from the beginning. I told him about the good stuff—sitting in stools at fancy stores like Neimans and Saks when I was six, watching Mom get makeovers for free because she couldn't afford to buy the makeup, and how when she was done, she'd put some lip gloss on me, which would make me feel just as grown-up and beautiful as her. And how, when I was seven, she had bailed on an audition for a Judd Apatow movie that Carrie had thought she was perfect for because it was at the same time as my ballet recital, even though she could barely see me because Madame Stravasky had put me as far in the back as possible because I couldn't do a plié without almost tipping over. And how, when I was eight, she had come up with this idea that, although we didn't have any money to travel, in order to teach me about different countries, we would eat at a restaurant that specialized in the food, watch a movie from there, and learn a bit of the language. (The fact that one of the phrases she always insisted on looking up was "What kind of wine do you have?" should have been the tip-off that she wasn't like other mothers.)

Those stories rolled off my tongue effortlessly, because they were all stories I had told reporters from *E!* and *People* over the years. It was the other stuff I had trouble with. The times she had been late to pick me up from somewhere because she had fallen asleep, or had just forgotten about me because she was too busy thinking about herself.

The way she would ask me for advice about things that I had absolutely no idea about—when I was eight she asked me whether she should have declared bankruptcy because of all her debt.

I don't know why I felt I could tell Walter my secrets, but they just came out. And once I started telling them, I couldn't stop. Walter just let me talk, and when I had to stop to blow my nose, he didn't make fun of the way I honked into the tissue. I didn't even hear any clicking in the background, as if he were typing on his laptop while I went on and on. He just listened.

I talked until my throat was so dry I needed to stop for a minute.

"Are you done feeling sorry for yourself?" Walter finally asked.

Not the response I was expecting. *"Excuse me?"*

"I said, are you done feeling sorry for yourself."

"I know what you said," I replied. "I'm just trying to figure out *why* you'd ask that. Because I am not feeling sorry for myself."

"Well, you're not in the solution."

"What are you talking about?"

I cringed as a huge crunching noise came through the speaker. "You're either living in the problem, or you're living in the solution," he said with his mouth full. Another wave of crunching crashed against my ear. Walter may have been polite enough not to eat while I was spilling my guts, but he was sure making up for it now. "And you, my friend, are living in the problem."

I wanted to snap that friends didn't tell friends they were feeling sorry for themselves, but I didn't. "And how is that?" I demanded.

"It's the three C's of alcoholism and addiction," he replied. "You didn't cause it, you can't control it, and you can't cure it. The only thing you *can* do is control your reaction to it."

This Twelve Step thing sure had a lot of slogans.

"What time is it?" he asked.

I looked at the clock. "Five."

More crunching. "If you leave now to pick me up, we can make the six o'clock meeting over on Montana. In fact, if you hurry, we might even have a chance to stop at In-N-Out before."

More food? Really? "Yeah, thanks for listening, but I'm not going to be able to do that."

"How come? Because you need to stay there to make sure your mom doesn't open that vodka bottle?"

I thought about lying before realizing that telling the truth was a lot less exhausting. "Well . . . yeah."

He snorted. "Good luck with that. If she's going to drink, she'll find a way to do it. Believe me. My dad's done it seven times since the first time he got sober. Well, seven times that my mom and I know of. It's probably more."

As annoying as Walter could be, it must have really sucked to have a dad like his.

"Meetings are a way for you to control your reaction to your mom," he went on. "*That's* the solution."

Whether it was because I was too tired to come up with excuses, or I was afraid I'd go deaf from the crunching, I sighed.

"Fine. Give me your address."

"Took you long enough," Walter said after he came out the front door of his house on Twenty-sixth Street—a house that looked just as normal and nicely landscaped as ours had—and got into the car. He looked at his watch. "Nope. Not enough time to go to In-N-Out," he sighed. He pointed to the bashed-up front fender on a silver BMW. "See that? That's what happens when my dad goes out to celebrate winning a case. One more DUI and he's going to have to hire someone to represent him to keep him out of jail."

I didn't know why it made me feel better that Walter's dad seemed as screwed up as Mom, but it did. Maybe because I knew that when he said he understood how I felt, or that he had been there, I could believe him.

Although it was a different church basement than the first meeting, it had the same musty smell, like old books and wet chalk. Some of the same kids who had been there that Saturday were there, and even though it had been a while ago, a few remembered me and asked how I was doing. As usual, I was tempted to lie, but instead what

came out was "Yeah, not so great." The way that they nodded—with sad smiles on their lips and eyes that said, *I get
it, but I'm not going to make you feel worse by throwing
out some dumb cliché like "Don't worry—things will get
better"*—allowed my shoulders to stop making out with
my ears and move back to their regular position. Within a
half hour into the meeting, my jaw started to relax, and
I stopped grinding my teeth. And while at one point I
reached into my bag to make sure my can of Play-Doh was
there, I wasn't tempted to go to the bathroom for a huff.
I even found myself laughing a few times. And when the
sharing got to me, instead of clamming up and passing or
trying to spin things so that I sounded better than I was,
I kept telling the truth. When I felt the tears coming, I
took the crumpled-up tissue from the Filipino girl sitting
next to me with a grateful smile and continued with my
story, going on and on until I saw Walter pointing at his
watch, mouthing, *Wrap it up.* After the meeting, when
kids crowded around me and offered me scraps of paper
with scribbled names and phone numbers *(Call anytime!—
Amy L.; Hang in there . . . it gets better.—Laila N.),* I didn't
just shove them in a pocket of my jeans and forget about
them so they ended up going through the wash; instead,
I placed them carefully in my wallet. And when a few kids
asked me for my number, I didn't change the last digit so
they wouldn't be able to get in touch with me.

I couldn't say that I felt good when I got home after

dropping Walter off. In fact, because of the number of French fries I had eaten at In-N-Out, I felt a little nauseous. However, I did feel that I was understood, which was something I hadn't experienced for a while (see: loss of best friends). And that I wasn't some freak, or the only one in the world who had a screwed-up family life. And because I believed them when they told their stories, there was the tiniest part of me that was willing to believe that things *would* get better over time.

Whatever it was that ran the universe worked fast. Because after school the next day, a miracle was waiting for me in the form of a freshly showered, made-up mother sitting across from her AA sponsor in our living room, the two of them sipping chamomile tea.

"Hey, Bu— Annabelle," she said when I walked in after being held hostage in the lobby by our neighbor, Miss Kowalsky, while she told me how she had rushed her cat O'Neill to the vet because he had almost died from a urinary tract infection.

"Hey," I said, happy to see her out of bed but still mad. "Hey, Willow."

"Hey, Annabelle. You good?"

I liked Willow. Mom told me that when she first got sober she had a purple Mohawk, so she had to buy a wig before she went on job interviews. Now her hair was long and black and shiny. "Sure," I replied.

She nodded. "Good."

"Do you want to sit with us and have some tea?" Mom asked hopefully.

I shook my head. "I don't think so." That was progress. The old me would've said yes just to keep the peace. But as someone had said in the meeting, "'No' is a complete sentence."

Her shoulders sagged a bit. "Okay."

They were still talking quietly when I turned out the light and went to bed. Part of me wanted to stand at the door with my ear against a glass eavesdropping, but I didn't. If Mom suffered from Disclosure of Inappropriate Information disease, I was just as guilty in that I was willing to listen. While I was glad that she was once again part of the human race, I didn't need to know why. It wasn't my problem.

Over the next few weeks something weird happened. Maybe it had to do with the fact that I had started going to Alateen meetings regularly and Mom was going to her AA ones again, too, sometimes twice a day. Maybe the timing was all just a coincidence. But it was as if the umbilical cord between us—the one that the doctor had apparently forgotten to snip when I was born—started to dry up and crumble.

For the first time, when I would glance up from my Lean Cuisine and see my mother, I thought of her as something separate from me. Now, when my mouth would open to finish her sentences, or I'd want to rush in to do something for her because it would've made things that much easier, I didn't. To her credit, she let up on me as well. She stopped trying to tell me what I wanted or thought (or if she did, she'd quickly catch herself and say, "You know what? Forget I just said that.").

That Wednesday night as I worked on a paper for English class, Mom knocked on my door—*she knocked on my door*—and asked if she could come in.

"Sorry to interrupt," she said.

"That's okay," I said.

"I was wondering if you could teach me how to use the printer," she said, "so I can print out my résumé."

"Your résumé?" I asked, confused. "You mean your credits on IMDb?" IMDb stood for Internet Movie Database and gave you information on actors' credits and mini bios of them, including birth dates that were a few years off.

She shook her head. "No, I just put together a résumé for my interview tomorrow."

"What interview?"

"At Promises," she said.

Promises had been the first of the fancy rehabs back in the day.

"To *work* there?"

She nodded.

"Wow. Well, that's . . . great," I said, trying to be supportive. In trying not to butt into Mom's business, I wasn't going to tell her that she didn't actually have any skills other than acting and accessorizing. "But Mom, if you have a regular job, you know you're not going to be able to leave during the day to go to auditions and stuff."

"Yeah, I know," she said. She shrugged. "I've decided I'm done with acting." She flashed a camera-ready smile, but her eyes were sad. "I just think it's time for me to do something different now." She smiled bigger. "I can be a walking example that when you get sober, your life just gets better and better!"

I looked around the room that was stuffed to the seams with furniture as the smell of cigarette smoke from the down-stairs apartment came through the radiator. It did?

A car alarm went off, and Mom cringed. "Or that at least you can stay sober through whatever life throws your way."

A second alarm joined the mix, which made a dog start to bark. Back when we lived in Santa Monica, the loudest thing you heard was the stone fountain from Japan that had been on our patio.

"So you're in a bit of a dry spell," I said. In the middle of the Sahara Desert. "It's not like it's going to last *forever*." It couldn't, could it?

She didn't look convinced. Maybe because I didn't sound all that convincing.

"Mom...you love acting," I said quietly. "It's your life."

She shook her head. "No. *You're* my life, Annabelle," she replied. "Or rather, taking care of you and making sure your tuition is paid and putting food on the table is my life." She walked over and hugged me. It wasn't the bone-crushing-push-the-air-out-of-you kind of hug that I was used to from her. "Do you know how grateful I am to have you?" she asked into my hair. "You really are the best, Annabelle. And for these last months that I have you before you go off to college, I want them to be as normal as possible."

"But we've never been normal," I said into her hair. "Why should we start now?"

She laughed. Her laugh sounded different nowadays. Deeper. Older. More real. "Okay, maybe not normal. But at least with some . . . *stability*. Listen, I had a career that most people only dream of. . . ."

I hated that she was speaking in past tense.

She let me go and smiled at me. "But now it's time to move on."

I searched her eyes for tears, but there weren't any. It was as if she had just said, "And now let's go have Skinny Cow ice cream sandwiches."

Maybe she was ready to move on from being an actress—but I wasn't ready to let her. My mother was never happier—or more herself—than when she was acting. And as much as I was trying to separate from her, watching her do that made me happy as well.

I couldn't let her quit. Especially not now.

Even if I had no idea what to do to stop her.

CHAPTER EIGHT

"I know this was my idea," I said to Walter as we sat in my living room a few days later staring at the receipt with Billy Barrett's number, "but now I'm thinking it might be a very, very bad one." I pulled the bowl of microwave kettle corn away from him. "And stop hogging."

"I'm not," he replied, pulling it back. "Plus, my doctor told me I need more nutrients."

"Then maybe you should try eating something that's actually *nutritious*," I countered. I wasn't sure how Walter had become the person with whom I spent most of my free time, therefore making him resemble something along the lines of a best friend, but he had.

"Look, you said it yourself," he said—stopping to try and catch some kettle corn in his mouth, but missing so the pieces joined the other missed pieces in between the couch cushions—"there was obviously a reason you didn't throw away that piece of paper."

"Yeah. Maybe because I couldn't be bothered to walk over to the garbage can at that moment in time?"

"Or maybe because your Higher Power knew that you were going to need it down the line."

I cringed. While the meetings were definitely helping, I still got weirded out when Walter or my mom started talking about a Higher Power aka God, as if He/She/It were living next door. That being said, it was a little bit weird that this was coming into play now.

Walter picked up the receipt and handed it to me. "Just do it."

I sighed. I had rehearsed my speech numerous times, but every time I tried to dial the number, I got cold feet. *Hi, Billy? This is Annabelle Jackson—Janie Jackson's daughter? You know, the ex–TV star who ended up driving the wrong way down the PCH a few hours after she met you in Whole Foods? Well, I'm not sure if you heard or not, but while she was in rehab she found out that she was totally broke and now she's paying our rent with tampon commercials.* It was usually at that point that I would have to stop rehearsing in order to take a huff of Play-Doh.

"Okay, well, I guess I'm going to have to help you," Walter said, picking up my iPhone and punching in the numbers.

"What are you doing?! Stop!" I yelled, trying to grab it away from him. When I heard the sound of ringing, I started to freak. And when I heard Billy's voice saying "Hello? Hello?" after Walter thrust the phone into my hand, I *really* started to freak. I didn't have to talk to him. I could just hang up. It's not like he would recognize the number.

"Hello?" I heard Billy demand as I stared at the phone. I could hear people in the background, as if he was in a café or something.

I pulled the phone closer to me, my finger poised over the End button. And then . . . "Is this Billy?" I asked.

"Yeah. Who's this?"

"This is Annabelle Jackson . . . Janie Jackson's daughter? We met you in Whole Foods a while back. . . . You probably don't remember, but—"

"Sure, I remember," he said.

At that, I stumbled. I had spent so much time practicing the part where I reminded him who I was that I blanked on what came next.

"Who is it, Billy?" a woman's voice demanded.

I heard him cover the phone. "I've got it, Skye," he said, slightly muffled.

I quickly pushed the Speaker button so Walter could hear.

"Is it another one of your *friends*?" Skye asked. "'Cause we talked about this with the therapist. Either you get rid of those *friends*, or we're over. For good."

"Yeah, and we also talked about the fact that you need to stop being so freaking paranoid that I'm scamming on every girl I say hello to, or it's over," he snapped.

Walter and I looked at each other. "This is *good*," he whispered.

"I think I should just hang up. This doesn't seem like the best time to—"

"So what's up, Annabelle?" he asked.

I quickly took it off Speaker. "I, uh, had a favor to ask you, but if this isn't a good time to talk, I could just—"

"You know the Apple Pan?"

Who didn't know the Apple Pan? It was an L.A. institution. "Of course."

"Well, I'm totally jonesing for their banana cream pie—"

"You always do that!" Skye cried in the background. "You *know* I can't have that because of the gluten and dairy thing, so you pull this passive-aggressive move and go there in order to avoid me because of your fear of intimacy!"

She was loud enough that Walter could hear her even without the phone being on Speaker. Jeez. If she were my girlfriend, I'd want to get away from her, too.

"Meet me at four?" he asked.

"Meet you. In person. At four," I repeated nervously as I looked at Walter, who nodded. "Okay."

I tried to convince Walter that if he were really a good friend, he'd come with me, but he was having none of it.

"Listen, I think the guy is awesome—I mean, I've already seen *Rad and Righteous* five times and actually paid full price for the tickets rather than only going at matinee times—but it would be weird if I went with you," he said as I dropped him off at home.

"But the whole thing is weird!" I cried. "Why not just have it be *weirder*?"

He put his hand on my shoulder. "You can do this, Annabelle. I know you can," he said as he got out of the car. Before he shut the door, he turned. "And if you would bring me a piece of banana cream pie afterward, that would be awesome."

I also loved the banana cream pie at the Apple Pan, but not when my stomach was so jumpy I was positive that if I swallowed a bite, I'd immediately upchuck it.

"Are you going to eat that?" Billy asked after he finished off his slice.

I shook my head. I was so nervous I didn't trust myself to talk.

"Then can I have it?" he asked, pulling his L.A. Lakers hat down a little lower as a couple across the room stared at us.

I barely had the "shh" part of "Sure" out of my mouth when he slid my plate over his way and started to eat the slice of pie. "I love this stuff. Makes me think of home."

I knew from articles that Billy was from Iowa. Or Nebraska. Or some other place where they had a lot of corn.

"So what's up? What'd you want to talk to me about?"

"Well, um—"

His iPhone dinged with a text. As he looked at it, he sighed. "Are there, like, sanity tests or something online that you can print out? "'Cause I'm definitely making the next woman I go out with take one first."

Well, that was good. That meant there'd be no way he'd want to date my mother. "I don't know, but that sounds like a good idea," I replied. "So what I wanted—"

As his phone beeped again, I saw him will himself not to look at it and to stay focused on me.

"I wanted to ask you—"

Finally, he gave in, picked up his phone, and sighed. "Oh, man. Rondo's out tonight because of his knee! That *blows*."

I nodded as if I knew who this Rondo person was. "Totally."

His eyes lit up. "You like basketball?"

"Huh?" I asked, confused.

"The way you said 'totally' when I mentioned Rajon Rondo's knee made it seem like you followed basketball."

"Oh. Well, I do follow it . . . a little . . . but not, you know, all the time," I said.

"Oh, man, I love it," he said. "I keep telling my agent to find me a script where I play a player. I played in high school, you know. I mean, I wasn't the *best* on the team, but I have a pretty awesome dunk."

"That's cool," I said.

"I'm thinking something where there's a role for Jack," he went on.

"Is Jack another player?" I asked.

He laughed. "No, I mean *Nicholson*," he replied. "Don't you think that would be awesome? If Jack played, like, my grandfather? Or maybe some old coach who comes out of retirement to coach my team and at first he's all up in my grill about stuff but later you find out that's only because he thinks I have all this potential?"

"Sounds great," I said.

"Yeah, I think so, too," he agreed. "So what is it you wanted to talk to me about?"

I was always amazed at how people with ADHD could move from subject to subject without missing a beat. I took a deep breath. The only thing I hated more than asking people for help was . . . actually, there *wasn't* anything I hated more than that.

"I . . . actually, will you excuse me for a sec?" I asked as I grabbed my bag and stood up.

Once inside the bathroom, I took out a can of red Play-Doh. (My blue can was tapped out because of how often I had opened it over the last few weeks.) As I started to take a sniff, I got a look at myself in the mirror. "Okay, you need to stop this," I said to my reflection as I chucked the can. "Not only is it pathetic, but if you get cancer, Mom's not going to be able to afford the treatment."

Billy was on the phone when I got back. From the number of "dudes" out of his mouth, I figured he was talking to one of his friends. Of course Billy was a dude kind of guy. Finally, he clicked off. "That was my agent. I freaking love her."

Or the kind of guy who called women "dudes."

"So what's up?" he asked.

"I wanted to talk to you about . . . my mom."

"Is she okay?" he asked, with concern.

I felt myself stiffen. Why was he acting as if he cared so much? He had met her only once. "She's fine," I said. "I mean, maybe she's not *totally* fine," I admitted. "But she's not not fine—you know, to the point where she's drinking again or anything like that," I babbled. "But . . . she's thinking of getting a job at a rehab."

"To do research for a role?" he asked.

"No. For, like, a new *career*."

He cringed. "But what about acting?"

"That's the thing—she wants to give it up," I said. "And the reason I wanted to talk to you is that I heard they haven't cast the role for the woman in your new movie. And I think she'd be perfect for it."

His eyebrows went up.

I took another deep breath to help me go on, wishing I hadn't thrown out the Play-Doh without first taking a sniff. "And even though I've never ever done this before—I *swear*—I was wondering if maybe you could talk to your agent or the producers or whoever, and see if she could come in to audition," I blurted. "I'm not saying to give her the part or anything, but just . . . give her a chance?" This was as excruciating as the cramps on the first day of my period every month. "Her

170

agent tried to get her in, but no one thinks she's . . . important enough anymore," I said quietly, staring at the floor. "And she could really use a break."

"I know she could," he said just as quietly.

Oh, God. This suddenly felt like the worst idea ever. "Like I said, I've never done this before." I fidgeted nervously. "In fact, I think it's totally gross when people do things like this, but—"

"I'll have my agent call the producer tonight. We'll set something up for Monday."

I looked up.

"Really? You'd do that?"

He shrugged. "Sure. Your mom's a great actress. And she's been through a tough time. Consider it done."

As I felt my eyes fill with tears, I looked back down at the floor. I was *not* going to cry in front of Billy Barrett.

———————————————————————

Once, when I was in the bathroom and picked up one of Mom's little daily meditation books (there were about ten of them strewn around the apartment, which prompted me to tell Mom that the next one she bought should be called *Meditations for Women Who Can't Stop Buying Daily Meditation Books*), I read something about how doing something nice for someone isn't all that spiritual. It's doing something nice and then not telling them that's the spiritual part.

Not that I had any plans to tell Mom about what I had

done. Although she was doing a better-than-average job at trying to act all upbeat about her life ("You know what, Bug? I actually *like* having all this free time, without the phone ringing. It's very therapeutic after so many years of having every second scheduled"), I knew that she was struggling. And if I hadn't known, the fact that her most recent purchase at Be Here Now was a book called *When Things Fall Apart* by some Buddhist lady named Pema Chodron—in which she had highlighted almost every paragraph and scribbled *Yes! Exactly!!!!* in the margins—was a good clue.

But then the abundance candle happened.

On Tuesday I walked out of school to find her waiting for me.

"Mom, you're...dressed," I said in surprise when I got to the car. I tried not to cringe at the latest bumper sticker: LET GO AND LET GOD. For the last few weeks, she had been alternating between three pairs of yoga pants and several T-shirts. But that day she was wearing her tightest jeans (even tighter nowadays, due to the fact that a lot of her free time was spent eating Skinny Cow ice cream sandwiches, which, despite their name, do not make you skinny), a lilac boho peasant shirt, and a pair of vintage brown cowboy boots. She looked like the old Janie Jackson—the famous one who used to end up in *People*'s Most Beautiful People issue.

She flashed a smile that would've lit the entire electric grid of L.A. "That's because we're celebrating!"

"You got it?!" I yelped.

"Got what?" she asked, confused.

Whoops. "What?"

"What?"

I had seen the "What?" thing in a movie once. It worked on Mom every time.

I quickly opened the car door and jumped in, sliding down a bit in order to hide from Olivia and Sarah as they walked out. Not that it would have mattered if they had seen me. Nowadays whenever we crossed paths, they just pretended not to see me. Mom saw them, though.

She turned to me. "I'm really sorry, Annabelle."

I felt my face get warm. "Just drive, okay?" Every time Mom tried to get me to talk about how my friends had dumped me, I refused. What was the point? Talking about it wasn't going to make me feel better. If anything, it was going to make me feel worse.

"I don't understand why you don't want to talk about it," she said. "It's very important to process emotions. Otherwise, they get stuck in your body. By the way, did you know that studies are now showing that cellulite might be caused by emotions that are trapped—"

"Mom, just go," I ordered as Olivia and Sarah got closer.

"Okay, okay," she said as she pulled out.

"So what are we celebrating?" I asked in order to change the subject.

"Well . . . we're celebrating the fact that I'm going in

173

to read for the Billy Barrett movie tomorrow!" she shrieked.

I gave what I hoped was a very believable shriek in return. "Mom, that's *awesome*! What happened?"

"The abundance candle is what happened!" she replied. "Remember when we were at Be Here Now, and I wanted to buy that candle?" she asked. "The one that came with the angel card? And you told me not to get it because you thought thirty-two ninety-five was a rip-off, even though Oprah had listed it as one of her favorite things?"

"Yeah. Because it *is* a total rip-off."

"Yeah, well, I had Enid buy me one when she was there the next day." Enid was this older woman who went to the same Tuesday AA meeting in Beverly Hills, the one Mom called the Shoes and Handbags meeting because it was filled with rich women. According to Mom, Enid had gotten drunk only once in her life but found the meetings so uplifting that she had been going for five years, even though she wasn't sure she was an alcoholic. "And I've lit it every night during my meditation," she went on, "and obviously it worked." She looked at me. "See what can happen if you just practice posi-tive thinking, Miss Nancy Negative?"

I couldn't believe she thought a *candle* had done all this. "Mom, you didn't get the audition because of a candle."

She turned to me. "What do you mean?"

"I mean . . ." What was I doing? It was so nice to see her happy again. Did I want to ruin it? At a meeting the other day the topic had been "Would you rather be right or would you rather be happy?" Frankly, I would've liked to have been both, but I was trying not to worry about being right all the time when it came to Mom and focus on just being happy. "It probably wasn't *just* because of the candle. It was probably because they realized that you're a great actress."

"Well, I'm sure that's part of it," she agreed. "But I think most of it was because of the candle."

I'm sorry, but sometimes it was hard not to want to be right. Did she realize how insane she sounded?

"Well, the candle and my vision board," she added.

Apparently, she did not. A vision board was a bulletin board on which you pinned up stuff that you wanted in your life. Kind of like an old-school Pinterest thing.

"So where are we going?" I asked, trying to change the subject.

"To Fred Segal," she said as we drove down Pico Boulevard.

Fred Segal was one of the most expensive stores in L.A. "For what?"

"For something for me to wear to the audition!" she exclaimed. "Even though, you know, it's probably not an audition. More just a meet-and-greet before officially offering me the role."

"Mom, we don't have any *money* for you to be buying new clothes," I said. "We barely have enough to pay the rent."

"Annabelle, I appreciate your concern," she said in her high-pitched I'm-the-mother-here tone. "But I'm the mother here, and I'll decide how the money gets spent."

"But we don't have any for you to spend!" I shot back.

She shook her head. "What do you think it's going to say to the universe if I stop trusting it and show up dressed in some rag?"

"The universe doesn't care!" I cried. "Because the universe did not get you this audition! I did!"

The minute the words were out of my mouth, I tried to breathe them back in.

She slammed on the brakes. Which, thankfully, happened to coincide with our hitting a red light. "What are you talking about?"

So much for being spiritual. "The reason you got the audition is because I went to see Billy Barrett and asked him if he could talk to the producers and have you come in," I confessed.

The light turned green, but Mom didn't move. "Why did you do that?" she asked quietly.

A horn blared behind us. "I don't know," I said nervously. "Because I didn't want you to quit acting. And it seemed like a good idea at the time."

"I can't believe this," she muttered, shaking her head as she began to drive. "Talk about humiliating."

"Yeah, well, how about a thank-you?" I shot back unspiritually.

"For what?" she snapped. "For butting into my business and not respecting my boundaries?"

Ever since rehab Mom had been big on the B-word and managed to work it into a conversation at least three times a day. "Since when have we ever had *boundaries*, Mom?"

"That's it—we're not going to Fred Segal," she said, slamming on the brakes and doing a U-turn smack in the middle of Pico Boulevard. Which, given her lack of driving ability, was impressive. I would have complimented her if we hadn't been in a fight.

"Good! BECAUSE WE CAN'T AFFORD IT!" I yelled.

"STOP SAYING THAT!" she yelled back.

The rest of the ride was spent in silence. At least until I couldn't bear the silence because it made the *Why are you such a bitch? Why did you have to do that? What's WRONG with you?* monologue in my head even louder and meaner, so I turned on the radio to KROQ. Until Mom reached over and clicked on her *Meditations for Calming Down in Traffic* CD, on which, over the sound of waves, a woman's gentle voice said, "There's no reason to get upset. You're exactly where you're supposed to be at this moment. And you'll get to exactly where you're going at the divinely appointed time." Until I turned it off because the monologue in my head was slightly less annoying than the anti-road rage lady.

I tried to open my mouth to say "I'm sorry," but it was as if it had been wired shut. Was I sorry? What I was was confused. In the past, if I had done something like this, maybe Mom would've gotten mad for, like, a minute or so, but then she would've been happy that I had helped and she would've gone into her what-did-I-do-right-in-a-past-life-to-deserve-the-best-kid-in-the-universe speech.

Because if I wasn't helping; if I wasn't being useful; if I wasn't saving the day, who *was* I? That's what I did. That was my role. I was never going to be as pretty or talented or famous as my mother. I was never going to light up a room like she did. So I had to do something.

"Do you want me to run lines with you?" was what I said in lieu of an apology.

No response.

"So now you're not talking to me?"

Nothing.

My stomach started to clench. She *knew* I hated when she wouldn't talk to me. Some kids got smacked by their mothers. I got the silent treatment, which, in my opinion, was just as bad.

"Fine. Don't talk to me. I don't care," I said, hating myself for caring as much as I did.

When we got back to the apartment, we stomped off to our respective bedrooms and closed the doors forcefully. (Because they were so cheaply made, you couldn't slam them or else they would literally fall off their hinges, and then you had to wait for Samir, the landlord/very-unhandy handyman, to come fix it, which, because he hated the fact that back in Iran he had been a doctor but now spent his time unstopping stopped-up toilets, made the whole thing very uncomfortable.)

As I tried to do my homework, I listened for the sound of Mom's door opening. When it came and I heard her banging around in the kitchen, I opened mine and walked out.

"It's dinnertime," she said icily. She opened the freezer, pulled out a Lean Cuisine, and threw it down on the counter. "But because you're so intent on running the show, I'm done cooking for you. You're on your own," she said as she pulled a can of chickpeas out of the cupboard and clamped the can opener on the lid.

It was a good thing I had learned how to "cook," i.e., push the buttons on the microwave, back when I was five. "Fine," I replied.

We stomped around in silence for a bit. "I was just trying to help," I finally said.

She looked up from the can, which, as usual, she couldn't get open because it didn't have buttons. "Annabelle, 'helping' is zipping up someone's dress," she said. 'Helping' is cutting the price tag off her sweater." She went back to butchering the can. 'Helping' is *not* tracking down a major star and begging him to allow your mother to audition for his movie after everyone's decided she's a washed-up has-been!"

"Yeah, well, *I* don't think you're a washed-up has-been!" I said as I broke down and grabbed the can from her before she hurt herself. "I think you're someone who's had really crappy luck lately and deserves another chance!"

She shook her head. "I've been thinking about it, and I don't think I should go in to audition."

"What?!"

She shrugged. "If I were supposed to, it would have happened organically, without interference from anybody. Plus, I told you, I want to work at a rehab."

"You'd rather stand outside a bathroom listening to people *pee* so you can make sure they give clean drug tests rather than star in a movie?"

She cringed. "Would I really have to do that?"

I shrugged. "I don't know. I saw it on *Celebrity Rehab* once." And then it hit me. She was scared. I put my hands on her shoulders. "Mom, you can do this," I said. "It's just an audition."

"But what if I don't get it?" she asked quietly. "Then what, Bug? "'Cause I have to tell you—I'm running out of ideas here."

"Well, if you don't get it . . . I guess the universe has other plans for you," I replied.

That was pretty freaking spiritual, if you asked me.

━━━━━━━━━━━━━━━━━━━━━━━━━━━━━━━━━

THINGS I PROMISE TO DO IF MOM GETS THE MOVIE
★ Throw out all Play-Doh and Barbie heads.
★ Stop stalking Olivia and Sarah's Facebook and

Twitter accounts and spending time making up stories about how much fun they're having even though I know for a fact that Olivia always exaggerates on her posts in order to make things sound better than they are.

★ Become one of those people who spends her weekends working with guide dogs for the blind or volunteering at nursing homes.

★ Make an attempt to make more friends rather than spending all my time with Walter, because even though I've gotten used to the fact that he's a very loud cruncher, I miss having girlfriends to talk about girl stuff with, other than the morning ride to school with Maya.

★ Stop making lists, because they don't really seem to help.

===

That night, I ran lines with Mom and found myself surprised at how good she was. I wasn't sure why—she had won a bunch of Emmys over the years. But something had changed. As we went through the scenes, it was as if she stood still and played a game of strip acting, slowly taking off one layer after another—humor, anger, defensiveness—until the lines blurred and I forgot that I was watching my mother and instead felt like I was seeing the X-rayed insides of this English professor who was so scared of getting hurt that she'd rather spend her time with the writings of a dead poet than with other human beings.

A few days after her audition, I got home from school to find her waiting for me at the dining room table reading her *Meditations for Women Who Think Too Much* book.

"Oh, good, you're home," she said, standing up. "Come on—we're going out."

"Where are we going?" I asked as I tripped over a meditation cushion and banged my elbow on an armoire.

"It's a surprise," she said, grabbing her purse.

"Where are we going?" I asked again as we drove east on Pico Boulevard.

"I told you. It's a surprise."

When we pulled into the King Fu parking lot, I turned to her, confused. Back before she was famous, King Fu had been the place where we had gone on every special occasion—birthdays, last days of school, Christmases with the rest of the Jews, even though we weren't Jewish. "What are we doing here?"

"We're having dinner!"

I looked at the clock. "It's four thirty."

"We're having an early dinner!"

Other than two old couples who spoke very loudly because they couldn't hear each other, we were the only people in there.

After we ordered (as usual, with the kung pao chicken and moo shu pork and vegetable dumplings and sweet and sour pork, we ordered way too much food. And, just the way it had been back when we used to come here, I was already worrying that the bill was going to be expensive), she smiled at me. "Bug, do you remember the last time we were here?"

I thought about it. "I think it was . . . to celebrate your getting *Plus Zero*."

A smile spread across her face.

"Oh, my God. YOU GOT IT?!" I screamed.

She nodded.

"YOU GOT THE PART???!!!"

She nodded again.

"IN THE MOVIE?!"

More nodding.

Although I was probably too old (and too heavy), I leaped out of my seat and jumped into her arms before she screamed, "Bug, honey, my back!" and I jumped down and instead lifted *her* up.

"YOU'RE GOING TO BE IN THE MOVIE?! REALLY?" I screamed as I plopped her back down once I realized that all her depression eating was making *my* back hurt as well.

"I AM!" she screamed back.

After we did a little happy dance (in addition to being almost deaf, the other diners seemed to be almost blind as well, as none of them were paying us much attention), she stopped and grabbed my shoulders. "Honey, this is all because of you. If you hadn't believed in me—" At that her lip started quivering. Usually when that happened I got super-uncomfortable, knowing she'd be starting with the crying any second, but this time I didn't care. Probably because I had already beat her to it.

"No, Mom—you did it," I replied, wiping my eyes. "I helped a little, but you went in there and nailed it. *You.* Not me. And not a candle."

"I still think the candle helped," she said.

"Okay, fine," I laughed. The whole thing was so surreal, I was waiting for a camera crew to jump out and tell me I was being punk'd. "So when does it shoot?"

"July. In upstate New York," she replied. "Bug, you're going to love it up there. Apparently, this little town called Hudson, where we'll be staying? Supposed to be so cute. It's two hours north of Manhattan, right across the river from Woodstock."

If this had been a few months ago, I would have fought her on going because I wouldn't have wanted to leave my friends. But seeing as I no longer had any friends, except for Walter and Maya, it sounded like it could be fun.

It wasn't until much later that I realized that her doing the movie meant that she'd be seeing Billy Barrett on a daily basis and pretending to be in love with him.

And for my mother, there was a very fine line between reality and make-believe.

CHAPTER NINE

A few nights later Ben took us out to dinner to Ivy at The Shore to celebrate. Ever since he had started seeing Alice, we had seen less and less of him. That night, when Mom came into my room to ask me how she looked, instead of just giving a routine "Great," without even looking, I actually took the time to check her out, and I was glad to see that she did look great. I knew it was silly because Mom's beauty only canceled out the fact that she was nuts for a limited amount of time, and then guys usually caught on to the truth and bolted, so the fact that Ben had been in our lives for so long meant that he was either (a) incredibly stupid (which he was not) or (b) would have loved her even if she wasn't a Most Beautiful Person. What was even sillier was the fact that I was still hoping they would hook up.

I spent a lot of the dinner trying to get everyone to play the "Remember When" game. (Remember when we

went to Martha's Vineyard that summer and ate steam-
ers and lobster rolls? Yeah, no, not the time Mom threw
up over the side of the boat because she'd had too much
sangria—the night before that. Remember when we took
a road trip up to Northern California and stayed in that
really pretty hotel, and Ben and I drove over to San Francisco because Mom had to stay in bed the next day after
the tour of the vineyard?) But even with that, things felt
weird. More polite. Like instead of its being our one thou-
sandth dinner together, it was our first.

In French there are two ways to say *you*: the formal
vous, which you use for strangers and bosses and old
people, and the informal *tu*, which is for family and close
friends. That night, the *tu*-ness that had always been there
between Ben and Mom felt like a thing of the past, and
Ben's "Sure! Of course!" when I asked if he would come
to New York to visit us during the movie came off as very
*un*sure.

As for Mom, she didn't seem to notice the fact that
things were weird.

She was too busy texting.

"Who are you texting?" I asked after Ben had excused
himself to go to the bathroom. "Willow?" For good or
for bad, now whenever Mom got stressed out, instead of
reaching for a drink or a pill, she texted her sponsor. (Good
for the rest of the world, bad for Willow.)

"No," she replied, pecking the keyboard with one

finger. ("Do you think they offer a class at the Learning Annex where adults can learn to text with both hands like you kids?" she had asked me the other day.)

"Then who? Eldin?" Eldin was an older African American guy from Mom's Monday night meeting who had become one of Mom's buddies.

I heard the *ding* of the response from the mysterious texter, followed by Mom's laugh. A real laugh. From her shrinking-by-the-day-because-she-had-sworn-off-carbs-because-the-camera-adds-ten-pounds belly. "Billy," she replied.

"Billy *Barrett*?" I demanded.

She squinted at the phone. "Tell me again what LMFAO means. I always forget."

Even with the text abbreviation cheat sheet I had made for her, Mom still struggled with that stuff.

"Since when have you been texting Billy Barrett?" I demanded.

She shrugged. "I don't know. A few days?"

"About what? The movie?"

"The movie, life, love . . . ," she said, as if it were the most normal thing in the world. "What does it mean, Bug?"

"What does it mean that you're texting some guy you don't even know about *love*? A guy who, by the way, has a *girlfriend*."

"No. The LNFAO."

"It's LMFAO," I corrected.

"Whatever. So what does it mean?"

"Did you hear me about the girlfriend part, Mom?"

She sighed. "I did hear you, Annabelle. And we're not talking about love in terms of *us*. We're talking about love in terms of, you know, the *concept* of it. Seeing that that's what the movie is about."

I shook my head. I had no one to blame for this but myself.

"So are you going to tell me what it means, or am I going to have to Goggle it?"

"It's *Google*," I corrected.

"Same thing. The Google will also tell me how to give someone a ringtone, right?"

"There's no 'the.'"

"What?"

"It's just Google. Not *the* Google. Or *a* Google. Just Google." Was it dumb to get hung up on articles like *the* and *a*? Yes. But I needed to have control over *something*.

"Fine. Google. So will it?"

"You want to give Billy Barrett his own *ringtone*?!" I cried. "Mom, you don't just give *anyone* a ringtone. It's a big deal to do that!"

"I'm thinking something by Katy Perry," she said. "Does it cost extra when the song is really popular?"

My forty-two-year-old mother wanted to use a Katy Perry ringtone for a guy who was sixteen years younger than she was and with whom she was having text conversations about love. I could only hope I made it to the bathroom in time before I threw up.

Before we could get into it more, Ben returned to the table and we continued pretending that everything was just like it had been pre–rehab/bankruptcy/Alice. To her credit, Mom put her iPhone away in her bag, but I could still hear the stupid text noise come through a bunch of times. (Really? Billy Barrett didn't have anything better to do with his time than triple-texting without a response?)

Outside, as we waited for the valets to bring our cars, Ben and I watched as Mom signed autographs and posed for pictures with some girls a little older than me.

He smiled. "It's nice to see her back in her element."

"Yeah. And with fans who aren't retired and living on Social Security," I replied. The fact that she was doing a movie with Billy had gotten her a lot of cred with younger people.

I cringed as I heard one of the girls asking Mom if Billy was as hot in person as on-screen and then turned to see Ben looking at me. "What?" I asked.

He shook his head. "Nothing. Come here," he said, pulling me toward him into a hug.

I wasn't big on hugs. Probably because with my mother, instead of making you feel safe, they had you fearing for your life as the breath was squeezed out of you. But I did love Ben's hugs. They were my version of the pills that used to litter Mom's bathroom. As soon as he wrapped his arms around me, I felt my body relax, which was great for two seconds, until my eyes began to fill with tears.

"What is it, Annabelle?" Ben asked. Even without seeing my face, he could tell something was wrong. Which, for some reason, made the tears come faster.

"Nothing," I replied, trying to keep my voice level.

"You're lying. Your voice went up at the end."

That made me even want to cry more.

He pulled me away from him and looked me in the eyes. "Tell."

"It's . . . things are all *vous*-y with you and Mom," I blurted.

"Huh?"

I wiped my eyes. "You don't love her anymore, do you?" I asked softly.

He pushed my hair out of my eyes. "What are you talking about? Of course I love her. I love both of you. You know that."

"No, I mean . . . you're not . . . *in* love with her anymore."

He looked away. "Annabelle, I was never . . . ." he started to say. But then he stopped and looked back at me. "No. No, I'm not," he said gently.

This time when my eyes filled up, I didn't try to stop them. I would have been lying if I didn't admit that this whole time, part of why I wanted Mom to get it together was so that she'd finally have the Movie Moment—when she'd finally realize Ben was her guy and she'd get in her car and, while some Death Cab for Cutie or Phoenix song played, drive as fast as she could to his office without getting a ticket (no one got tickets during Movie Moments)—and profess her undying love to him in front of everyone.

"Are you in love with Alice?" I asked.

"I . . . care for her a great deal," he replied, staring at the sidewalk as if one of those visions of the Virgin Mary had just appeared, like in those articles in the *National Enquirer*. (At one point, back when Mom was still really famous, there was something in there about how the Virgin Mary had appeared in our house because Mom was a descendant of her.)

"You love her."

He sighed. "Yes," he said quietly. "I love her."

Ben was not one of those super-sensitive guys—like Per, the Swedish sculptor whom Mom had dated during her Scandinavian phase—but I could have sworn his voice cracked a little as he said it.

I felt something crumble inside of me. Like when something dries out to the point where it just turns into dust, even though a second earlier it had looked solid. Luckily, our car pulled up then so we didn't have to talk about it anymore. Which was good, because, really, what was there to say? *Wow, I'm so happy for you guys—even though this totally screws up my master plan of you and my mother getting together now that she's finally getting it together. Great—so I guess I should stop pretending that you're my father, huh? Hey—if you guys get married, do you think maybe you can fix up a room for me to crash at when Mom is driving me nuts?*

As much as I hated Mom's bumper-sticker collection, I was grateful for them at that moment; they gave me something to focus on as I willed the tears not to fall. I cleared my throat. "Well, that's good. You should love her. She's cool. Thanks for dinner," I said quickly as I turned to bolt to the car.

Ben grabbed my arm. "Annabelle."

Don'tcryyoucannotcrywhateveryoudodon'tcry, I said to myself as I turned to face him. "Yeah?"

"It doesn't change anything," he said. "You know that, right?" He sounded like he was pleading.

Actually, it changed everything. I shook my head and got in the car.

———————————————————————

One of the great things about a parent getting sober was that after years of their being so stuck in their own head, thinking about themselves, they were finally able to notice when something was bothering you.

"Annabelle, we need to talk about something," Mom said solemnly, breaking the silence as we drove up Olympic Boulevard toward home.

I pinched my thigh in order to stop the tears from coming. "Can we talk about it later?" I pleaded, pinching harder.

"No, we can't," she said firmly." Bug, I know that we've talked about this before—"

"Actually, Mom, we *never* talked about it," I snapped. "That's part of the problem. Because maybe if we had, then things would be different right now—"

"What are you talking about?" she asked, confused.

"I'm talking about— Wait, what are *you* talking about?"

"The trainer issue."

"What?"

She took another deep breath. "I know you're worried about the money stuff," she said, "and when I told you a few weeks ago that I was considering starting back up with Brian"—Brian was Mom's very expensive personal trainer—"you gave me a look like I had just suggested I sell one of my kidneys, but I just don't think I can trust myself to do what needs to be done to get myself into top shape before shooting begins without having to be accountable to someone."

Amendment: Some parents, when they got sober, got out of their heads and noticed when something was bothering you. Mine? Not so much.

"Don't look at me like that, Annabelle," she went on. "I know you think this is all vanity, but it's not. Being fit is part of my job," she said defensively.

I shook my head. "Amazing," I laughed. This time when I pinched my thigh, it wasn't to stop the tears—it was to prevent myself from screaming at her.

The next day I stood in front of the fountain at the Grove—the giant one pulsing in time with a Celine Dion song that made me want to jump in and refuse to get out unless they turned it off. What did people wish for when they weren't busy wasting their wishes on other people? Did you start small? ("I hope they have some black-and-white cookies left at Diamond Bakery across the street on Fairfax.") Or did you just go all out? "I'd like a boyfriend who looks like Ryan Gosling but has the personality of Jesse Eisenberg because Ryan Gosling is too cool and would intimidate me.")

Behind me I heard the unmistakable noise of way too many pieces of popcorn being shoved into a mouth at one time. "What are you doing?" asked Walter. We had become such good friends that even, when his mouth was full, I understood him. Plus, he asked that question all the time.

"I'm . . . not doing anything."

"You were going to say something," he said suspiciously.

"No, I wasn't."

"Yes, you were. I heard the pause in between the 'I'm' and the 'not.'"

I rolled my eyes. Walter may have wanted to do special effects for movies when he grew up, but he would've made a great detective.

"What were you going to say?"

"Nothing. Forget it." Although I was constantly being surprised at how much I had in common with the kids in Alateen (marking vodka bottles with Sharpies in order to check the level was something I had been particularly embarrassed about until, when I finally admitted it during a meeting, there was a bunch of knowing laughter), there was some stuff that felt so stupid I'd be afraid that if anyone ever knew, they'd think I was nuts.

"I *hate* when you do that 'Nothing, forget it' thing," he said.

He did hate it. Just like I hated it when people did it to me. "Okay, fine," I said, "so you know when you throw a penny into a fountain?"

He shook his head. "I never do that. In fact, I try to avoid pennies whenever possible. I bet if you Googled it, there's stuff about how touching all that copper gives you cancer or something—"

"I meant, in *general*," I said. "The *idea* of throwing a penny into a fountain."

"Oh, yeah."

"Well, for, like, the last five years, every time I've thrown one in—"

He wrinkled his nose. "I hope you wash your hands after you do that."

"Walter."

"Okay, okay. Sorry. Go on. So every time you've thrown one in—"

"I've . . . wished that my mom would stop drinking."

He shrugged. "That makes sense."

"And . . . that she'd realize she's supposed to be with Ben, and then they'd get married and everything would be fine." I waited for him to start laughing, but he didn't. He just sniffled because of his ever-present postnasal drip. "But now I realize how stupid it sounds." Not to mention it didn't work.

He shrugged. "Don't beat yourself up. Magical thinking is just part of the deal."

"What do you mean?"

"Wishing on pennies. Needing to sit in the same chair at meetings. We all have it," he said. "Well, at least, you know, kids who grow up like we do. I don't know if the normies do it." "Normies" were what alcoholics called non-alcoholics. Or, in our case, what we called kids who grew up in homes where you weren't constantly worrying about whether your dad was going to burn down the house if he passed out with a lit cigarette in his hand. Or where you taught yourself to use the stove when you were six so you could make breakfast for your three-year-old sister because your mother's hangover was so bad she couldn't get out of bed. "When I was eight, I did this thing for a few weeks where I would only eat orange foods because one weekend when I drank a half gallon of orange juice, my dad stayed sober the entire time," Walter admitted. "So I thought if I just stuck to orange stuff, it might keep working."

"So what'd you eat?"

He shrugged. "Cheetos, oranges, butternut squash, carrots. Lorna Doones—"

"Lorna Doones aren't orange."

He shrugged. "No, but they're *beige*. Which is in the orange *family*."

I laughed.

"It didn't work, by the way," he said. "A week into it my dad got another DUI. And my fingers were stained orange from the Cheetos." He sniffled and made a noise that sounded as if he was about to hack up a hairball. "Listen, you can wish on pennies or not step on cracks—I know this kid named Kevin? He used to do that, the no-cracks thing, and talk about annoying. It took *forever* to get down the street with him—anyway, you can do all that, but it doesn't make a difference. What's going to happen is going to happen."

I nodded. I knew he was right. But instead of feeling bummed out that I had even less control over life, I felt warm and fuzzy inside. The kind of warm and fuzzy that came when you took the risk to tell someone something that you were sure they would laugh at, and instead he understood. As I looked at Walter—an occasionally annoying, no-concept-of-boundaries-when-it-came-to-other-people's-food, loud-talking, postnasal dripper—I realized I was going to miss him when I was in New York. Because his parents were on the verge of splitting up. ("I mean it this time, Walter," his mother had been telling him for the last few weeks, the way she had for the last four years. "I really do.") They had decided, in a last-ditch effort to try to work things out, to rent a house in Nantucket, because once upon a time, when they were young and didn't have any kids, they had gone there on vacation and had had a really good time. (According to Walter, they had made similar trips to Florence, Italy, and Cabo San Lucas, Mexico, to try to do the same thing.) Which meant that Walter and his younger sister, Allison, were going to Florida, to visit their grandparents. Thank God for Skype, although he (and Mom) were already on me about how I was going to have to find some Alateen meetings in New York. ("There may be cows there, Annabelle," Mom had said the night before, "but there are meetings as well.")

Walter and I may have been friends for only a few weeks, but in a lot of ways I felt closer to him than I did to my old ones. The same ones who, as we turned around to leave, I saw coming out of Anthropologie and right toward us.

"Omigod! Annabelle!" Olivia cried as they drew closer, juggling three bags. Anthropologie used to be my favorite store as well, but now I was all about bragging to anyone who would listen about my new pink-and-white Diane von Furstenberg–rip-off Mossimo dress that was marked down twice at Target. "That is so weird. Sarah and I were *just* talking about you!" She turned to Sarah. "Right? Weren't we?"

Sarah nodded. "Yup, we were. Totally."

They had their backs turned to Walter, as if he wasn't even there. "This is my—" I started to say.

"We wanted to catch you at lunch, but we couldn't find you," Olivia cut me off.

I hadn't been in the cafeteria because Maya had been out sick, which meant I had no one to sit with. Instead, I sneaked off to my favorite handicapped stall to eat my tuna sandwich and have a panic attack in peace.

"So how are you? What's new?" Sarah asked, stepping in front of Walter.

When I had first started going to meetings, Walter had shared about how he often felt invisible, especially around his parents because they were such big personalities. As Sarah did that—just turned her back on him like that—I knew that he was probably feeling awful. Just like I had around them for the last few months.

I grabbed his arm and pulled him over next to me. "This is my friend Walter," I announced.

"Hi," he mumbled.

Olivia and Sarah looked at each other. "Your friend?" Olivia asked, her mouth twitching as if trying not to laugh.

"Yeah. *My friend*," I replied. Out of the corner of my eye, I could see Walter stand up straighter.

"Um, okay..." she said, as if the idea was totally insane. "Anyway, what are you doing Friday night? My dad got us tickets to Mumford and Sons, and I think I can get another one."

"I have plans." I didn't, and I loved Mumford & Sons, but I would rather have listened to them with really shitty earbuds than gone with those two.

"What about Saturday? There's a Crossroads party," Sarah said.

"Omigod, it would be so fun if we all went together!" Olivia said. "We'll get Maya to come, too. It'll be just like old times."

Did they know how transparent they were?

"I can't believe you're going to get to hang out with Billy Barrett!" Sarah said. "That is totes rad." Whenever Sarah tried to use slang, she sounded like a foreigner for whom English wasn't her first language.

Olivia shot her a look. "But that's not why we want to hang out with you," she said, trying for the save. "It's because . . . we miss you. *Obvi.*" She sounded a little more normal when she tried, but not much.

"Oh, wow. That's really sweet of you guys," I said. "I wish I could say the same, but actually . . . I *can't.*" I watched as the smug smiles on their faces started to deflate, like Sarah's bra when she took out the padding. "And I wish I could say it has been nice running into you, but, you know, I can't say that either." At that, they were flat, like Sarah's chest. "So I think we're gonna go. Come on, Walter."

I would have killed to see the looks on their faces as we walked away, but it felt even better not to turn around.

CHAPTER TEN

MAIN DIFFERENCES BETWEEN LOST ANGELES AND
UPSTATE NEW YORK

★ The stars you see are in the sky, not the
supermarket.
★ Subaru Outbacks and Foresters are the equiv-
alents of Mercedes and BMWs.
★ The ads on the radio stations sell Jesus, not Botox.
★ When you're forced to stop to let a fox cross
the road, it's the four-legged kind.
★ Starbucks is considered on par with fracking, in
terms of screwing up the environment.
★ There is no need to set the alarm on your
iPhone when you have a cow as your next-
door neighbor.

That last one I learned the first morning we were there,
three hours before I had planned to get up.

"That cannot be a cow," I murmured as I got out of bed in the 1922 farmhouse in a town called Clermont—population 1,726—that the producers had arranged for us to stay in during the movie. Because it was still dark, I managed to add another bruise to my collection as I whacked my knee on an antique sewing machine on my way to the window.

It was. Still mooing. And not only was there a cow—there was a goat as well, nuzzling up to the cow. Which, had I been awake, I would have found very cute.

Mom came running in, wearing a black silk nightgown. "What's going on?" she yelled. "What's that noise? Is someone out there? Is it a pap?"

I stumbled back into bed and covered my head with a pillow. "It's not a pap. It's a *cow*."

"A *cow*?"

"Uh-huh," I said sleepily.

"A real cow?"

It mooed again. "It would appear so," I said through the pillow.

"Oh, my God. How fabulous is that?!" she exclaimed. "That's going to make the whole country thing so authentic!"

I pulled the pillow tighter around my ears. Did she have to sound so awake?

"What's that thing next to it?"

"A goat," I said, turning over and placing the other pillow on the back of my head. "And I don't think they're ours. I think they belong to the neighbors." At least I hoped they did. Otherwise, we might be in charge of feeding them, and I highly doubted they liked Lean Cuisines.

"You do know that cows are considered sacred in India, don't you? They bring very good luck," she said. "I learned that in yoga class."

Realizing that going back to sleep wasn't an option, I sat up. "Great. But we're not in India," I said over the cow's bellowing. Although with how different upstate New York was from L.A., we may as well have been in a foreign country.

"Well, I'm sure they're good luck everywhere," she said, climbing into bed with me. "How'd you sleep? Isn't the quiet *magnificent*?"

"Actually, I found it kind of loud," I said. It was weird not to go to sleep with the sounds of car alarms or Persian music. Instead, it was chirping crickets and buzzing cicadas, and, in the case of my right ear, one lone mosquito that I couldn't get no matter how many times I slapped at it.

"Yeah, me, too," she agreed. "Still, it's the *country*!" she said, squeezing me to her before she jumped out of bed. "Come on—let's go get breakfast."

I squinted at the clock. "Mom, it's six o'clock. Nothing's going to be open."

"Of course it is! People get up really early here," she said, grabbing my arm. "To work the land!"

I guessed I could cross farming off my Potential Careers list because I was so not a morning person.

They got up early if they worked at Stewart's, a combination gas station/mini-mart. Which, once we drove around for a while, I discovered was the only thing open that early other than the Mobil XtraMart across the street.

"Ooh, these look good!" Mom said, pointing at something that looked as if it had wanted to be a scone about two weeks earlier but gave up somewhere around the biscuit stage. She smiled at the woman behind the counter, who was sporting a slight beard. "These aren't gluten-free by any chance, are they?"

I cringed. *"Mom."*

"Glu what?" the woman asked, confused.

"Nothing," I said, jumping in. "Do you have iced coffee?"

"Yep," she replied, staring at Mom.

"Great. We'll have two of those," I said. "Thanks."

As she walked over and started pouring something out of a milk carton with "iced coffee mix" printed on the side of it, Mom cringed. "I don't even want to think about all the chemicals that are in there," she whispered. "When we get back in the car, you'll Goggle that *New York Times* article about the best places to eat in the area."

"Google," I corrected.

"That's what I said."

"Half and half?" the woman asked.

"Half and half? Do people still drink that stuff?" Mom asked.

"*Mom.*"

"What? Do you know what that stuff does to your arteries?" She gave the woman a Janie Jackson smile. "Actually, do you have soy?"

"Soy sauce for your *coffee?*" the woman asked.

If this was how the next six weeks were going to go, we were in serious trouble. "How about nonfat milk?" I jumped in.

She pointed to the dairy section, which held gallon-size milk cartons. "You could buy one of those, I guess," she said, "and put some in."

"We'll just have some regular milk, if you have it," I said, before Mom could say yes.

"Bug, you know I can't digest lactose."

"It's one time," I said. "You'll live."

"Did I see you on TV the other day?" the woman asked as she handed us our drinks, which were now so light they looked like milk with a splash of coffee.

Oh, no. It was starting.

Mom smiled some more. "You may have," Mom said. "A few years ago I was on a sitcom called—"

"No, it was one of them judge shows," the woman said. "Not *Judge Judy.* That other one."

I started to laugh but, once Mom gave me a dirty look, quickly turned it into a cough.

"No, sorry," Mom replied. "I've never been on one of those."

"Oh," the woman said, disappointed.

I took a sip, totally prepared for it to be disgusting. "Oh, my God—this is *awesome*!" I said, amazed.

"That's because it's probably all sugar," Mom whispered. She turned to the woman and flashed another smile. "Well, thank you! So nice meeting you!"

"Mm-hmm," the woman replied, eyeing my mom suspiciously.

"I thought people in the country were supposed to be nice," Mom said as we got back into the green Subaru Outback that the producers had arranged for us to have while we were here. "That was more of a Manhattan attitude."

"Maybe they're not used to seeing people fully made up and accessorized at seven o'clock in the morning," I replied, sipping at my iced coffee. I wasn't even done with it, and I already wanted another one.

As we drove down Route 9G toward Hudson, which, according to my Googling, was considered the "Brooklyn of the Hudson Valley," I had to admit that with the wide-open smog-free blue sky and glowing purple Catskill Mountains, it was pretty gorgeous. Other than the one dead deer, two dead skunks, and multiple squirrels we passed on the way. ("Honey, it's the country. You get used to it after a while," Mom said, as if she had any experience with it. "Plus, it's a good reminder of the ongoing cycle of life and death.")

"How *adorable*!" Mom chirped when we got to War-ren Street, Hudson's main street. "It's like something out of a movie!"

It did look like a movie set. For something set in the early 1900s. With the small, square row houses and Victo-rian townhomes, I almost expected Annie to come march-ing down the street singing "Tomorrow." As we walked, I saw that every other storefront was a gallery or antique store. "There's a Pilates place and a yoga studio," I said, relieved. Not like I'd be going to either, but it was comfort-ing to know that we weren't completely lost in time.

Next door was a little café called The Cascades. They didn't have soy, either, but they did have nonfat milk, which made Mom happy. Not to mention these ginor-mous coconut-blueberry muffins that made me happy and made her eyebrows go up when I ordered one. Plus, the waitress, Wenonah ("WE-nonah, with a hard *e*—not Wynonna with an *i*-sounding *y*, like that country singer," she informed us when she introduced herself) recognized Mom right away. As she plopped herself down at our table and started to gush about how much she had related to this TV movie Mom had done early in her career, in which she had played a woman on the run from her abusive hus-band because literally almost the *exact same thing* had happened to her, back in '95, when she was married to her first husband, whom she couldn't really talk about because of, you know, *legal* things, I excused myself to go to the bathroom. When I came out and saw that Wenonah was still yakking away, I walked to the front to grab one of the free magazines I had seen when we walked in.

"You've never been here, huh?" a voice asked as I thumbed through a glossy magazine called *Chronogram* that, along with music listings and art openings, also had a large selection of eco-builders and hypnotherapists.

I turned around to see a guy a little taller than me with blue eyes and brown hair that looked as if it hadn't seen a brush for a while. He was wearing paint-stained khaki shorts and a T-shirt that read HUDSON: THE UN-HAMPTONS (AND LET'S KEEP IT THAT WAY). Unlike the guys I knew from L.A., who were lean from years of soccer and lacrosse, this guy had a cuddly look to him. Almost like if you were to squeeze him in the right place, he'd let out one of those squeaks like a stuffed animal.

"How'd you know that?" I asked suspiciously.

"Because anyone who's been here knows that once Wenonah corners you, you're in trouble," he replied. He smiled. "I'm Matt."

The gap between his two front teeth made me smile back. "Annabelle."

"So you a weekender?"

"A what?"

"Do you live in the city and just come up here on weekends?"

"Oh. No, I actually live in L.A.," I replied. "I'm just here for the summer. With my mom. She's . . . working up here." I wanted to see how long I could hold off on the per-haps-you've-seen-my-mother's-mug-shot-on-TMZ? thing.

"At Bard?"

Bard was a college near Tivoli, which was about ten minutes from the farmhouse. Mom had made sure to tell me the producers had mentioned there was a nice gym there, in case something about the country air turned me into someone who liked to work out. "No. She's, uh, shooting a movie."

I waited for him to start with the third degree the way people usually did—especially people outside of L.A.—but all he did was nod after he waved to the woman behind the counter. "Cool," he said as she slid a cup of coffee across the counter toward him.

So this is what it felt like to be normal. At least until the cook came out and barked at Wenonah to leave the customers alone and get back to work, which meant Mom was free to walk over to see what I was up to.

"Oh, my God—what a *life* that woman has had!" Mom announced as she joined us. "This is why it's important to get out of the fishbowl of Hollywood, Bug—not just to be in nature, but to meet people who are such . . . *survivors!*" She held up a scrap of paper. "I got her e-mail address. I think if I have some time, I'll interview her. You know, for research, in case I ever do another battered-woman thing again." She turned to Matt and flashed him a smile. "Hello, I'm Janie Jackson."

I searched his face for recognition, but there didn't

seem to be any. "Matt Wallace. Nice to meet you. So are you making a documentary?"

"A what?" she asked, confused.

"Annabelle said you were making a movie," he replied. "There's a lot of documentary filmmakers up here, and because you just said you wanted to interview Wenonah, I thought maybe—"

Mom laughed. "Ohhhh. You meant a *documentary* documentary." She shook her head. "No, no—I'm making a *movie* movie. With Billy Barrett?"

He nodded. "Ah. Yeah, I heard some of the girls in Swallow talking about him the other day. I've never seen his stuff, but he sounds like a pretty big deal."

Mom looked at him like he was an alien. "You haven't seen a Billy Barrett movie? Do you even . . . *go* to the movies?" Mom asked.

"Mom."

"Oh yeah. All the time," he said. "Over at Upstate. In Rhinebeck. They also have one in Woodstock."

I had seen that in the *Chronogram* magazine. They had all the independent stuff.

"They had this great documentary last week about fracking," he went on. "If it's still there, I highly recommend it."

Mom turned to me. "Do I even want to know what fracking is?"

"I'll tell you later," I replied.

"Do you have a TV?" she asked.

He shook his head. "No. I watch stuff on Hulu and Netflix, though."

She relaxed. "Good. That explains it."

I shook my head. I wondered if there was a clinical term for people who had an overwhelming need for people to recognize them. Other than "actress."

"Well, I should get going," Matt said. He flashed another gap-toothed smile. "Maybe I'll see you around."

"Yeah," I said, hoping I sounded like what the magazines referred to as "inviting but not desperate."

"Nice meeting you, Mrs. Jackson."

I tried to cover my laugh with another cough.

"Oh, honey, it's never been Mrs.," Mom laughed. "Janie's fine."

After he was gone, Mom turned to me and raised her eyebrow.

"What?"

"Nothing," she said, her lips twitching as she tried not to smile.

My face felt all hot. "Then why are you looking at me like that?"

"I'm not looking at you any way."

On TV, parents tried to discourage their kids from dating, nervous to see them grow up. Not my mother. Although she never came right out and said I was a freak because I wasn't sneaking off to Planned Parenthood to try to get the morning-after pill, I knew the fact that I wasn't boy-crazy was somewhat of a disappointment to her. After yet another fight about the whole thing, we had decided the subject was off limits which, for some reason, made me feel like even more of a loser.

The truth was, not only was I still a virgin, but I had made out with a boy only once. In Sarah's garage with her cousin Sam, who was visiting from San Francisco. He was cute in a post-weight-loss Jonah Hill way, but it didn't end well. When we first started making out, it wasn't horrible—his lips were soft, and he didn't jam his tongue down my throat like I had heard from Maya sometimes happened. (Before she decided she liked girls, Maya had made out with a lot of guys.) But then he started jamming his tongue in my ear. *Hard.* To the point where I told him if he didn't stop I was afraid he'd damage my eardrum. I didn't say it to be mean—it was more that I just didn't want to go deaf—but he took it that way. (The fact that he called me a bitch under his breath as he stomped off, knocking over a rake in the process, sort of tipped me off.)

Sure, I wanted a boyfriend, but watching over Mom had always been a full-time job, so there never seemed to be time. Plus, if the way you acted in a relationship was hereditary, I was screwed. The minute Mom got into one, she became all obsessive and clingy and started reading every horoscope online to try to figure out what was going to happen in the future; then she'd make an appointment with her psychic to try to figure out how not to screw it up. Being in love didn't look like fun to me. It looked as if it would bring on even more panic attacks.

"He's probably got a girlfriend, Mom," I said as I turned around and started to walk out of the café.

Which would be both a relief and a bummer at the same time.

The next day, after dropping Mom off at an AA meeting at a church in Hudson, I went over to the Spotty Dog, a bookstore/pub on Warren Street.

Other than the guy working behind the bar, there was no one else there. I checked out the photography section. For a small bookstore, they had a surprisingly large collection, including the Francesca Woodman one Ben had bought me. Even though I already knew the photographs by heart, I took it off the shelf so I could browse through it. As I walked toward the back, I passed the self-help section and paused. Usually, I avoided that stuff at all costs, but after glancing to make sure the guy behind the counter was still busy with his issue of the *Believer,* I ran my fingers along the books until I came to the Relationship section and grabbed a book called *Thirty Days to Calling in the One.* It wasn't like that Matt guy was the *One*—I'd probably never even see him again—but it couldn't hurt to learn more about what to do if, indeed, I wanted to call in the One. Or Someone. Or Anyone.

I had just finished reading about ways to feng shui your living space to invite in love and had moved on to the chapter about how to unblock your energy field when a shadow came over me.

"Whatcha reading?" a voice asked.

Oh, God. I knew that voice. If I hadn't recognized it from the *Rad and Righteous* ads, I would have known it from the voice mails that Mom had saved on her iPhone, which I had listened to the other day while she was in the shower. (When I told Walter about that, he suggested I pray to my Higher Power to have my nosiness removed.) I quickly moved the book behind me and jammed my back against the shelf to keep it in place while reaching for the Francesca Woodman.

"Billy, hey. Just, uh, this," I said, holding it up.

"Dude, I love Francesca Woodman!" he exclaimed, grabbing it from me.

"You know who Francesca Woodman is?" I asked, surprised. She wasn't one of the big names, like Cindy Sherman or Diane Arbus or Gregory Crewdson. She was more like the angsty Sylvia Plath of photography.

"Yeah. My art consultant bid on one recently at an auction for me, but we didn't get it." He started to flip through the pages. "I'll show you my favorite."

Now that I thought about it, it made sense. Most of her work consisted of nude self-portraits she had made when she was in college. I couldn't believe I was going to have to stand here and look at nude photos with Billy Barrett. Although that would have gotten a lot of traction as a Facebook status update or a tweet.

He stopped flipping and held the book out. "This one."

I looked at it. "Really?" I asked, surprised. It was a photo of her in a clawfoot bathtub. Her face wasn't visible, but her long dirty-blonde hair hung over the back of the tub.

"Yeah," he said, studying it intently.

"That one's my favorite, too," I replied.

He smiled. "Right on. She reminds me of Ophelia in this one, for some reason."

"Ophelia from *Hamlet*?" I asked dumbly.

"Well, yeah. I mean, what other Ophelias are there?"

I don't know why it surprised me that he would reference Shakespeare. The guy *was* an actor, and *Hamlet* was one of the most famous plays in the world. But Billy was better known for explosions than running around a stage in tights.

"Especially in light of, you know, what happened to her at the end," he went on.

"You know about how she died?" I asked, even more surprised.

At that, he turned to me. "What do you think? That the only thing I read is *Maxim* or something?"

I guess the slight pause as I racked my brain trying to think of a response was answer enough. "Yeah, well, you wouldn't be the only one," he sighed.

Way to make a girl feel guilty. But what was I doing feeling bad for Billy Barrett? He did not need my sympathy.

"So are you waiting for your mom?" he asked.

And just like that I no longer felt bad. He didn't really want to talk to me. He was waiting for her, too. "Yeah."

"What time is her meeting over?"

I pressed harder against the shelf to keep the book from slipping. "How do you know she's at a meeting?" I demanded.

"We were texting a little bit earlier."

I wasn't sure if it pissed me off to watch his face turn red as he said that, or if I should be grateful that he felt somewhat weird telling me that. "Did you know that when you get sober, they suggest you don't get into a relationship for, like, a year?" I blurted out.

The way he stared at me made me think that he knew what I was saying with that little tidbit of information. "Yeah, I've heard that," he replied. "I have a bunch of friends in the program. Sounds like it's probably a good idea."

Radiohead's "Creep" began to blare from his phone, which I remembered was Skye's ringtone. He ignored it.

"You sure you don't want to get that?" I asked.

"Nope, I'm good," he said as he turned off the ringer.

"It's okay if you want to," I said.

"Nope, it can wait," he said firmly.

Right then my own phone beeped.

*OKAY ALL DONE CAN YOU COME GET ME BECAUSE
I STILL CAN'T FIGURE MY WAY AROUND HERE!!!!!
THANKS BUG XOXOXOXOXOX*

Reading my mother's texts—almost always composed entirely of caps, Xs and Os, and zero punctuation marks, other than an overabundance of exclamation points—was sensory overload. "I need to go," I said.

"Right on," he said. Maybe if you had a total crush on him (like 99 percent of the female population in the world), the "Right on" thing would seem cute, but every time he said it, I wanted to throttle him. "See you at that dinner thing tonight?" Usually, before a movie started shooting, the producers had a dinner so that the key cast members could meet and hang out with the director.

"Oh, you're going to that?" I asked, trying to hide my disappointment. Of course he was going to that—he was the star. And what was I doing? It was one thing to *think* about how I had no interest in getting to know this guy, and even less interest in my mother getting to know him, but it was a whole other thing for the filter between my brain and mouth to break down so that he knew it as well.

"Yeah," he replied with a little laugh. "Is that okay?"

"Of course it is," I said. "I didn't mean . . . you know, I think I'm still jet-lagged," I mumbled.

He looked at me for a second. "This is probably going to make me sound like a total ass, but whatever," he said. "The fact that you don't like me—"

"I never said I didn't like you."

"'It's actually kind of awesome," he went on. "I mean—again, gonna make me sound like a jerk—but when everyone is always kissing your ass? It gets boring real fast."

"I wouldn't know. I don't really have that problem," I said wryly.

He smiled. "But it doesn't mean I'm not going to do everything I can to change your mind about me."

PLACES TO SHOP FOR MOVIE KICKOFF PARTY-APPROPRIATE OUTFITS IN L.A.
- ★ Fred Segal
- ★ Anthropologie
- ★ Any boutique on West Third Street near the Grove
- ★ The holy trinity of Saks/Neimans/Barneys

PLACES TO SHOP FOR MOVIE KICKOFF PARTY-APPROPRIATE OUTFITS IN UPSTATE NEW YORK
- ★ H&M
- ★ Kohl's
- ★ T.J. Maxx
- ★ Marshalls
- ★ Target

"Bug, you are so right—Target is *incredible*!" Mom exclaimed as we went through the racks of sundresses that in L.A. would have been considered too casual to wear anywhere else but to Target, but up here were totally appropriate to wear to a fancy dinner.

"Mom, you've been to Target before," I said quietly as two women over near the bathing suits looked over to check out who the nut was who was only just discovering the genius that was Target. "We used to go all the time before you got the show."

"I know, honey, but I don't remember the clothes being this fabulous." She laughed. "Not that I remember much of the last eight years, seeing that I was either passed out or doped up most of the time."

I cringed. Honesty was one thing. Honesty in front of complete strangers in a discount store about your deepest darkest secrets was a whole other.

"Volume, Mom," I whispered.

She held up a leopard-print dress. "What about this?"

"We're here to find something for me, remember?" I replied. "You have five suitcases full of stuff at home."

"I mean for you."

I wrinkled my nose. I was so not a leopard girl. Even a print was going out on a limb for me. I was all about solids. Solids were safe. They blended in. Didn't call attention to themselves.

Mom took me by the shoulders. "Honey, it's time for you to shake it up a bit," she said gently. "I know that up until now, most of your life has been spent taking care of me—"

I felt my stomach start to flip-flop as her lip started to

quiver. She had to pick here for one of her Moments? Really? "Mom, can we talk about this later?" I asked quietly.

"Oh, God, Annabelle. I know I'm supposed to stop beating myself up for everything I put you through, but it's just so *hard*," she moaned, swiping at her eyes, which were now indeed leaking tears. "I mean, you're my *life*, Bug." She grabbed my arms tighter. "You know that, right?"

Apparently, we could not talk about it later. "I do," I said, trying to extract myself from her death grip. I looked around to see more people staring at us. "And now half of Target does as well." I cringed as I moved her hand away and used her cardigan to dry off my now-sticky arm.

"What was I saying?" she asked as she took out a mirror and checked to make sure her eye makeup hadn't smeared. You had to give it to my mother—for someone who was a big crier, she had perfected the art of being able to do it so that it left no messy evidence.

"How I was your life."

"No. Before that."

"That I need to shake things up a bit."

"Right." She grabbed my arms again. "I'm serious, Bug. I've been thinking about this a lot, and I don't want you to turn into one of those characters who ends up alone because she's devoted her life to taking care of a parent. Like that woman in the English movie we watched last week. The one who snapped when they kept calling her a spinster."

"Mom, I'm only sixteen—"

"I know, I know, but, sweetie, you need more of a social life," she said. "The fact that you've never had a boyfriend...it's not...*normal.*"

I felt my stomach start to burn. I couldn't believe she was bringing this up again. She knew the subject was off limits. As was my weight, and why I didn't want to get a bikini wax. She grabbed a purple wrap dress and held it up to me. "What about this? This is cute."

I pushed it away. Only my mother could totally insult me and try to dress me in the same exact moment. "Oh, I'm sorry," I snapped. "I guess I was too busy checking on, you know, whether you were still *alive* to worry about hooking up and getting pregnant like you did."

Her eyes flashed before she took a deep breath. "Okay. I deserve that," she said quietly.

"And what do you know about normal?" I demanded. "Our life is not and never has been normal, Mom."

"Hey, we barbecued last night," she said. "That's a normal thing to do—"

"And we almost burned the house down because you didn't check to make sure the propane tank was hooked up correctly!" I cried.

"I meant the dinner *after* that part was normal," she said. "That salmon was excellent." She examined the dress

221

again. "Bug, seriously, why won't you try this on? It's ador-able."

"Because I don't want to. It's too low-cut."

"Annabelle, I keep telling you—the body is nothing to be ashamed of! Especially since you've cut back on snacking," she said. "I haven't said anything because I know it makes you mad when I comment on your weight, but sweetie, you're looking fabulous. Really."

My mother may not have won an Oscar yet, but she was the queen of backhanded compliments.

She threw the dress in the cart. "Then if you don't get it, I will. All I'm saying is that you don't need to take care of me anymore, honey." She moved my bangs out of my eyes. "I'm okay. I'm going to be okay," she said gently.

I wanted so badly to believe that, but it was hard. Why was it so hard?

"It's time for you to have fun again," she said quietly. "I just want you to be open to it."

I wanted that, too. I just didn't know *how*.

"Okay?"

"Okay," I agreed.

She smiled. "Good. And we're cutting your bangs before the dinner tonight. You never know who you might meet."

CHAPTER ELEVEN

HOW THE EVENING BEGAN
- ★ Five outfit changes (Mom)
- ★ Three warnings that if she changed her outfit one more time we'd be lucky if we made it there for dessert (me)
- ★ Four different variations on the same hairstyle (Mom)
- ★ Two mumbled recitations of the Serenity Prayer in order to ward off a fight (me)
- ★ One tearful call to her sponsor saying she didn't know how she was going to make it through the dinner without a drink because post-rehab her evenings had been spent either in meetings or at home (Mom)
- ★ Numerous updates on what time it was (me)

"Honey, forty-five minutes is not late," Mom announced as we walked into the back garden of Ca'Mea on Warren

Street after I had finally wrangled her into the car. "You know, I've been thinking about it, and I think your obsession with being on time has to do with the whole being-a-child-of-an-alcoholic thing."

The last part just happened to coincide with a lull in the conversation so that you would have had to have a hearing problem not to have heard it clearly. Which meant that pretty much everyone in the garden—about twenty people—all turned to stare at us.

"What she say? Alcoholic? I thought she stopped with the drinking, that one," said Giovanni, the Italian cinematographer who I came to find out later that evening had twenty-five grandchildren because his family was very Catholic and didn't believe in birth control.

"Oh, she did," said a tall thin guy with little round glasses who was so pasty that I wanted to shove him in a tanning bed with a few sandwiches. From his English accent and some photos I had come across during a Google search, I could tell this was Alistair, the director. He was wearing peach-colored linen pants and a tight white tank top—which was way better than the very tiny, very tight Speedo he'd been photographed in while he was on vacation in Ibiza with his florist-to-the-stars boyfriend, Henrik. "I saw a photo of her coming out of an AA meeting on one of the blogs." He turned to Barry, a fat bearded guy who was chewing on a straw. Barry was one of the producers, and from the few times I had met him, I now realized the pained expression on his face—a cross between indigestion and nausea—seemed to be his resting state.

"Barry, she is still sober, is she not?" I heard Alistair ask. (I'm not sure if there was any scientific evidence to back it up, but, like me, Walter also had supersonic hearing, which led me to believe that that was a by-product of the whole kid-of-an-alcoholic thing.) "Because I'm telling you right now—my healer said my nervous system is still recovering from that last film I did, and I refuse to put my health in jeopardy. Even for a Billy Barrett movie."

"Of course she's still sober," Barry assured him, not even bothering to take the straw out of his mouth. At dinner, he had mentioned that the straw was because he was quitting smoking. ("Yeah, for the last five years," Dina, his ex-assistant/now-wife/co-producer said, rolling her eyes.) He turned to Dina as she popped a piece of bruschetta into her mouth whole. The other night, after watching her scarf down not just her own meal but also Barry's—not to mention part of Mom's—Mom and I had decided that her gazellelike appearance was maintained with some good old-fashioned bulimia. "You didn't see her drink anything at dinner the other night, did you?" he asked her.

"Nope. Just club soda," I heard Dina reply. "I even picked up her glass and took a sip when she was in the bathroom to check."

By this time they weren't trying too hard to keep their voices down. Not that it mattered, as Mom was busy oohing and aahing over Giovanni's wife's little dog, which looked like a drowned rat. One actress cliché that Mom did not fall into was a love of small, bedazzled dogs that could be carried around in designer carriers—in fact, she sometimes had nightmares about them. ("Usually when I overdid it on the Klonopin," she said.) Like any good actress, however, she knew that even more important than the director, the person to win over was the cinematographer. You did not want to piss off the person who was in charge of filters and lighting, unless you wanted every wrinkle and mark on your face to be magnified.

I grabbed a red juicy tomato topped with basil and mozzarella off the tray of a passing waiter and bit into it. Not having to lie awake anymore worrying about whether Mom was going to be able to pay the rent with tampon voice-overs was great, but my second favorite thing about her doing the movie was that between the party and the on-set catering, I could eat as much as I wanted and not have to worry about how much it cost.

"I wondered if I'd run into you again," a voice said. A male voice. With a twinge of a New York accent. The very voice that I had played over in my head the last few nights before attempting to convince myself that the sweet and funny things it might be capable of saying were probably reserved for another girl.

I turned around to see Matt, in jeans and a cornflower-blue button-down shirt that made his blue eyes even bluer.

"Well, I guess you don't have to wonder anymore," I said. Was that lame? It sounded lame. And was I going to second-guess everything I said to him? If so, that would be exhausting.

"It's Matt," he reminded me, as if there had been any chance I had forgotten.

"Oh, I know," I said quickly. Too quickly. Way too quickly. This is why I stayed away from guys. Well, this and the fact that I didn't need to fall for someone and be let down by him. My mother had broken my heart enough times over the course of my life that I didn't need anyone else doing it. "Annabelle. I mean, I'm Annabelle."

He smiled. "Yeah. I know."

Yet again the gap between his teeth did it to me, and I smiled back. "Are you—" I started to say.

"A guest here?" he finished. He smiled. "Nope, I'm working. I find that cater-waitering really informs the process of painting. All the great ones did it. Rumor has it Picasso could balance four trays at a time."

"Yeah, I've heard that," I said. "And when he dropped them, that was the start of cubism."

He laughed. "Nice," he said, impressed.

What was I doing coming up with comebacks on the spot? And, like, semi-smart ones at that? That was so not me. "So you're a painter?"

"Yeah. Well, studying it at Bard. Just finished my freshman year," he replied. "But mostly I just sit there staring at the canvas paralyzed with anxiety over the fact that I've chosen a career where, after thousands of dollars of debt in student loans, I'll probably never make any money, forcing me to ultimately take a job as a telemarketer and move home and live in my mother's basement."

I cringed. "Wow. That sounds—"

"Like your worst nightmare?" he suggested. "'Cause it's mine. Especially the moving-home-with-my-mother part."

I laughed before looking over at my own mother, who was now demonstrating her signature pratfall for a couple who looked to be in their early forties, both dressed in black, with matching hip nerd glasses. I had a feeling they were the couple who wrote the movie. And who, from the way they exchanged a baffled look, didn't seem to find it as funny as most of America had.

"Your mother's very . . . colorful," Matt said.

"That's one word for it," I sighed. "And she's not even drunk."

He motioned to my cheek. "You have some basil on your cheek."

Of course I did. I swiped at it.

"The other side."

I swiped again.

"Still there."

I swiped harder. Actually, it was more like I scrubbed at it.

"Got it," Matt said.

"Actually, it's part of my outfit," I said. "I thought the

green went well with the red." I motioned to the jersey dress that Mom and I had found when we stopped at Kohl's post-Target crisis. It was cleavage-lite, which made me happy, but short enough to please Mom. "Kind of a Christmas-in-July theme."

"Well, the outfit's working." He smiled. "Even without the basil."

I was too busy turning the same color as my dress to be able to think of a comeback—witty or not—to that. But even if I could have, I wouldn't have gotten it out because just then Billy arrived.

"Hey, Annabelle," he said with a smile.

"Hey," I replied. "Billy, this is Matt. He's a painter."

"And your cater-waiter for the evening," Matt added.

Billy laughed. "Been there, dude. *A lot*. Back in the day when everyone in L.A. was on a Middle Eastern kick. Do you know how hard it is to get the smell of baba ghanoush out of your hair?"

He definitely got an A in charm.

As he told us a story about dropping a tray full of two thousand dollars' worth of caviar at an Oscar party, Mom looked over from her conversation across the garden. When she saw Billy, her smile got so big that it erased all of the little stubborn lines that Botox never seemed to be able to get.

"Hey, will you excuse me for a second?" Billy asked. I turned to see that he was looking at her in that way they

were always talking about in those Harlequin romance nov-
els that Esme read—as if Mom was the only person in the
room.

Before I could say anything—like maybe something
along the lines of "So, Billy, what's your position on fracking?" or "Have you ever thought of narrating a documentary on global warming, because even if it were just your
voice and not you, shirtless, killing terrorists, I bet it would
attract an audience that wouldn't necessarily pay attention
to that stuff"—Mom appeared.

"Hey, you," she said as she stood in front of the three
of us. Unlike me, she didn't have any sort of food particle
hanging off her cheek.

"Hey," Billy said, dazed. Is that what happened when
you were really into someone? You sounded stoned?
Because I had to say, it was not very attractive. Although
the other person, being equally high on hormones, probably wouldn't notice.

"Hey, Mom—you remember Matt, right? From the
café the other day? You know, the day you met that
woman Wenonah?" I babbled. I could have kicked myself
for not having bought some Play-Doh at Target earlier.

"Of course. Nice to see you again," she replied, not
seeing him at all, because she was too busy making out
with Billy with her eyes.

"Nice to see you, too," Matt said. He turned to me. "I
think I should go . . . you know . . . work."

"Right. Sure," I said, trying not to sound disappointed. Of course he didn't want to hang around. This was a guy who preferred documentaries to sitcoms, read real news instead of gossip blogs, and had never seen a Billy Barrett movie. I'd want to get away from it, too, if I could.

"You look beautiful," Billy said to Mom as he mauled her right back with his eyes. "You both do," he added.

While any girl my age—or woman or gay guy or dog, really—would have had an epilectic seizure if Billy Barrett had called her beautiful (and, after she recovered, begged him to say it again so that she could tape it with her phone and make a ringtone out of it), it pissed me off. How many times had I been in this position?

WHAT HAPPENS WHEN MOM HOOKS UP
   ★ Mom hooks up with guy.
   ★ Guy says nice things to me and buys me little gifts in order to impress Mom.
   ★ Guy gets bored with pretending to like kids, causing him to stop putting on fake smile whenever he sees me and instead looks annoyed and impatient as he tries to figure out how long it'll be before I'm gone and he can get Mom into bed.
   ★ Guy starts to realize Mom's a bit of a nut and begins to pull back.

★ Mom catches on to the fact that guy is pulling back and starts getting clingy because, according to her, she's got abandonment issues.

★ Mom starts to get a little stalkery.

★ Guy realizes Mom's not just a bit nuts but a total freak and dumps her.

★ Mom takes to her bed for a week with a bottle of Stoli in one hand and a bottle of pills in the other.

★ Rinse and repeat.

"Oh, you're sweet," Mom said.

"Hey, I'm just stating the facts," Billy said.

I pulled on her arm. "Everyone's starting to sit down for dinner."

"Okay," she replied, not moving.

"We should go, too, don't you think?"

"You go sit. I'll be there in a second."

"It's okay. I'll wait. I'm not that hungry," I said, even though I was. I knew I was being annoying. But I couldn't help it. I felt like, if I stayed, maybe I could prevent what I already knew in my gut was going to happen.

"Go sit, Annabelle."

"I'm good."

She tore her eyes away from Billy and glared at me while I tried my best to look innocent.

"Annabelle's right. We should probably go sit," Billy agreed. "Plus, I'm starved. I could eat a side of beef. If, you know, I ate beef." He looked at us. "I just found out PETA wants me to be the voice for a bunch of PSAs they're doing about vegetarianism," he said proudly. "I'm so psyched."

"Omigod, that's fabulous!" Mom exclaimed. The same woman who, the other night, had torn into a hamburger (minus the bun, of course) and announced that it was better than sex.

It was starting. The morphing herself into a carbon copy of the guy she was into, except with boobs and a better ability to accessorize. Ben was the only guy she hadn't done the pretzel thing with, the only guy she knew she could be herself with, and he'd love her anyway.

She took a deep breath. "But, Billy, if we're, you know, going to be friends, there's something you should know."

"Yeah?"

"I love meat," she confessed. "I actually eat a lot of it. And . . . I don't plan on stopping."

Okay, that was big.

Billy nodded. "That's cool. I totally support a person's right to choose around that issue."

"Just so you know, I do go out of my way to make sure it's grass fed. Obviously."

"Good, good," Billy said. "And, you know, I hope you're cool with the fact that it's just not my thing—"

233

"Oh, completely! I totally respect and admire that!" Mom assured him.

He gave her one of those smiles that kept getting him on the Sexiest/Most Beautiful lists. "Right on."

They were flirting over the discussion of *beef*. And yet they had this way of making it sound cute. Mom had taken the risk to do something differently—i.e., not be a love-junkie pretzel—and it had paid off. Shouldn't I be proud of her? This is what I wanted, right? For her to change and, in changing, get better? So why, instead of being happy for her, did I feel as if I was about to have a panic attack?

Mom and Billy could have spent all of dinner flattering each other about, say, Billy's efforts to help revitalize New Orleans ("I know that's really Brad Pitt's thing, but the city holds a real special place in my heart from when I went there for Mardi Gras my junior year of college"), or the fact that Mom had decided that once the movie was over, she wanted to put her efforts toward starting a wellness and self-esteem school-like place in Mexico. ("I'm a terrible flier, especially now that I can't take Xanax, and it's a lot closer than Africa. Not to mention that between Madonna and Oprah, they've kind of got that continent covered.") Instead, they let everyone else join in and compliment them as well. Because it was a Hollywood crowd, everyone knew how to do it in such a way that it all sounded very sincere. Like when Barry told Mom with a straight face that he agreed that inspirational bumper stickers were a terrific way to spread good energy on a daily basis, especially in a place like L.A., where there was so much traffic.

As for me, I spent my time trying not to appear painfully aware of where Matt was at any given second. I kept shifting my body in such a way so that he was always in my peripheral vision, but never so that I'd be face-to-face and have to talk to him. Although he didn't seem to have an issue with it, I felt self-conscious about the fact that he was on his feet bringing out course after course of Italian food while I was sitting at a table with people who were complaining about how difficult it was to fly on a regular plane once you had flown on the Paramount private jet (Barry and Dina). Even back in the day when you couldn't pick up a magazine with a (non-mug-shot) photo of Mom on the cover, I had never felt comfortable listening to rich white people bitch about rich white people problems.

After dessert—tiramisu and profiteroles, which, in true Hollywood fashion, everyone picked at except for Billy and me—we cleaned our plates—people started to leave. As Mom and Billy talked I kept looking toward the door, half of me hoping that Matt would come out before we left. The other half prayed he wouldn't, because the idea of his saying something like "Well, nice seeing you again" and nothing else felt worse than leaving without saying good-bye. Finally, after the dishes were gone from the table and everyone else had trickled out so only me, Mom, and Billy were left, Matt came rushing out, having exchanged his cater-waiter preppiness for a faded NYU T-shirt and the same paint-flecked khaki shorts from the other day.

"You're still here," he said.

It was probably me just projecting my own feelings, but I could have sworn he sounded relieved. "Yeah," I said, trying to keep my voice neutral.

"I don't know what you're doing now . . . I mean, I know it's a little late . . . although being from L.A., you probably don't even go out until around now," he said. "Even though my dad says that people in L.A. go out early because they like to get home early so they can get to bed and get up and do yoga at six o'clock in the morning—"

He was talking a lot, and fast. Faster than he had at the coffee shop. Was he talking a lot because he was nervous?

"Oh, I love early-morning yoga classes!" Mom said.

"Me, too," Billy said. "I took this sunrise class on the beach once when I was in Hawaii? I think it was one of the most spiritual experiences of my life."

"Omigod, I'll *bet*," Mom gasped. "Where do you like to go when you're there? The Big Island or—"

How had my conversation with Matt suddenly become one about how Mom and Billy had yet another thing in common?

"Anyways, there's this music-reading-performance thing at the Basilica—the arts center place down near the train station?—that a friend of mine is doing, and I thought you might want to check it out," Matt blurted out.

I could feel my stomach start to do warm-ups. This guy—this really cute guy—was kind-of-sort-of asking me out.

"You know, as a way for you to meet some people around here," he added.

The warm-ups stopped. He was just being nice. Still, date or no date, here was my own opportunity to do things differently. To say yes and be social instead of hanging out at home watching over my mother. "Oh. Thanks. That's really nice of you," I said, "but—"

"What a generous invitation!" Mom exclaimed. She turned to Billy. "Don't you find the friendliness of country people just so *refreshing*?"

I sighed. If Matt had taken back his offer based on that alone, I wouldn't have blamed him. Luckily, when I glanced up at him, he looked amused rather than offended. "I have to drive my mom home," I went on. "She's not so great driving in the dark."

"Who are we kidding," Mom snorted. "I'm not even that great stone cold sober in the daylight."

That was true.

"I could drive her home," Billy offered hopefully. "Clermont's just over from Germantown." I hadn't seen it, but over dinner Billy had been talking about the converted barn with thirty-foot ceilings that the producers had rented for him for the shoot. It sounded amazing.

The three of them waited for my response. What was I waiting for? This was what I wanted, right? What I had used my wish on at the fountain at the Grove that day, after realizing that the one about Ben and Mom had officially passed its expiration date—to have a life? Just then I heard Walter's voice in my head telling me—actually, ordering me—to "act as if." I could act as if hanging out with cute boys with gaps between their teeth was something I did on a regular basis. I could act as if I wasn't nervous that I'd say or do something stupid. I could act as if I wasn't worried what would happen if my mother invited a hot guy sixteen years younger than her into our house after he drove her home.

I could act as if it was okay that, for a few hours, I stopped trying to control not just my world but everyone else's around me.

"Cool. That sounds fun," I said.

It's one thing to be cooped up in your bedroom on a Saturday night, scribbling in your journal about how you are so over the fact that you're missing yet another party because you need to babysit your mother, so pissed that the pen breaks and ink gets all over your hand. But it's a whole other thing to be given your freedom. Because as much as you've wished for freedom, once you have it, you don't feel exhilarated. You want to hide in the bathroom of the Basilica.

"I don't know what the men's room is like," I said to Matt as I walked out of the ladies' room after realizing that

238

if I stayed in there any longer he was going to think I had serious digestive issues. "But it's really cool in there." The whole place had a vintage industrial look.

"It used to be a glue factory. Now they use it for art shows and music stuff," he explained.

We walked over to the edge of the main room where a tatted-up bald guy wearing an I'M PART OF THE ZERO PERCENT AND PROUD OF IT T-shirt was doing a spoken-word thing about the evil of the ego and how the world would be a much better place if meditation was made mandatory by law.

"And to give guys like that a chance to try to impress girls by making them think they're all deep so they might get lucky and hook up," he said.

I laughed. "I guess hipsters are everywhere."

But Matt wasn't a hipster. He was hip in that he wasn't hip. In fact, during the walk down Warren Street to the Basilica, I discovered that he had this way of nervously rambling on, which reminded me a little of the actor Jesse Eisenberg. Who I just happened to find really cute. I didn't really mind the rambling. It took me off the hook from having to talk too much.

"I'm assuming you've been to Swallow?" he asked.

I nodded. Swallow was a coffee place up on Warren that was swarming with hipsters. "Yeah, I guess you can't work there unless you have a very bushy beard."

He laughed. "Yes. And chunky black-rimmed eye-glasses."

"And a passion for foreign magazines," I said.

"Or—even better—a dog-eared copy of something by Freud or Kafka, which you keep on the counter at all times and then, when people come to place their order, you tear yourself away from it but not before making sure they see the cover first."

"And listen to jazz," I said. "Or world music. And when asked where the band is from, you don't say Nicaragua. You say *Nicarrrrragua* with a rolled *r*."

He nodded. "Right. And even better if it's playing on an actual record player instead of a CD or iPod," he yelled over the feedback of the electric guitars that the bald guy had added to his performance.

This was fun. So fun that as we were going back and forth, I eventually stopped trying to imagine what Mom and Billy were doing at that moment and whether she had invited him in. And whether she remembered what the AA people said about how it wasn't a good idea to get into a relationship your first year sober. And whether Skye was texting Billy so that he remembered that he had a girlfriend.

"So I guess I should introduce you to some people," Matt yelled as we moved to the side of the room.

"Okay," I said, disappointed we couldn't keep bantering.

"But the thing is, I'd really rather just get out of here so I can save whatever's left of my hearing and walk over to the river and just talk more because, honestly, most of the people here are asshole poseurs who, even though I don't know you well, I don't think you'd like," he said. "Plus, even though I sort of know them, I don't *know* them know them, and therefore, when I introduced you, they'd be thinking 'Do I even know this guy?' and then it would be this whole awkward thing."

"Okay," I laughed.

"Okay to which part? Okay to leaving and going for a walk, or okay to wanting me to introduce you and have it be awkward?"

I giggled. When was the last time I had giggled? "The walk option."

He smiled. "Excellent."

I tried to will my hand not to get clammy after he grabbed it in order to lead me through the maze of bushy beards (guys) and nose rings (girls mostly, but also some guys) in order to get out. Or to think about how his hand was an interesting mix of rough and soft and what it might feel like if he happened to, I don't know, touch my face with it.

I was disappointed when he let go of my hand once we got outside, and pretended to pay attention as he told me the history of Hudson and how it used to be the red-light district for the politicians in Albany, which was forty-five minutes away. But really what I was doing was thinking about how good it felt to be doing something so . . . *normal teen-ager*–like. That is, hanging out with a boy and wondering if he was going to try to kiss me at the end of the night.

As we sat on a bench under the full moon, I tried to act nonchalant, as if this were something I did on a regular basis instead of never. Just like I tried to act as if guys always wiped off benches for me before I sat down the way he did. It reminded me of the scene in this old movie *Say Anything* where John Cusack stopped a barefoot Ione Skye from stepping on glass as they walked home after a party. Mom and I had decided that scene was number six on our "Top Ten Romantic Scenes in Hollywood History."

He turned to me. "So there's something I should tell you."

Really? He couldn't have waited until when he dropped me off to bring up the fact that while he thought I was really cool, the truth was he had a girlfriend and he wanted to get that out in the open because it was totally obvious from my face that I found the way he rambled on nervously was cute instead of dorky?

Before he could go on, my phone rang. I took it out of my bag and looked at it. Mom. "I'm sorry. I just need—"

"No worries," he replied, sounding a bit relieved that he had a short reprieve before he had to come clean about the girlfriend.

"Is everything okay?" I asked when I answered, my standard greeting to my mother.

"Hi, honey. Are you having fun?" she asked.

"I am. You got home okay?"

"Yup. Did you happen to see the moon by any chance? Is it not totally gorgeous?"

Seriously? "Yup. So what's going on?"

"You know, I totally forgot to write down my new-moon affirmations," she went on. "But if I remember correctly, you have about twelve hours afterward as well, so I might be able to—"

"Sooo...did you need something?" I asked impatiently.

"Yes, I wanted to know where you put that tea we bought yesterday. The pear one. We're going to try it."

"Who's we?"

"Billy and me."

"He came in?"

"Yes. For tea."

"How long is he staying?"

"He's staying for as long as it takes for us to drink a cup of tea, Annabelle," she said in her I'm-the-mother tone.

"In the cabinet to the right of the stove."

"Thank you."

"What time do you want me home by?" I asked before she clicked off.

"What do you mean?"

"Well, what's my curfew? I forgot to ask before."

"Curfew? I don't know. Billy, what do you think a good curfew time is for someone Annabelle's age?" I heard him mumble something in the background. "He says eleven thirty, but that's in ten minutes, so that's not going to work. Plus, that sounds a little strict to me. Why don't we say, I don't know, one?"

"How about twelve thirty?"

"Okay. That sounds good. But I don't want you to rush if you're having fun," she replied. "You know I trust you."

I sighed. I'm sure that tomorrow she'd present me with a box of condoms. "Yeah, I know. Bye," I said as I clicked off and turned off the ringer. I turned back to Matt. "Sorry about that. So what was it you wanted to tell me?" I figured it was better just to get it over with so he could take me home and I could go to my room and make a list of all the reasons why Matt's girlfriend was different (read: better) than me anyway.

"Okay, so I Googled you," he confessed. "After that morning at The Cascades."

I waited for the rest of it—the part about the girlfriend. But he didn't say anything. He just looked at me anxiously. "That's it? That's what you wanted to tell me?" I finally asked.

"Yeah," he replied. "Is it weird that I did? That I told you, I mean?"

I shrugged. Maybe there was no girlfriend. "Why is it weird? You're just being honest about what everyone does but doesn't admit." And because I hadn't known his last name, when I tried Googling him, it hadn't netted me anything of use other than some Twitter accounts that didn't seem to be his.

"Anyway, I read about what happened . . . you know, with the DUI, and the money . . ."

Genius. As much as my mother tried to force me to go

have a life, she ended up coming with me no matter what. "Yeah, well . . ." I said, trailing off. Because, really, what was there to say about it?

"Sounds like it's been a rough couple of months."

I guess there was that to say about it.

"But it seems like things are better now," he said. "And she seems happy with Billy Barrett."

"Wait . . . what? With? Oh, they're not *together* together," I corrected. "They're just doing the movie together."

"Oh."

"'Oh' what?"

He shrugged. "I just . . ." He shook his head. "Nothing."

"Why? Did it *look* like they were together?"

He shrugged. "Well . . . yeah. Kind of. Or, you know, on their way to it."

I shook my head. "She's sixteen years older than he is. Plus, he has a girlfriend. Well, sometimes. They're on and off a lot. Her name's Skye. She's a screenwriter. She tweets a lot." Who was the one rambling now?

He shrugged. "Okay."

I so wanted to ask him what the "Okay" meant. Was it "Okay—I understand now and I believe you," or was it "Okay—you sound like a crazy person so I'm going to figure out a way to change the subject"?

Instead, I took out my iPhone and took a shot of the moon reflecting on the river.

"You like photography?" he asked.

I nodded. "Yeah. It's kind of my thing."

He pointed at the phone. "Can I see some of your stuff?"

I hesitated. I always felt weird showing it to people. I handed the phone over, trying not to squirm as he scrolled through the photos.

"Wow. You are *good*," he said, impressed.

I shrugged. "Not really. It's just different filters, you know, from Instagram, Hipstamatic . . . stuff like that."

"Those things scare me," he said. "I was never good at math."

"What do camera apps have to do with math?" I asked, confused.

He shrugged. "I have no idea. It just seems . . . mathlike to me. But seriously—these are really cool. They're . . . different. He smiled. "Like you."

Was that a good thing or a bad thing? I was glad it was dark so he couldn't see me blush. "So tell me about your family," I blurted.

His smile vanished. "I'd rather talk about math," he said wryly.

I laughed again.

He went on to tell me about how he was the youngest of two kids ("My sister did the smart thing and moved across the country for college and stayed there") and he had grown up on the Upper West Side of Manhattan. His mother was a book editor, and his father was a novelist and a professor at NYU. They lived in the city until his parents got divorced. ("The thing my father hates more than anything in writing are clichés," he explained, "but then he went and turned into one when he started having an affair with one of his students and bought a Harley.")

They had originally started coming upstate on weekends when his parents were still married, but after the divorce, his mom had moved them up full-time, and he'd finished his last two years of high school here. ("You know you're no longer in the city when your classmates drive pickup trucks with NRA bumper stickers and spend their weekends hunting for deer instead of private-school girls.") He had lived on campus this past year, but was back at home for the summer with his mom.

"I'm surprised you're not sleeping yet," he said. "My life story has a way of doing that to people."

"Are you kidding? I love it. It sounds so . . . normal."

"Yeah, don't worry—I can promise you it most certainly is not," he said. He looked at his watch. "I should probably get you home."

"Yeah, I guess." I hoped I didn't sound as disappointed as I felt.

He smiled. "You're really easy to talk to."

I smiled back. "I know." I cringed. "That's not what I meant. What I meant is that *you're* easy to talk to."

"I knew what you meant."

I smiled. That was the great part. I felt like he really did.

We pulled up to the house to find a royal-blue pickup truck in the driveway.

"Sweet ride," Matt said. He put his car—an old silver Volvo station wagon ("The other official upstate car, after the Subaru," he had explained when he opened my door for me; it took a few tries because, as he said, the car was so old it had arthritis)—in park and turned off the ignition.

Even with my limited (read: zero) experience with dating, I had to believe that turning the car off instead of letting it idle was a good sign. Like he wanted to keep talking. That, or he was really conscientious about saving gas.

"Is it yours?" he asked.

"No, it's Billy's," I replied. I knew this not because I had seen it in person, but because I had seen a picture of it on SimonSez the day before. Apparently, what car Billy Barrett drove while on location was news.

"Ah."

Again, I refrained from asking what the "Ah" meant. "Ah," as in "You *say* nothing's going on with them, but if he's still there at twelve forty-five, that 'nothing' is soon going to be a 'something' . . . if it's not already," or just a regular old "Ah"? And had I been this neurotic prior to the last four hours, or had it always been there, lying in wait? And did everything that entered my brain have to be in the form of a question from now on?

We sat there staring at the dashboard. Was he going to kiss me? Did I want him to kiss me? Exactly how much of what I had eaten had garlic and onions? And when would the question thing stop?

"So," he finally said.

"So," I repeated.

"So I should probably let you go in."

"Yeah. I guess," I agreed, really not wanting to. At least until I looked at the house and saw my mother's honey-colored head behind the curtain in the window watching us. "Oh, God," I said out loud. And then, as if she could hear me, she moved the curtain aside and actually *started waving*.

He laughed. "That's sweet."

I looked at him as if I had eaten a piece of bad fish.

"In. . . . some . . . alternate . . . universe?" he suggested.

"Yes. In a galaxy far, far away," I replied. I looked back at the window to see that now Billy had joined her at the window. "Okay, I really should go," I said quickly, grabbing for the door, only to find it stuck.

"It gets . . . stuck from the inside, too," he said, reaching across me to open it. "Hey, so are you going to give me your number?" he asked as he jiggled it.

I was so relieved, my spine felt like it wanted to melt. Asking for my number meant he'd call so we could see each other again. Unless he didn't call. Which, I knew from movies (and Mom), was a very good possibility. "Sure. It's—"

"Maybe wait until I get this open and take out my phone—"

"Right. Sorry."

"Don't be sorry," he said, still jiggling. At this point his chin was somewhere around my boobs, but I didn't dare move for fear of the situation becoming even more awkward than it was at the moment.

"Sor—" I started to say again before catching myself.

"Annabelle?"

"Yeah?"

"This isn't going to work."

My spine snapped back to attention. We hadn't even gone out again, or even talked on the phone, and he had decided that already. And *told* me. Which I guess was better than his not telling me, but still. "Yeah, I guess you're right. I mean, I'm only here—"

He let go of the door and sat up. "I'm going to have to open it from the outside," he announced as he started to open his own and get out.

I shook my head as I watched him walk around the car. There was no way my nervous system was going to be able to handle this. Finally, I was out of the car. After glancing over at the window to see if Mom and Billy were still spying on us, I gave him my number, and we stood there.

"I'm really glad you came out tonight."

"Me, too," I agreed.

"It was fun."

"Totally." If this turned into something, was I going to be like Mom and just agree with the guy about everything?

He put his hands on my shoulders and started to lean in. He was going to kiss me? Right there? With my mother and Billy watching? He aimed for my cheek. Which was sweet, and would have been even sweeter if I hadn't decided to move my head at that exact second so that the kiss—and his chin, and somehow his teeth—ended up in the middle of my skull.

"Ow—" he said.

"Oh God—I'm so sorry!" I cried.

And then, as if things couldn't get more awkward, the front door opened.

"Annabelle, do you want to invite Matt in for some tea?"

I patted my head to check for blood, while Matt felt his tooth to see if it had chipped. "We're good, Mom!" I called back.

"Or some of that lemonade? With the ginger and the honey? I know it's not good to have sugar so late, but it's really good."

"Did you want lemonade?" I asked, not wanting to be rude but hoping he'd say no.

"Thanks, but I should—"

"I know it's not really a summer thing, but I think I saw some hot chocolate packets in the cupboard," Mom went on. "Unless Matt doesn't like preservatives. I don't either, you know, but with some things I think it's okay. Like hot chocolate."

"—go," Matt finished.

"Yeah," I agreed quickly.

"I'll call you."

"Okay."

He leaned in to kiss me on the cheek again, but then seemed to think better of it and just squeezed me on the shoulder instead. I stood there as he pulled out, a smile plastered on my face as if I did this kind of thing all the time. I gave one last wave before turning around and going into the house.

You would've thought, as actors, Mom and Billy would have at least *pretended* they hadn't been watching me, but there they were, still at the front door.

"That was so *cute*, the way he went to kiss you and missed!" Mom exclaimed as I walked in. She turned to Billy. "Wasn't that so cute?"

To his credit, he looked uncomfortable. "Ah, I guess so?"

I tried not to think about what they'd been doing, or how late it was and the fact that he was still here.

I walked toward my room. "Good night."

"But I want to hear all about it!" Mom called after me.

I was sure she did. As I got ready for bed, I was relieved to hear the sound of Billy's truck on the gravel as he drove off. A few minutes later, once I was settled in my bed with my notebook, I heard Mom stop in front of my door.

"Annabelle, are you still awake?"

I kept quiet.

"Bug?"

Still quiet.

"I can see the light underneath the door," she said. "But in trying to not be codependent and respect your boundaries I'm just going to leave you alone. But if you *do* want to come tell me about your evening, I'll be up for a little while, so feel free to crawl into bed and tell me."

"Crawling into bed with you is not very respecting boundaries–like," I called out. "In fact, most people would probably consider that kind of creepy, Mom."

"Fine. Well, maybe you'll want to talk about it in the morning. Good night."

"Night," I replied. After I heard her walk away, I picked my notebook back up to make a list.

REASONS NOT TO GET OVERLY EXCITED ABOUT MATT, EVEN THOUGH IT WAS SUPER–EASY TO TALK TO HIM AND HE SEEMED TO BE AS INTO ME AS I WAS INTO HIM

★ I'm here for only six weeks, which means that even if he *did* call, and we *did* hang out again, there's really no future in it, and therefore it would just make it that much harder when it was time to leave, and then I'd go back to L.A. and spend way too much time Facebook-stalking him.

★ He probably thinks that because I'm from L.A. and my mother is an actress, I'm a slut and therefore, if he calls, it's probably just because he thinks I'll sleep with him.

★ If we did hang out, and it *did* start to get physical, once I told him I wasn't going to sleep with him—because to sleep with someone you already knew you had a limited shelf life with felt dumb—he wouldn't want to hang out anymore.

★ Because he seemed like a smart guy, he was smart enough to know that Mom was an equal opportunity embarrasser, and therefore, if we ever spent time in front of her, he'd be in her line of fire.

My phone dinged with a text.

At the risk of being shunned and stoned by the male race for not waiting at least 12 hours—or even 1—to send this text, I was wondering if you were busy tomorrow after-noon, and if not, if you wanted to hang out.

I smiled.

Sure, there were a million reasons *not* to get excited.

But I still couldn't help myself.

CHAPTER TWELVE

I woke up the next morning to find Mom in the kitchen, dressed in running clothes and cooking something. And not just pushing-buttons-on-a-microwave cooking, but something that included a pot and a spoon and a flame on a stove.

"What's going on?" I asked warily as I watched her move the pot and almost light her arm on fire.

"Good morning, sleepyhead!" she chirped as she turned to smile at me. "You finally decided to get up and join the living, huh?"

I took the ground coffee and milk out of the fridge and went over to the coffeemaker to brew it, only to find it already brewed. "Mom, it's only eight." I poured myself a cup and took a sip. She had even done the thing I had taught her, where you put some cinnamon in the coffee before you brewed it. "Wait a minute—did you even go to sleep last night?"

"Of course I did," she said, ladling out whatever was in the pot into two bowls. "And I couldn't sleep so I got up at five thirty and went for a run and then decided to make breakfast."

Okay, who was this body snatcher and what had she done with my mother? She placed the bowl in front of me before taking the seat across from me. I couldn't believe it. My mother had made *oatmeal*. From scratch, not from a packet. My whole life I had dreamed of her making me things like oatmeal and rice pudding and mashed pota-toes—things that weren't fancy but smacked of comfort and would keep you anchored when everything around you was swirling and you were worried that you were going to float away. And not only that, but she had added walnuts and berries and a spoonful of brown sugar.

"That's how you order it at John O'Groats, right?" she asked. "With the berries and the walnuts and the brown sugar?"

"Yeah," I said quietly. I felt my eyes start to fill. All that time when she was drinking, when I thought she was so out of it she never noticed anything, she had. I stood up and started to walk to my room.

"Annabelle, where are you going? What did I do wrong?" she called after me, confused.

I came back with my camera. "You didn't do anything wrong," I replied as I took the lens cap off and focused in on the bowl, pleased that the light that was coming in from the window highlighted the texture of the oatmeal, and the grains of the sugar, and the little bumps on the raspberries.

"You're taking pictures of *oatmeal*?"

"Yeah," I replied, snapping away.

"Do you want me to hold the bowl? So I can be in the picture, too?"

I couldn't help but laugh. "No, thanks," I replied as I snapped away.

When I first started getting into photography, I read a lot of interviews with different famous photographers. I was amazed to learn how many shots they took in order to get just a few that were decent. Maybe that was what life was about—you just kept doing it until you got somewhere within the zip code of "right."

And then—there it was. The shot. The bowl, with Mom's hand next to it, her nails short and unpolished. I loved them like that. More than when they were covered with her signature glossy red. I clicked the shutter.

"So are you going to tell me about your date with Matt last night, or are you going to be passive-aggressive and reply with one-word answers until I eventually go away?" she asked.

"It wasn't a date," I said as I put the camera down and started eating. I cringed. "How much salt is in this?"

"None. It's sugar," she said, holding up a clear jar.

"That's salt."

"Oh."

She had tried. I got up and took out a waffle to nuke.

"So are you going to tell me?"

I shrugged. "It was fun."

"What'd you do?"

"Hung out and talked." At least my answers were three and four words instead of the usual one or two.

"What'd you talk about?"

"Stuff."

"That's a one-word answer."

I smiled. "I know." It wasn't that I didn't want to tell Mom about Matt. I did. It was that I didn't want to have to watch her get all excited that I had met someone and could finally hang up my HEREIN LIES AN UTTER AND COMPLETE FREAKAZOID WHEN IT COMES TO GUYS T-shirt, only to have to put it back on after he decided I was, in fact, a freak and then disappeared. "What did you and *Billy* do?"

"We talked."

"About what?"

She shrugged. "Swimming with dolphins, therapy, what happens to you when you die, whether it's worth it to have a manager in addition to an agent or if it's just a waste of money."

I hated even to think it, but it sounded like they were meant for each other. I grabbed the waffle out of the microwave and took a bite standing up. "Did you kiss?"

"*No*, we did not kiss," she said. "But what if we had? Would you have been upset about that?"

"What about Skye?"

"They're broken up," she replied. "In fact, if you go onto SimonSez, there's a photo of her canoodling with Channing Tatum's stunt double at Soho House."

"Canoodling or just sitting next to each other?"

"*Canoodling* canoodling," she replied.

Huh. I'd have to check that out. "Well, what about the fact that you were sixteen years old and already having sex when he was born?"

She cringed. "You don't have to put it like *that*."

"Well, you were."

"Seriously, Annabelle—what if something did end up happening between Billy and me? Not that it has, but what if it did?"

"Then I would say...maybe you'd want to do a Google search and take a look at all the girls he's been with over the years and see for yourself that he met most of them on the sets of his movies, and that when they were done shooting, he was pretty much done with them as well."

She shook her head. "That was when he was younger. He's really looking for true intimacy and commitment now. That's what he's working on in therapy."

"If what you mean by 'younger' is 'three months ago,' then knock yourself out. Plus, you're not supposed to get into a relationship for a year, remember?"

"That's just a *suggestion*," she replied. "Not an order. Willow says it happens all the time. She met her husband when she was thirty days' sober."

I joined her at the table with my waffle. "You mean her *ex*-husband? The one she was married to for six weeks?"

She tore off a piece. "Listen, I know you think Billy's just some hot guy who just spends his time hanging out at clubs and surfing and tweeting, but he's not," she said. "I mean, yes, he does that stuff, but there's a lot more to him. He's a good guy, Annabelle. I'd really like it if you gave him a chance."

"Why does it matter if I give him a chance if, after this is over, I'm never going to see him again?"

"Because who's to say that's going to be the case?"

"The bloggers who like to call him Billy 'Location Doesn't Count' Barrett?"

She gave a little laugh. "I would think you of all people would know that you can't trust what those guys say."

That was true.

She took my hand. "Honey, I know it's hard to trust people. But just staying closed up and not letting yourself take risks because there's a chance you *might* get hurt . . . that's not really a way to live, you know?"

When you put it like that, no.

But was she talking about her or me, or both of us?

THINGS I'M NOT USED TO
- ★ My mother making breakfast for me.
- ★ Having a Conversation-with-a-capital-C with Mom that did not turn into a fight.

★ People following through on things they say they're going to do.

So when Matt called at eleven o'clock that morning, which is what he'd said he'd do after I had texted him back that, yes, I'd like to hang out the next day, I was surprised. Pleasantly surprised, for sure, but surprised.

I walked into the living room to find Mom studying her script as she did crunches while a recording of herself reciting Emily Dickinson's poems blared from the iPod speakers. When it came to work, her power to multitask was beyond impressive.

"Since you have your hair and makeup tests this afternoon, I'm going to go out and do some exploring, okay?"

"Okay," she replied. Even with the crunches, her voice was completely normal. I, on the other hand, sounded like I was two breaths away from dying when I tried to talk while exercising. "Alone?"

"No."

"With Matt?"

"Yes," I sighed.

She was so coordinated with her multitasking that even the clap and squeal she gave upon hearing the news didn't screw up her rhythm. "Where are you going?"

"Some hike over in Woodstock," I replied. "What time will you be back from the camera tests?"

"They got moved to tomorrow."

"Oh. What are you going to do then?"

She shrugged. "I don't know."

"Are you going to go to a meeting?"

She got up and started to do some squats. "Maybe."

"Are you going to hang out with Billy?"

"I don't know, Annabelle."

"I can call Matt to see if we can do it tomorrow instead," I said. "He already told me he's not working until Thursday and—"

"You're going," she cut me off. "Now go get dressed," she ordered. "And then I'll do your makeup."

MORE THINGS I'M NOT USED TO

★ Being asked questions instead of listening to a running monologue.

★ Being listened to when answering the question, without the other person's mouth twitching because they're in such a hurry to be the one talking again.

Which is why, when Matt picked me up at one (the time he said he would), the drive over to Woodstock felt more like a police interrogation than a conversation. They weren't hard questions, or stuff that was all that personal. It was standard small-talk stuff: What kind of music do you like? (Me: '70s stuff, i.e., Joni Mitchell, Neil Young, Fleetwood Mac. Him: emo-ish, but not annoyingly-so indie stuff, i.e., Bon Iver, Band of Horses, The Shins.) What are some of your favorite movies? (Me: smart indie rom-coms where people ended up living happily ever after but not sickeningly sweetly so, and some vintage Nora Ephron stuff. Him: Mark Duplass Mumblecore stuff, in which people talk a lot about relationships but, despite all the talk, still can't manage to do them all that successfully.) What reality show are you most embarrassed to say you watch on a regular basis? (Both of us: *My Strange Addiction*, which was weird and comforting at the same time.)

But after I'd answer, he'd remain quiet, as if taking in what I'd said and reflecting on it before responding. It was hard to get used to that. In our house, "reflecting" was only used in terms of mirrors.

"So this is Woodstock," he announced as we drove into a little town full of cafés and shops.

"It doesn't look very hippyish," I said, as we passed an upscale clothing store.

"It's not," he agreed. "It's so expensive now that the only people who can afford to buy houses are people from Manhattan who work in finance."

After driving about a quarter mile up a mountain, we got to Overlook and parked. Across the street from the parking lot, I saw a bunch of brightly colored flags fluttering in the wind. "What's that?" I asked as I grabbed my camera bag.

"Tibetan Buddhist monastery," he replied, as he reached into the backseat to grab a couple of baseball hats. He took a Boston Celtics one and put it on my head. "It gets pretty hot out here. You like the Celts?"

"That's baseball, right?" I asked, my stomach fluttering a bit as he adjusted the hat. Was it weird that he hadn't asked first if I even wanted a hat? Or was it nice that he felt comfortable enough with me just to put it on me? And why, oh *why*, hadn't I popped off the head of the Ken doll that I had found in a box in the basement the other day when Mom sent me to check if there were any gardening tools. She had woken up with a *"hankering* to garden" (she actually used the word *hankering* before I told her that no one in modern-day America really said that); I reminded her that she had killed every houseplant we ever had.

He cringed. "I'm going to pretend I didn't hear that. It's basketball."

"Right. Now I remember," I said, totally lying.

"Don't worry—I'm not a sports freak," he said. "Basketball's the only guy thing I'm really into. It's the only thing that makes my grandfather think I might actually be straight."

I laughed as I reached into my bag and took out my camera and snapped a few shots of the flapping flags. I turned to him. "I promise I won't be that annoying person who stops every two seconds to take pictures."

He shrugged. "It's cool. If I had your talent with that thing, I would, too."

I felt myself blush. A few minutes into the hike, I was glad to have the hat. Not only did it help with the sun, but it made the stream of sweat that was pouring down my face after a few minutes of what was turning out to be a pretty steep climb less evident. *Note to self,* I thought as I struggled to keep up with him, *if a guy ever suggests another physical activity as a date again, tell him you have really bad allergies and therefore your doctor has suggested you stay inside in air-conditioning at all times.*

Occasionally, I'd stop to take a photo. Random things — a Yoo-Hoo bottle cap. An uncapped pen next to a log. A dusty, dried-up snakeskin. (That one? Made me nervous.)

"I like how you focus on small, specific things," Matt said as I zoomed in on an empty crumbled Marlboro Lights box.

"Yeah, I've never been big on regular pictures," I admitted. "You know, like, 'And here's the Eiffel Tower' and 'This is the Statue of Liberty.' I like things that just . . . jump-start the memory. So that when you look at it later, what comes in is more how you felt rather than what it looked like."

He cocked his head as he thought about it for a second before slowly nodding. "Jump-start the memory. I like that. That's good. It feels like a title for an exhibition or a show of your pictures or something."

There *was* something in there. Not that I'd ever be good enough to have a show.

He scratched the side of his nose and took a deep breath. "So there's something else I should tell you."

This was it — the girlfriend he hadn't mentioned last

night but needed to now so I didn't get the idea that this was a *date* date, and not just an outing between two people who simply didn't have anything better to do today. I was glad I was wearing the hat. Hopefully, it hid the disappointment.

"What?" I asked, wondering if, after he told me, I'd have to continue the hike or if I could come up with an excuse about why I needed to get back.

"I, um, came across your Tumblr last night," he confessed.

The relief that a girlfriend was still nonexistent quickly morphed into feeling like my insides had just been X-rayed. "How'd you figure out it was my Tumblr?" I asked suspiciously. "It's anonymous." And the reason it was anonymous was so that no one would find it.

"I know. But I decided to put in a Los Angeles tag, and then I figured it out from that series of photos you did where you contrasted your old house with your new apartment," he explained. "It sounds stalkerish, I know," he admitted. "But I'm not. Really. *I swear*," he said. "It's just . . . I'm a little OCD-ish, and I have insomnia sometimes. I think it may have been because I had an iced Americano at six. For some reason I always think that something about the ice will water it down and make it less caffeine-y, you know? But it doesn't. And I've experimented enough with drinking it at different times over the years to know that three p.m. is the latest I can drink any sort of coffee drink and not have it interfere with my sleep."

Wow. Matt was a total BWNer (BWN = babbles when nervous = a term Walter and I had come up with to describe the kids in Alateen who kept going on even when the "spiritual timekeeper" had signaled that their three-minute share was up).

"I'm babbling," he said, as if reading my mind.

I shrugged. "That's cool. I like babblers," I said with a smile.

"You do?"

I nodded. It was a bit of a lie. Usually, I found it annoying. Mom had a black belt in babbling. But with Matt, it wasn't annoying, it was . . . sweet. And not only that, it was . . . attractive.

"Good," he said, sounding relieved. "Anyway, I debated about whether to tell you I had found it," he said. "Not just because of the stalkerlike quality of it, but also because of the anonymous thing of it all. But then, once I found it, I felt like not telling you would be a lie. Not a lie lie. More like one of those sins-of-omission things."

I nodded. That's what I had a black belt in.

"Anyway, you're really talented, Annabelle," he went on. "Like . . . *really*."

I shrugged. "They're just weird shots." They were. Super-random things, like a homeless person and a hipster standing on the corner of Abbot Kinney in Venice. Walter's hand grabbing a fistful of fries at In-N-Out. A collection of Indian goddess statues at Be Here Now.

He shook his head. "I don't think they're weird," he

said. "It's as if . . . they're puzzle pieces or something. Like you know they're part of this bigger picture, but you're not sure how they fit together." He plucked off a white blossom from a tree and twirled it in his fingers. "It's, like, although you don't exactly understand what's being said, you get the sense that it's a little bit complicated." He smiled. "Like you."

At that, my smile evaporated. Last night I was just different. "*I'm* complicated?" I wasn't complicated. My mother had used up all the complicated chips.

"Well, yeah. Not in a bad way. In a *good* way." He held out the blossom to me. "It's a compliment. I promise."

———————————————————————

I love when someone you don't know well suggests something to you—a book, a movie, a band—with the line "I think you'll really like it," and they turn out to be right. There's so much potential in that victory—not just because you've discovered something you like, but because there's the opportunity of being understood.

The chance of being gotten.

So when Matt had suggested we go to Overlook because there was something he wanted to show me because he thought "you'll like it," I was intrigued. We had spent only a few hours together, but I already felt as if I wanted to be gotten by him. Even if the idea of being known sometimes made me feel like throwing up.

When we rounded the corner and I saw the building in front of us, I smiled, immediately knowing that this was what he wanted to show me. It was an unfinished concrete building. The foundation was there, and arches where the windows would go, and stone steps, but it was more like just the skeleton. Like a Polaroid photograph that, midway through developing, decided to not go any further.

"It's the Overlook Mountain Hotel," Matt said. "The third version of it. The other two were made of wood and burned down, and then they ran out of money while building this one and just stopped. It's cool, huh?"

"It's *amazing*," I said as I ran up to it and started snapping away. It looked like something out of a fairy tale—both creepy and comforting at the same time. I doubted I'd be able to capture the feel of it in a photo, but I wanted to try.

"It's one of my favorite places around here," he said as he stood in an archway.

The way the light was shining through the trees on him gave him a halo effect, like something out of a religious painting. "Hey, is it cool if I take some shots of you?" I asked. Because I hated having my picture taken, I always asked first. Except with my mom. I never asked her, because I always knew what the answer was.

"Sure," Matt replied.

I focused in on him. I was glad he didn't do what most people did when they knew they were having their picture taken, which was immediately change their expression to try to look how they thought they should, which was never natural or real and therefore ended up in the trash folder. After a few shots I pointed to an old clawfoot bathtub. "Go sit in there."

He gave me a look.

"You're an artist," I said. "It's an artistic idea."

"Okay, okay," he laughed, folding himself into the tub.

His legs were so long it looked as if he was going to explode up and out of it. As I clicked away I moved closer and closer until soon I was standing over him. After I was done I put the camera down but didn't move. As we looked at each other, I felt like I was at the top of a roller coaster before that first drop. So this was what people meant when they talked about a Moment with a capital *M*.

"You do realize that as soon as you let me out of here, I'm taking some of you," he finally said.

Moment broken. I brought the camera back up to my face. "No way."

"How come? It's only fair."

I shook my head. "I like to be *behind* the camera, not in front of it."

"Okay, Jackson, you're off the hook for today, but I promise you at some point *I* will be the one holding the camera and *you* will be in front of it."

"At some point" implied a future. With him in it.

I smiled.

CHAPTER THIRTEEN

After the hike—which included a visit to a fire tower, which Matt admitted he had never been to the top of, despite numerous attempts to climb it, because he had a slight ("Maybe not slight—more like crippling") fear of heights—we stopped for lunch at this place, Luna 61, in Tivoli, near Bard. After a quick glance at the vegetarian menu (pad thai noodles, stir-fry, sweet potato and goat cheese enchilada), I decided it was my new favorite restaurant in the area. And then, after one bite of the owner Debra's homemade banana cream pie, I amended my decision: it was my favorite restaurant anywhere.

I kept waiting for our conversation to hit a lull. To get to that moment when an awkward silence fell over the table like a cheap itchy blanket that we found ourselves unable to untangle ourselves from, where no matter how many topics we tried, we couldn't throw it off and get back to easy flow. That's how it had always been for me with guys I knew in the past. I would play this slow game of verbal strip poker—take off an earring with this story, a ring with that memory—but soon enough the messy truth of my life started peeking through and the guy somehow intuitively knew it was time to start backing away and to find someone who was . . . less complicated.

But that didn't happen with Matt. The conversation kept flowing through lunch and over the ride home. It was so easy that as we turned onto my road, I was even thinking that maybe I'd be the one who suggested we get together again. Sure, I'd be blackballed by all those magazine advice columnists who were always saying you needed to let the guy do everything or else you'd scare him away (if he was going to be scared away that easily, did you really want him?), but who cared. Especially because off in the distance, whatever happened between us already had an expiration date of forty-seven days and fifteen hours. Not that I had counted.

"So," he said as he put the car in park and turned off the ignition.

"So," I repeated. Would it be weird to invite Matt in? Did it just scream, *I'm asking you in because I'm hoping you might kiss me even though I still don't know for sure that you're not with someone?* Yeah, asking him in could be weird. "Do you want to see our cow?" I blurted. The minute it left my mouth I cringed. As if *that* wasn't weird?

He looked confused. "You have a cow?"

"Well, no, it's not ours," I corrected. "It's the neighbor's, but it likes to hang out at our fence. She's nice. We named her Mabel. My mom thinks that's a cow-sounding name. She even answers to it. Kind of." Who was the babbler now?

"Sure, I'll come see your cow." He cringed. "Although that sounds kind of creepy when you say it out loud."

We were just about to turn the corner into the backyard when we heard Led Zeppelin's "Ramble On" come pouring out of the windows of Billy's pickup truck as he pulled into the driveway. My mom was sitting next to him.

So that's why I hadn't gotten any texts from her.

"Omigod, they're so good!" Mom said as she tumbled out of the truck with a bunch of bags full of produce. "Who is that again? Lynyrd Skynyrd?"

Billy cringed. "I can't believe you just mixed up Skynyrd and Zeppelin. I'm going to have to pretend I didn't hear that."

Mom laughed. And not one of her fake tinkly laughs she used when she was flirting with a guy. This one was simple and genuine. Which alarmed me even more than the alternative.

"Dude, I'm going to have to make you a classic-rock playlist," he went on. "To educate you. Maybe even track down some concert at, like, the Pomona Fairgrounds, with some band from the seventies to take you to when we're back in L.A."

Okay, (a) the guy called my mother *dude*. And (b)—as if (a) wasn't bad enough and a (b) was even necessary—Billy was talking about hanging out with my mom when the movie was over and we were back in L.A. He wasn't supposed to say things like that. That was not "Location Doesn't Count"-ish.

"Hi, Bug. Hi, Matt," Mom said when she saw us. She held up a bag. "We decided to barbecue and went over to Adams in Kingston. Bug, you wouldn't *believe* what a great market it is. And you know you're not in a big city when there's barely any frozen food in the place! Matt, would you like to stay?"

Really? She was doing this in front of everyone without asking me first? It wasn't like she had had a lot of experience trying to be the cool mom in front of a boy her daughter liked, but still—we had never missed an episode of *Gilmore Girls* back when it was on. From that alone, she knew the right and wrong things to do. She knew she had to check with me first.

"Oh. I . . . uh . . ." He looked over at me, but I just kept staring at the ground. On the one hand, I didn't want him to go (see: lamely asking if he wanted to see my cow). But like people were always talking about in Alateen, it was one thing for a parent to stop drinking. It was a whole other to change habits and patterns that had been etched deeply because of the parent's drinking. Like, say, being afraid to have friends over when you had no idea whether your mom was going to be drunk, or get drunk, and what she was going to do or say in front of your friends. Yes, my mother was sober, and, yes, with every day that went by she was showing me that she was, indeed, changing, but it was hard to trust that it was going to last. I had gotten pretty good at moving through life with my breath held, afraid that if I dared to exhale my life would all come crashing down. You can't give that up after a week, or a month.

"I can't," Matt finished. "In fact, I need to get going." He turned to me and flashed me a generic smile, the kind you wear when being introduced to a friend's somewhat-senile grandparent. "Fun hanging out with you today."

"Yeah, totally," I said, hoping I didn't sound as bummed as I felt.

I waited for him to say something about getting together again, but instead he patted me on the arm (could that be any more of a kiss of death?). "See you around."

See you around? There was a bigger kiss of death—and it was that.

"Sure," I replied.

As he walked to his car, I made a beeline into the kitchen so I could head off the disappointment that was starting to churn inside me by stuffing my face. Luckily, I knew there was one last slice of the banana bread I had made. (Now that Mom was back in full Weight Watchers/Jenny Craig/Eat for Your Blood Type mode, I was well aware that every time I wondered how something I baked disappeared so fast, I had only myself to blame.)

"Hey, Annabelle," Billy said as he sat at the kitchen table. "Your mom told me you made this banana bread?" he asked as he held up the last sliver of it.

And now this was happening? "Yeah," I sighed.

I watched longingly as he popped the last piece in his mouth. "It's *awesome*," he said as I went to the freezer to get out some of the frozen Momofuku Compost Cookies that I had made the day before (when your cable is out, other than read, there's not much to do when you're stuck at home in the country but bake). But they weren't in there. "Where are the Compost Cookies?" I asked as Mom sailed into the room in a silky rose-colored boho caftan thing (any fewer than three wardrobe changes a day signaled depression). It was more Morocco than country, but the color made her blue eyes even bluer, not to mention made her boobs look perkier, which might have explained why she chose it.

"The cookies with the potato chips and pretzels and toffee pieces?" Billy asked. "Those were killer." He patted his zero-percent-body-fat eight-pack. "Although I had no business eating all those when we're four days away from camera."

I looked at Mom.

"I put them out with the tea last night," she explained. "I wanted to show him what a great baker you are."

"Dude, you totally are," he said. "Hey, you know what you could do? Find a cookbook by whoever is considered, like, the most popular baker in history and then start a blog and make all the recipes and then turn the whole thing into a movie, like they did with that Meryl Streep one."

"*Julie and Julia*," Mom said. "We loved that, Bug—remember? We watched it that time I had that awful stomach flu?" She meant the stomach flu that was really low-grade alcohol poisoning. "It was so cute."

"Maybe it could even be something for my production company," Billy went on. "I know everyone's going to expect me to do these action things, or raunchy *Hangover* comedy things, but I want to mix it up a bit, you know? Appeal to that female demo as well."

"I think that's very smart," Mom agreed. "It just makes me so mad how Hollywood tries to pigeonhole us. In fact, I was thinking of writing something for the *Huffington Post* about it—"

As they continued talking, I looked at the two of them, sitting at the table together with a vase of wildflowers and a pitcher of lemonade between them, like something out of a magazine ad. I had to admit they did look good together. But I wanted it to be just *on*-screen, not off.

Billy ate all my homemade baked goods, thus forcing me to go down to the basement and wade through spiderwebs, rusted garden tools, and a pile of what were probably mouse droppings to get to the box with the Ken doll so that I could try to deal with my anxiety that way. (It didn't work. My highly developed olfactory senses revealed that Mattel must use a different kind of plastic for their male dolls, which lacked the same sort of soothing effects.) And when he got excited about something—like the fact that he, too, enjoyed the occasional episode of *Too Cute* on Animal Planet—he called females *dude* when demonstrating said excitement. ("Dude! I love that show! That one with the Jack Russell puppies? Seriously too cute.") And he took a long time to tell a story because he was a stickler for getting the facts right. ("Once, when I was in sixth grade . . . no, wait . . . it may have been fifth. . . . yup, it was fifth because I remember Whitney Barbano sat in front of me 'cause of the alphabetical thing, and I had such a crush on her because she had this jet-black braid . . .") But even with all that, I had to give him props for putting aside his strong feelings about vegetarianism to grill Mom and me the most amazing burgers I had ever had in my life.

"My mom would kill me if she found out I was sharing the Barrett family secret with you guys, but whatever, she's not here to find out," he said when Mom asked what it was that made them so good. "Two words: *grape jelly.* Well, in this case, five: sugar-free grape fruit preserves—because that's all I could find in your fridge."

"They're pretty awesome," I agreed.

"Yeah? You think so?"

It was kind of sweet the way he sounded like the answer really mattered to him. Then again, he was also an actor. Maybe he was just trying to impress Mom. I nodded. "Almost as good as Father's Office." That was my favorite burger place in L.A.

"Omigod. *Dude.* I *love* that place! Well, I did until I stopped eating meat." He jumped up. "You want me to make you another one? I can make you another one."

"Oh, that's—"

"Seriously. It's no big deal," he said, already throwing one on the grill.

I shrugged. "Okay, thanks." I looked over at Mom, who mouthed *Is he not so sweet?* and shrugged. He was sweet. They were all sweet in the beginning. Especially at the beginning of filming, before they caught on to how nuts she was.

After he brought it to me—well-done, but not well-well-done, which was usually how people did it when you said well-done—Mom poured us all some more lemonade. "So, Annabelle. Tell us about your day with Matt."

"It was fun," I said, taking a bite of my burger. *Until the part when you showed up and he got all weird and bolted, obviously never to be heard from again.*

She turned to Billy. "For the most part Annabelle is very articulate and communicative—all her old report cards say something to that effect. But when it comes to talking about boys, I get one-word answers."

"*Mom.*" And she wondered why.

"Annabelle, you want another piece of corn?" Billy asked. "It's good, right? There's something about grilling it in the foil that—"

"So when are you seeing him again?" Mom broke in. She sighed. "I remember *my* first boyfriend. . . ."

A triple: interrupting, embarrassing me, *and* making it about her. "Mom. I just met him. He's not my boyfriend."

She turned to Billy. "Annabelle hates when I try to talk to her about boys."

"Well, yeah, I can understand why," he laughed.

Mom's smile—the one that seemed permanently etched on her face whenever he was around—flickered. "Excuse me?"

He shrugged. "It's obvious that you're embarrassing her. Look at the way her ears are turning pink."

My ears got even warmer. I wasn't sure what was worse: being talked about like I wasn't there, or having Billy Barrett notice my utter and complete mortification.

Mom laughed. "I'm not *embarrassing* her."

Billy's eyebrows shot up.

"We're just *talking*," she said lightly. "Annabelle and I talk about everything. We're very close."

"Yeah, but maybe this is something you want to talk about *later*," he suggested gently. "Like when I'm not here."

If there was anything that made Mom go into diva mode, it was when someone tried to give her parenting tips. Billy didn't sound drama king–ish, like he was stirring it up looking for a fight, but even Ben didn't dare call her on the way she dealt with me. His response was always to change the subject as quickly as possible and divert her attention to something else, like how when a kid fell, you tried to distract him before he could compute that he had fallen and had a meltdown.

I watched Mom watching Billy, who wasn't watching either of us but was instead putting mustard on his veggie burger, as if everything was cool and they were just having a conversation instead of standing on the brink of a huge drama. As he brought the burger up to his mouth, Mom did her guppy imitation (mouth open, mouth shut; repeat) before closing her mouth. She stood up. "I'm getting a sweater. Does anyone need anything from inside?"

We shook our heads before I went back to focusing on the grilled red pepper on my plate. I was confused. On the one hand, I was grateful to Billy for cutting Mom off at the pass—he was right, she had been completely embarrassing me. But at the same time I was also annoyed. Billy barely knew Mom. And he certainly didn't know our relationship. Sure, maybe what she and I had was a bit—okay, more like a lot—dysfunctional, but it was our dysfunction.

"Sorry for butting in like that," he said as he polished off his burger.

"It's okay," I said. I took a breath. Maybe it was okay. In Alateen kids were always talking about how when you first started doing something differently, it sometimes felt wrong, because you were so used to things being done the screwed-up way. I waited for him to say something more about it—*why* he had said it; how he *felt* about having said it; what it *meant* that he had said it—but he didn't. Instead, the Rolling Stones' song "Wild Horses" started playing, and he went off on a story about being at some fancy resort in the Caribbean where Keith Richards had a house and this Victoria's Secret model was being introduced to him and asking what it was like to have been in the same band as John Lennon.

Was it a guy thing, this not analyzing and talking something to death? Or was it just what semi-healthy people did?

Mom came back out with her sweater and an apple pie from Migliorelli's farm stand. I studied her face, but there were no visible emotional bumps or bruises from his comment. She was back to looking happy and relaxed and all the other things she never used to be unless she had had at least four drinks in her. After dessert, we carried the dishes into the kitchen, and Billy started to wash them.

"You don't have to do that," I said.

"It's cool. You would've thought that with two older sisters I would've gotten through life without ever having washed a dish, but it was the opposite," he said. "They made me do *all* of them."

Billy Barrett doing dishes. If I were a different kind of

person, I so would've grabbed my camera and snapped a picture and sent it to *Us Weekly* for their "Stars—They're Just Like US!" feature. Instead, I grabbed a dish towel so I could dry.

"Hey, do you have plans tomorrow?" he asked as he handed me a plate.

Although I hated myself for it, I had snuck a look at my phone more than a few times during dinner to see if Matt had texted. He hadn't. "Nope."

"Well, I was supposed to go in for wardrobe stuff, but it got rescheduled," he said as he scrubbed a bowl, making sure it was actually clean. The few times Mom had done the dishes, you could be assured that when you'd go to get a glass, there'd still be a lipstick stain on it, or flecks of dried food on a fork. "So I was thinking of heading down to the city and hitting some galleries. I thought that if you didn't have any plans, you might want to come with me," he said. "There's some shows in Chelsea that are a little Francesca Woodman–like that you might enjoy."

Spending the day with Billy? *Alone?* On the one hand, I had been wanting to go into the city to check out some art. Mom wasn't a good person to go with because her way of looking at art was to walk in a quick circle around the room and then pick and choose which she could see hanging in our house. ("Don't you think it would be so cute to have this photograph of the woman in the bathtub hanging over a bathtub?" she had once asked when we went to a show at a gallery in Venice. "Very meta.") But on the other hand, I couldn't even begin to imagine what the bloggers would write about Janie Jackson's daughter hanging out with Billy Barrett if they found out.

He scrubbed harder. "But it's cool if you don't want to," he added, not looking at me. "I get it."

Okay, it was getting more and more difficult to think Billy Barrett was just another dickish star when he went and got all human and nervous like this. "No, I'd like that," I said. "I mean, I'd have to ask my mom first—"

"I already ran it by her," he said. "She's good with it if you are."

Wow. Mom hadn't said anything during dinner. She actually let it be between him and me and didn't insert herself into it. This was huge. I wasn't quite sure how to react to that. "Oh. Okay then. Sounds like a plan."

He looked over at me, another big smile on his face. "Really?"

"Sure."

"Awesome!" he exclaimed. "Dude, we're gonna have a *blast*."

So this was what it was like to be optimistic all the time. As for me, I was already worried about what would happen when we ran out of things to talk about ten minutes into the drive.

CHAPTER FOURTEEN

THINGS MOST PEOPLE PROBABLY DON'T KNOW
ABOUT BILLY BARRETT THAT I NOW DO

- ★ Despite the fact that he's high on the list of the richest movie stars, he likes to save money. We took the train to the city because, according to him, parking is a huge rip-off in Manhattan. And we didn't even sit in business class, even though it was only ten bucks more.
- ★ He hums to himself without knowing he's doing it, which—next to whistling—is one of my biggest peeves. Also something he does.
- ★ He says "Really? You think so?" more than anyone I know, which means the whole Zen "I just try and accept where I'm at and not compare myself to anyone else or look for outside validation, you know what I'm saying?" thing that he pulls out in interviews is more wishful thinking than reality.

Maybe because the Chelsea neighborhood of Manhattan is filled with an absurd number of hot guys (which, seeing that it was ground zero for gays and galleries, made sense), but with his San Diego Chargers baseball cap and Ray-Bans, Billy blended in and wasn't mobbed. And probably also because it was Chelsea, when he *was* recognized—in a few galleries, when he took his sunglasses off—there wasn't any screaming or wailing or cell phones whipped out to snap photos. There were a lot of double takes with a moment of recognition before the New York I-don't-care-who-you-are-I'm-cool-too-especially-because-I-work-in-an-art-gallery blank-faced expression returned.

"Is it me, or is being snotty a skill you need to have to work at these places?" Billy whispered to me as we looked at some stuff by William Eggleston. While I'd seen some of his stuff before, Billy knew all about him and educated me not just about him, but where he stood within the context of modern photography. It was like when you went to a museum and used those headset guides, except Billy was funnier and used the phrase "'It's, like, you know...'" a lot. (He also owned some of his work, which, seeing that it could be found in many museums, obviously cost a lot.)

But it wasn't all blending in. When we were done in Chelsea, we decided to walk around the Village, and that's when I got to witness just how insane people were about Billy. Sure, there were tons of people asking for autographs (not only did he sign them all, but he posed for pictures—

including one with the owner of a Korean deli, which he said he'd add to their Wall of Fame right under Snooki from *Jersey Shore*). That I expected. But the girls bursting into tears at the sight of him in Starbucks? That was creepy. ("Oh man—I *hate* when they cry," he said nervously as a girl who looked to be about my age began to wail.) And when we were browsing at the Strand, a bookstore that Matt had mentioned the first night we hung out, a woman who looked to be in her early thirties ran into the bathroom, came out a second later, and thrust her bra toward him.

"Does that happen . . . a lot?" I asked as he yanked me into the Philosophy section. ("I've learned that this is one section where I'll be left alone," he explained.)

"Not tons, thank God. But enough. Once there was a lady in, like, her sixties who did it." He shuddered. "That's the sense memory I use whenever I'm doing a scene that calls for me to be all creeped out."

He looked at the books I had collected as we browsed. *How to Be a Woman* by Caitlin Moran. Tina Fey's *Bossypants*. *Looking at Photographs* by John Szarkowski (Billy said it was like the New Testament for people who were into photography). *Portnoy's Complaint* by Philip Roth.

"*You're* reading Philip Roth?" he asked. "Wow. I haven't even read him yet."

"I didn't mean to pick that one up," I said, trying to grab it back from him.

He opened the book jacket and started reading the flap. "This one's the one that's supposed to be pretty outrageous, right?"

I grabbed for it again. "I just . . . I'm not going to read it. . . ." I sighed. "Matt was talking about it the other night. It's his favorite book, so I thought I would . . ." I shook my head as I took it out of his hands and threw it on a table. "Whatever. It was a stupid idea."

"What's a stupid idea?" Billy asked. "The book, or Matt in general?"

I paused. I had been thinking it could be helpful to get a guy's take on this stuff. And other than Matt, and the cashier at Stewart's with whom I now had a close personal relationship because of my newfound addiction to their iced coffee, Billy was the only guy around here I knew. I guess I could've e-mailed Ben, but he and Alice were in Europe (a few days in London with her parents, and then a week on the Amalfi Coast in Italy to recover from the experience of being with her parents, Alice had written me in an e-mail), and I didn't want to bother him. It used to be that I went to Ben for everything, from what to do about Mom to which was a Phillips screwdriver—the flat-head one or the pointy one?

However, since the *tu*-to-*vous* change, while we still e-mailed and texted a bunch, he was no longer my go-to person for every little thing. Google was. Our e-mails felt more official—like letters from camp filled with descriptions about what I had done, where I had gone, what I had seen. But how I *felt* about what I did and where I went and what I saw—that I now left out. As for Walter, we texted or FaceTimed every day, and if it had been a question about Spider-Man or Batman or any other action figure-turned-blockbuster-movie, he was the guy, but stuff about relationships with people of the opposite sex whom you weren't related to? Not happening. And Maya—I had spoken to her once since I left L.A. To say she was my best friend felt like a lie now. Even to say we were friends felt like a stretch.

So it was either do some more Googling, which only confused me due to the completely opposing advice you'd get in the search results *(Call him!!! Whatever you do— DON'T call him!!! Call 1-800-PSYCHIC to find out whether you should call him or wait for him to call you!)*; pray about it and hope I got some sort of sign (if God was as awesome as everyone in Alateen said, I didn't understand why He/ She/It couldn't just leave a typed note under my pillow with very clear and specific directions as to what to do); or—my favorite, and the one I had the most experience with—sit on the couch and try to figure it out myself. ("I hate to tell you this," Walter had said early on in our friendship, "but 'figure it out' is not one of the Twelve Steps or slogans.")

I shrugged. "All of it."

He nodded. I waited for him to say something, but he

didn't. Radiohead's "Creep" started to blare, and he took out his phone and tapped Decline, sending Skye to voice mail.

"Is this one of those reverse-psychology things?" I finally asked.

"What do you mean?"

"You know, where you ask me a question, and I answer but not with, like, a *real* answer, and you don't badger me because you think your *not* saying anything will ultimately make me talk about it," I replied. "Because sometimes Mom does that."

He laughed. "Why does that not surprise me?"

My mouth opened to defend her before realizing there was nothing to defend. The truth was it totally pissed me off when she did it. But protecting my mother—making excuses for her, even for the stuff I hated—was second nature. And when I looked at Billy, I realized it wasn't a slight, because the smile on his face was full of acceptance, the kind you have when you totally see that someone is perfectly imperfect, aka human.

"Are you a Buddhist?" I asked. I knew from all the self-help books that were strewn around the house that the Buddhists were very big on the acceptance thing.

"Well, not, *officially*," he replied. "I mean, I've read some books. And the last time the Dalai Lama was in town I got to hang with him at a fund-raiser. But my ADHD makes it really tough for me to meditate. How come?"

I shrugged. "No reason."

"Listen, if you want to talk about Matt, that's cool. But I'm not going to push you into it. You've already got one person doing that to you. Don't need another," he said with a wink.

"Good. Because I don't. Want to talk about it, I mean."

"Cool," he said, pulling his cap down and putting his Ray-Bans back on. "Let's get out of here then."

That was really it? No pushing me on the issue? Just letting that be the end of the story? It was so . . . drama-less. And he was an actor. None of this made sense to me.

"Okay, fine—I'll talk about it," I said a little later as we left the International Center of Photography and started walking back to Penn Station. Although I tried to stop him—saying the books he had bought me at the Strand were more than enough—he had insisted on buying me a Lomography camera in the store there.

"About what?" he asked, confused.

Maybe that was a sign that I shouldn't bring it up. Sure, he was nice, and definitely a guy, but still, I liked the sitting-on-the-couch-and-figuring-it-out option better. "About . . . Matt."

"Ah. Right. So what's up?"

"What's up is—"

"Creep" began to blare again. The easygoing smile on

his face disappeared, replaced by annoyance. "Annabelle, I'm really sorry to do this—" he started to say.

"Not a problem," I said. This was good. Not only was I saved from telling him about Matt, but I also got to eavesdrop on his conversation with Skye.

He took a deep breath and pushed Answer. "What is it, Skye?" he asked gruffly. Even though he had turned his head away from me, I could still hear her shrill voice coming through the phone. "*No*, my not answering your calls is not my way of passively-aggressively breaking up with you," he hissed. "Because *we're already broken up.*" She started in on him again. While I couldn't make out what she was saying, I could hear the hostile machine gun–like *rat-a-tat-tat* of the words. "What photos of you at Soho House?" *Rat-a-tat-tat.* "I didn't see them." More. "Because, Skye, unlike you, who is addicted to that garbage, I don't spend my time surfing stupid gossip blogs so I can *read about myself.*"

The *rat-a-tat* was replaced by a sonic boom. "Listen, feel free to make out with whoever you want. I don't care." Back to the *rat-a-tat-tat*. "I'm not saying that to compensate for my guilt because I'm making out with Janie. Because I'm not *making out with her.*" He looked at me. "Sorry," he whispered. "What? I said 'sorry.'" More. "No, not to you—why I would say sorry to *you*?" More. "I'm not with Janie—I'm with . . . you know what? It's none of your freaking business who I'm with!" *Kaboom.* "Skye? Thanks for the update on how you're moved on. That's great. I'm happy for you." More. "And I think that's fantastic that this is the last call you'll be making to me. So maybe, this time, unlike the *seventeen others* over the last week, it actually will be." More. "Okay, I'm hanging up, Skye. Hanging up." More babbling. "Seriously, Skye, this is me hanging up. Okay. Whatever. Good-bye."

After he clicked End, he turned the Power button off and shoved the phone in his pocket and shook his head. "That's what I get for drinking tequila that night I met her," he sighed. "Hey, when you're twenty-one and start drinking? Do yourself a favor and steer clear of that stuff. It'll save you a whole lot of trouble."

"So are you guys *really* broken up?" I asked. "Or just, you know . . ."

"Yes, we're broken up!" he cried. "Did you not hear me? Why would you think differently?"

I shrugged. "Because in the Hollywood Yearbook edition he did a few weeks ago, SimonSez voted you guys Most Likely to Break Up and Get Back Together by Lunch."

He looked embarrassed. "Yeah, well, that was before." He looked at the inside of his left arm and began to scratch at little red blotches that were popping up. "Things are different now," he said firmly.

Before what? Before meeting Mom? And why were they now different? Because that smile that came over his face when he talked about Mom actually meant he really liked her? And even though she was crazy, she wasn't nearly as nuts as Skye? And exactly how long would I obsess over that after I got home? And what kind of list could I make to help with the anxiety about what would happen if I was right?

He scratched harder. "Great. She gave me *hives*. I get them when I'm stressed."

And who would believe that Billy Barrett ever got stressed? That was something that, you know, human beings had to deal with. Not megastars.

We walked for a bit without saying anything before he whipped out his phone. "I can't *believe* I'm doing this," he muttered as he turned it on and waited for it to boot up. Soon, the screen was filled with a photo of Skye and a guy who, although he wasn't as cute as Channing Tatum, definitely had as awesome a body. And they were indeed canoodling. He turned it off again and shoved it back in his pocket. "I don't want to talk about this anymore," he said firmly. "Back to what we were talking about . . ." Maybe he'd forget. ". . . Matt."

Busted. I shrugged. "That's the thing—there really isn't anything to tell. I don't think he likes me. You know—in a *canoodling* way."

He snorted. "'Canoodling' meaning can't keep your hands off someone in a public place?" He shook his head. "She *knows* that Soho House is like my living room! He took a deep breath. "But we're not talking about that.

We're talking about you. And I'm here to tell you that Matt likes you."

"How do you know?"

He shrugged. "Because I saw the way he was looking at you that night at the restaurant."

"How was he looking at me?"

"Like he liked you!"

Why did I think this was going to be a long conversation? "Okay, I don't know what that means," I said. "Plus, he's not acting like he does. That whole thing at the house, and Mom inviting him . . ."

"You mean he hasn't tried to kiss you?"

I felt my cheeks turn red. Way to cut to the chase. "I didn't say *that*." I looked over at Billy, whose eyebrows were raised. "Okay, fine. You're right."

He shook his head. "He's not going to kiss you for a while."

"How come?"

He shrugged. "You're either going to have to make the first move," he said, "or you're going to have to make it really, really clear to him that you like him."

"What? Why?!"

"Because it's obvious that he's the nerdy, sensitive type—which, before you get all mad at me for saying that, I'll have you know is the number one growing type at the box office, according to my agent," he replied. "And you're intimidating."

"I am so not intimidating!" I cried.

"You are."

"How?!"

"Because you're strong and smart and funny and gorgeous."

It was never easy for me to accept compliments ("Bug, *yeah, but* is *not* an okay response when someone compliments you," Mom was always chastising me. "*Thank you* is."). But at that moment, coming from Billy, it made me feel physically ill.

He stopped walking. "Is that weird that I just said you're gorgeous?" he asked, worried. "Because I didn't mean to, you know . . . I mean, you *are*, but I'm not, you know . . ."

I waved him off. "I know. I get it." I knew that Billy Barrett wasn't interested in me. He was interested in my mother. And although he had never been my type to begin with, because he wasn't a sensitive nerd, as I got to know him and discovered he was kind of sweet, and very human, it made him even *less* hot, if that was mathematically possible. *Talking to him is like talking to an older brother*, I thought. I cringed. That wasn't a good image, because of my mom. A neighbor. He was like . . . a neighbor.

"Look, I know you've had a lot to deal with over the years," he continued.

I felt my back go up. Exactly how much had Mom told him about what things had been like? I didn't need Billy Barrett feeling *sorry* for me.

"And I get how that would make it hard to let your guard down and trust people. But sometimes that whole protection thing . . . it can come off, like, I don't know . . . that you're not interested. . . . you know what I'm saying?"

No, I didn't know what he was saying. I had never been in this position because I had been too busy spending my time holding mirrors up to my passed-out mother's mouth to check for signs of life. "But what about that whole *Rules* thing?" I blurted out.

"Huh?"

"The thing about how you're supposed to sit back and let the guy call the shots, and play a little hard to get, and not return their texts right away, and all that stuff?" I cringed as I listened to myself. When you said it out loud, it sounded even more stupid than it did when you read it.

"Aw, man," he groaned. "Really, Annabelle? You're one of those *Rules* girls?" He sounded disappointed. Like I had just announced that when I was old enough to vote it would be Republican.

"I have no idea what kind of girl I am!" I cried. "It's not like this happens a lot for me!" Like, say, ever.

He shook his head. "That's just game playing," he said. "Pretending to be someone you're not. Like those girls who have two bites of lettuce when you go out to dinner and then, once you've been together for a while, you walk out into the kitchen at two o'clock in the morning and find them scarfing down pickles and olives and maraschino cherries." He shuddered. "That was intense. But back to you. Listen, look it from his point of view. Here you are, this hip and cool chick from L.A. —"

"I don't think *hip* and *cool* are two words that immediately come to mind when people think of me—"

He held his hand up to shut me up. "—who's just blown into this little town in upstate New York because her mother is filming a big Hollywood movie—"

"It's not *that* big a movie," I corrected. "I mean, if you weren't in it, it would be more of an indie, and—"

"—and probably has a ton of guys falling at her feet back home."

I rolled my eyes. "As if."

"Guys with a lot more going on than he has."

"He's got a lot going on," I said defensively. "He just won some award at Bard in the Art Department."

"That's great," Billy said, "but I'm telling you, if he's a creative type, he's definitely insecure. Maybe not so much about his work, but about everything under the sun. Goes with the territory." We stopped in front of a Mister Softee ice cream truck. "Chocolate or vanilla?" he asked.

"Chocolate," I replied, too exhausted to fight him on letting me at least pay for my own ice cream.

He handed me my cone. "Add to that that he's a *guy*—which means he's already a little bit scared and somewhat clueless when it comes to reading people—and you've got yourself a situation where he'd rather chew off his arm before he makes a move when he's not yet entirely sure you're interested in him and risks being rejected by you."

I looked at him. "Really? Is that true?"

As he took a bite of his cone, some chocolate ice cream plopped onto his shirt. "Totally."

"So what am I supposed to do?"

"Well, you can start with asking him to go do something instead of wait for him to bring it up," he replied.

"But what if he has a girlfriend? He might have a girlfriend."

He shook his head. "He doesn't have a girlfriend."

"How do you know?"

"Have you asked him?"

"No."

"Why not?"

"I don't know. Because that's . . . a really personal thing to ask someone."

"Do you hear yourself right now?"

I thought about it. "Yes. And I sound ridiculous."

"I'm glad we're in agreement about that," he said. "Why don't you start with that? With asking him if he has a girlfriend?"

"But what if he says yes? Then I'll feel beyond stupid, and it'll be really awkward," I replied. "If I do that, I'm going to have to have my own car so I can leave right away and get home—"

"And what if he says he doesn't have a girlfriend?"
That was even scarier.

===

Maybe it was all the walking. Or all the food. Or the soothing rhythm of the train as it barreled north, and the glow of the sun as it set on the Hudson River. Or maybe it was because after so many years of keeping my distance from people, this new experience of letting people see bits and pieces of myself was becoming addictive, like the Play-Doh. Whatever it was, when Billy glanced up from making notes on his script and asked me what I was doing, I didn't close my laptop and say "Nothing" before he could see.

"Uploading some photos," I replied.

He looked interested. "Yeah? Can I see?"

This was a guy who collected art by people whose work hung in museums. Why on earth would I show him my stuff? He'd probably say it was good, because really, what else was he going to say, but he wouldn't *mean* it.

I held the laptop out toward him. As he took it and settled back in his seat, I settled back into my own and gazed out the window, trying not to pick at my cuticles as I stared at the landscape as it whizzed by.

"What is this? Your blog?" he asked after a while.

"Tumblr. Yeah."

He nodded and went back to going through the photos. Finally, he looked up. "Annabelle, these are terrific."

I felt myself turn red. "No, they're not."

"They are. You have an amazing eye for composition. And you totally capture the absurdity of L.A." He pointed to one. "Like with this one. The one with the bag lady going through the Dumpster next to all these beemers and Mercedes-Benzes."

I had taken that near a parking lot where all the cars were valeted for Ivy at The Shore. It was one of my favorites.

"Have you taken a lot of classes?" he asked.

"I haven't taken any."

"Really?" he asked, surprised.

I nodded.

"How'd you learn?"

I shrugged. "Just started shooting."

"Have you entered any contests or anything?"

"No. There's this fellowship thing this summer at CalArts in a few weeks that sounded cool, but I didn't apply."

"How come?"

I shrugged. "Because I had to come here."

He looked up again. "Your mom said you couldn't go?"

"No, I mean, I didn't even tell her about it." I sighed. "I'll apply next summer."

"They just asked me to be on the board there."

"CalArts? They did?"

He nodded. "Do you have other stuff? Other than this blog?"

I did. I had the photos of Mom. The ones I had started taking when she went to rehab and began getting well. The ones that showed all the stuff I had never been able to talk about before Alateen because I was too embarrassed and ashamed.

The ones I had never shown anyone.

I reached for the computer and clicked on a file called Negative Space. There it was—everything you ever wanted to know about Janie Jackson but were afraid to ask.

I wasn't sure why, of all people, I was showing it to him. Was it a warning? *This is the kind of baggage we at Casa del Jackson travel with*. Or was it a dare? To see if, after knowing this, he would stick around.

I watched his face as he studied each photo in the folder.

A lipstick-stained crystal glass filled with vodka and melted-down ice cubes next to an amber-colored prescription bottle with one pill left.

An unmade bed with smudges of mascara on a pillowcase.

A bunch of feet in a circle—scuffed-up Nikes with frayed laces next to perfectly pedicured toes peeking out of Christian Louboutin sandals next to black patent-leather Mary Janes with white lace anklet socks—during Family Weekend at Oasis.

Mom's hand clutching her thirty-day-clean-and-sober coin.

Mom signing an autograph outside our new apartment

building as the movers unloaded a grand piano. (Which, by the way, neither of us knew how to play.)

The head of an Emmy Award peeking over a cardboard moving box.

Occasionally, he'd cringe. Or his eyes would widen. There was a sigh. And a few bittersweet smiles. If I had had some Play-Doh in my bag, I so would have gone into the bathroom. Instead, I just had to sit with the anxiety and not try to fix it, or make excuses for her.

When Billy was done, he handed the computer back to me. I waited for him to say something—anything—but instead he gazed out toward the river.

Finally, he turned to me and cleared his throat. "You know, my dad . . ." He cleared it again. "He drank." He shrugged. "For all I know, probably still does."

"But I thought . . . I mean, all the articles talk about how great your parents are," I said, surprised. "How they've been together forever, and how your dad's your best friend."

"That's my stepdad," he replied. "My mom married him when I was seven, so he raised me. But my real dad?" He shook his head. "That's another story. And my business manager has paid him a lot of money not to tell it." He pushed his hair away from his forehead and leaned toward me. "See that?"

On his left temple was a thick white scar.

"That was courtesy of the remote control when I jumped in between my mom and him after he got on her for overcooking his steak." He laughed ruefully. "I was lucky. My oldest sister's got a scar from a cigarette burn on her forearm."

I thought about what Walter once said about his grandmother. How she liked to say that if everyone were to put their problems in the middle of the table, we'd probably all take our own back. My mother may have been selfish, and self-centered, but other than smothering me to death with hugs, she had never laid a hand on me.

"I know your mom can be a little nuts sometimes," he said quietly, "but I think it's great for both of you that she's not drinking anymore. You both get a real shot at things, you know?"

I nodded. I did know that. Just like I was starting to learn that—also like they said in meetings—you can't judge a person's insides by their outsides. All the articles and interviews made it seem as if Billy had had a perfect childhood. But I guess there was a reason he was paid so much money as an actor—he was excellent at pretending. "Is that why you pushed for her to get the movie?" I asked.

He looked out the window again. "I don't know," he finally said. "Maybe that was part of it. But I also thought—think—that she's a great actress. And that now that she's sober, she'll be an even better one."

In the past, hearing something like that would've pissed me off and made me all defensive, as if he were feeling sorry for us. But now I realized it was what kids in the meeting called a "God shot"—these moments of coincidence when you were given a gift. It didn't matter how Mom had gotten the movie—it mattered what she did with the opportunity now that she had it. In the past, she used to pass out when she was studying her lines, but that wasn't the case anymore. Now she was prepping for it like they were the SATs.

"Has your mom seen these photos?" he asked.

I shook my head. "No way. She'd kill me."

"Why would you think that?"

I shrugged. "Because."

"But it's the truth," he said. "How can you go wrong with the truth?"

That sounded good in theory, but when you were so used to living surrounded by lies, doing things differently sometimes felt impossible.

When Billy and I got home from New York and Mom saw that the trip had accomplished what I figured she had hoped it would do—i.e., we had bonded—her reaction was not what I expected. She got all quiet and weird and said things like "Well, that sounds like you had a lovely day" in a *Downton Abbey* kind of voice that was so polite that it came off as if, actually, she didn't think it was so lovely. And that, actually, she seemed a little angry that it had gone so well. "What's up with that?" Billy asked after she was done with her English countess performance.

"With what?" she replied innocently.

He cocked his head and looked at her, but all she did was give him the generic smile she gave to weird potential stalker-esque fans in order to not encourage them.

"With that."

"I have no idea what you're talking about," she replied. She yawned. "And while I'm so glad you guys had fun today, some of us had to work, so some of us are pretty tired."

"Okay, then I guess some of us should get going," Billy said.

"Probably a good idea," she agreed.

He looked over to me for help, but I was too busy giving her my patented *seriously*-you're-doing-this-*now*? look.

He shrugged. "Okay." He turned to me. "Thanks for hanging out today, Annabelle. It was fun."

"Yeah. I . . . yeah." I was confused. Like by saying too much, and admitting I had a good time, I was somehow dishonoring Mom.

"See you around," he said, maybe to me, maybe to her, maybe to both of us.

"That's it? You're leaving?" Mom called after him as he started to walk toward the door.

He stopped and turned. "You just said it was probably a good idea if I left."

"I know, but I didn't mean for you to . . ." She stopped, her mouth set in a straight line. "Fine. Yeah. You should go."

He stared at her for a second. "Here's the thing, Janie. I'm a simple guy, you know?" he said. "So when someone says go, I go. I'm not smart enough to read minds or to figure out when 'go' really means 'stay.' You know what I'm saying?"

She stared at him. "Yeah, I know what you're saying," she finally replied.

"Good," he said. "Good night, then."

Whoa. In all the years, with all the boyfriends, I couldn't remember any guy ever calling Mom on her shit before. Not even Ben. After Billy walked out, she turned to me.

"I can't believe he just did that," she said, all wounded. "Can you believe he did that?"

I shrugged as I walked toward the kitchen. "I think it's cool."

"You're taking his side?!"

I thought about it. I guessed I was.

CHAPTER FIFTEEN

REASONS NOT TO BE A RULES GIRL WHEN IT CAME
TO MATT

- ★ I was in town for only six weeks. If this was
  going to be anything, it made sense that it
  would be an accelerated AP schedule.
- ★ If he came up with some lame excuse as to
  why he couldn't get together, then I had my
  answer and could move on to obsessing about
  something else. Like what I was going to do
  in the fall when I went back to school and
  was faced with the fact that I had no friends
  other than Walter and half a friend in Maya.
  Or why I had just taken Billy's side instead of
  Mom's and whether that made me an awful
  daughter.

I was just about to add *If it backfires I can blame Billy*

when I realized that these lists weren't actually helping. I got a little bit of a relief for the time it took me to write them, but that was it. If anything, what they did was keep me in my head and out of life, a combination that was starting to feel more and more uncomfortable. Maybe it was because, as I had learned in meetings, while the alcoholic was powerless over alcohol, I was powerless over my thinking. But while it made sense that the reason I didn't participate in life before was because so much of my time was spent watching over my mother, I didn't have that excuse anymore. I couldn't blame her for the fact that I was holed up in my room instead of being out with friends, or meeting boys. I could only blame myself.

I didn't want to have to do that. I put down my red Pilot Razor Point (Was I proud of the fact that when Billy asked me if I had a pen he could use to sign an autograph, I had lied and said no because that would have meant the list-making pen was being used for non-list-making purposes? No. But if I had lent it to him, then I would have had to throw it out afterward), tore the list out of the notebook, and ripped it in two. And then, because I wasn't struck by lightning, I tore another one out and did the same thing. And then another. The whole thing was so invigorating that I reached for my iPhone and scrolled down to Matt's number. *Hey. It's me. Annabelle*, I started to type.

I stopped.

"Oh, come on. If you're going to do this, then do it," I said aloud. I clicked on his name and listened as it started to ring. Maybe I didn't have to, like, *do it* do it. Maybe texting was good enough. Between that and ripping up the lists, I was—

"Hey," he said just as I was going to hang up. He actually sounded excited to hear from me. Or did he? Other than Walter, I barely talked on the phone anymore, so I wasn't sure.

"Oh, *hey*," I said, pleasantly surprised, as if he had been the one who called me.

"What's up?"

"Not much," I replied. I waited for him to say something before remembering that in standard telephone etiquette, it was usually up to the person who had made the call to speak. "Actually, that's not true," I corrected. "What's up is that I was wondering if you wanted to maybe do something at some point when you're not busy. I mean, you probably *are*, because you live here, and you have friends, and a job, and stuff like that. . . . But if at some point you find yourself . . . not. Busy, I mean. And if you want to."

"How about tomorrow?" he asked before I could keep going.

"Tomorrow," I repeated.

"Yeah."

"Oh. Tomorrow. Well, tomorrow is the first day of shooting, so I should probably go to set—" Mom hadn't asked me to go with her, but it seemed like a good thing to do.

"Okay. Then how about—"

"But I don't have to go all day!" I blurted out. "I could just go in the morning and then meet you in the afternoon. I mean, if the afternoon works for you, and you're not busy." I cringed.

"Afternoon works for me," he replied. "Meet you at Swallow?"

"Okay," I replied. This whole thing had gone so easily it felt that much more complicated.

———

No matter how many times we ran lines together, there was something about seeing Mom in costume and makeup, truly becoming the character she was playing, that always amazed me. Now that I knew what I did about all the lying she had done back when she was drinking, it made sense that she was so good at pretending. But still, the fact was, when she was on set and all traces of herself evaporated, it kind of scared me.

As I watched her on set the next morning, dressed in a simple navy shirtdress (she was so committed to the role, she didn't even balk at the fact that it was cleavage-free) and flat sandals, her hair in a bun, with minimal makeup and black horn-rimmed glasses, I totally bought the fact that she was a tenured professor with a Ph.D. and was an expert on Emily Dickinson. As her students sat there mesmerized while she recited *Hope is the thing with feathers/That perches in the soul/And sings the tune—without the words/And never stops at all*, I was right there with them. And when they shot a scene back in her office, during which she opens a drawer and finds an airplane-size bottle of vodka stashed away, I held my breath as I watched a host of different emotions play across her face within fifteen seconds—surprise, fear, temptation, longing, resolve—before she throws it into the garbage.

Just like I bought that instead of being a Hollywood heart-throb who hung out at Soho House canoodling, Billy Barrett was just a normal, working-class guy. Now that I had spent some time with him, that wasn't so far off the mark. From the expressions on the faces of the crew as he shot his first scene—where, dressed in a flannel shirt and faded jeans, his face all scruffy, he pleaded with someone at the bank to give him a loan so he could keep the tavern that had been in his family for three generations—I wasn't the only one who was surprised to find that his acting abilities reached beyond being able to wrestle a bad guy to the ground or jump out of a burning building right before a bomb went off.

Just like, when they finally did their first scene together, in the bar, when he asks her what he can get her, and she pauses before ordering a cranberry and soda, I totally bought the chemistry between them.

"I'm starting a pool as to when the two of them take the

on-screen stuff offscreen," I heard the prop woman whisper behind me as we watched them banter back and forth.

"If they haven't already," one of the makeup guys replied.

I wanted to whip around and tell them they had not, but it was one of those moments where you couldn't look away. They were too good together.

"And ... cut," ordered Alistair.

Even with the immediate surge of movement—lights being dragged away, cameras being moved off to the sides, crew members hustling about like an army of overgrown ants—it took a second for Mom and Billy to break character. Instead, they stood there with goofy looks on their faces until Mom almost got hit in the head with a giant light. After that she dragged him over to where I was sitting.

"I need to make an amends to the two of you," she announced. Ever since rehab, nothing was just an apology anymore—now, because of the Twelve Step thing, it was always an amends, and it was always very official. "My behavior last night when you guys got home was inappropriate."

"No worries. Everything's cool—" Billy said.

She held up her hand. "Please, let me finish. It was not cool. It was inappropriate and rude and—"

"Janie, I get it. I do. Really. But it's over, okay?" he said. "So just let it go."

The two of us looked at him, confused. Letting things

go was not something we in the Jackson family had a lot of experience with. Holding on to things like a dog with a bone so that we could then throw them into each other's faces over and over again? That we were good at.

"So you're not mad?" she asked.

He shook his head.

"Really?" she asked doubtfully.

"Yes, really. But if you keep asking me that, I will be soon." He shifted his weight. "And I have to pee. Bad." He turned to me. "You hanging around for lunch?"

I shook my head. "No. I'm . . . going to go meet Matt."

He nodded. "You call him or he call you?"

I felt my cheeks flush. "I called him."

I guess he could've said "I told you so," but he didn't. Instead, a small smile came over his face. "Right on. Have fun."

After he walked away, Mom turned to me. "Did you ask *Billy* for guy advice?"

"*No,*" I lied.

She did that thing where she furrowed her brow as much as the Botox would allow it.

"Maybe," I relented.

She continued to wait.

"Fine. Yes, I did."

I waited for her lower lip to start quivering, the number one sign that a meltdown was forthcoming. (Other signs included blinking a lot, pacing, and taking deep breaths faster and faster).

Regardless of her amends, after what happened last night, I was sure she'd freak out. But the quivering didn't come. Instead, she did her guppy imitation before nodding. "Well, I think that's . . . just great," she said.

"Really?" I asked doubtfully.

"Yes, really."

I was doing the same exact thing to her that she had done to Billy. Was the drama-queen/making-mountains-out-of-molehills gene hereditary? "Okay then," I said. "I should go. You know, to meet him."

"Right. Of course."

But I didn't move. Something was happening in that moment. With every word, that cord between us was being stretched more and more, and I knew that if I turned around and left, maybe it wouldn't snap in half, but it would tear; and that tear would start to fray, until ultimately what we used to have would be gone.

"It's okay? That I don't stay?" I asked quietly, hating myself for giving her the opportunity to guilt me into it.

She smiled. "Yes, you don't need to stay, Bug. I'm okay. I promise."

For the first time in I don't know how long—maybe forever—I believed that was actually the case.

═══════════════════════════════════════

As Matt and I waited for the bushy beard–clad, David Foster Wallace-reading, Benjamin Franklin spectacles-wearing guy behind the counter at Swallow to get us our coffees (though not without a pained look, as if our request was seriously interfering with his reading time), he turned to me. "So did you have any ideas as to where you might want to go?" Matt asked. "Because I was thinking, if you didn't have anything special in mind," he continued, "I've mapped out a barn tour."

"A barn tour," I repeated. That wasn't something you heard a lot in Lost Angeles.

"Yeah. I was thinking about how the day, when we were driving over to Woodstock and we passed that red barn on 9G, you mentioned how you had always thought barns were cool and how, when you were little, you had wanted to live in one, so I was thinking, if you brought your camera . . . Did you bring your camera?" he asked as he leaned over and peeked into my bag. "Yup, you did." He smiled. "I was hoping you did. . . . Anyway, I was thinking that maybe we could, I don't know, go on a barn tour so you could take some photos. We don't have to . . . just, I was thinking . . . if you felt like it."

Growing up with my mother, anything I said—my likes, my dislikes, my fears—were immediately run through her what-does-this-have-to-do-with-me? filter. So when I mentioned something in passing like "I've always thought barns were really cool," it's not as if I expected anyone to hear me, let alone use up disk space in his brain to remember it. And then do something about it.

Just then, I flashed on a line in the script from the movie. Billy's character tells Mom's character that people think it's things like flowers on Valentine's Day, or a necklace on an anniversary, or dinner at a fancy restaurant for a birthday that symbolize love, but it's not. It's the day-to-day things, like letting them control the remote when you're watching TV in bed together before you go to sleep, holding their hair back when they have the stomach flu and they're throwing up, or giving them a free pass to be pissy and make a really big deal about the fact that you didn't replace the empty toilet paper roll when you know they had a bad day.

I knew I barely knew Matt, and that after the next few weeks, I'd probably never see him again, so it wasn't like it was *love* or anything, but having someone organize a barn tour for you was a sign of *something*. If just someone who would be a really good friend.

I watched as he turned red. "Forget it. I knew it was a stupid idea. I mean, you're from L.A. Why would you want to drive around looking at *barns*—"

I grabbed his arm. "I would like nothing more than to go on barn tour," I said.

"Okay, go-to comfort food?" he asked as we stood in front of a gray barn on 9G in Germantown.

I fiddled with my lens so I could get the willow tree in

317

the shot. "Rice pudding," I replied. I loved the Trader Joe's brand. When Mom was in rehab, I had bought so many they filled up an entire brown paper bag at the checkout. I fired off a few shots. Usually I got self-conscious about shooting when I was with people and tried to hurry up, but with Matt I didn't feel that way. "You?"

The way he did with all the questions we had thrown out to each other over the course of the afternoon (because it was somewhat like making a list, I very much enjoyed it), he didn't answer right away. Instead, he took his time to think about it, sometimes cocking his head from side to side as if weighing the different possibilities.

Snap. Without looking at it, I knew it was a good shot.

"Sunflower seeds," he finally said.

"That's your *comfort* food?"

"Yes. Mixed with peanut butter. And Hershey's chocolate syrup."

I focused in on his face again. Tighter this time. God, he was cute. "And do you make this concoction a lot?"

He stared into the camera, his gaze steady and strong. "Yes."

I gently pushed the button, listening to the click before lowering the camera. "Well, I eat a lot of rice pudding."

―――――――――――――――――――――――

"Most embarrassing moment," he yelled down from the

roof of a red weathered barn in Chatham. With the promise of some Momofuku Compost Cookies, I had convinced
him to climb up and had gotten some cool shoots of him
lying on it spread-eagled so he looked like a starfish.

I laughed. "With *my* mother? Too many to count," I
called out. "But I think having her mug shot come up as
the first image when you Google her name is probably the
winner."

He nodded. "Yeah. That would be tough to beat."

As he shimmied down from the roof, I tried not to
think too much about what it would feel like to have his
arms around me instead of the drainpipe.

"Why are you shaking your head?" he asked as he
landed in front of me with a thud. Close.

"Huh?"

"You're shaking your head like you have water in your
ears or something."

Busted. "Oh. No, I just . . ." I waited for him to step
back, but he didn't. It was like the moment at Overlook.
Now was the time to ask him if he had a girlfriend. I cleared
my throat. "There's something I wanted to ask you."

"What?"

"I . . . wanted to ask you . . . what . . . your most embarrassing moment was."

He leaned down to tie his sneaker and then plopped
down on the ground. "Probably the first time I kissed a
girl."

I joined him on the ground. "What happened?"

"Nerd asthma attack."

I laughed. "What is nerd asthma?"

He plucked a dandelion from the ground and started twirling it. "Nerd asthma is what happens when a nerd—i.e., me—has to go in a closet with a girl during Seven Minutes in Heaven."

"You're not a nerd."

"Ah, but I am," he said. "I just have you *fooled*."

"So what happens during a nerd asthma attack?"

"Exactly that," he said. "You get in a situation where your inner nerd gets activated, and you get nervous, and your asthma gets triggered, which makes it very difficult to continue kissing."

I tried to cough away my laughter.

"It's okay. You can laugh," he said.

"I'm not laughing," I replied, trying to keep a straight face.

"Well, you should. You have a great laugh."

I felt myself blush. "So does it still happen?"

"The nerd asthma?"

I nodded. And scooched over toward him the teeniest, tiniest bit. Like so teeny that if he called me on whether I was throwing myself at him, a jury would find me not guilty.

He shook his head. "No. Not so much. Well, except for that time when I was in the bakery in Tivoli at the same time as Brice Marden. He's a painter," he explained.

I waited for him to say something else. Or do some-thing. Like, say, kiss me. But he didn't. I waited, and then I waited some more.

Just like I had waited for Mom to get better. And for her to realize she loved Ben. And for Olivia and Sarah to apologize after they dumped me. And for the nine hun-dred other things on the running list I kept in my head of what I needed to happen so that I could finally be happy and start living my life.

I was so sick of waiting.

"I have to tell you something," I blurted out.

He paled. "You have a boyfriend, huh?"

"What?"

"I figured." He shook his head. "Man, am I glad I didn't try to kiss you right now. I mean, having this conversation isn't fun, but that? Would've been *awkward—*"

"I don't have a boyfriend," I interrupted.

"You don't?"

I shook my head. "Do you?"

"Do I have a *boyfriend*?"

"No! A girlfriend."

"No," he replied.

"Oh."

"Did you think I did?"

"I don't know. Did you think I did?"

"Well, yeah."

"Why?"

He shrugged. "Because. Because you're beautiful, and smart, and funny, and cool."

Wow. Billy really did know about this stuff.

"Well, I don't," I said firmly.

"Well, that's good," he said just as firmly.

I nodded. "I'm glad we had this conversation then."

"Me, too."

We sat there in silence. "So . . . what do we do now?" I asked.

He handed me the dandelion and then put his hands on my cheeks. "I think we do this," he said, as he leaned in to kiss me.

CHAPTER SIXTEEN

PROS OF HANGING OUT WITH A GUY, WHERE KISSING IS ONE OF THE ACTIVITIES YOU PARTAKE IN TOGETHER
(AKA A GUY YOU'RE SEEING BUT YOU ARE AFRAID TO SAY YOU'RE SEEING, EVEN TO YOURSELF, BECAUSE YOU'RE SURE THAT WILL SOMEHOW JINX IT)

★ Kissing
★ You don't have to wonder if he's going to try and kiss you.
★ The good mood you're in from all the kissing makes it easier to tolerate your mother.
★ The good mood thing helps when you get home to find your mother's co-star has taken a slice of the triple-berry buttermilk bundt cake that you made for the guy you're kissing.
★ You no longer feel like a freak because, for the first time ever, there's a guy in your life whom you're kissing on a consistent basis.

★ You want to keep revealing more and more of yourself to him because every time you take the risk to let him in on who you really are — the good, the bad, the crazy — he doesn't come up with a lame excuse as to why he has to get going. Instead he looks . . . honored.

It's not like I told Matt *everything* (see: Play-Doh, Barbie heads). But I did tell him what it had been like with Mom. And how I had spent my wishes on hoping she and Ben would get together. (Unlike Walter, Matt did not have issues with the unsanitary nature of pennies. But living in the country, his version of that was chucking stones in the Hudson River.) And about being dumped by Olivia and Sarah. And how, while I was happy that Maya had met Jade because they were totally in love, I sometimes hated Jade for taking her away from me. What I found was that every time I talked about this stuff — whether with him, or with Walter, or in a meeting (I had found an Alateen meeting over in Rhinebeck, where, although the kids may have looked different than at my meetings in L.A. — less diverse, more knowledgeable about chickens and how to dispose of mice in the most humane way — they thought the same way and had the same feelings) — it took away the power the stuff had to make me feel crappy.

When I kept regrets and secrets and shame inside me, each incident had a way of expanding, weighing me down more and more. But when I shared them, it was like popping a balloon with a pin and watching it deflate. Sometimes the relief was immediate; sometimes it came over time. In L.A., people were big on this thing called the Master Cleanse, where you drank this combination of lemonade and honey and cayenne pepper, and it was supposed to clean out your insides and you lost a few pounds before you gained them all back in a day by bingeing on Hostess Donettes (Olivia was a big fan). This was my version of a cleanse. An emotional one, where every day I let go of a little bit more of the weight of the world that had settled on my shoulders over the years.

And in return, I learned who Matt was. We went to the Blue Plate Restaurant in Chatham, which, in addition to being known for their meat loaf, was the place where his parents had told him and his sister they were getting a divorce. We drove past his old high school, where some pickup-driving, quality-time-with-their-dads-meant-going-hunting guys had accused him of being gay because he was into painting and had beat him up under the bleachers of the football field. He took me to the waterfall in Stuyvesant, to which he'd escape when his mother and sister would fight about the fact that his sister's way of getting back at her father for leaving them for a twenty-year-old was to have sex with anyone who smiled at her.

But while Matt let me into his life, the one place he wouldn't let me into was his house.

One afternoon, on the way home from the movies in Great Barrington (a double feature of Richard Linklater's *Before Sunrise* and *Before Sunset* starring Ethan Hawke and Julie Delpy), he stopped at his house in Ghent because he said he had something for me.

Like most of the houses in the area it was an old farm-house. It wasn't super-fancy, and it could've used some fresh paint, but it had a down-to-earth charm. Even the unruly manner of the black-eyed Susans and hydrangea in front was sweet. I much preferred the upstate look to the perfectly manicured lawns of L.A., which were as anorexic and lacking in character as the people who owned them.

"Great," he mumbled when he saw the cobalt-blue Subaru Forester in the driveway. As he pulled up behind it, I could see it was stuffed with magazines, clothes, a busted chair, and a lamp.

"Is that your mom's car?" I asked.

"Yeah," he sighed, putting it in park. "I'll be right back." He turned the radio on and punched some buttons until a country song filled the air. "You can listen to the radio."

"Wait," I called as he jumped out.

"What?" he asked impatiently.

Why was he acting so weird? "I . . . have to pee," I said. I overdid it with the free refill Diet Cokes at lunch. Plus, I really wanted to see his house.

He glanced at the house and then back at me. "Can you just wait two minutes and then we'll go to the Mobil station and you can go there?"

He wanted me to pee at a gas station?

"It's just that my mom is weird about people coming over unannounced. It's a Southern thing. She likes to be all formal and put out drinks and snacks and stuff." While he was open about so much in his life, the subject of his mother was one that he reverted to one-word answers when I asked about her. I knew that she was from New Orleans, and that she was a book editor, and that after the divorce she had developed a bad habit of feeding stray cats and naming them, but that was about it. I knew what it was like to be badgered when you obviously didn't want to talk about something, so I didn't push, but I was dying to meet her.

"Okay," I said, disappointed. Why *would* he bother to introduce me to his mom? I was leaving soon enough. Sure, we had been hanging out every day; our make-out sessions were getting longer and heavier to the point where, had we lived in the same place, and had this had a future, I probably would have started Googling which forms of birth control were least messy/had the fewest number of side effects. But I still wasn't sure how he felt. Maybe it was just a way to pass the time and avoid having to go to his studio because he was having painter's block. ("Look, I may not have experience, strength, and hope to share when it comes to dating," Walter had said as we had FaceTimed the night before, "but I know enough to know that the chance of that not being true is ninety-nine point nine percent." I then went on to ask what made him feel there was a point one percent chance that it was true, upon which he threatened to hang up.)

Stop getting so attached. You're leaving in a few weeks, I said to myself. I had decided that needed to be my mantra: *Attachment = trouble.*

He looked relieved. "Thanks. I'll be right back." As he ran toward the house, I saw a curtain open and a head peek out. I couldn't see her face, but she stared at me for a bit before slowly letting it fall closed again. When he came back out and got back in the car, there was no trace of the gap-toothed smile that I had gotten so used to; the one that I felt a surge of victory about every time I said something that made it appear. His mouth was set in a straight line, and before I could even get my seat belt buckled again, he was backing out the driveway and we were out of there.

"You want me to pull in?" he asked as we neared the Mobil station.

"It's okay. I can wait until I get home," I replied.

He nodded and kept going.

I wasn't particularly musical, or athletic, but the one talent I had developed over the years was the ability to read a room. Or, in this case, a car. And while Matt may have been only two feet away from me, it felt like a thick wall of glass had somehow materialized in the last few minutes. He was still there, but he—everything that made him Matt—had been boiled away. It was like what used to happen with Mom. So I did what I usually did in those situations: I tried to fix things, and went into overdrive. I began to babble on about everything, which, because of the sheer volume of it all, was really about nothing, and then, once I realized I was babbling about nothing, I kept going, in hopes of making it about something. During this car crash of a car ride, Matt would occasionally throw out an "Oh, yeah?" or a "Really?" or an "Interesting," even though none of what I was saying was interesting. If anything, it was all very *un*interesting.

About twenty minutes into the ride—after I shared my thoughts on such topics as the lack of ethnic restaurants in the upstate area (prompted by a restaurant called Park Falafel & Pizza that we passed as we drove through Hudson); how weird it would be to have your house become a historical landmark after you died and know that people were going to traipse through it on a daily basis (when we passed Olana, where the painter Frederic Church had lived); and the difference between fables, folk tales, and fairy tales (as we passed a sign for the Rip Van Winkle bridge, which I decided was a folk tale)—I had exhausted myself. I shut up, in hopes that he'd pick up the slack, but he remained quiet.

"Is anything wrong?" I asked as we passed into Germantown.

"Nope," he replied without looking at me. "Why would you ask that?"

I shrugged. "I don't know."

We went back to not talking. Until I couldn't help myself. "Did I . . . do something?" I asked quietly.

At least I got a quick glance out of that one. "Of course not. Why would you think that?"

"I don't know," I repeated.

"Well, you didn't."

I nodded and stared out the window.

"I just remembered that I need to pick up something from the framer over in Kingston," he said as we crossed over into Clermont.

"Okay." I liked Kingston. There was a Target there.

"So I'm going to drop you off and get going, if that's okay."

"That's fine," I said tightly. I had been thinking of showing him the series of photos that I had been doing of Mom when we got inside—the ones I had shown Billy—but now it seemed like a bad idea.

Needless to say, there was no making out when he dropped me off. Not even a kiss on the cheek. Instead, I pasted on a fake smile and said "Well, see you later!" as I reached for the door.

"Wait—this is what I needed to stop at my house for," he said, holding out a CD case. "I know the CD thing is kind of old school," he said, handing it to me, "but it felt more personal than just e-mailing you a playlist." Inside the jewel case was a CD, and a liner with a painting of black and white and gray shapes.

"Did you paint this?"

He nodded. "It's an abstract version of the Overlook Hotel. In Woodstock."

My heart—which over the course of the ride had been returned to where it usually stayed, behind bulletproof glass—stretched open a bit. Back in L.A, in a box in my closet in the apartment on Darlington marked ANNABELLE—PERSONAL, was a notebook full of lists that included one titled "My Ideal Guy," which I had made one night when I couldn't sleep. Somewhere around number 12 was *Someone who makes me CD mixes*. "Thanks," I said.

"You're welcome. Talk to you later."

I *hated* the "later" thing. As Mom said, men, like dogs, had no sense of time, which meant that fifteen minutes and fifteen days were the same thing to them.

Once inside I went straight to my room and starting rummaging through the different compartments of my suitcase, praying that somehow one mini Play-Doh can had managed to stay hidden during my periodic sweeps to rid myself from my addiction to noxious fumes. If the car had been there, I would have driven across the river to Target, but it wasn't, so I was stuck.

I turned on my laptop and slid in the CD. Stretching

out on my bed, I closed my eyes. Maybe the songs he had chosen would shed some light on things.

SONGS ON MIX CD AND POSSIBLE MEANINGS

★ Billy Bragg/"Must I Paint You a Picture?" — The "little black cloud in a dress" line was genius, but was that what he thought I was?
★ The Clash/"Should I Stay or Should I Go" — Granted, this was probably on here because we had heard it in Swallow one afternoon and had to leave because we were laughing so hard while watching the barista move his chin in a robotlike manner. Or maybe it was because he thought I was putting out mixed signals?
★ Pixies/"Where Is My Mind?" — The song was about questioning your sanity. Enough said.
★ Radiohead/"Give Up the Ghost" — Granted, I had mentioned to him that it was my favorite Radiohead song, but it was also about letting go of things.
★ The Strokes/"You Only Live Once" — While the tempo was upbeat, upon the second listen I discovered the lyrics were pretty negative ("Some people think they're always right/ Others are quiet and uptight").

I was on my third listen of the song, realizing it was also positive ("Sit me down/Shut me up/I'll calm down/

And I'll get along with you") while trying to figure out if I was supposed to sit down and calm down, or if he was, when I heard Mom's car turn into the driveway, followed seconds later by Billy's truck.

A few moments later the door opened and I heard Mom *click-clack* (she was pretty much the only woman in the entire Hudson Valley who wore heels) her way to the kitchen.

"You can't just run away like that, Janie, when someone tries to talk to you about something you don't want to talk about," Billy yelled as he came through the front door.

"I did not run away! I *drove* away. There's a difference!" she yelled back. I heard the opening and slamming of cabinets. "All right, if I can't drink over this, there sure as hell better be some baked goods lying around," she grumbled. I cringed as I heard the fridge open. "Ha. Jackpot," she said.

I walked out of my room to find her standing over the sink shoveling in the last slice of the peach pie I had made two nights before. The slice that I had been planning to have once I read Matt's mind via the CD. "What's going on?" I asked nervously. It must have been really bad because Mom never ate carbs during shooting.

"So they got some photos of us—big deal," he said. "It's not like we were *doing* anything."

"But they'll spin it like we were!" she cried. "Are you so naive that you don't know how the tabloids work?!" She smacked the side of her head. "Wait a minute—you're only *twenty-six*. You're *supposed* to be naive."

"Oh, so this is what it's about?" he asked. "The age thing?"

Because I was getting more and more nervous, I walked over to the drawer and got a fork and joined Mom at the pie. At first I wasn't sure she even knew I was there, until we got into a fencing match with our forks.

"You say that like it doesn't matter!" she said, pushing my fork way out of the way to get the last bite.

"Because it doesn't!" he yelled back. "It's just a number!" He glanced at me. "And it's not like there's anything going on between us anyway."

"But everyone will *think* there is," Mom replied. She shook her head. "I can see the headlines now—*The Cougar and the Cub*!"

"What if there was?" Billy asked.

"What if there were posts all over the Internet?" Mom asked. "Then I guess my publicist wouldn't feel bad about the fact that, other than my arrest, he wasn't able to get me any press in the last year," she said wryly.

"No. What if there *was* something going on between us?" he asked quietly. "For real. Not just on-screen."

"But there's not," she replied nervously.

"But what if?" Billy demanded.

She shifted her weight. "I'm sorry, what was the question again?" Mom may have been a big advocate of clear and honest communication when it came to other people, but when it came to herself? Not so much.

He stared at her.

334

"I don't want to have this conversation in front of Annabelle," she sniffed.

"Fine." He turned to me. "Annabelle, do you think I could speak to your mother alone?"

I turned to go.

"Annabelle, stay here," she ordered, grabbing my arm.

He sighed. "Really? This is how you're going to play it?"

Mom looked like a bug-eyed kitten hanging on to a tree. If the kitten had some piecrust in the corner of its mouth. "Well, you do know something about *players*."

He looked at her like he couldn't believe what she had said. Which made sense because I felt the same way.

"*Mom*—" I knew it was none of my business, but I couldn't help myself.

Billy held his hand up. "It's okay. Don't worry about it. There's obviously nothing to talk about," he said as he turned on his boot and started to leave. "See you around."

After he left, she turned to me. "Can you believe he just left like that?"

"Can I believe it?!" I said angrily. "I can't believe he didn't leave any earlier! What was that about?"

"You're taking *his* side?!" she demanded.

"You mean the side of the sane person in the equation? Yeah."

"You didn't even want me *talking* to him, Annabelle. And what, now you're rooting for us to end up together?" She shook her head. "Make up your mind here," she muttered.

She was right. I hadn't wanted her talking to him in

the beginning. Mostly because I was afraid that if they had gotten together, I'd have to sit back and watch as the same thing played out the way it always did. She'd fall madly in love and throw herself into the relationship, and then, as time went on, he would see that the real Janie Jackson wasn't the beautiful, sexy, kooky, fun person from talk shows and magazine articles. She was difficult and moody and needy, and that need would start to suffocate him—just like it suffocated me.

But the difference was, once he got sick of her crazi-ness, *he* could bolt—I could not. I had to stay and pick up the pieces of her heart like I always did when it got smashed—a heart that she always gave over too quickly, to men who weren't worth the gift to begin with. I would have to help put her together again, listening to her vows about how next time it would be different; next time she'd pick someone who could be there for her—for us—and we'd live happily ever after.

If, like they said in meetings, the definition of insan-ity was doing the same thing over and over again and expecting different results, then my mother had pretty much spent my entire life totally insane. But what I had witnessed since she had met Billy was that things had shifted. *She* had shifted. I had watched as she and Billy had become friends and gotten to know each other. He had seen her when she was happy and on. But the difference was that this time she had also allowed him to see her on her not-so-good days. The days when the sadness wasn't just confined to her eyes but bled out into all of her. Not to the point where she took to her bed and stared at the wall, but when she got quiet and didn't try to snap herself out of it. And the difference with Billy, unlike the others, was that it didn't scare him. He didn't act like somehow the fact that she was human was some betrayal, like she wasn't holding up her end of the deal. If anything, in those moments, as I watched him watch her being human, holding my breath to see if that would be the thing that made him pull back and leave her—leave *us*—he seemed to like her more. More than when she was up and on and acting as if she was still the star of a sitcom.

I never loved her more than when she was like that— when she was being real—and I realized right then that Billy did, too. Loved her. Loved her not in a Hollywood way, but in a true way—the kind of love where you let someone have their moods and their moments, but you're also not afraid to call them on it.

"Yes," I said.

"Yes what?"

"Yes, I'm rooting for you guys to end up together."

Had I just said that aloud? From the shocked look on Mom's face, I guess I had.

"But—"

I held up my hand. "Hey, I'm just as surprised as you are," I said. "But he loves you, Mom. I can see that. I mean, he's totally willing to put up with you. And before you go getting all offended, I mean that in the best possible way."

"But what about the age thing?"

"I don't know." I shrugged. "He may be a lot younger than you, but he's pretty smart about a lot of things." I walked over and took her hand. "He's a good guy, Mom."

She squeezed mine. "I know that," she sighed. "That's what's so terrifying."

"Maybe it'll work out and maybe it won't," I said, "but it seems like, if you're going to shake things up, you may as well go full force."

She wrapped her arms around me. "Oh, Bug—how'd you get so wise?"

I shrugged as I hugged her tight. "I don't know. Trial and error."

"I love you, Bug."

"I love you, too."

I waited for her to ask me how much, but she didn't.

Maybe she finally knew.

CHAPTER SEVENTEEN

The thing is, once you start going outside your comfort zone and taking risks (some people would probably call that living life), a weird thing starts to happen. Something gets flipped, and soon enough the thing that keeps you up at night and reaching for your notebook to make a list is the fear of not taking one. Once you've accumulated experience that shows that not only does the risk taking not lead to your world blowing up, but it actually makes your world bigger, it feels more uncomfortable to stay small.

So after my talk with Mom, I finished listening to the CD, and she drove over to Billy's house to apologize and who knew what else. (While I may have been okay with their being together, I wasn't at the point where I could deal with an actual visual of what might be occurring along with that without getting creeped out.) But even after listening to the CD a second time, I was no further along in my quest to figure out what Matt was trying to say or how he felt about me or what had happened that made him zip himself back up during the car ride home from his house.

I woke up to a buzz at around two a.m., on top of the covers with the lights still on, and immediately grabbed my phone. I felt myself relax a bit when I saw through half-open eyes that there was a text, only to come to full attention when I saw that it wasn't from Matt—it was from Mom, saying that she was spending the night at Billy's.

I felt the familiar whir as the adrenaline started to rev up inside of me—yes, I had essentially given her my blessing, but it didn't mean she should actually go and do it. But just as quickly as it started, it slowed down. Why shouldn't she give Billy a chance? Getting all mad at her for doing what I said she should do was just a way to avoid feeling bummed about the fact that Matt was acting weird and hadn't called or texted. I waited for the anxiety to rev back up, but it didn't. Instead, it conked out completely.

One of us should be happy, I thought as I turned out the light and got under the sheet.

I was at the kitchen table, eating pancakes—pancakes I had cooked in a pan on the stove instead of in the microwave—when I heard the door open.

"Bug?" she called.

I braced myself. It was too early to deal with her manic chatter that happened after she hooked up with a guy and was first in love. Especially when I was wallowing in Bumville because I had woken up to zero texts or e-mails from Matt.

"In the kitchen," I called out.

I heard the sound of Billy's footsteps following hers.

"Hi, honey," she said as they walked in.

I studied them to see what was different, but other than Mom's hair being a little messed up, they looked the same.

"Hey," Billy said.

"Hey."

He pointed to the pancakes on my plate. "Mind if I have some?"

And obviously nothing had changed with him. "Sure," I replied.

He went to the drawer and took out a fork. Instead of breaking off a piece, he took an entire one.

Yup. Still the same.

"So what are you going to do today?" Mom asked as she poured herself some juice.

I shrugged. "I don't know."

"I saw there's some new shows up at some of the galleries on Warren Street," Billy said as he polished off the pancake.

This was how it was going to be now that they were together? So . . . normal?

"Maybe I'll check them out."

"I'm going to shower," Mom said.

After she left, Billy grabbed some iced tea and joined

me at the table. He pointed at my iPad. "Mind if I check the baseball scores?"

I pushed it toward him, amazed as he skimmed the sports page of the *New York Times* as if this was just another morning and not the one after the first night that he and my mother had probably had sex for the first time.

"You okay?" he asked as he looked up to find me staring at him.

"Uh-huh."

"Is this weird for you, the fact that your mom spent the night at my place?"

"A little weird."

He nodded. "I can understand that."

"But not a lot weird," I said.

A few minutes later Mom came back, showered and dressed. "Okay, Bug—we're off," she said, kissing me on top of my head. "I'm speaking at a meeting tonight in Hudson, so I'll be home around nine."

Billy stood up. "I think I'm done on set around five, so if you want to go catch a movie or something, text me."

Things seemed exactly the same. Who would have thought?

Obviously, there was a new world order in place.

I could have just waited for Matt to get in touch with me, and then, when he did, pretended that everything was cool and not bring it up for fear of somehow making him uncomfortable or, even worse, mad. That's what the old me in the old world order would have done. But the new me—the me who was getting used to taking risks; the one who, as much as I tried to hold back and not fall for a guy who in three more weeks would live 2,886 miles away from me, I had totally fallen for—couldn't just sit back. The new me in this new world order wasn't going to count on waiting for Matt to maybe feel like talking at some point in time. This version of me was going to point-blank ask him what was going on. And not via text. But by calling. On the phone. Right after I went to Stewart's to fortify myself with an iced coffee.

Once back home, slurping the last of my iced coffee while watching George the goat (Matt and I had named him after watching a George Clooney movie on cable one afternoon) nuzzle Mabel the cow (had everyone around me hooked up?), I clicked on Matt's number and prayed for voice mail.

No luck.

"Hey, I was going to call you," he said.

Uh-oh. It was not a happy, excited "I was going to call you." It was the kind of "I was going to call you" that you'd get from a doctor right before he told you that you had three months to live.

"You were?" I asked nervously.

"Yeah, I feel like I owe you an apology."

"For what?" I asked innocently. I wasn't earning any

343

points in the point-blank event for that one, but whatever.

"For how I got all weird when we got to my house."

"Oh. You weren't—" I stopped myself. "Yeah. That's actually why I was calling you. To see what that was about."

He sighed. "I feel like I haven't been completely honest with you."

Oh, God. That was even worse than the "I was going to call you." Hadn't we already been through this with the girlfriend thing? In movies, that was the kind of sentence that was usually followed by "I have a wife and three kids." At least it was in the Lifetime one Mom and I had watched together the other night in her bed when she couldn't sleep because she was nervous about the scene she had to shoot the following morning, which took place in bed after she sleeps with Billy's character for the first time. ("Thank God you didn't make me sell those arm weights at the estate sale, Bug," she had said.)

"See, my mom . . . she's got . . . some issues," he said.

That was the big deal? "Join the club," I laughed.

He didn't. "No, I mean it," he said seriously.

"What kind of issues?"

"I'd rather tell you in person. Meet me at the waterfall in an hour?" he asked.

━━━━━━━━━━━━━━━━━━━━━━━━━━━━━━━━━━━━

On the drive over, I decided I wouldn't do what I usually did, which was play out all the different scenarios of what

Matt might say, and how I would feel when he did, and what I would say in return, so that I showed up having had the experience way before it happened and acted according to my version rather than the real one. Instead, I took what they called in meetings "contrary action," and called Walter.

"What's the matter?" he asked suspiciously when he answered.

"Nothing. Why would you think something was the matter?"

"Because now that you have a boyfriend I barely ever hear from you."

"Okay, (a) he's not my boyfriend, at least not officially," I replied, "and (b) that's not true! We talked two days ago."

"No—*you* talked two days ago," he replied. "About him. And then when you were done, you said you had to go." I was used to Walter getting all grumbly and complain-y, but this was different. Underneath the grumbling I could hear the hurt. Which made me feel awful. I had become his Maya.

"Walter, I'm so sorry—"

"Whatever."

"No, it's not whatever," I said. "You're right—I've been a shitty friend, and I'm sorry. I'm glad you told me."

"Apology accepted," he sighed. "Just try not to be that girl, okay? I *hate* when people ditch their friends when they start dating someone.

"So what's going on?"

"Not much." Sure, it was a lie, especially in light of Mom and Billy hooking up, but I didn't want to talk about that. "What about you?"

"Not much."

"What movies did you see this week?" Some kids, during the summer, read as many books as possible. Walter had decided he was going to watch a movie a day until school started.

"Okay, so on Monday, I watched this Japanese horror movie," he said. "It was so creepy. You wouldn't have made it through the first fifteen minutes. And then on Tuesday . . ."

I smiled as I listened to him go on. By the time I got to Stuyvesant, my nervousness and the hurt in his voice were gone, and things felt back to normal. Well, as normal as the fact that my best friend was a fourteen-year-old gamer and film geek.

"Okay, I need to go," he said. "I'm meeting someone."

"Who are you meeting?"

"A . . . person."

Wait. What? "Is it a girl person?"

"I am neither going to confirm nor deny that."

"Is it Amanda from the Saturday meeting?" He always denied it when I asked him, but I knew he had a crush on her from the way he always called on her first to share and gave her the Twelve Steps to read when he was chairing a meeting.

"It might be."

"It is!"

"I didn't say that."

"You don't have to," I laughed. "I can hear it in your voice."

He gave a heavy sigh. "I liked it better when we talked about you," he grumbled.

POTENTIAL ISSUES I DECIDED MATT'S MOTHER MIGHT HAVE

★ She drank.

★ She was a kleptomaniac. (The mother of this girl in my grade, Frannie Berkowitz, was a kleptomaniac. So bad that her father had made a deal with the Holy Trinity of Barneys, Saks, and Neimans that when they saw her coming, a security guard would follow her around and make note of everything she stole and then just send him an itemized bill.)

★ She suffered from depression.

★ She had a gambling problem.

★ She was obesely overweight.

★ She was anorexic.

If I had more time, I could've come up with a bunch more, but that was all I could get through from the time it took to park and make my way to Matt. However, even if I had had all the time in the world, I doubt I would've guessed what it turned out to be.

"Okay, when you said hoarder, do you mean like *hoarder* hoarder?" I asked after he told me.

"Yeah," he said, not looking at me as he ripped a clump of grass out of the ground.

"Like *TV*-level hoarder?"

He pulled up another clump. "It's not like there are *dead cats* lying around, but it's bad."

"How bad?"

He couldn't look at me. "Bad."

At this rate, it would be next week before I pulled the full story out of him. But I knew what it was like not to be able to look someone in the eye; to be in that place of wanting more than anything to be able to share the truth of what was going on, while at the same time feeling like to do so was a complete betrayal that might make your world as you knew it come crashing down.

I put my hand on his cheek and steered his face up so that he was looking at me. "You can tell me," I said quietly.

His eyes darted to the side a few times before he focused on me. "I know I can," he whispered.

And with a deep breath, he did.

He told me about his mom. How before becoming an editor, his mother had written a novel that had gotten a lot of attention and great reviews but that she never wrote another one after that because his father felt that one writer in the family was bad enough.

How after the divorce, in an attempt to make herself feel better and give herself a new start, his mother had started buying things. New clothes. New dishes. New sheets and comforters. Then, when Matt's father announced he was marrying the woman he had been having an affair with, and his mom moved them upstate full-time where they had more room, it started getting worse. Antique silver candelabras she got at a garage sale and planned to polish up but never got around to. An old butter churn she found at a flea market in Ghent that she was going to make into a table but never did.

Then, when the woman got pregnant, his mom started getting more out of control. Boxes of books off eBay. Record albums for fifty cents from an antique store in Hillsdale to go along with the turntable she had bought at a thrift store in Great Barrington. While their house was big—five bedrooms—soon enough her office was packed with stuff that once purchased often didn't even make it out of their bags and boxes. Then, when Matt's sister went away to college, her bedroom was taken over as well.

The bigger his father's life got (a new wife, two more kids, a *New York Times* bestseller) the smaller his mother's became—swallowed up by more and more stuff. He talked about not being able to breathe when he came home, and the nightmares he had where there would be an earthquake and everything would roll into his room and smother him. And yet, like in my life with Mom, to the outside world, it all looked okay. The lawn was still mowed; the bills were still paid (well, in our case, they weren't, but we hadn't known that, thanks very much, Barney). The elephant in the room may have grown bigger and bigger over the years, thanks to a steady diet of crazy, but as long as it was well dressed and didn't pee on the carpet, what was the big deal if it was there?

Sure, if anyone had come over and had seen how out of control things had gotten, something would have had to have been done, but there was an easy solution to that: just don't invite anyone over. He said it had been some-what manageable back when the clutter had been con-tained to rooms that had doors, and he could just make sure they were all closed before a friend came over; but in the last two years, things had started to spill out into hallways and onto counters. A year before, for Christmas, he and his sister had bought his mother a gift certificate for six sessions with a personal organizer, but before the first three-hour session was over, the woman had taken Matt aside and told him that she couldn't help them and that he should look into getting his mother professional help. Other than their handyman, she was the last person from the outside world who had been in the house.

"I didn't expect my mom to be home when we stopped by there yesterday," he said. "And I was scared she was going to come outside and invite you in, and it would turn into this whole deal." He shook his head. "I keep thinking that if I just plan well enough, I can keep this stuff under control, you know? And if I keep it under control, it'll somehow give me enough time to come up with a solution and fix it."

Boy, did I know that one. I nodded. "I get it. Believe me."

He took my hand. "I know you get it," he said quietly. "That's why I wanted to tell you. And because to not tell you felt, somehow, like . . . a lie."

That's what I was learning. That leaving stuff out was sometimes just as bad as making stuff up.

He pulled me down so we were lying on the grass. As we held hands, not talking, I watched the cotton candy clouds move across the blue sky, listening to the steady rush of the waterfall in the distance and the soft rustling of the giant trees as they swayed in the breeze. I thought of a list I had made about a year earlier during one of Mom's deeper depressions—the one where I was holding the mirror up to her mouth to check her breathing a few nights a week rather than a few nights a month—called Perfect Moments. Like the time when I was six and had the stomach flu and Mom held my hair back as I threw up and then rubbed my back as I drank ginger ale. And reciting the lines from *The Way We Were* with each other as we lay in her bed and ate popcorn. And listening to the studio audience clap and whoop at the end of the taping of the pilot for *Plus Zero* when Mom took her final bow.

As I lay there, the sun on my face, so relaxed I wasn't

even worried about tick bites that might have led to Lyme disease, I knew that this moment would be added to the list.

The first perfect moment my mother was not a part of.

Matt rolled over and propped himself up on his arm. "I didn't plan for this to happen."

I rolled toward him and propped myself up as well. "Telling me about your mom?" I asked.

"No. I mean, yes, that, too, but I'm talking about you and me," he replied. "After that first night down by the river, I thought that it would be fun to hang out with you while you were here, but I didn't plan on, you know . . ."

I felt a switch flip on in my stomach. "What?"

He looked at me—really looked at me, in a way that I never felt seen before. Instead of breaking my gaze, I kept still and *let* him look at me, not worrying that he'd see something less than perfect; not fidgeting so that by being a moving target I was less likely to be found out and he'd leave.

The corners of his mouth lifted into a smile.

"Falling in love with you," he said.

I would have been lying if I had said that, sometimes right before I fell asleep, I hadn't thought about this moment and what it would feel like and what I would say and what it would mean. What I hadn't counted on was how it wasn't those five words that cracked my heart open—it was how his voice shook when he said them, and how his hand got all clammy. It was how a little crease appeared between his eyebrows and lines appeared on his forehead as he held his breath, waiting to see how I'd react, as if pleading for me not to laugh or cringe or reject him. As if he were saying, "Okay, I just unzipped my skin and this is what's underneath and I'm really putting myself out there, so think carefully about what you say because your response is going to be singed on my brain forever."

Which is why I said the only thing I could think of.

"Well, I love you, too."

CHAPTER EIGHTEEN

After I got my period the first time when I was twelve, for the two weeks following, everything I did was commemorated by saying "This is my first fill-in-the-blank since I got my period." This is my first shower/breakfast/algebra test/time I've had to pour cold water on Mom's face to wake her up since I got my period.

And the same thing happened after Matt and I said "I love you" to each other.

This is the first Stewart's iced coffee I've had since officially being in love. (Bought approximately forty-five minutes later because of whatever weird chemical they put in it to get you hooked.)

This is the first slice of Debra's banana cream pie Matt and I have shared at Luna 61 since we said "I love you" out loud. (Eaten that evening because love makes you hungry.)

This is the first time I have walked into my kitchen and found my mother and Billy Barrett making out since I have joined the ranks of people who say "I love you" to people of the opposite sex.

That one—which happened on day three of being officially in love, when I walked into the kitchen to get some carrot cake—was the first time I had seen Mom and Billy kiss off set, period. Even with my love high—the blissed-out, perma good mood that made it so that I did not curse out drivers who decided to pass me because they felt I was going too slow down Route 9, even though I made a point of going five miles over the fifty-five-mile speed limit—it was more than a little weird.

"Bug. I didn't see you," Mom said after I cleared my throat.

Most likely because she was too busy going for the gold in Tonsil Hockey. Is that what Matt and I looked like when we made out? I hoped not because it was not at all attractive. "I just wanted to get some carrot cake," I said, making my way to the fridge.

"Oh, I think I may have had the last piece," Billy said sheepishly. "Sorry."

Now that it seemed as if he was going to be in our lives for an extended period of time, I was going to have to set some ground rules around the food stuff.

I walked to the window and pulled back the curtain. "Still no paps?"

"Nope," Billy said. "We've been ignoring each other on set."

One of the things I had been worried about when Mom and Billy hooked up was that the paparazzi were going to stake out the house like they had after her DUI, making it look like an airport rental car lot with their Pontiac Grand Ams and Chevy Cavaliers. But one glance at TMZ showed that summer seemed to bring out more bad behavior in celebrities, so they were busy with an overabundance of cheating scandals and drug busts.

I grabbed a rice cake and went back to my room to finish uploading the photos I had taken that afternoon over in Athens and Catskill. It gave me the creeps to be over there—Matt said that he had always thought of it as a place where, if you pushed hard enough, you'd find bodies buried in the wall—but the old Victorian houses with their peeling paint made for cool photos, especially if you pimped them out with Hipstamatic and Instagram. Over the last few days Matt had been hounding me to let him take a picture of me. A few times he had even succeeded, while I was driving—but I quickly made him delete them. I may have been in love, but I wasn't so checked out that I was willing to change my stance on photos of me.

As I uploaded one of a porch that looked like it was about to crumble into dust, my e-mail dinged. Now that Mom was so busy, she had stopped sending me videos that were made up of stock shots of sunsets and smiling babies and Olympic runners set to songs like "I Believe I Can Fly" and "That's What Friends Are For." ("Bug, it's not spam," she would say when I would complain. "It's very motivational stuff that can change your mind-set and your energy field and the outcome of your entire *day*!") But because Walter's birthday was coming up in a few weeks, that had been replaced by links to various movies and video games that he thought might be good gifts for me to get him. ("Not only would the Criterion versions of *The Royal Tenenbaums* and *Rushmore* bring me hours of enjoyment, but they would bring *you* enjoyment, too, 'cause I'd even let you watch them with me!" he had written in an e-mail the night before.)

This e-mail, however, wasn't from Mom. Or Walter. It was from CalArts, congratulating me on being chosen as a high school fellow for their August intensive.

Which would have been great . . . *if I had applied.*

I remembered my conversation with Billy on the train ride back from New York. He and Ben were the only ones who knew about that fellowship—and Ben wasn't on the board of CalArts. Since that day, Billy and I had had a bunch more talks about my photography—mostly his telling me how good I was, and how I should really put my work out there, especially the stuff I had taken over the last few months that had to do with my mother, and me shrugging it off and coming up with excuses about why I didn't want to.

He thought I was afraid of rejection. But it wasn't so much about submitting stuff and being turned down. It was more about the fear of being seen and known. Sure, in the last few months with meetings, and with Walter and Matt, I was getting more and more comfortable opening up to people, but even then I could still control the information and the flow of closeness. But putting my work out into the world—especially the Mom stuff—was different. If I did that, I couldn't control people's reactions, and I couldn't be there every single minute to explain and defend and justify Mom or myself or our relationship. Plus, if I went, it would mean leaving Mom. For a month. Other than when she had been at Oasis, we had never been apart for longer than a few nights.

After cursing myself for not having any Play-Doh (Was it really *that* awful to have a sniff once in a while?) I ran into the living room, where I found Billy rubbing her feet as they watched TV. That had been one of the things that had made me think he was the real deal, because her feet, with all the bunions from years of high heels? Nasty. Even back when we had money and she used to offer to pay me if I would rub them for her, I said no.

I held up my iPhone with the e-mail. "How could you do this?" I demanded angrily.

"Is this about the carrot cake?" Mom asked. "Annabelle, I've been doing my best to not say anything about this, but I'm getting a little concerned about the baking," she said. "Honey, I need you to tell me—are you baking out of *happiness*? Or is this a way of acting out because you've got some food issues? Because if it's acting out, then maybe when we get back to L.A. I could get Beverly from my Thursday women's meeting to take you to an Overeaters Anonymous meeting so you could see if you relate at all—"

"I don't need to go to OA!" I yelled. "I need *him* to butt out of my life!"

"Whoa. Calm down," Billy said. Calmly. Which pissed me off even more. "What did I do?"

"What did you *do*?!" I demanded. "Mm, I don't know. How about the way you used the fact that you're rich and famous to force some stupid college to agree to let me into their stupid program even though *I told you I didn't want to go!*"

"What are you talking about?" She turned to Billy. "What's she talking about?"

At least he had the decency to look busted. "I thought they would get in touch with me first," he said quietly. "So that I could—"

"So that you could what?" I snapped. "Figure out the best way to tell me that you had found a way to ship me off?" Billy had to have known that if I took the fellowship, it meant leaving Mom here for a month by herself. "You didn't do this because you believe I have talent! You did this so that you can be with my mother without her dumb daughter in the way!" I shook my head.

"Annabelle, that's not true," he said. "Let me explain."

"I'm going to ask again. What is going on here?" Mom demanded.

"What's going on is that when he asked to see my photos—obviously because he was just trying to earn points and make me like him so that I wouldn't freak out if you guys got together," I said, "I was dumb enough to show them to him, and even more dumb to believe him when he said they were good."

"Because they *are* good!" he said. "They're incredible."

"You showed Billy your photos? You never show *me* your photos," Mom said, clearly hurt.

She was going to make this about *her*? Seriously? "Because you never ask to see them! You ask me to take your picture, but you never ask to see any other pictures!" I cried. I remembered how Dr. Warner's eyebrow had gone up when I had told her that I was fine with the fact that Mom showed no interest in my photography; that it was probably a good sign of boundaries. When she said that it looked like my mother was frightened by my photography, because it was something apart from her—something where, had I put my work out into the world, then I would no longer be hidden in her shadow, where she could keep me close so I didn't leave her—I had gotten really mad. Probably because, yet again, she was right and I couldn't handle it. "And then he went and made CalArts give me a spot in their high school program!"

Mom thought about it. "Well, is that so bad?" she asked. "I mean, it sounds like he was just trying to help—"

There it was. Now that all those dumb hormones

had been kicked up, she was doing her thing where she chose a guy over me. Why couldn't she just go through menopause already? "I didn't ask for his help!" I cried.

"I know you didn't," Billy said. "And you're right—I had no business doing that. I just . . . you're *really* talented, Annabelle. I know what it's like to be afraid of letting your-self believe people when they say that—"

"I'm not afraid," I snapped. "What was I thinking even showing you in the first place? That stuff was *personal.*"

The maternal part of Mom's reptilian brain—the part that knew when to check if I had a fever, or knew when I was sneaking cookies before dinner—lit up, and she turned to Billy. "What exactly were those photos of?"

"Mom, no! It's nothing like that. They were just pho-tos of . . . things."

"What *kind* of things?"

"Photos I had taken when you were in rehab," I said. "To try to make sense of how I felt." I looked at Billy. "But unlike *some* people, maybe I don't have this overwhelm-ing need to have the entire world tell me how great I am. Maybe I just want to live my life like a normal person, without attention."

"And maybe by showing your work, you can help peo-ple!" he retorted.

"How is my stuff going to *help* people?!"

"By making them feel understood! And less alone!"

"Yeah, well, if I ever wanted to do that, it needs to be my decision!" I yelled. "Plus, I'm here for the summer. The program starts in a week! What am I supposed to do, just up and leave?"

"This program is now?" Mom asked.

I nodded. "Yeah. For the month of August."

"You'd leave me?" she demanded.

I sighed. Again. More about her. "You don't have to worry." I looked at Billy. "I'm not going anywhere."

A RANDOM LIST OF THINGS I DON'T LIKE
- ★ Prejudice or discrimination of any kind
- ★ Right to Lifers
- ★ People who cut in line
- ★ Teva sandals (Matt has a pair, and he says they're really comfortable, and I let it go because I'm in love with him, but I'm sorry, they're just *wrong* from an aesthetic point of view.)
- ★ Kale (I've tried. I really have. But it has a weird aftertaste.)
- ★ When you go to someone for support because you know they'll agree with you. And then they don't.

As I drove to Target (I'm sorry, but if there was ever a time to get back on the Play-Doh train, it was now), I called Walter to download what had happened.

362

I had a feeling that he wouldn't give me a "Oh, poor Annabelle . . ." pep talk, because that wasn't what Walter did. What Walter did was listen to me—sometimes crunching away on Sun Chips, sometimes smacking gum, sometimes glugging down Coke, sometimes, if I was lucky, remaining quiet—and then when I was done, he'd wait a second before giving a heavy, semi-annoyed sigh and say "Are you done?" Sometimes I wasn't, so I'd go on a little bit longer, and then I'd say "Yes, I'm done." And he'd say, "Okay, so now that you've told me why you think the other person is wrong, what's *your* part in all this?" That would totally piss me off because I didn't have much interest looking at *my* part— because to discover I had a part meant that I was not perfect and all sorts of other things that I disliked. But eventually after some grumbling, I'd talk it through and find my part and instead of making me feel worse, figuring out which of the less-than-admirable behaviors off my greatest-hits list had been in play actually made me feel better, because in being aware of it, I could try not to do it the next time.

So when Walter told me that, no, he didn't agree with me that Billy was a total control freak who was trying to ruin my life and maybe him getting me into the photography program was an H.P. thing (H.P. = Higher Power = God = Walter's paranoia about saying it out loud and people thinking he was some sort of religious freak if they knew he believed in God) since I was too scared to take steps to do it myself, I wasn't too surprised and I didn't get mad. What I did do was thank him for the feedback and say that I was about to lose reception because I was going through that weird intersection at 9 and 9G, where things got wonky. Which was not a total lie, as I would be going through the intersection . . . in about fifteen minutes.

After I hung up and turned around (I had gone this long without Play-Doh, why ruin it now?), I called Matt, who was nearby in Tivoli finishing up a cater-waiter gig at an event at Bard.

"Obviously because I love you, I find it cute, but you do realize that some people might think hanging out at a booth in a gas station is kind of weird, right?" he asked as we sat at the one in Stewart's a few minutes later.

I shrugged as I sipped at my iced coffee. Since we had sat down the straw had not left my mouth; it was like an IV drip.

"So what's going on?"

I unclamped my teeth from the straw and told him what had happened. Matt was a good listener because he gave you just enough facial feedback (a slight nod here; a small smile there) to let you know that he was paying attention, without giving so much that you were tempted to stop talking every few moments and say, "Wait—how come you just raised your eyebrow like that?"

"So that's what happened," I said before I clamped my mouth back onto the straw.

Matt nodded and scratched the side of his nose while he thought about what he was going to say. Walter did the same thing—taking a second before giving a response. So did Ben—but in his case, he would stroke the bottom of his chin, which, because he hated shaving, would always make a scratchy sandpapery sound. I had thought about calling Ben about this, but I wasn't sure how much he knew about what was going on between Mom and Billy. Plus, Ben was not my Ben anymore. Actually, now that I thought about it, Billy had become my Ben this summer. At least until a few hours ago.

"I mean, I'm sure there are probably a few ways that I could have handled it differently—" I started to say to fill the silence of the thoughtfulness. "But still—"

"I think you should go," he said.

"—even if I . . . Wait a minute. *What?*"

He chugged some of his water. Unlike me, Matt was not a fan of Stewart's iced coffee. In fact, when he had tried mine, his response had been along the lines of "Is this all chemicals, or is there actually coffee somewhere in here?"

"I said I think you should go."

"Why?"

"Because it's an amazing opportunity."

"But . . . he did that without telling me. . . . Don't you think it's wrong?"

He shrugged. "Well, sure, it probably could have been handled better," he agreed. "But you wouldn't have agreed

365

to apply." He grabbed my hand. "I know you're pissed and don't want to hear this right now, but Billy really cares about you, Annabelle. And as weird as I know all this has been for you, I think you feel the same way."

"But . . ." I bit the side of my tongue to stop the tears that were getting ready to do a swan dive from my eyes. "If I went that would mean . . . leaving you," I said quietly.

He sighed as he squeezed my hand. "I know. And that would totally suck. But you're a real photographer, Annabelle. You need to start owning that. And I don't want to be that guy who stands in the way of that." He shook his head. "That's what my dad did to my mom. Look, it's not like you weren't going to leave anyway," he said.

I sighed. I knew that.

"So it would just be happening a little earlier than planned," he went on. "What is it your mom always says? You make your plans and God laughs?"

I nodded. She did like that expression. Thankfully, she hadn't found a bumper sticker of it yet.

"When do you have to give them an answer?"

"Wednesday." I sighed.

"So you have two days," he said. "Just think about it."

I was still angry about the whole situation. But I did think about it. I thought about it; I read my daily, weekly, and monthly horoscopes on the sites that Mom considered to be the best ones; I did tarot card spreads on it using facade.

com. I was so desperate for an answer that if I had had a Magic 8 ball, I would have tried that as well. I guess I was more like my mother than I thought. But the more I tried to figure it out, the more confused I got.

I was in the middle of trying to meditate, in hopes of being hit with an answer, but was spending most of the time opening one eye to check the clock to see how much time had passed, when my phone buzzed with a text.

BUG CAN YOU PLEASE COME MEET ME FOR LUNCH TODAY!! IT'S IMPORTANT!! THANK YOU!! XOXO

My mother overdid it with everything. Especially with caps and exclamation points.

"You didn't tell me this was the scene you were shooting!" I cried, holding up the schedule of what was being shot that day as we stood in the cramped wardrobe truck later, with Mom wearing nothing but her underwear. I had avoided the set ever since I went to meet her for lunch one day and she was shooting a scene where she gets sick from chemo. She was so good and so believable that it freaked me out.

Georgina—the wardrobe woman—and her assistant scurried around gathering up an assortment of hospital gowns for her to try on. Like all wardrobe people I had met, they didn't even blink when Mom stripped down in front of them.

"I know I didn't," she said calmly as she stepped into one of the gowns. "Because I knew you wouldn't come if I did."

Georgina turned to the assistant. "I'm thinking strapless bra. So the drooping isn't so noticeable."

I could see how insulted Mom was, but she had been doing this long enough to know that the three crew members you never wanted to get on the bad side of after the D.P. were wardrobe, makeup, and hair, so she kept her mouth shut.

"You want me to watch you *die*," I said.

She shrugged, holding her boobs up over the gown in an attempt to de-droop them. "What can I tell you. I thought maybe it would make you appreciate me more," she replied, tweaking my nose.

I laughed. At least she was honest. Warped, but honest.

"But seriously, there's something I do want to talk to you about."

A production assistant rapped on the door. "Ten-minute warning," she yelled out.

"Go sit," Mom said. "And we'll have lunch in my trailer afterward, okay?"

I was in the midst of making small talk with the script supervisor while Alistair and the D.P. fought about how to shoot the scene (according to Mom, having come from the theater, Alistair didn't think that moving the camera was all that necessary, which had resulted in a few days' worth of very slow footage) when Billy walked on set, trailed by a P.A. trotting behind him like a puppy.

When I saw Billy, I did the mature thing: I shifted in

my seat in hopes that he wouldn't see me so I wouldn't have to talk to him.

"Hey, Annabelle," he said as he came up to me.

"Oh, hey," I said, as if surprised to see him. The script supervisor—who, like almost all the female members of the crew—had a huge crush on Billy, got up and made some excuse about how she had to go see someone about something.

"I texted you a few times," he said. "To see if we could talk about this."

"I know. I just . . . I was just so . . . *mad.*" Dr. Warner would have been proud of me. Mad was not something I did. At least not admitting it out loud. I much preferred to let it build up inside of me so that it resulted in stomach problems.

He nodded. "I get that. And you should be. I was totally out of line. But Annabelle, you need to know this: it had absolutely nothing to do with wanting to get you out of the way—"

"I know it didn't," I replied. He didn't have to ask me if I wanted to go to the movies, or for hikes, but he had. A lot.

Before he could continue, the hair and makeup people descended on him. "Can we talk about this more later?" he pleaded.

I nodded.

I watched him as he walked away. Yet again, Billy Barrett was proving to be a nice guy.

I was not an easy cry. Not in life, and especially not when watching movies. (Mom, on the other hand, was an easy cry—especially now that she was sober and had "gotten her feelings back," which meant even more balled-up used tissues strewn around the house for me to pick up.) But as I watched Mom die in Billy's arms over and over on the steps of what was supposed to be Emily Dickinson's house but was really a Jehovah's Witnesses Kingdom Hall, my sniffling turned into full-out ugly cry gulping, to the point where I had to excuse myself and go hide in the bathroom and sob under a mural of what the caption said was "life in paradise, from the *Knowledge* book." (Apparently, paradise included people of all races, in addition to koala bears and tigers.)

It was as if every single acting class and every session with every coach she'd ever had paid off in that one scene. Instead of being sappy, or not sad enough, the chemistry between Mom and Billy was spot-on. It was funny and sexy and true, and every time she smiled at him right before she closed her eyes for the last time, your heart broke over and over and over as you realized how much it sucked that after only just finding each other, they had to say good-bye. They were so good together that even though Alistair had no vague, passive-aggressive feedback to give, he just kept saying "And again" while subtly wiping at his eyes. ("The English just *hate* showing emotion,"

Mom was always saying. "That's why I had to break up with Ewan, remember him?")

And I wasn't just crying out of relief that Mom was so good. She was. So good that, as much as I worried I was jinxing it, I was ready to start looking for something to wear to the Oscars. With every take, I realized that even though she drove me crazy, and had no sense of boundaries, and totally embarrassed me, and was constantly making everything about her, one day—hopefully not for many, many years—I would lose her.

As far back as I could remember, every time Mom tucked me in, after I had run out of excuses to keep her there (another story, a glass of water, checking my group of stuffed animals to make sure none were in danger of suffocating during the night), after she had gotten me to tell her I loved her all the way up to God, past God, past God, she would take my cheeks in between her hands and she'd say "*You*—Annabelle Meryl Jackson (the Meryl was for Meryl Streep, her favorite actress of all time)—are my heart." She said it so many times that for the longest time I thought it was another term for "I love you." As I got older—especially when I was mad at her—I'd roll my eyes when she said it, or try to push her away. Not only did I find it corny, but I'd feel a pressure in my own chest. A pressure to make sure that everything worked out and we were okay, because if we weren't, somehow her heart would stop beating and she would stop loving me.

But now I saw, I *was* her heart. I was hers, and she was mine. Sometimes I was able to make myself believe that if I didn't love her and need her so much, it would make it that less painful when we fought, or when she got drunk, or when she was depressed. Or if I didn't let myself love her so much, then maybe it wouldn't hurt so much when the day came when she did die, the idea of which was so horrible to me that every time it crossed my mind I physically had to shake my head to rid myself of it.

As I sat in the bathroom of the Kingdom Hall, blowing my nose into some scratchy toilet paper, something happened. I just knew at my very core that Mom was Mom, and no matter how many self-help books she read and how many AA meetings she went to and how many hours she spent meditating, the chances of her changing into one of those moms you see on TV—the ones who know how to cook and make hospital corners with the sheets and are always running on time—was never going to happen. And that—after years of not being okay—suddenly . . . was.

My mother was nuts, and her favorite hobby was processing her feelings in front of others. ("You know what I call that? *Mental masturbation*," Walter liked to say before giving a *Beavis and Butt-head* laugh.) And my first response would probably always be to roll my eyes when she started crying in public, but that was all part of the deal. Because on good days, my mother was the sun. She was warm and bright and enveloped everyone and everything around her with this amazing feeling of potential. And she wasn't just my sun. From the way I sometimes caught Billy gazing at her when she wasn't looking, she was his as well.

She was the sun, and when the day came when she did close her eyes for the last time, it would get dark. So dark that I couldn't think about it. But finally, I didn't have to think about it right then, or every minute of the day. Because as long as she didn't pick up a drink or a pill, it probably wouldn't get dark for a very long time. For now, she was still here. And that day, as she did her thing in front of the camera—which, as she liked to say, was when she was utterly completely 100 percent herself—the sun was shining brighter than it had in a long time. It made me feel warm and safe, like I had the other day when I stretched out and felt it on my body while I was at the waterfall with Matt, and he rolled over and put my face between his rough soft hands and kissed me for a very long time.

Which was why, after I splashed some water on my face, I was going to go to her trailer and give my mother a huge hug, and as I did, as I let my body go limp, as I let her hold me as tight as she wanted to, I was going to tell her that not only did I love her all the way up to God, past God, past God, but that I forgave her. For everything.

And for the first time I was going to truly mean it, with all my heart.

And then I was going to tell her that I was going back to L.A for the CalArts thing. Because like Sting sang in that song, "If you love something, set it free."

Because it was time for both of us to do that.

CHAPTER NINETEEN

It used to be that after Mom did a big scene, the first thing she'd do when she got back to her trailer or dressing room was dig out the bottle of Stoli she kept stashed away and have a drink. That would then be followed by holding whoever was unlucky enough to come in hostage as she dissected her own performance and worried that it wasn't good enough, and how she should have done this or that different. When the alcohol kicked in, she'd start to calm down, and soon enough it was no longer her fault that she had screwed up—it was the director's, or her co-star's. Then, if she got buzzed enough, she'd stop talking about it and move on to other important topics, such as did the hostage think that it was time for her to get her lips done because, while she had been putting it off because she was afraid of looking like Meg Ryan, they did seem to be getting thinner.

When I saw Mom in her trailer after the death scene, she was curled up on the couch playing Words with Friends with Al from Chattanooga, Tennessee.

"Hi, Bug." She smiled as I walked in. She looked exhausted, but in a good way. I guess dying over and over will do that to you.

"Hi," I said as I walked over and snuggled up to her and took her arm and curled up under it.

"So what'd you think?" she asked anxiously.

I pulled her arm tighter around me. "I think you were amazing."

A huge smile came over her face. "Really?"

I nodded.

I couldn't tell who was hugging who harder. Maybe it didn't matter.

"So I wanted to talk to you about something—" she started to say.

"And I have something to tell you, too."

"So what I wanted to say was . . . Wait, would you like to go first?" she asked.

I shook my head. "No, it's okay."

"Are you sure?" she asked. "I'm really trying to work on my self-centeredness this week."

I loved my mother, but it was going to take more than a week to put a dent in that one.

"It's okay. You go."

"Okay." She took a deep breath. "So here's the thing, Bug. I understand why you're upset about what Billy did. And I don't blame you. And just so you know, I told him that," she said. "But . . . I think you should go."

What?

She started tickling my arm. "I know how much you love photography," she went on. "And I'm sorry I haven't been more supportive of it." She sighed. "I think it's that when you're off doing it, you're so involved with it, and so good at it, and it's something that I don't know anything about and . . . I don't know . . . I feel . . . left out. It sounds crazy, but when you're doing it, it has this way of making me realize that you're growing up. And that soon you'll be gone."

I moved closer to her. "No, I won't."

"Honey, you *will*! Because that's what happens in normal families!" she cried. "In normal families, kids get to be kids instead of taking care of their parents, and then they grow up and leave and start their own lives!"

"So we're not normal!" I shot back. "Who cares? Normal is boring anyway." What was I doing? This was what *I wanted*. To finally get out from under her and lead my own life.

Didn't I?

She clutched my arm. "You need to go pursue your dreams, Annabelle. You deserve that."

"But what if—"

"What if what? What if Billy and I break up? What if I get depressed? What if I drink?"

"Well . . . yeah," I said quietly.

She shook her head. "I'm not planning on any of that happening. But even if it did, *it's not your problem*." She started to cry. "It was *never* your problem, and I am so sorry you had to take that on."

I was crying, too. "It's okay."

"It most certainly is *not* okay." As she wiped her eyes, mascara got all over her face. "I really want you to go, sweetie. Do you understand me?"

I nodded.

"So you'll go?"

I nodded again.

She smiled. "Good. Now what was it that you wanted to tell me?"

I knew that what my mother had just done was huge, not just for her but for us. And even though that sins-of-omission thing was a real gray area for me, I decided to let her believe that she was the bigger person in this one.

Because she was.

I shook my head. "I can't remember," I replied.

On our last day together, Matt brought me back to Overlook Mountain in Woodstock, where we had gone that first afternoon.

"Whatcha thinking about?" he asked as we hiked up the mountain. The mountain that, only a month ago, I had been huffing and puffing up but was now barely breaking a sweat. This outdoors thing was growing on me.

"Just about how much has changed in a month," I replied. Matt and me. Mom and Billy. Billy and me. Ben and Alice, who I'd just found out the night before via text had gotten engaged. I hadn't planned for any of it, and yet now I couldn't imagine my life before it. I mean, I *could*, but I didn't like to because it had been depressing.

"Pretty wild, huh?" he asked as he took my hand.

I nodded, not trusting myself to speak. I had promised myself that I would not be that girl who cried when saying good-bye to her summer love. It was way too Nicholas Sparks.

When we got to the half-built hotel, he ran ahead.

"What are you doing?" I called after him.

"Just checking something," he called back. "Good. It's still here."

As I walked up behind him, I saw that it was the bathtub that I had made him get into so I could take his picture. I smiled. That had turned out to be a great photo. In fact, it was the one I planned to frame and put on my nightstand when I got back home.

He turned to me. "Okay—get in."

"What?"

"Get in the tub." He held out his hand. "And hand over the camera."

I shook my head. "No way."

"I told you I wasn't going to let you get away with the no-pictures thing," he said reaching for it while I tried to hold it behind my back. Soon he gave up and started kissing me instead. That, I did not fight him on.

After a while, he pulled back. "Please?"

Just like that first day in the café, I couldn't help but smile back when I saw his gap-toothed grin.

"Fine," I sighed, handing it over and climbing in.

He took some shots and then stopped and moved the camera to the side. "Maybe you want to try . . . I don't know . . . pretending you're not standing in front of a firing squad?"

I laughed. "Okay, okay."

I wasn't sure if one of the hallmarks of being in love was that no matter how corny the person's jokes were, you found yourself laughing, but that's how it was for me. Soon enough I was relaxed, not caring how close he got with the camera, even though I was well aware I had a giant zit on my chin.

"Hey, Annabelle?" he asked as he focused.

"Yeah?"

He moved the camera aside. "I love you," he said, before refocusing.

I smiled. "I love you, too."

At that, the shutter clicked.

Without even seeing it, I knew it was the best picture of me ever taken.

———————————————————

If my life were a movie or a book, then I would've spent my last night with Matt. Maybe, if it were a particularly romantic movie or book, I would've even slept with him, so that when I got back to L.A., I could do the "This is the first time I'm flying/driving down the 10 freeway/eating an In-N-Out Double Double with Cheese as a non-virgin."

But I didn't.

Instead, I spent my last evening with my mother. Eating Lean Cuisines in her bed watching *Terms of Endearment*. Over the last few weeks, she had caved and gotten hooked on Stewart's iced coffees, so we drank those as well.

Although we had done this a million times before, this time was different. It was different because *we* were different—both individually and together. We were just as connected as before, but that umbilical cord—the one that, on good days, felt like an anchor and, on bad days, felt like it was strangling me—was gone. What held us together now was a faith that no matter what happened, we—individually and together—would be okay.

After the movie was over, and we had finished drying our eyes, and she told me for the nine millionth time about how, the night she went to sleep after deciding to cancel the abortion appointment, she then dreamed about a little girl with brown curls, I stood up.

"I'll be right back," I said.

I went to my room and got my laptop and then crawled back into bed with her. Opening the Negative Space file, I showed her the photos that I had shown Billy on the train. The ones that showed my mother at her ugliest and most beautiful. Her worst and her best. Who she had been and who she was becoming.

The ones that told a story that no journalist or gossip blogger could write.

Her story. My story. Our story.

The story I would not have traded for anything in the world.

EPILOGUE

There's a photo I keep on the night table next to my bed in my dorm room in Boston, where I'm in my first year at college.

It's a photo of my mother and me taken on Zuma Beach in Malibu one afternoon last February that Billy took. She's wearing a vintage one-shouldered cherry-red Halston dress. Straight and simple, hugging every one of the curves on her forty-four-year-old-body that she has finally come to love (or at least *like*) rather than attempt to diet away. Her honey-colored hair is being whipped by the wind as she leans her head back and laughs.

In the photo, I am not in front of her or behind her, like I am in our other family photos. I am next to her, in a long royal-blue embroidered satin dress with a slit up the leg that I bought for thirty-five dollars in Chinatown one Sunday after dim sum with my friends. New friends I'd met that fall. Friends who don't care that my mother is famous, or a recovering alcoholic, or living with the guy who was just voted *People*'s Sexiest Man Alive for the third year in a row. In the photo, my brown curls are piled on my head, just about to break free of all the bobby pins and spill down my back, which I will then not pin back up and my mother will not say a word about.

In the photo, I, too, am laughing. But not the kind of laughter that comes out of making the best of a horrible situation, or because it's either laugh or burst into tears and not be able to stop. It's the kind of laughter that comes from the deepest place in your belly, the kind that's about nothing and everything. The kind you wish you could bottle and take out and sniff when you're having a bad day.

The kind of laughter that happens only when you're with your best friend.

If you were to put a magnifying glass up to the photo, you would be able to see how tightly my mother and I are clutching each other's hands—so hard that you can see the veins in our wrists pop out. Her hand, with its short buffed clear nails, and mine with red polished ones.

But in this photo—taken hours before my mother won the award for Best Actress at the Academy Awards—we are holding on to each other not out of fear, not because we're circling the drain and if we let go, that's the end of the story. We're holding on because we choose to.

And because this is just the beginning.

There is another photo on my night table as well.

It was taken at a photo gallery in Venice a few months ago, at the opening of the exhibit of the photos I had taken of Mom. The exhibit was called *If You're Going Through Hell, Keep Going*, something that Winston Churchill, the prime minister of Great Britain, had said, and had been suggested to me by Matt during one of our nightly Face-Time sessions after I got back to L.A.

Every review included a line that I'd probably gotten the show because I was the Daughter Of Janie Jackson, but that's not the truth. The truth is that one afternoon, I was sitting at Om My Gawd trying to focus on an English paper but instead thinking about a conversation I had had with Billy the evening before as we cooked dinner in the house he and Mom had bought together in Laurel Canyon. A conversation, much like the one we had on the train back from Manhattan, where he had told me that it was time to share my work with the world because maybe it could help someone else.

That afternoon I packed up my laptop and walked next door to the Pink Gallery. The owner, Nicole, happened to be there, and happened to have time to look at the photos on my laptop. She offered me a solo show before she'd even gotten to the ones where Mom's face was visible— before she knew I was a Daughter Of anyone of importance. Billy did, however, help me edit them.

This photo is of me and the people I consider my family.

Matt is on my left. In one hand he holds the bouquet

of tulips and lilies he brought me because I had once mentioned in passing, during one of the first times we hung out, almost two years ago, that they were my favorite flowers. And with his other hand, he holds mine. To my right is Ben, with his arm around my shoulder, looking like a proud father. Something he was to me for so many years, and something he would soon be to the little boy whom Alice—standing next to him, with her very pregnant belly—would soon give birth to.

Because he's shorter, in front of me is Walter, with whom I still FaceTime or talk almost every day so we can share the craziness in our heads between meetings. As he likes to say, thankfully we're not both sick on the same day so we can help each other out.

Behind me is Billy—who, as much as I tell him not to, still calls me *dude*, and still eats the last of anything I bake—with his hands on the tops of my shoulders, the glint of the platinum of his wedding band visible.

And next to him, with her head peeking over my other shoulder, not trying to take center stage but completely willing to stand in the background, is my mother.

Glowing.

And looking so proud I'm afraid she might burst.

PROM.

The best dress. The best shoes. The best date. Cindy Ella Gold is sick of it all.

Her anti-prom letter in the school newspaper does more to turn Cindy into Queen of the Freaks than to close the gap between the popular kids and the rest of the students. Everyone thinks she's committed social suicide, except for her two best friends—the yoga goddess India and John Hughes-worshipping Malcolm—and shockingly, the most popular senior at Castle Heights High and Cindy's crush, Adam Silver. But with a little bit of help from an unexpected source—and the perfect pair of shoes—Cindy realizes that she still has a chance at a happily-ever-after.

"A big heart + an insanely keen sense of humor = exactly the sort of book I love to read!"   —Lauren Myracle, *New York Times* bestselling author of *TTYL* and *Thirteen*

PRINCESS, MEET FROG . . .

Dylan Shoenfield is the princess of L.A.'s posh Castle Heights High. She has the coolest boyfriend, the most popular friends, and a brand-new "it" bag that everyone covets. But when she accidentally tosses her bag into a fountain, this princess comes face-to-face with her own personal frog: self-professed film geek Josh Rosen. In return for rescuing Dylan's bag, Josh convinces Dylan to let him film her for his documentary on high school popularity. Reluctantly, Dylan lets F-list Josh into her A-list world. But when Dylan's so-called Prince Charming of a boyfriend dumps her flat, her life—and her social status—come to a crashing halt. Can Dylan—with Josh's help—pull the pieces together to create her own happily-ever-after?

"The perils of popularity are showcased in a lighthearted contemporary novel filled with snappy dialogue."   —*Publishers Weekly*

WHO'S AFRAID OF THE BIG BAD WOLF?

When Sophie Green goes to spend Spring Break at her grandmother's house in Florida, she never dreams she'll end up catching the eye of the hottest guy she's ever seen. As much as Sophie craves excitement, she's a seat belt–wearing, three-square-meals-a-day, good girl at heart. . . . She doesn't even have the guts to wear Dark As Midnight nail polish. But Sophie dreams of being the girl who isn't afraid to live on the edge. So when a motorcycle-riding hottie calls her "Red" and flashes her a wolfish grin that practically screams Danger, what else is a nice girl to do but jump at the chance to walk on the wild side?

"Robin Palmer takes a classic fairy tale and spins it on its head! *Little Miss Red* is funny and full of heart. You won't be able to put it down."

—Jen Calonita, bestselling author of the
Secrets of My Hollywood Life series and *Sleepaway Girls*

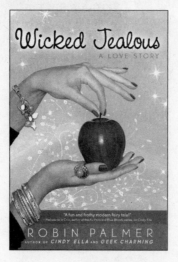

WHO WANTS TO BE THE FAIREST ONE OF ALL, ANYWAY?

With her snow-white skin and habit of hiding behind her long black hair and Tastykake Butterscotch Krimpets, Simone Walker is used to being The Weird Fat Girl at L.A.'s Castle Heights High. That is, until she's adopted by a troupe of Zumba-ing fairy godmothers, discovers the perfect French vintage look, and sheds more than a few pounds. With the help of the seven college guys she's just moved in with for the summer, her happily-ever-after seems almost within reach. But with her soon-to-be-stepmother scheming on the sidelines, Simone quickly realizes that people aren't always what they seem. Is there more to her than what the mirror on the wall shows? Will she figure it out in time to find a Prince Charming who loves her for who she really is?

"Wicked Jealous is a modern-day fairy tale that has everything a girl needs—romance, comedy, and seven hot college guys."

—Jen Calonita, bestselling author of the Secrets of My Hollywood Life series and *Sleepaway Girls*